Falling
like
EMBER

Falling
like
EMBER

Christina L. Schmidt

Falling Like Ember
Published by Besser House Publishing
Centennial, CO

Library of Congress Control Number: 2015954004

Schmidt, Christina L., Author
Falling Like Ember
Christina L. Schmidt

ISBN: 978-0-9968969-0-0

LITERARY CRITICISM / Science Fiction & Fantasy
FICTION / Romance / Paranormal

QUANTITY PURCHASES: Schools, companies, professional groups,
clubs, and other organizations may qualify for special terms when
ordering quantities of this title. For information, email
info@besserhousepublishing.com.

♪

For the ones who lack character, kindness,
positivity, loyalty, and strength, thank you for
inspiring me to write characters who strive for
these qualities. I have hope for you, because I
hold onto hope for myself. For the ones who
are hurtful, may you find healing.

For the ones who see life as a soundtrack,
this is for you.

Prologue

Album: The Greatest

Track: One

Late one Saturday night in August, fourteen-year-old Lux Tazo was too restless for sleep. She twisted her long, mocha locks into a thick braid while her sapphire eyes gazed at the ceiling. Unable to sleep, she tiptoed out of her bedroom in search of a glass of water. But the voices of her parents and older sister downstairs in the den stopped her.

"I just couldn't see what the judges saw. To me it was like Polka, and I was hoping for Bluegrass or the Blues," Arrabelle said. "I love the Blues."

"Arrabelle, you have not had a blue day in your life." Mr. Tazo chuckled.

"I didn't see polka dots; I saw messy," Mrs. Tazo interjected.

"It's called *abstract*," her husband corrected.

"If that's all she produced in two months at camp, I'm not

sure I want to send her back next summer," Mrs. Tazo continued as though she hadn't been interrupted.

"That's not the issue; she doesn't seem to have motivation," Lux's father said. "Not like you did at her age, Arrabelle. She's not fighting for anything yet."

"Hopefully this new school will change that," said Mrs. Tazo.

"Okay, so tell me about the school," Arrabelle suggested. "All I know is that Jackson's going to be teaching there."

"Jackson, your best friend from high school?" Mr. Tazo asked.

"Yes. It's Briar Heights Academy, right?" Arrabelle said. "He's heading up the art program."

"Lux adored Jackson when she was younger," he said. "This is wonderful."

"Here's the brochure," Mrs. Tazo said. "They take four hundred and eighty students, so there will be no more than one hundred and twenty kids in her grade. The concentrations are fashion, art, dance, theatre, voice, songwriting, music, film, and creative writing."

"School goes from 8:00 to 4:00," Mr. Tazo added. "She'll have five classes a day, with no more than twenty students in each class. Plus, there are so many extracurricular activities to choose from. We're hoping she'll choose at least two."

"What are the extras?" Arrabelle asked with a hint of doubt in her voice.

"Ones that will matter in university," her mother said. "Rugby, lacrosse, golf, tennis, swimming, skiing —"

"The motto is 'Fight For Your Life?'" Arrabelle said, cutting her off, "and the mascot is the Cunning Fox. None of this really sounds like Lux. She's...chill. Have you already paid for it?"

"The structure is what we like most about this school," Mrs. Tazo explained. "They will keep her busy. We're not at home as much as we were with you, Arrabelle."

"I've never heard of CRT," Arrabelle continued.

"We liked that, too. She'll be forced to socialize."

"CRT is Common Room Time. The entire school eats lunch together at the same time. And every day after the lunch period, each grade gathers in their respective Common Room before the afternoon classes," Mr. Tazo said. "Dr. Jacobs, the principal, explained it as an opportunity for the three C's: communicate, collaborate, and connect. They think it's important to socialize everyone in one place in order to avoid cliques."

"We saw a Common Room when we got a tour of the school. It's like a large living room enclosed in floor to ceiling windows," Mrs. Tazo said. "There are board games and books, couches and chairs, and a coffee station. It's well done."

"I just think that these competitions and this school is placing her on *that* track, you know?" Arrabelle said. "They'll encourage her to attend an art school instead of a real university. I'm not sure this is what you want for her." She sighed loudly. "And what happens if she doesn't succeed? Wine, anyone?"

Lux hid behind a plant at the top of the grand staircase. The click of stiletto heels grew louder. Arrabelle's shadow rounded a corner into the kitchen, and a moment later, a cork popped.

"What if Lux does want to go to art school? It's so specific," Mrs. Tazo whispered loudly. "We don't even know how good she really is, and she'll *hardly* be in any shape to take over the spa someday. This is just like what happened with Arrabelle and her obsession with music. It took so much persuading to show her that wasn't the path for her. What are we doing wrong?"

"Our efforts to direct Arrabelle's career path haven't quite paid off, anyway," Mr. Tazo said. "And don't kid yourself darling; you'll never trust the spa to anyone."

"What if Lux turns out to be one of those starving artists?" Mrs. Tazo said. "I'm not paying for a flat in the Village while she putters away on a canvas, hoping her designer friends will promote her work in their studios. If only she had Arrabelle's social skills. It's her personality. That's what worries me. Maybe she should see a therapist. Should I call Dr. McRoberts in the morning? Or maybe Dr. Trevino?"

Lux sank to the floor and covered her face. Her heart began to beat loudly in her ears.

"There's nothing to worry about yet," Mr. Tazo reminded his wife. "She's young. We agreed that Briar Heights Academy is the best, hands down. She needs to excel in creative arts in order to be there, so we'll encourage it for now."

"What's wrong with Harper High?" Arrabelle asked, returning to the conversation.

"Arrabelle, it's a *public* school. You attended Harper because there was no decent private school within an hour in any direction," Mrs. Tazo said. "I suppose I do want wine."

"Fine, then. Whiskey for me," Mr. Tazo muttered.

Lux heard her mother move into the kitchen.

"Daddy, Lux doesn't know her potential yet. She'll need to make connections, promote herself, and focus on her appearance. I hate to say it, but that's a big factor," Arrabelle said. "I could style her."

"I don't doubt she could do whatever she wants to when she's ready. Just because she doesn't wear stilettos to Wednesday dinner, like you did at fourteen, doesn't mean she doesn't care."

"She wears a lot of black —" Arrabelle cut herself off and hesitated.

"You're wearing a black shirt right now."

"This black *shirt* is a designer button-up fitted *blouse* off the runway."

"And I suppose I paid for it." He chuckled.

"She just doesn't have *your* appeal, Arrabelle," Mrs. Tazo interrupted when she returned. "But then again, I don't know anyone who does. What were you saying?"

"Lux's outfits," Arrabelle said.

"No. We were discussing Lux's future." Mr. Tazo cleared his throat.

"Oh, you should have seen what she wore to Wednesday dinner, Arrabelle. She looked like a vagrant." Mrs. Tazo giggled.

"That's what I'm saying," Arrabelle said sighing loudly. "If her work brings her into the public eye, she will be judged, and she's just too sweet."

"Listen, she was so pleased taking home that award today. Who am I to take that away from her?" her father said. "Maybe someday she'll surprise us all with something out of this world. But for the next four years she belongs at Briar Heights Academy, and let her dress how she wants!"

"You're right. She doesn't need to know the truth yet," Arrabelle agreed.

"And Arrabelle, while we're here," Mr. Tazo continued, "let this be a friendly reminder that you aren't to get too comfortable in your little music management job. Good night ladies."

Lux quickly stood up and backed away from the top of the stairs before her father saw her. She rushed back to her bedroom and locked the door. Feeling foolish and heartbroken, she cried herself to sleep.

An internal debate stole the joy from Lux's few remaining days of summer. She felt like an intruder within her family, and there was nothing she could think of to do about it. She felt confused more than anything. Should she say something? Should she try to change who she was? She spent every waking hour searching her heart for answers, clarity, freedom. She felt pain. She knew if she gave up painting she'd be lost; she wouldn't be herself. Would it be worth it? Could she trade her passion for her family's acceptance? She realized the answer was no. While she couldn't force herself to give up painting, she did decide it would be a good idea to find a new creative space. She no longer felt comfortable painting in her home. So over the next few days, she gathered her art supplies and re-staked her claim on the old tree house in the backyard. She covered the walls with inspirational quotes from artists she admired, and she promised herself everything would be okay somehow.

The next Wednesday crept up on Lux: the first day of freshman year at Briar Heights Academy. She embarked on the one-mile jaunt through Juniper Creek. Her neighborhood, dating back to the mid-nineteen hundreds, was adorned with elaborate brick homes centered on pristine lawns. Large trees swayed in the wind and dark clouds hung low in the sky. While she was distracted with worried thoughts about the rest of her life, a boy nearly knocked her over.

"Sorry, don't fall! I was just trying to catch up," the boy explained, grasping her arm. "Hi, Lux."

But she did fall.

She'd never before noticed what a smoke show Ember Sweeney was: his vivid jade eyes; his wavy, espresso hair (definitely a 'first-day-of-school' cut); his perfect teeth and killer smile; and his newly developed honey-drip voice. Smoke show.

Lux and Ember had been neighbors for five years, but in grade school he'd studied at Briar Day, while she'd attended Morrison Prep. Both had been busy with extracurricular activities so they hadn't spent time together.

"I didn't mean to run into you. It's so windy." Ember grinned as he caught his breath and matched his pace with hers.

"Ember Sweeney," Lux stated. She eyed him inquisitively. Her arm tingled where he'd grasped it.

"I saw you in the paper," Ember added. "I know, I read the paper. Anyway, awesome painting." He nudged her pointedly.

"Thank you," she replied, taken aback.

"And you're going to Briar!" he said, crossing his arms proudly over his chest. "That part was in the paper, too. I guess I should have assumed. This is big time."

"Yeah, so you are too?" she asked.

Ember nodded. "The whole band got in."

"This is paramount!" Lux's breath caught in her throat. She knew now wasn't the time to be a kitten about making new friends, especially someone like Ember Sweeney.

"What's your class schedule?" he asked. "Do you want to walk together every day?" He continued before she could answer. "Do you know Duffy Raven?" Then he took one of the paintbrushes surfacing from the side pocket of her messenger bag, twirled it between his fingers, and acted as if it was a drumstick.

"I have a lot of art classes," Lux explained, watching the paintbrush in his hands.

"Right." He nodded. "Painter." He handed the brush back to her. "Well, the band comes over every day after school. We could all hang out."

They walked in silence for a moment. Lux wanted to say something else but couldn't think of anything. It wasn't long before he spoke up again.

"Is anyone else in your family artistic?"

"I guess not," Lux said. It felt lonely to admit. "Arrabelle really loves music. I guess that's the closest thing we have."

"Oh, I think she's friends with Astor," Ember remarked.

"Astor Dane?" Lux asked, intrigued. "I practically grew up with him and Jackson Nickel. They were best friends with Arrabelle in high school."

"You're lucky. Maybe we'll be best friends in high school," Ember blurted out, walking a bit faster.

"Maybe," Lux agreed. She rushed to catch up with him.

The wind had died down, but it began to rain softly. Ember zipped up his jacket.

"Here, let's share my umbrella," she offered. He moved in closer and held the umbrella over them.

"So what about you? Are your parents into music?" she asked.

"Not like I am," he said. "Well, I'm not sure about my mom. She left us a long time ago."

"Oh. I'm sorry," Lux said.

Ember simply winked and smiled at Lux, but didn't say anything.

When they walked through the main doors of Briar Heights Academy, Ember closed the umbrella and handed it to Lux. They turned to face each other.

"This is it." He grinned.

Anxiety swept over Lux. "See you." She waved. As she walked away from Ember, her heart melted. Her heart had never melted before.

"Lux?"

"Yes?" Lux whipped around to see that Ember hadn't moved.

"In case I don't see you, we can meet here after school," he said.

A hopeful smile spread across her face and she nodded. Students passed between them, and she lost sight of him.

Lux arrived at her new locker and saw Anya Jensen, who'd attended Morrison Prep with her. She was tall with caramel hair and alexandrite eyes. Even though Anya's concentration was fashion design, the girls still had two of their five classes together. They quickly caught up on the details of each other's lives from over the summer. When Lux mentioned Ember, Anya already knew all about him; apparently he was a big deal, especially for a freshman.

"They did surprise shows all summer in Old Towne!" Anya informed her. "There's a park right by my loft, and they were there at least once a week. Anyway, and more importantly, talk to me about painting. How was summer camp?"

"Camp was amazing," Lux admitted for the first time. "I did get first place in the competition."

"I love how surprised you act!" Anya said, and laughed.

On the way back to her locker at the end of the day, Lux passed by Ember, surrounded by a group of guys and a horde of giggly girls. One blonde girl was standing very close to him. He broke away from the crowd as soon as he saw Lux.

"Don't be a kitten, Ember. Who's this?" one of the guys asked, peering over Ember's shoulder.

"You'll learn to ignore Jamison," Ember said, and winked.

"Wait! Ember, what's your song?" Jamison persisted.

"Oh!" That stopped Ember. He turned around and paused for a moment. "'Rich Woman.' Robert Plant and Alison Krauss."

"'Don't Mug Yourself.' The Streets," Jamison said. "Go, Luther."

"Elefant. 'Sunlight Makes Me Paranoid,'" said a boy behind Jamison. He stepped forward for a better look at Lux and then turned to the boy next to him. "What about you, Tanner?"

"'River,'" Tanner said, glancing uncertainly at the guys.

"Sarah McLachlan?" Jamison snorted.

"Going through your mom's MiniDisc collection again?" Luther said.

"I'll see you guys at home." Ember waved at them as he led Lux away from the guys, who had begun to argue. She turned around for another look at his friends and was met with watchful stares from the girls.

"Every day we discuss the music we've been listening to," Ember explained, as they reached Lux's locker. "Lately we've been sharing the first song we listened to that day. Or sometimes it's the most significant. Sometimes inspirational. And then we listen together and discuss during practice. We've been focusing on a lot of older stuff from the past few decades, all different genres and styles."

"Sounds like what my sister used to do," Lux said. "She and

Astor and Jackson, I mean Mr. Nickel. All they did was listen to music together. They went to shows every week."

"What's the first thing you listened to this morning?" Ember asked.

Lux had listened to a song Arrabelle had once sent her. She'd set it as the alarm on her phone. "'The Greatest.' Have you heard of Cat Power?" she asked, suddenly nervous that Ember might judge her for how little she knew about music.

"Yes!" he said excitedly.

She stuffed homework in her messenger bag while Ember compared Cat Power to a few other bands he knew of, and they left school together.

They talked about music all the way home. Lux didn't feel like an expert on anything, but Ember seemed to relate to everything she did know. They stopped in front of his house. "I think you'd like a lot of what Duffy listens to," he said. "Want to come in?"

"I can't," she said, wondering, but failing to ask who Duffy was. "I have this family dinner thing every Wednesday. And now I have to dress to impress." She shrugged. Ember's face fell.

"And we have an audition at the Sour Enchantment tomorrow night," he said. "Maybe Friday?"

"I love Friday," Lux replied.

"It's a date," Ember said. "And if tomorrow goes well, the band will book our first show there!"

"That's paramount!"

"Yeah! Have you been?"

"Not yet! My sister hangs out there when she's in town," Lux said.

"I'll take you there," Ember concluded.

He walked to his front door and turned to wave again. Lux was on cloud nine. She turned to walk home.

"Lux."

"Yes?" She swiveled around as she had earlier that day in response to his voice.

"Why do you need to dress to impress? Who's going to be there?"

"Oh. Just my family."

"Oh. You look nice now."

"Thanks."

Lux looked down at her outfit, damp from the rain. Her off-the-shoulder black top acted like a dress over her black and white striped leggings and buckled leather boots. Her long necklace sprouted a black feather, which matched the black flapper band around her head. Her hair was twisted into a messy braid and fell over the front of her right shoulder. And then she gazed at Ember. His scuffed boots, dark jeans and layered shirts were completed with a thick leather wrist cuff watch and a worn leather belt with a rustic buckle that matched the boots. His hair had relaxed since morning, as he constantly ran his fingers through it, but his eyes were still bright.

"Okay. Bye," she said.

"See you in the morning," Ember said.

Neither of them moved. Finally, Lux began to walk backward, still facing him. Then she turned without another word and ran the rest of the way home. Once she was safely inside, she jumped up and down gleefully on the couch, chucked her headband across the room while her hair tossed about, and screamed into a pillow, thankful that nobody was home to see her excitement.

Thursday was a beautiful, colorful blur. The fact that Ember and Lux didn't have much time together in or away from school only made them more drawn to one another. They searched for each other in the hallways between classes. He found her at lunch and made the whole table move down so he could sit with her. And while both were kept in the company of other classmates during Common Room Time, they kept eyes and smiles on each other.

Ember was waiting by Lux's locker after school. Lux and Anya approached, and he promptly introduced himself.

"Anya, hi. Fashion design, right?" Ember high-fived her. "You're on student council and president of the fall fashion show? And you play lacrosse. I'm Ember."

Anya didn't bother to hide how impressed she was that Ember knew this about her.

"I know who you are," she replied simply. "We'll be friends."

They were interrupted by the four Guerrero sisters and the rest of the Lacrosse team, who bombarded Anya with equipment, and asked her to help them carry things out onto the field.

"I'll call you tonight, Lux," Anya said, as she walked away with the team. "Bye Ember!"

"So what about tomorrow?" He nodded his head, smiling confidently, and ran his fingers through his hair.

"Tomorrow?" Lux asked, scanning her mind for every word that had been exchanged between them in the previous thirty-six hours.

"Yeah, in the morning. Can I see you before school?"

"Yes." Lux's ears were ringing, and she could feel the pink in her cheeks. She'd planned to get up early anyway and start painting a new idea that had surfaced in her mind that day. But for him, it could wait.

They met in Ember's front yard the next morning while the sky was still black. Lux yawned. She'd been awake all night thinking about him. He handed her a flashlight.

"Good morning," he said, in a way that made her wish she could meet with him every morning. They turned on their flashlights and headed down Juniper Pass.

They reached a small park a few blocks away and approached the bridge over Juniper Creek. It was silent, except for rippling water below them. They sat down on the bridge. Ember reached into his messenger bag and removed a thermos, two coffee mugs, apples, and croissants.

"Breakfast; and hopefully a sunrise if we can see it through the clouds," he said. He handed her a cup of coffee; she'd never had coffee before.

They ate slowly and yawned a lot. The horizon began to change and the first hazy light appeared. Lux examined Ember's face. He met her gaze and smiled. He reached for her hand.

She leaned her head on his shoulder, and decided it didn't matter what her family thought of her. Ember made up for all of them.

"Ember?" Lux stared into his eyes, shining from the morning light.

"Lux." He moved in closer.

She suddenly became very aware of the taste on her tongue, which no longer resembled minty toothpaste.

"I'm glad I met you." She turned away as she said it, just as Ember moved in to kiss her. His lips brushed her ear, and they both backed away. He let go of her hand.

"Me, too. We'll always have the sunrise," Ember replied after a long pause.

She wanted to laugh, but she also wanted to cry. Or run. But she couldn't move. He began to hum a tune that felt familiar, maybe simply because it was his voice, or maybe she'd heard it before. She wasn't sure. But it was comforting, so she didn't run.

They sat on the bridge for another hour and eventually talked, with a safe distance between them that eased Lux's coffee-breath anxiety. Ember led the conversation and asked a lot of questions, and before Lux was brave enough ask if they were on an official date, the day was upon them.

They cleaned up breakfast and walked to school. They fell into a discussion about their new classes and teachers. So far, Lux hadn't remembered a thing she'd learned in any of her classes, but she loved everything about school. The day dragged on and flew by and was exciting and overwhelming and perfect.

The last class was cancelled because of the school welcome assembly. Lux wandered down the hall looking for Ember, but he was nowhere to be found. She wondered why he hadn't planned for them to sit together, but before she had the opportunity to dive into her thoughts, Anya arrived at their lockers. She was accompanied by Francesca and Nicolette Guerrero, the Lacrosse team co-captains, whose arms were full of equipment.

"Lux, can I leave these in your locker?" Francesca asked. "I won't have time to run all the way back to the gym because I have to be the first one on the field after school. I want to impress Coach Spurz. And I don't want to miss this show!"

"Of course," Lux answered. She opened her locker. She kept looking down the hallway for Ember, but his entire crew seemed to be missing. She walked with Anya, Francesca, and Nicolette into the auditorium. They sat with the two youngest Guerrero sisters, Gabriella and Isabella, who'd saved seats for all of them.

"I'm Dr. Jacobs and I'd like to officially welcome you home to Briar Heights Academy. I enjoyed meeting with each of you during summer orientations. I hope and trust your first few days have given you a good idea of what your time here will be like. This is an environment structured for creative minds to excel and discover additional opportunities that will prepare you for college and professions beyond. You're all here for specific reasons, and we know you'll each produce magnificent, meaningful pieces, whether on film, stage, fabric, canvas, audio, or sheet music. You'll make sacrifices and fight to be understood outside these walls, but you will find your place and your purpose." Dr. Jacobs paused and smiled encouragingly. "Look around you. Your peers are not your competition. They are your support. This is your team."

Anya nudged Lux's arm and pointed to the stage. "There's Ember," she whispered.

Ember was sitting at a piano behind Dr. Jacobs. Lux realized she'd underestimated this boy: the only one performing at the welcome assembly for a school of fearless performers. Why hadn't he told her he'd be performing today? Shouldn't he have practiced in the morning instead of spending his waking hours with her? Then she could have started her painting, too. Butterflies erupted in her stomach.

After Dr. Jacobs finished his opening speech, having explained that the Briar Heights Academy motto, "Fight For Your Life," really meant "Fight for the best quality of life you can hope for," the lights dimmed, and a spotlight shone on Ember. He introduced himself and talked about the background of the ballad he'd written over the summer. Everyone in the auditorium was captivated.

"Bring him home and your parents will forget about any flaws they see in you," Anya whispered. "He's long-term."

Lux knew Anya had intended her comment to be positive. But for some reason in that moment, the Tazo family's whispered words violently tumbled to the front of her mind. The walls of uncertainty that had fallen with ease over the past few days instantly built themselves again, stronger this time, and higher. Her talent was a flaw. She was a burden. But, why? Lux watched Ember perform and was suddenly blind to what he could possibly see in her. Her confidence drained. She became anxious and ashamed and sank down in her seat.

"I'll be right back," she whispered to Anya.

She escaped the auditorium and ran. She couldn't catch her breath or stop the tears once she'd found sanctuary in a bathroom stall near the Sophomore Common Room. Eventually the assembly ended and school let out. A crowd of girls entered the bathroom and formed a line. When Lux heard Ember Sweeney's name mentioned, she hastily dried her face. She found her way back to the freshman hallway and was bombarded by Anya.

"Why did you leave!" Anya exclaimed. "He dedicated the song to the girl who won the award. And then he said, 'To many more sunrises.' He dedicated his song to you!"

Lux shook her head. This confused her even more.

"Wait, have you been crying? What's wrong?" Anya blurted out. But she was distracted by the Guerrero sisters retrieving and organizing the Lacrosse equipment. "Hold on. Don't leave," she said, then stepped away to help the girls.

Lux stole a glance down the hall with the hope of making some, or any, connection with Ember. She needed something from him, but she didn't know what. He was at his locker surrounded by his friends, as usual. But what she saw tore her heart. She had to look again. She couldn't form a clear thought. His arms were wrapped around the blonde girl Lux had seen with him earlier in the week. Then he kissed the girl on the forehead. Lux's stomach lurched. She ran without looking back, ignoring Anya's shouts ringing down the hallway.

She ran all the way home. The drizzle that had lingered all week finally turned into a storm. Soaked to the bone, she wept. Her tears blended with raindrops and thunder silenced her sobs. She locked herself inside the walls of her dark, colossal home. She did not understand anything.

Lux still hadn't moved from the couch in the den when the doorbell rang nearly an hour later. The door creaked loudly when she opened it. Startled, even though it was who she expected it to be, she shut it again quickly.

"Lux!" Ember's muffled voice came through the door. "Are you okay?"

She wiped her face dry and opened the door again. Behind Ember, street lamps were already giving life to the growing darkness.

He stepped back when he saw her.

"Weren't you at the assembly? What about our date tonight?" Ember asked, his voice shaking slightly. "What's wrong? What happened?"

"I...couldn't," Lux stammered, confiscating fresh tears.

"Why are you crying?"

"I'm not who you think I am. And you're not who I thought you were." She pictured the blonde girl. "I don't even know you. What was all of this, us, about? Who do you think you are!"

She slammed the door in his face. All she wanted to do was run into his arms and let him hold her. But she couldn't, because now she knew that he was holding someone else.

"What happened?" he shouted at the door. "Lux!"

She locked the door and walked away, blocking Ember out and barricading herself in. She cried hard into the pillow she'd screamed so delightedly into only two days earlier. Ember knocked on the door again and again, but she didn't answer. She felt sick to her stomach. She'd run from him in a shame that she couldn't explain. Eventually the knocking stopped. She was devastated, too sad even to climb up into her tree house and express it the only way she knew how.

After a sleepless night, Lux came to the conclusion that she'd have to be clear with Ember Sweeney about how she felt and what she knew. She had enough people in her life making a fool of her, and he wouldn't be another. She knew she'd see him again very soon. So she practiced a speech and held back her tears.

Sure enough, he was waiting in his front yard when Lux left for school Monday morning. He rushed over to her with a note in his hand.

"Lux. I'm so glad to see you —"

"I can't see you anymore. I know we live next door to each other, but it was never a problem before, so we can pretend like last week never happened," Lux said quickly. Her voice shook. "Like you never ran into me. Like I never fell for you."

"But, why?" Ember's face crumbled. He shook his head.

"I saw you with that girl!" she shouted. "You made a fool of me!" This wasn't part of her speech.

"What girl?! There's no girl!"

"She's blonde."

"Duffy Raven? She's my best friend. Like, my sister."

"Well..." Lux's speech had vanished. She was lost. And she realized Duffy wasn't the issue. "I don't trust you. I don't understand. And I don't even want to. So please stay away from me. Pretend we never met. Leave me alone. If there's any good in you at all —"

"That's not fair. There is good in me...but I can't leave you alone. Duffy is my friend! I like you...I —"

"It's not you then, or her, okay? It's me!" Lux cried. "I can't be around you! I don't know who I am! And I don't want anyone to tell me! I'm not good enough for you. So just leave me alone. I have to figure it out alone."

"That's a lie," Ember said weakly.

"Promise me. Pretend we never met."

"No, I will not."

"What will it take for you to forget I exist?" Lux asked pointedly.

"Stop it." He took the note in his hand and shoved it in his back pocket.

"Fine, then. I just don't like you."

He said nothing. They both knew she was lying. She looked into his eyes and saw pain, and she wept. She'd inflicted it, but she couldn't undo it. She wouldn't. As much as she wanted to, this was for the best.

"I hate you Ember Sweeney. Don't ever speak to me again."

Finally, he nodded. "You need love."

"No, I don't."

He took a step back and slowly retreated into his home.

She didn't see him again for a very long time. Weeks, at least. And by then, the cold reality had sunk in for both of them. Something changed in him because of her. An edge appeared, like a cut. He was wounded, and no girl would ever get so close again. Yes, there would be girls. Always. But deep within the subconscious of his heart, Ember would hope to hurt them all, just enough, so that distance would remain. He would never forget how she'd hurt him, and he would never get hurt like that again.

Lux hated herself for what she'd done, but he was better off. She was a mess. She was a disaster. She believed lies. She couldn't be herself because she didn't know who that was. How could someone like him care for someone like her? It didn't add up. The worst thing about it all was that she never stopped feeling for him. His song began to play in her heart. She was haunted.

ONE

Album: Colour The Small One

Track: Three

Lux woke on the dreary morning of October first, reluctantly wondering about Ember Mason Sweeney. She grabbed
her phone from the bedside table to check the time and found
a group text message from Piper Speedman, film student and
BHA's official informant.

> Piper: Guess who is back with Blondie... Is this the
> FIFTH time they've dated?! Can't they just make it
> forever already?!

She dropped her phone to the floor. Whimpering, she hid
back under the covers. "Blondie" and Ember were inseparable.
Two years had passed since Lux had fallen for him and then
ruined everything by rejecting him. She didn't quite know why

she'd done it. And because of that, she felt she couldn't fix it.

Ember was complicated for a high schooler. He was mature: humble, kind, and a musical prodigy; therefore, disciplined. He was an intimately kind writer of words in yearbooks and on Sour Enchantment bar napkins, where his band held a residency. He played piano, guitar, and drums, but he was really known for his voice and the lyrics he wrote. Lux didn't stand a chance of getting over him, and really, there was no argument that she should try. But she never talked about it. Every day she vowed to believe she'd never known him. Sometimes it worked.

Lux sat up in bed and tried to ignore the dread festering in her stomach. Maybe it was normal to feel this way. The weather certainly agreed. Icy rain spattered against the windowpane and streamed methodically to the base of the glass. The breeze gave wings to drenched ginger and ruby oak leaves sporadically departing from the ancient trees, and they danced beautifully, pirouetting to their death. She wanted to paint the scene, but it would have to wait.

She rifled through the assortment of black in her closet. She glanced back out the window, and chose an outfit that could handle both rain and three classes worth of splattered paint. She pulled on a charcoal thermal shirt and over it, her favorite black hoodie with blue birds sewn on the arms. It read "LITTLE WING," the LITTLE separated from the WING by a wearied zipper. Arrabelle had gotten it for her years ago. Lux didn't know the significance of the words one way or the other, but it was cozy. She then chose an old pair of black and white striped leggings, which reminded her of her favorite Tim Burton film. They would go under her favorite black skinny jeans, which were decimated by rips and tears, because she'd been wearing them since the eighth grade.

"Lux! You have ten minutes!" Mrs. Tazo shouted cheerfully from downstairs. She had no idea just how annoying she was in the morning. Lux knew she had ten minutes, but she humored her mother; parents often assumed their children were too caught up with friends and love to properly keep track of things like time. But Lux kept track of time. She would pass Ember's house in eleven minutes and walk one block ahead of him on the nineteen-minute walk to school.

She decided to hurry so she could get to school early and track down Piper Speedman. But she stumbled as she threw her left leg into her jeans, and her toe caught on a frayed hole at the knee. Mid-stumble, she caught a glimpse of movement in Ember's kitchen and flung herself unwillingly against the frigid window. Her face landed against the glass with a splat, framing her mortified expression in plain sight of Ember himself. He gazed, bewildered, through his kitchen window and bit into an apple. Lux was mortified.

"Lux Grace Tazo!" her mother shouted again. Lux nervously pried her mouth from the window, leaving fog and a bit of drool on the glass, and shook her head in disarray. She then proceeded to carefully straighten her hoodie and gracefully button her jeans, again whimpering under her breath. She did not look back. With her cheeks deeply flushed, she adjusted her messenger bag over her shoulder and slunk from the scene.

"Take this to go." Mrs. Tazo handed a small can of pineapple juice to Lux, scrutinizing her, while holding a phone to her ear. "I'm taking the spa staff to dinner at seven. Will you be at Anya's? You need a jacket. A scarf, at least." Mrs. Tazo scurried around the kitchen, glancing back at Lux. "Your face is red."

Lux rolled her eyes.

"It's Thursday. I stay at Anya's on Fridays. We're going to the Sour Enchantment for a show. Tonight, I need to finish my Women's Literature presentation."

"Of course I know it's Thursday. And please, go shopping this weekend. Honestly, you look like a hobo." Mrs. Tazo threw her free hand out toward Lux. "Anya doesn't dress like this!"

"I just wanted to be warm, and it's *Boho*. Bohemian. Anya's an aspiring designer, *as you know*. We're different." Lux shrugged.

"Well, have her dress you, then!" Mrs. Tazo said. "What if they have to switch to uniforms because of girls like you?"

"Anya likes how I dress. She thinks I'm trendy. Bohemian is a legitimate style. But, by the way, this particular outfit is considered "grunge," which was trendy in the 1990s, and Anya approves of that, too."

"At least let Arrabelle style you. I'll have her come by Saturday and take you to the Grove. If Anya's busy, bring Piper. She's classy, too. Though she only ever wears jeans."

"I don't want to be styled by Arrabelle."

"I'll have dinner delivered at six," Mrs. Tazo said, changing the subject. "You'll be home by then, right?" She ripped the tags off a yellow and gray striped scarf and matching mittens and followed Lux toward the front door. "Dad has a deposition that needs to be finished tonight. Text him if you need anything, since my dinner is technically a meeting." With a quick, exasperated grin, she nodded toward Lux's grimy, bubblegum pink sneakers. "Tie your shoe." She couldn't refrain; her face twitched.

The laces on Lux's right shoe were held together with an old, hardened piece of green gum. The left shoe was untied. Lux gazed down at what she was wearing and finally at her shoes. Her heart sank.

"You know, I'll just pick up new ones today. Size six, got it," Mrs. Tazo chirped. "And as far as Bohemian goes, all that means to me is that you spend hundreds of dollars on oversized things that hide your figure, like wraps and cardigans, which you're not even wearing today. You just look…"

Lux tuned out her mother's voice.

The thing was, Mr. and Mrs. Tazo were perfect. The perfect couple. The perfect parents. The perfect friends with the perfect careers. The perfect home. The perfect appearance. And they had one perfect daughter named Arrabelle, who resembled a Barbie doll: pink stun-gun in her manicured hand, and always a new, unsuspecting boyfriend in her shadow. Mrs. Tazo was currently developing a new sea salt product line, the successor to the Arrabelle series, which would surely *not* be named Lux. A handful of celebrities were already lined up to promote the future product, so the fact that Lux bit her paint-stained fingernails and constantly forgot to show up for her pedicure appointments drove Mrs. Tazo *perfectly* crazy.

"I know, you think I look like I belong in public school. Whatever that means," Lux said matter-of-factly. She was fairly certain her mother believed Briar Heights Academy was a European Boarding School, and not a creative arts school that accepted and embraced every student as unique, no matter who or what they wanted to be. She tied the scarf around her neck and pulled on the mittens. She would not tie her shoe, but that was on principal alone. She was about to argue that she didn't want new shoes at all. But Mrs. Tazo opened the front door, and three hauntingly familiar voices echoed down the street. The guys.

Tanner Vanderbilt, Luther Warwick, and Jamison Kincaid were Ember Sweeney's best friends. They were all in a band together called Falling Like Ember. They all looked the same to Lux: tall and lanky with muscular forearms that were quite ready for tattoos, dark faux-hawks, and distinct, confident voices that carried over crowds. Intimidating. And everyone in Briar Heights knew of them. The guys had one other best friend: Blondie, a.k.a. Duffy Raven. She was much quieter than the guys, petite, and her vanilla latte hair contrasted with her soft amethyst eyes and olive skin. Lux thought Duffy was the prettiest girl in school, so it made sense that Ember kept her close. Duffy was not officially in the band even though, like Ember, she was known at BHA for having a remarkable singing voice.

Lux wandered outside, forgetting about her mother completely. She unlatched the ivy clad wrought iron gate belonging to 38 Juniper Pass, which looked like the entrance to a secret garden. She started down the cobblestone street, adjusted her messenger bag again, pulled her hood over her head, and followed the alluring and intimidating boys at a safe distance. Two of the guys were gripping guitar cases, and the other was twirling drumsticks. They marched up the steps that belonged to 27 Orchard Way, and were greeted by Mr. Sweeney, a charming, older version of his son.

Even after they'd joined Ember in the parlor, Mr. Sweeney held the door open for Lux. He waved. She'd come to a stop in front of the yard without realizing it. She gasped and scampered away. Even though they were neighbors, Lux knew she and Ember were worlds apart.

Thursday's homework load couldn't have been any heavier, with upcoming exams in four of her five classes, an unexpected three-page Medieval History paper, and an additional Latin quiz, which would take place Monday. Lux had been troubled all day with thoughts of Mr. Sweeney holding the door open for her. Should she have accepted the invitation? What was the worst that could have happened?

Lux perked up when she saw Anya waiting by their lockers with a mischievous look on her face.

"You've got news. What is it?" Lux yearned for a distraction from her mind. She studied her tall best friend's face. Then she realized she'd never found Piper to verify the rumor.

"It's about you. Oh, and here." Anya handed Lux a tattered journal they shared for writing letters to one another.

"What?" Lux said, caught off guard. She slid the journal into her messenger bag.

"Something paramount happened today." Anya swept her hair away from her face. Her eyes shined. "I want to explain before —" she stopped and her gaze darted past Lux.

"Explain what?" Lux crossed her arms defensively. She had a bad feeling about what Anya was about to say. Anya enjoyed being mischievous, and sometimes she didn't think things through. Students rushed by them, eager to leave for the day. Lux knew them all and was friends with most, but in the moment, she recognized no one.

"It's *okay*. And before you ask if I'm up to my matchmaking shenanigans again, look — here comes your smoke show..." Anya grabbed Lux by the shoulders and turned her around so she was face to face with Ember. He was smiling directly at her. There was no mistaking it. He slowed down and looked her over.

"Just smile!" Anya whispered into Lux's ear.

"Moonbeams and fairy tales," he said, and chuckled. "All she ever thinks about." His voice melted into the air between them, and he winked at her.

"What?" she said.

Ember hesitated. Suddenly alarmed, he looked to Anya, who nodded confidently. "Your hoodie. Jimi Hendrix? Little Wing. Anyway, careful, your shoe's untied." He disappeared again into the whirlwind of students. Lux stumbled back, and Anya caught her. What he'd said was irrelevant. Because the fact that he'd spoken to her at all made no sense. She turned and glared at Anya. Anya grabbed Lux's hands excitedly and resisted jumping up and down.

"I talked to Ember Sweeney today and he said that their album is almost finished except for one track and — album art! He said he wants someone he knows, someone from our school, to design the cover. And he chose you! We were by Mr. Nickel's classroom, and I showed him what you've been working on, and he loved it, Lux! He wants to talk to you about it! He wants to *talk*! I think he's pretty scared of you though, so he's working up the courage."

Lux had never heard Anya speak so fast.

"I knew it would happen eventually. Haven't I been telling you for two years? It's perfect..." Anya sighed happily. She still had no idea that Lux had once told Ember she hated him, and that was why they didn't speak.

"Don't say *perfect*," Lux whispered. She sat down and leaned against her locker. The scenario didn't add up. After two years of secretly admiring the boy she'd so severely denied, someone who'd remained so close, yet so far away, it could not be this simple. She felt very strongly that any artwork of hers Ember had seen was not good. Not good enough. Not good enough for him. And she knew there was no way they could move forward without a formal reconciliation, one in which she apologized and confessed the real truth.

"So, I can't read the look on your face. Are you mad? Please don't be, I was just trying to help! What's wrong? He really loved the idea — what?" Anya threw her hands in the air.

"It's personal!" Lux shouted.

"Your paintings are on display all around school," Anya argued.

"Never mind. I'm not, they're not...enough." Lux hid her face in her hands.

"Enough of what? I was only trying to help. He wants to meet with you. I told him you'd be at home this afternoon, but I'll tell him to forget it," Anya said.

"I don't want your help. I'm not like you!" Lux's eyes burned. "You can't just force yourself into people's lives and try to fix everything."

"What are you talking about?" Anya asked dejectedly.

"Not everyone gets a happy ending!" Lux shouted.

"You think I don't know that?" Anya whispered, and took a step back.

"Just leave me alone. I want to be alone."

Lux stood up and filled her messenger bag with books. She couldn't look at Anya; she was afraid of what she might say next.

"Maybe one of these days you *will* be all alone," Anya said, her voice trembling. "You'll wake up old, and you still won't know yourself because you'll still be letting other people control your happiness." She turned swiftly, but hesitated. "That was low, Lux. I don't have a family. I am alone. I'll never see my parents again. And I would never wish that for you. But I try to be happy. Whatever it is, get over it. Get it out of the way so you can be free and live." And she was gone. Lux knew she'd broken Anya's fearless heart.

Lux felt awful. Anya was an orphan, but she never talked about it, never complained about it. In fact, she never seemed to complain about anything. Lux could see the downward spiral she was trapped in but didn't know how to get out. She'd been running for a long time and now realized something: she needed to stop and turn around and run back. She needed to undo the past. But how?

On the walk home Lux didn't even think about her exchange with Ember, although she did think about the first song she listened to that morning, which she'd done every single day for the past two years. She just wanted to send him a simple text.

Lux: Sia. Breathe me.

And maybe he would write back in paragraphs. And they would have a connection again.

TWO

Album: Unclear Sky - EP

Track: Three

"Kiddo," Mr. Tazo whispered, and rested a hand on his daughter's shoulder. While struggling to concentrate on homework, Lux had fallen asleep huddled against the bay window in the kitchen. "It's late; go to bed."

She rubbed her burning eyes and looked around the kitchen, disoriented.

"What time is it?" She'd been in the middle of a nightmare, screaming at Ember to stay away from her. She'd wanted to say something entirely different, and couldn't control her words. She swallowed the painful lump at the bottom of her throat.

"It's the middle of the night." He grasped Lux's arm to help her stand and accompanied her to the stairs. They both knew Mrs. Tazo had come home and gone to bed at exactly 9:45 pm, like she did every single night. She hadn't checked on Lux.

Lux glanced at her father and noticed him clearly for the first time in what felt like a long time. More silver than usual was poking out from his untidy, normally short, salt-and-pepper hair, matched by the graying stubble on his face. He was aging. Standing a few steps above him on the stairs, she reached forward and touched the hair by his temple. He looked different, but maybe it was just the dim lighting in the dead of night.

"Dad, do you color your hair?" she asked, and yawned.

"When your mother makes me, yes. But I missed my appointment last week."

"I like it this way. You could grow it out. You'd look cool." Lux giggled.

"In that case, I'll think about it. But I'm not sure it's worth enduring your mother's and sister's nagging."

"Good point. I wouldn't wish that one anyone." Lux rolled her eyes, yawned again, and turned for the stairs. "Night."

"Lux?"

"Yeah?"

"Is everything okay? Friends? School? Us?"

She considered what time it was, how tired and sad she truly was, and the unfinished homework she'd fallen asleep in front of. She sighed. "Of course."

Restless sleep accompanied Lux through the rest of the night while she dreamt of laughing strangers with umbrellas. The stranger's faces turned into Ember and then into Anya, who shook her head in disapproval and cried. Lux tossed and turned. Her blankets tangled around her arms and legs. Just before dawn, she sat up in bed and stared out the window at Ember's house. If this was how her nights were going to be, she decided she'd rather not dream at all.

Friday morning started off normally enough. Following her mother's usual shrewd appraisal, Lux meandered through the parlor gazing down at her grubby shoes. *Careful, your shoe's untied*, played over in her mind in Ember's voice.

She rounded the corner onto Ember's street and noticed a shiny pink cruiser bicycle parked in his front yard. Duffy Raven's bicycle. So early in the morning? Lux walked slowly. Nobody caught up with her. She was alone. The enormous trees on either side of the street bowed in toward her. Leaves began flying wildly around her as the wind picked up, and she shivered fiercely. It then occurred to her, for no reason in particular, to take a detour. A detour meant a longer walk to school. It also included a peculiar view of something most people in Briar Heights never spoke of. She reached the crossroads that led to school or the countryside and took a left instead of the usual right. The cobblestone ended. The road ahead was broken and holding hostage deep puddles of worm-infested water. A fog crept up the vacant street.

Then she saw it, its backdrop a thick forest, and its surroundings a serene park. The Lara Rehabilitation Clinic. Dim lights flickered. The outside of the building looked quite beautiful; it was the inside that everyone was afraid of. Lux found herself walking up the path toward the wrought iron gates. The grounds were groomed, and vines crept up and over the stone wall that kept everyone out. Or in. She grasped one of the wrought iron bars of the gate and peered inside. Drops of rain rested on thick blades of grass. She felt her shoulders relax, and her foggy breath moved slowly through the barriers of the gate. Maybe this was where she belonged.

"Can I help you?"

Lux whirled around with a breathless scream and instinctively shoved the tall, dark haired man towering over her. He took a few steps back, and she glanced back only for a better look before running for her life. She fought for breath, but seemed to have none. The strong wind in her eyes caused tears to stream down her flushed cheeks. Where was Anya at a time like this? Oh, right. A bell rang in the distance; school had started.

The halls were empty when Lux reached school. Her pounding heart plummeted. She pictured Anya avoiding her the way she,

Lux, had avoided Ember for so long. She supposed she'd end up alone again today. No show at The Sour Enchantment. No midnight milkshakes at Apples and Worms Diner. No sleepover. She was still shaking so visibly that she decided to hide in the nearest bathroom until she was calm. She thought about her decision to undo the past and was more confused than ever.

Lux found her way to Abnormal Psychology even though there were just a few minutes remaining. The teacher, Ms. Rehberger, stopped short at the sight of Lux in the doorway. The entire class turned to stare. Lux felt her eyes bug out.

"Are you okay, Ms. Tazo?" Lux didn't realize how disheveled she must look, but Ms. Rehberger rushed over to her.

"Uh…" Her mouth became very dry. She felt her eyes dilating and her face sweating. She felt there was no other choice but to run from this situation as well. So she did. But Ms. Rehberger chased her down the hall.

"Lux, *stop*. What happened?" Ms. Rehberger persisted. Lux saw the indisputable worry on her face and decided it was safe to be honest.

"I went by Lara on the way to school," Lux began, avoiding eye contact. "I don't even know why. It was awful." Ms. Rehberger pushed her black framed glasses up on her nose, and swept her blonde waves from her face. She relaxed her shoulders a bit, but crossed her arms, waiting for the rest of the story.

"I just wanted to see what it looked like. I was standing at the gate, and there was a man —"

"An inmate?" Ms. Rehberger interjected dramatically. "You didn't go inside, did you?"

"I, I don't know, he, I —"

"What did he do to you?"

"Nothing! He scared me, so I just ran away."

"Lux. Are you *sure* that's all that happened?"

Lux nodded. Ms. Rehberger motioned for Lux to follow her back to the classroom. "Promise me you'll stay away from the Lara

Clinic, all right?" The entire class was peeking out the doorway now, listening in on Ms. Rehberger and Lux. A multitude of whispers erupted in a ghostly echo through the hallway.

"I think I will go to the nurse," Lux said.

She convinced the nurse her parents didn't need to be called and proceeded to spend the rest of the morning resting on a cot in a cold, dark room.

By the time the lunch hour arrived, everyone in school knew that Lux had been at the Lara Rehabilitation Clinic. Some understood her to have been committed, and others believed her to be the victim of an attempted kidnapping by a hallucinogenic patient. It was strange to hear so much gossip about herself. Through all of this, Anya was nowhere to be seen. This bothered Lux more than anything, even more than the group text message Piper had sent, accidentally including Lux and spreading the rumor in the first place.

Lux finally emerged from the nurse's office after CRT. She didn't want to miss Advanced Canvas III. She knew everyone would be more focused on their projects than on her. Even Dylan Black, who sat next her, and was probably her best friend in the art program, would know better than to address any rumors while they were in class. This was their quiet time.

"I'm giving you homework," Mr. Nickel, Lux's favorite teacher of all time, suggested in his British accent. He glanced at her bland canvas, perched on an easel. She gawked at him. Nobody else was getting an extra assignment.

"I can't figure out your method," he said, lowering his voice. "You were known for luminosity when you embarked upon your studies here. But this, compared to *your* style...this is dark. It's missing something. I feel you sometimes forget I've been noticing your work since you were about five years old."

"Maybe my style is changing," she replied, crossing her arms. She didn't appreciate him playing the "I've known you forever" card.

"Don't misunderstand me, this is remarkable work," he said, "but I think your work reflects you, and this is telling me something's the matter."

Lux looked away. "So what's my homework?" She knew she could trust him. He'd been a part of her life since she was in kindergarten and was like a big brother. He understood her. Mr. Nickel was still in his twenties and a charming hipster whose friends were rock stars. To say he was popular with the students at BHA was an understatement. And his best friend was Astor Dane, owner of the Sour Enchantment, which only added to his appeal. But Lux had one hang-up: he was also best friends with Arrabelle Tazo. Lux couldn't talk with him about family.

"Where has your light gone?" Mr. Nickel didn't wait for an explanation but nodded toward the door, as if he knew where her light had gone. "Let's take a walk."

She followed him out of the studio, and they walked to the Sophomore Common Room. On one wall, among other works of art, was an intensely bright painting Lux had completed her sophomore year, titled "A Moment of Clarity." It had won the grand prize in a competition that Mr. Nickel had forced her to enter and which she'd hidden from her parents. Lux sat in a plush chair across from Mr. Nickel, facing away from her painting.

"I want to ask you a question." He moved forward to the edge of the couch. "And I know you well enough to know whether you answer truthfully. What's going on at home?"

"We can't talk about home," she said immediately. "You know that."

He moved back on the couch and relaxed, mindlessly scratching his newly groomed beard. He frowned and finally cleared his throat.

"But we can. I'm always on your side." When Lux didn't answer, he continued. "Anyway, it's time to be looking seriously at universities, specifically the Art Institute. Your resume needs more credentials, and I want to help you."

"*This* is you." Mr. Nickel motioned to the painting. "I can't keep forcing you to compete. You need to step out on your own."

Lux looked at the painting. It made her want to cry.

"I'm not going to contact your parents, but —"

"Maybe my light *is* gone," Lux said finally, choked up.

"Then we must find it," he answered promptly. Lux nodded. "Lux, I'd hate for you to realize how much I care about the lives of my students, because I am very cool, and I do have a fulfilling life of my own." He winked at her. "But I do pay attention, especially to you, and I hear a *lot* of rumors around here."

"Well, don't believe them, Jackson," she replied, with a hint of annoyance.

"Hey, come on," he said, frowning. But he shrugged after a pause. "We're going to find your light. Deal?" Lux nodded. "Brilliant. Hey. I'm always here for you. We're family."

They walked back to the studio in an unusual silence. A few classmates, whom Lux would normally call friends, whispered when she, still accompanied by Mr. Nickel, approached her work station, the slate colored paint dripping and drying on the canvas.

"*By* the way, I spotted Ember Sweeney in here yesterday looking at *your* work." He tapped her shoulder. "He's searching for cover art for his band's new album. If you don't know who he is, find him and introduce yourself. I mean, I'm sure you know him; he's *Ember Sweeney*."

"Keep your voice down," Lux hushed Mr. Nickel. He looked momentarily confused, then smiled broadly. He patted her shoulder.

"Well, he obviously already knows who you are." He winked.

"He's my neighbor," Lux said, swiftly turning to her painting and blushing fiercely.

"Lovely. Well, take the opportunity. Show him why you're right for him," Mr. Nickel concluded. "Anyway, your homework. I'm sending you home with one canvas and three colors of paint. Pink. Yellow. Gold."

"What? Ew! No." Lux glared at Mr. Nickel. "Pink?" She pictured

Duffy's bicycle.

"Bring me something brilliant." He grinned. "Paint your five year old soul. Go back."

Lux shook her head. She was too annoyed to cry.

"Mr. Nickel, what's the first song you listened to today?" she asked, wanting to change the subject, and wanting the attention away from herself.

Mr. Nickel took his phone from his pocket, opened the messages, and gave the phone to Lux.

Astor: Still Fighting It. Ben Folds. Remember when we used to listen to this in Arrabelle's car?
Jackson: That, and The Get Up Kids. Mass Pike!

Lux handed the phone back to Mr. Nickel. She knew the song. She could still remember overhearing Astor, Jackson, and Arrabelle belting it out in Arrabelle's bedroom. He patted her back and walked to the front of the class.

"You okay, Lux?" Dylan asked softly. He didn't look away from his canvas.

"Yeah. Thanks," Lux said. She stared at her unfinished work.

When the fifth and last class of the day rolled around, the stories about Lux had spun out of control. The latest was that she was going to be committed to Lara after school that night. The absurdities were settling in her mind like cement. Grim thoughts crept in again; she needed to undo so much.

Students wandered into Medieval History lazy and happy because it was Friday, but every one of them eyed Lux upon arriving. She instead tried to think about other things like...Ember. Only he could occupy her mind from what was happening around her. *Ember Sweeney is my neighbor*, she thought. *Ember is...such a smoke show. Ugh, whatever. He's okay...and nice, and he said hi to me yesterday...or acknowledged me, anyway. For the first time in two years. Even after I told him to forget I exist. But, why?*

Ember is dating Duffy. I think, maybe. Ember will be at The Sour Enchantment tonight. He's always there.

Nearly the entire school would be at the Sour. It's what everyone did on Friday and Saturday nights. Lux wondered what it would be like if she went to the show alone. It wasn't like she didn't have other friends. She had a lot of great friends at school. She could go with the Guerrero sisters, but they would ask questions.

Lux spotted Anya at the lockers. She reached into her messenger bag and handed over the journal. "I didn't see you today. I was looking for you." It had been Lux's turn, anyway. She'd written a rare and heartfelt explanation of her outburst. "I'm really sorry," Lux said quietly. "It's been a hard day. I'm sorry."

"I took care of it. I found Sweeney and told him to forget it," Anya explained briskly. "I know you're haunted by him and by your own talent, and while I don't understand, I should have respected you." Lux found her stomach sinking once again, and her face reflected it. "That's what you wanted me to do, right?" Anya looked both frustrated and worried.

"I guess," Lux said. "Everything's just a mess. I don't know how to fix it. I don't know how to undo everything."

Anya set her jaw. "First of all, you can't undo anything. You have to start new. I wish I could undo what happened to my family, but guess what? All I have to work with is this moment." She shrugged. "Anyway, ninth grade was a long time ago," she said. She swapped out books in her locker. "Ember doesn't even remember what went wrong between you two. He's just confused. Typical guy. He thinks —"

"Wait, you two talked about *us*?" Lux sputtered. "What did he say?"

Anya threw her hands up in surrender. "STOP! That's enough, Lux!" Anya was angry now. "Of course we talked about you. He's been wondering for two years what he did to make you hate him. He didn't think you'd want to talk to him, and he was *right*! But

I said you *would* talk to him, because I wanted to help you," she said, exasperated. "That's it."

"I don't hate him," Lux argued.

"Then stop acting like it!" Anya shot back.

Then, like the day before, Lux turned and was face to face with *him*, Ember Sweeney. His arm around none other than Duffy Raven. Everyone paused. Time slowed. Even the next words out of Duffy's mouth moved slowly. "'The Fear You Won't Fall.' Joshua Radin," she said, glancing at Lux. Anya eyed Ember, then Lux. Lux watched Ember and Duffy together, and Ember noticed.

"'Let It Be Me.' Ray LaMontagne," he said. Then he deliberately tightened his grip around Duffy. Lux backed into her locker. With a soul-melting grin, Ember observed her in a way that made her wonder if she'd forgotten an important piece of clothing that day. He surely couldn't be eyeing her for the same reason every other student was, because they were all avoiding actual eye contact. His direct stare penetrated deeper into her heart than she could handle. Then Duffy smiled and waved at her, too. What.

"Sour Enchantment tonight!" Ember announced then, and everyone in the hallway cheered. He turned back once more for a good look at her.

"What will it take for you to believe, Lux?" Anya whispered. They stared after Ember.

"Who communicates in lyrics and song titles, anyway?" Lux exclaimed. "I mean, movie quotes, maybe. But it's like they have their own language. And is Blondie invisible to you? Duffy Raven. The coolest, prettiest girl in school. It's always gone back to her since the beginning," Lux argued dolefully. "And even if she wasn't in the picture, he's dated half the girls in school."

"Sure, dated. And broken up with. He's reckless. But he's never looked at any of them the way he looks at you. You're the one he always wanted," Anya said. "You're mysterious. Anyway, you *know* the girls he's dated have asked *him* out, not the other way around."

"Except for Duffy. And I'm not mysterious," Lux said.

"You're definitely cryptic. I haven't *officially* heard that Ember and Duffy are dating. Like I've told you so many times before, I think they're like siblings," Anya said. "I for one, ignored Piper's gossipy text, just like I ignored her again this afternoon when she said you've gone crazy. Side note, it's a good thing you don't care about social media. You're everywhere right now. Plus, I thought Duffy was with one of the guys in the band now."

"But I saw her bike at his house this morning!" Lux exclaimed. "They're together all the time, including right this very minute."

"Guess what, Ember Sweeney's never asked me about Duffy Raven! He asked me about Lux Tazo; so there. Are we going to the Enchantment tonight, or not?"

Lux sulked. She couldn't resist turning in Ember's direction again. "Haven't you heard? I'm about to be committed to the Lara Rehabilitation Clinic." She rolled her eyes.

"I did hear something like that." Anya smirked. "And if you were, I'd visit you. What's the real story?"

"I needed you today! I have been alone in this place, hearing the most bizarre accusations, and then Mr. Nickel tried to talk —"

"I'm here now. What happened?" Anya repeated calmly.

"Basically, I walked by Lara and some guy freaked me out, so I ran. That's it. Maybe I'm a little bit scared that I do belong there," Lux said, staring at the ground. "But, yes, Sour Enchantment. And midnight milkshakes. Arrabelle's stopping by the house tonight, so I have to see her first. I'll have her drive me to the Sour. Rodrigo's playing, right?"

"You must not have heard, since you're more popular than him today. Rodrigo cancelled last minute. Falling Like Ember is headlining." Anya chuckled.

"Popular, ha." Lux rolled her eyes, but caught sight of Ember again at the end of the hall. He turned and looked at her. They locked eyes. It was the connection she'd needed two years ago when she doubted his intentions in the first place. She shivered.

"You know, maybe Duffy Raven is the prettiest and most popular girl in this school — to *you*. But everyone here is just who they are. Maybe *you're* the prettiest and most popular to someone else. You never know who looks up to you. So you have to care. You have to try. You're so damn talented."

"Thanks, mom."

"Come on, we know your mom wouldn't say that," Anya continued, determined. "But really, be nice to yourself. You're awesome. What are you going to do with what you have? It's your choice. There's nothing I see in Blondie that's better than what I see in you. It's not like that. You know, I have Astronomy with her, and she's really nice," Anya added.

Lux said nothing.

"See you in a little! *Falling Like Ember!* Apples and Worms! Sour Enchantment!" Anya sang and skipped away. Lux began to feel strangely optimistic. She started to smile but tried to frown, and she couldn't.

"Don't run," an unmistakable voice spoke softly. "Please." Ember Sweeney was a few steps behind Lux and cautiously gaining on her. She jumped. This was the second time this had happened in one day, but she was too startled to run this time. His jade eyes glowed with endearing curiosity. He smiled warmly, but uncertainly, and shrugged off his pea coat. He handed it to her, and she obliged with a shy, unexpected smile.

"I just want to know one thing. Will you be at the Sour Enchantment tonight?" he asked. Lux pursed her lips and nodded; her voice had abandoned her.

"Good. That's really good; I was hoping you would be," Ember said. He sounded nervous. They walked in unison down the cobblestone street. No words were spoken, only quick glances stolen.

Lux wondered if she should offer a casual "I'm sorry" and apologize for something along the lines of ripping his heart out, and for lying about hating him. But she didn't. Ember's hands were shoved in his pockets and he was shivering. Lux held her messenger bag protectively.

"So, I'll find you there tonight." Ember shrugged and smiled. They'd stopped in front of his house. The lights were on inside and music blasted out the windows. Duffy Raven's pink bicycle was leaning against the fence again. Lux took off Ember's coat and handed it back to him.

All I have to work with is this moment. Lux heard Anya's voice in her mind.

"You know, I was thinking about that first week of ninth grade," she blurted out. *Goodbye* was what she'd meant to say. She cringed. Ember's eyes grew wide. He opened his mouth to speak, but Jamison opened the front door then. He stopped when he saw Lux and Ember together, dropped the apple he was holding, and ran back inside.

"Let's talk about that tonight," Ember said. "I have something for you. It'll be at the show."

"Okay," Lux replied quickly, short of breath. She turned and ran home.

Upon reaching the front door, Lux couldn't find her house key. She rummaged through her messenger bag but found nothing. She must have left it hanging in her locker. The garage code didn't work. Arrabelle had forgotten it a week earlier and tried it so many times that it had locked, and it hadn't been reset yet. Lux left her messenger bag at the door and ran all the way back to school, adrenaline carrying her along. A storm was moving in, the weather growing darker and colder by the minute. Her face began to sting as the wind whipped her hair against her cheeks, but something had stirred her heart. She couldn't stop smiling.

She made it back to school in ten minutes. The vintage street lamps surrounding BHA were already lit, illuminating nightfall. Everything was beautiful again. She went inside, moving quickly past the faculty offices, corridors, and the Junior Common Room. The place was nearly empty. She opened her locker and, sure enough, the key was there. She stuffed it into the pocket of her long cardigan and headed back the way she'd come in.

"Wait, what?" Lux stopped short outside the Junior Common Room. Her painting that Mr. Nickel had discussed with her earlier in the day had been moved there. It hung above the fireplace and a spotlight shone on it.

"Lux, what are you doing here so late?" Mr. Nickel appeared from down the hall with Mr. Besser, head of the film department, and Mr. Jorgensen, head of the music department. Lux pointed to the painting, her jaw hanging open. She said nothing even when the teachers greeted her.

"Looks lovely here, doesn't it?" Mr. Nickel said. "Oh. I talked with Astor Dane just a moment ago. Astor had just spoken with Ember Sweeney, and Ember forgot his school bag in the auditorium. I said I'd bring it to the Sour tonight. But you're his neighbor, right? Could you drop it by?" He smiled. Lux's jaw continued to hang open. Eventually she nodded.

"Is she okay?" Mr. Jorgensen asked.

"She's brilliant," Mr. Nickel replied. "She's splendid. I heard she'll be at the show tonight, too. Is that right, Lux?"

"Yes." Lux finally found her voice. "I'll be there."

"See you tonight, then." Mr. Nickel smiled. "Oh, and Ember's bag is on the desk in my office. The door is open."

"Got it," Lux said in a daze, and waved goodbye. She wandered into Mr. Nickel's office and spotted the bag. She adjusted it over her shoulder, feeling important and amazed and nervous. Then she returned again to the neighborhood of Juniper Creek.

Instead of delivering the messenger bag to Ember's house, Lux found herself taking it home with her, which she hadn't intended to do. She walked through the dark house, through the sage-scented kitchen, and opened the French doors, which led to the cozy backyard. Well, it would have been cozy if it hadn't been windy, raining, and typical October cold. She entered the backyard and stared up at her favorite place in the world.

Lux's treehouse was beyond compare. It had originally been named Tazo Castle and given to Arrabelle as a birthday gift. But

Lux inherited it when Arrabelle got her first car. The three-room structure was carpeted and had electricity and heat. It also had a bell for room service, a dumbwaiter, a tire swing, and a rope ladder. Boards were nailed to the tree trunk for steps. Lux preferred this over the rope ladder. The main room was round with a domed ceiling, and opened into two additional rooms. Incidentally, one window offered a perfect view of the Sweeney home. Reluctant tears and deep secrets were hidden inside the tree, but more importantly, so were hopeful dreams and enduring inspiration.

Lux adjusted both messenger bags across her shoulders and climbed up the crooked steps that led to the treehouse. She crawled into the round room and dropped the bags on a beanbag near a doorway leading to another room. She switched on a lamp and the floor lights, walked to the kitchenette, and plugged in a tea kettle.

She propped open the south window, the window with the view into Ember's house. She stared at Ember's messenger bag next to hers, a piece of them both lying together in a perfectly sweet heap. Reunited. In Tazo Castle. She couldn't help but smile and panic in unison. The only thing better than this would be Ember himself in the tree house with her. After the day she'd had so far, she believed it was possible. Anything was possible.

THREE

Album: So Tonight That I Might See

Track: One

Lux sipped her tea while she pondered looking through Ember's messenger bag. She sat down next to it and slowly pulled it closer. The side pocket was open with wrinkled papers threatening to spill out. She peered inside. Between books and homework was an album on vinyl, *Raising Sand* by Robert Plant and Alison Krauss. She removed the vinyl from the case, powered up her turntable, and played a few seconds of each track before returning to the beginning. She liked it very much. She laid back and stared at the ceiling. When she'd made it through at least half of the album, she returned the needle to the second track. The music drew her in; it was Ember Sweeney.

Lux sat up when she noticed that something had fallen out of the bag. It was a journal, titled *Notes for Falling Like Ember*. She was afraid to pull back the cover and discover its contents, so she set it down, but a note fell out of it and into her lap. It looked as though it had been in the pocket of someone's jeans for months. Somehow that was more intimate than the journal, so she ignored it and opened the journal.

Nobody would ever have to know. She opened the first page; it contained four jumbled sets of handwriting. She paged through the journal recognizing lyrics and names of people she knew. The pages included notes, ideas, plans, significant words, confessions, and images. She saw Anya's name and closed it again immediately, her heart beating heavily. She knew it was time to get the bag back to Ember. She had to see him again.

Lux turned to pick up the note, planning to place it discreetly back into the journal, but her mug of tea tipped over and spilled all over it. Ink soaked through instantly. She gingerly pulled the soaked note from a small puddle, saw L U X soaked through, and gasped.

Loud voices suddenly rang through from next door. Lux got up quickly and looked into the windows of Ember's house. Duffy was in the kitchen watching smoke billow through the open window. She was holding a pan of burnt cookies. Luther, Tanner, and Jamison were also there, teasing her and laughing.

Suddenly Luther stopped laughing at Duffy and observed Ember critically. "Ember, where's the journal? We have to be at the Sour in two hours, and we still have to practice *your* song...if you're still set on doing it."

"I forgot my bag at school," Ember said apologetically.

"Why would you leave the journal with Ember? He loses everything," Jamison cut in.

"We need to practice!" Ember raised his voice and ran his fingers through his hair.

"Okay," Luther said. "What are everyone's songs today?"

"'Cupid De Locke.' Smashing Pumpkins," Jamison said.

"'Shadows.' David Crowder Band and Lecrae," Tanner added.

"Thrice. 'The Lion and the Wolf,'" Luther said, as he sat on the counter.

"'Trouble is a Friend.' Lenka," Duffy said. She leaned on Luther's leg.

"'Love Will Come Through' by Travis," Ember said. "She's going to be there. She told me!" He sighed loudly and left the kitchen.

"Oh, sure. She told him! They talked." Luther rolled his eyes. "Maybe he can bunk with her at Lara," he muttered, and followed Ember out of the kitchen.

"No, they were talking. I saw them in the front yard," Jamison said matter-of-factly as he bit into a burnt cookie.

Duffy's eyes widened. "Wait, what? Why didn't he say anything!"

Jamison replied by spitting the cookie back out onto the pan.

Lux felt the warmth drain from her face. She wasn't prepared to answer any questions, but she had to see him face to face; she had to know their walk home together had been real. The song ended and the third track began.

The wind had picked up. Thick branches began thumping loudly against the tree house. Lux hastily shoved the journal back into Ember's messenger bag; then, she adjusted both of their bags over her shoulders.

She made her way out of the tree house and started down the rickety steps. She paused and gazed around curiously. Time had slowed. The vast, winding tree branches seemed to be reaching for her. The rising moon was casting shadows in every direction. The voices next door had faded, whipping into the wind and getting lost in the atmosphere.

The note! Lux hesitated and moved back up the uneven steps, holding tight for balance, both messenger bags weighing her down. She climbed inside the entrance of Tazo Castle and pulled the note toward her with her fingertips. She shoved it in her back pocket and nearly lost her balance in doing so. If only she'd turned the backyard lamp on; she could see nothing and the shadows were disorienting. But each step down brought her closer to Ember. Her life was about to change; she could feel it. The next time she looked into his eyes, their life together would begin.

Her thoughts wandered to Ember's captivating smile and his words, *your shoe's untied.* She smiled dreamily, just as she felt her shoelace catch on the edge of one of the jagged steps. It wouldn't budge. She hesitated nervously when she realized just how high up she was. She tried to wiggle her foot out of the shoe. She was stuck.

A colossal wind blasted against Lux's body and the weight of the messenger bags shifted. The gust rose up again and violently shook the branches above, releasing dead leaves in a shower over her. They scattered uncertainly toward the ground. Her heart raced.

In a slow horror Lux watched her own body continue to move against the will of her trapped foot. She lost her grip and fell backward, out from under her shoelace. Her body twisted around, then jolted. She heard a spine-tingling crack and a chilling cry of pain. She plummeted toward the dark, uninviting earth, reaching for anything to stop her fall, but she only grasped wind. It was a long fall. The messenger bags floated weightlessly away from her body. The music played on.

The wind delivered sharp raindrops and a chilling autumn storm. Lux's plans were arrested. She couldn't explain why she had Ember Sweeney's possessions. She wasn't there to hear the earth-shattering scream when Arrabelle turned on the lamp in the backyard an hour later. She didn't see Ember and his friends run to her house to find out why an ambulance was in the driveway.

The music played on. It traveled away from Tazo Castle and off to other places, places never heard of before, places with moonbeams and fairytales and shadows.

Blaze was being summoned. By someone he'd given his heart to long ago. Someone he would be tied to for eternity. Each heavy step he took toward her was accompanied by a fearful shudder. Ignoring her would end much worse than facing her now. But he was afraid of her. He was the only one she wanted, the only one she'd ever wanted. But he would never be enough.

He was far in the forest now. The natural light had diminished. He slowed down and caught his breath when he reached the tunnel down to Venia's Lair. The massive, hollowed tree was marked by strands of long black hair, which hung knotted over a branch. His heart sank. He climbed inside the hollow, which smelled of foul darkness. When had this become them?

He plummeted down the sinister tunnel, and his breath halted in his chest. A crimson glow ahead of him grew bigger and brighter the faster he fell. He couldn't slow down or turn back. Every return to her felt worse than the first, because it always felt like the last.

Tree roots cracked beneath Blaze where he landed. Every joint in his body was furious with pain. He sat up and looked around the dank and seemingly endless lair, which was lit crimson like a darkroom. He pushed away jagged branches and removed a sharp slice of wood from his punctured shoulder. Blood spilled; a thick stream trickled down his arm. He moved out from under the tree hollow and brushed dirt and slithering maggots off his body. He stood up and walked toward her hiding place.

He reached the crumbling building, abandoned of warmth and life. Only shards of windows remained in place as if a bomb had blown through. Drooling bats swooped overhead in small groups, ducking in and out of the structure, as if protecting Venia. An odd pair of miserable looking creatures was guarding the door: a mangy lion and a battered wolf, both gnawing on molding meat. They lifted their salivating mouths in unison, staring coldly, growling at Blaze. Then they stared at each other.

"Come in, Blaze." Venia's hideous voice slimed its way out of her rotting throat in a haunting song that echoed through her living quarters. Her flesh was weak. Her spirit was in limbo between vigorous and vanishing. The door creaked open. Blaze stopped breathing but continued to walk, trying his best to ignore the creatures now flanking him. "Yes, come inside."

"H-hello —" Blaze bowed slightly. Venia responded with a psychotic, shrill laugh that was felt more than heard. He imagined she would eventually grow mad enough to rip her head from her own body, demand it to form wings beneath her snarly hair, and fly away with the bats. The bats, which housed her demons. Lethal demons. But for now, she was sitting on her throne in a far corner, head attached.

"You and I, we're about to make a deal. Fetch her. Your return to me before darkness falls will be your agreement." Venia tapped her decrepit fingernails on the arm of her throne, making shrill clicking noises.

"It's a *her?*" Blaze suddenly raised his head in unanticipated hope, failing to ask exactly what their deal was. An idea surfaced, but he wasn't quite willing to acknowledge it. "It's her, isn't it? I don't believe it, finally. She's here. It's…you."

"You must take exceptional care of her. I need her in one piece, at her very best. Full of trust and love and hope. She's the one." Venia's voice cricked. "Cause her to desire you like she's desired no one and nothing else. But you must not give her your heart in return." Venia chuckled darkly. "Lie to her. Trick her. Lead her on."

"Venia. Do you remember…remember you and me? How we were before the war. Is there truly no hope?"

"Her fate hasn't been decided yet. That's why she's here! And this is my opportunity. How dare you bring memories into this place! Go NOW!" Venia's scream rattled the room.

Blaze ran. Screaming and growling followed him until he reached the entrance. He scrambled desperately into the open.

He fell in a heap on the forest floor, breathing hard. He grabbed fistfuls of foliage and breathed it in. Finally, he stood up and composed himself. He would fetch the girl, and he knew exactly where she would be.

She would be at the Crossroads. The place where he would steal her heart and she would discover she'd stolen his long ago. It would be nearly impossible to carry out what he'd been instructed, but he must. He must lie. If there was any hope of saving her. If there was to be any hope at all: hope for the future, hope for the past, hope for an eternity where time was but a glimmer and souls could be restored.

FOUR

Album: Raising Sand

Track: Two

Lux had stopped tumbling down. Now she was rising up. Her eyes were closed, but she could feel cool air sliding against her body, which helped to ease the intense pain she was experiencing. Then she was weightless and stopped moving at all. Time was nowhere to be found. Gravity was nonexistent. She was floating, although her head was still spinning wildly. The agonizing sensation momentarily left her. And then she felt tremendous pain everywhere. And then nothing again. Uncontrolled emotions filtered swiftly through the stores of her mind, picking and sorting memories, moments; tossing, saving, protecting, and neglecting. Behind closed eyelids, she began to see faces. Her heart became very full, and then vastly empty. So empty, she wished for a ceased existence. She screamed, but her voice wouldn't work. She cried, but she didn't know why.

When she was finally able to open her eyes, Lux was met by a brilliant blue sky. Above her head was a mound of rust colored clouds. She continued moving upward, drifting slowly and aimlessly like a balloon. Just as she was about to bump into the clouds, two thick vines reached down from inside them and wound around her wrists. She tried to break free. She took as deep a breath as her weak body would allow and tried to focus. The object holding her in place was not a cloud, but a pile of autumn leaves suspended in the sky. This made no sense. She tried again to free herself. No luck. She looked around helplessly.

Below her were sprawling, grassy fields. Beyond the fields in one direction was a thick forest, and in the other direction, snow-capped mountains. A sparkling stream flowed uphill from the forest to the base of the mountains. The direction of the stream seemed odd, but not impossible. She was, after all, suspended in the sky by a pile of leaves. Off the mainland was a larger body of water with small islands scattered throughout. A burning orange sphere of light reflected off the water and rested just above the highest point of the mountain. Lux had never seen such a sunset: gold with pinks and yellows that bled into rich greens and soft blues. It was a work of art. A hydrating breeze blew past, causing the leaves above her head to rustle. Then she heard something somewhere in the forest.

"HELP!" she shouted desperately, finding that her voice worked once again. She tried with great difficulty to catch her breath. "Help ME!"

"There you are," ventured a deep, soothing voice. A man, somewhere between youth and age, had appeared below Lux.

"I'm stuck!" She writhed, frustrated.

He continued to watch her. A smile slowly framed his face.

"Calm down," he said. She didn't like his soothing tone.

"Let me down!" Lux shouted, surprising herself.

He promptly reached up, which, as it turned out, wasn't very far at all, twisted the leaves bound to her wrists, and released her.

The ground shook violently. A thunderous boom sounded like a cannon as she landed in a pitiful heap. She struggled to sit up, but a force she couldn't see held her against the ground. She felt pressure, something both pushing and pulling her into the earth. And then she felt an exchange take place. A weight set in. Something had latched on to her.

"What's happening?" she whispered.

Clouds rolled behind the mountains. The sun seemed to freeze. Birds chirped in the distance as though nothing had happened, and the steady flow of the river murmured.

The man held out a strong arm and pulled her to a standing position. The spot on the grass where she'd landed looked as though it had been burned. She stumbled back when she looked into his eyes for the first time. They looked like graveyards, but she knew them. She'd been there.

"What was that?" she asked.

"It was you," the man suggested matter-of-factly. This enraged Lux for no reason she could understand at all. She threw her hands on her hips.

"Where am I? Who are you?" She was again startled by her own voice. The man smiled and looked up at the sky.

"I can't believe you're really here." He chuckled to himself. Then, very abruptly he took Lux's arm and pulled her toward the forest. She stumbled after him as if she weighed nothing in his wake. But she still felt something, a presence, a heaviness.

"Stop! Wait!" Lux screamed. He stopped. He faced her, an intrigued expression on his face.

"Where are we?" Lux demanded. They were now deep in the forest, but some light was still shining through the trees. "Who are you?" She observed his sculpted, protective features. He was tall, with shaggy dark hair and piercing eyes. He wore a tattered, sleeveless top, which was stained with dirt. His frayed dark blue pants were held in place with a thick rope for a belt. Hanging from the rope on his right side was a small sword, and his feet were bare.

"I'm so sorry," he said. "I keep forgetting you don't know me here. You're sure you don't know me?"

"What? No. I don't know you!" Lux shouted, annoyed. She glanced at his arms again.

"I'm Blaze," he said. Then he took a deep breath, winked, and nodded reassuringly. Lux did a double take. His mannerisms were familiar, too. Maybe she did know him. But she couldn't. The more she thought about it, she didn't know anyone. Or anything.

"You're not here by mistake," he said firmly. "You are meant to be here right now. This place is keeping you safe. I will keep you safe." He ran his fingers through his hair.

"But where is here?" she asked. "And what are you keeping me safe from?"

"You're in Boreloque."

"*Boar*-lock?" Lux sounded out the word, uncertain.

"Yes, Boreloque." Blaze answered. "It's beautiful, isn't it? It's where you're brought to prepare when you're not quite ready for something. A place to grow."

Lux looked around, wondering what he meant. She had to admit that Boreloque was breathtaking. The forest seemed alive; it was enchanting.

"It's like a fairy tale," she murmured.

"You may be on to something," Blaze agreed, and shrugged. "Your tragic scenario does mirror one quite perfectly. And we do have fairies here."

"I'm not tragic!" She argued.

"Whatever you are, I have business to attend to: a dear friend to visit. In fact, I'd love nothing more than for you to meet her. She's my best friend."

"*Her?*" Lux wasn't sure why this annoyed her. She didn't like it. But Blaze took her hand and once again, she felt a trace of familiarity.

"She's delightful. And I'll tell you more about Boreloque and me once we get there. Is that okay?"

"Do I have a choice?" Lux asked. She held back when he tried to move forward.

"No. You don't," he said. They stared at one another, and finally he grinned. "I don't remember you ever being this feisty."

How could she not have a choice? What if she didn't want to be with him? What if she wanted to be on her own? But she didn't actually want to leave him, she realized as she considered her options. And what did he mean by using the word "remember" in association with her? They'd only just met. Too many thoughts. And, wait —

"Fairies?"

Lux glanced up at the light shimmering through the trees, but there was a flash and the light disappeared. She was in darkness. Her veins went cold. Her entire being shook and she fell to the ground. The pain was immense. Worse than before. She heard distant, panicked voices. Her bones ached and every inch of her flesh felt ready to give up. Ice coursed through her body and stopped at her heart with a heavy jolt. The voices became almost deafening. She covered her ears, but the sound didn't go away. She recognized at least one of the voices. So much pain....

And then it was gone. Silence.

She opened her eyes. Blaze was kneeling over her and grasping her shoulders.

"Look at me. Are you okay?" he asked urgently. Lux didn't know what had happened, but now she felt fine. In fact, she felt nothing. But she couldn't ignore what she'd heard.

"Did you hear those voices?" Lux asked.

"I only heard your cry," Blaze said. They stared at each other. He pulled her to a sitting position. "Listen, you've got to stay with me. We have things to do. Important things."

"I'm Lux." Her name had finally come to her. She'd heard someone scream it, and she knew it was her own, because she felt the need to answer. Something flashed in Blaze's eyes. He nodded and smiled.

"Let's take a walk, Lux." He took her hand again, and they continued through the forest.

Sun-stained branches hovered protectively, shifting slowly in the breeze. They reached a massive tree stump, which towered over them and was illuminated by the setting sun. Blaze pounded his fist against it five times. Lux heard a crumbling sound and looked around and then down. The ground began to shift and open around them. The tree stump became an island. She could see far below to where the roots had slithered.

Blaze pulled Lux into his embrace. "We're going to jump."

"But I'm afraid of heights!" she shrieked.

"No you're not!" He laughed. They fell together into the opening in the earth, and she screamed.

"Trust me!" he shouted. They slid rapidly down a smooth tunnel. Lux's stomach rose up past her chilled heart and caught in her throat. Her terror turned to exhilaration. Tiny lights faded in and out along the tunnel walls. Vines blossomed around the lights, producing white and golden petals.

They landed quite suddenly, and found themselves in a round, warmly lit room. The low-domed ceiling was shaped by tree roots. Dripping candles were melted down in crevices in the walls, causing the entire room to glow. Flower petals sprouted along edges of the ceiling, and untrimmed vines hung above their heads. Lux circled the room, her fingers meticulously following designs etched onto the roots.

"This is where Pleiades lives," Blaze explained, while catching his breath. "You'll love her just as much as I do." He approached Lux, smoothed her hair, and straightened her clothes. "Ready?"

She nodded, although she doubted whether she'd like whoever Pleiades was. They moved into the next room.

A confident face in a wispy, white, sleeveless dress appeared in the doorway. She giggled effortlessly. She, too, had a rope for a belt hanging around her waist, but no weapon to accompany it. A headband rested on her head like a halo and matched the golden residue on her lips.

"Well, come in." Pleiades' glazed eyes widened at the sight of Lux. "I've been waiting!"

"Lux, this is Pleiades." Blaze nodded importantly. He smiled at Pleiades, who turned and led them into yet another candlelit room.

"Welcome to Boreloque, Lux," Pleiades sang in a carefree voice.

"Thank you," Lux answered politely.

"Now, have a seat my darlings," Pleiades laughed and stole another sip from the goblet she was holding. "Strange seeing you two together like this, I must say. It's been so long."

Blaze rolled his eyes at Pleiades. She smiled, curtsied, and waited expectantly for them to sit. Blaze sat down on a large chair and folded his hands, and Pleiades promptly pushed Lux into the empty space next to him. She swirled the contents of her goblet under Lux's nose and offered it to her, but Blaze instantly backhanded it away. The glass shattered against tree roots protruding from the ground.

"Not *yet*. What are you thinking?" Blaze glared at Pleiades. Pleiades smirked, fell into her own chair, and faced them.

"What am I thinking? I'm thinking I'm trapped. I'm thinking there's nothing but a wall between us! And walls can be broken," Pleiades pondered. "You're not the only one, Blaze."

"But I'm *the* one."

"Actually, she is," Pleiades said, pointing to Lux. "Anyway, I was just trying to help. Protective already. You'll never change." Pleiades winked. "But that's the whole point, isn't it? It's important for her to see who we are here."

Lux didn't even hear Blaze and Pleiades because she was too busy thinking about the scent of the drink Pleiades had offered her. It had smelled of coconut, orange, vanilla, espresso, and maybe a hint of nutmeg.

"Now, first things first," Pleiades said. "What size is she? She'll need clothes." She eyed Lux. "And where has she been so far?

Twilight Trees? Dreamer's Lane? Folly Falls?" Pleiades asked.

"Just here. I wanted her to meet you first," Blaze explained. "Will you continue on with us?"

"Blaze, remember that we don't know her heart. You can't control the outcome, even if you know the past." Pleiades smile faded. "Even if you think you know the future. You will have a difficult choice to make."

Pleiades wandered to the far side of the room where cyan colored goblets lined a shelf. She grabbed a new goblet and pulled the handle of a spout protruding from the wall. A foamy shimmering substance flowed into the cup, and the scent wafted back to Lux.

"She needs your help," Blaze said. Pleiades sat down and observed Lux.

"And she will be helped." She took a sip of her drink. "Lux, what do you remember?"

"I don't know," Lux said, distracted. "What's that you're drinking?"

Pleiades took another dramatic sip and smiled brightly. "Come find out."

Blaze stood up then, grabbed Pleiades by the arm, and pulled her into the other room. Lux immediately wondered if she could sneak a goblet. But before she could decide, they were back.

"Lux, listen carefully." Pleiades glared at Blaze. "You're in love. Actually, in a state of uncertain, unrequited love."

"Love?" Lux felt her face warm. "No...no."

"*Where* you arrived in Boreloque matters," Pleiades continued, "and you arrived at the Crossroads." She paused again for another drink and glanced at Blaze. Lux felt a sudden urge to look at Blaze, too, but she found she couldn't.

"What's the Crossroads?" Lux inquired. Nobody answered.

"Okay, maybe this was a bad idea," Blaze said, and held his hand out to Lux. "Let's go."

"Get it together, Blaze," Pleiades warned.

"Don't I need new clothes?" Lux asked.

"You're fine," Blaze said brusquely, "and you're uninvited, Plei."

"Go ahead, then," Pleiades scoffed. "But, you can't protect her. Not from me, not from anyone. Especially not from yourself." She placed her goblet in Lux's hands. "She has to know how to survive. At least do her that kindness." Blaze grabbed the goblet and handed it back to Pleiades.

"We'll see you at the park," he said. "Let's go, Lux."

Lux followed Blaze back to the room they'd arrived in. There was a door she hadn't noticed before that opened into a dark tunnel. When they stepped inside, the door closed them in. She felt them moving upward, and a moment later they were back in the forest.

"Cove. That's what Pleiades was drinking. It makes you forget." Blaze glanced at Lux and added, "you don't want to forget."

"But there's nothing I remember *now*," Lux admitted. They'd reached the edge of the trees. A field of lavender lay before them.

"If you drink the Cove, I can't guarantee you'll be able to go back to where you came from," Blaze said.

"What if this place is better than wherever I came from?" she said, already feeling a sense of attachment. "Would you want me to stay?"

Blaze continued through the field, ignoring her question.

Lux heard a rush of rustling branches then, and Pleiades appeared at the edge of the forest. She rushed toward them with a fiery look in her eyes. Lux could smell the Cove on her tongue.

"Does he know you're in love with him? Does he know you dream about him? Hope he will choose you? Wish you were his? Would you sacrifice everything to be with him? Know your answer, Lux. You arrived at the Crossroads. You're a thief." Pleiades tapped her finger roughly into the sensitive flesh below Lux's neck. "You stole a heart. So watch yourself, because I'm watching you. And I'll protect *him* until the end. You. Need. Us. And when it comes time for you to do the right thing," Pleiades pointed to

Blaze, "you'd better do the right thing."

Lux was stunned.

"Pleiades, go home," Blaze said calmly. "Have a drink. We'll see you at the park. Okay?" He nudged her away and wrapped his arm around Lux.

"Don't get your hopes up, Blaze. I'm sorry." Then she disappeared again into the trees.

"Coming?" Blaze asked and began to walk again. Lux caught up with him. What had Pleiades meant by all of that?

"Don't worry, she's just jealous that I uninvited her to join us. Sometimes, no amount of the Cove can appease her. When she doesn't get enough, she begins to remember things." Blaze lingered on the thought. "It's tricky. She knows you, but she's forgotten why."

"What, are you two a thing?" Lux asked. She felt insulted, but didn't know why.

"She's my friend," he said simply. "My best friend."

They'd neared a river. A fresh breeze swept up the tips of the grass and tossed the blades lazily from side to side. The air was thick and warmer than it had been in the forest. Lux stretched out her arms out and breathed in sea salt and gardenia. She sat in the grass and pulled her remaining shoe off, too distracted to wonder or care why she was wearing only one. She stole a quick glance in Blaze's direction. He sat down next to her and stared into the water.

"I'm not a thief," Lux said, determined.

"But, yes you are." Blaze smiled and nudged her shoulder. "We're all thieves. That's how we ended up here."

She must have known Blaze much longer than just today, or however long she'd been in Boreloque, which somehow felt like both one solitary moment and the richness of a lifetime. She looked around and realized that time wasn't passing. It couldn't be. The sun still hadn't moved.

Pain momentarily returned to her body in the form of a dull

buzz, and Lux began to sense that it was coming from somewhere other than her flesh.

"So, anyway," Blaze said, and stood up. He had been quiet for a very long time. "I won't sugarcoat this, although you should know that in Boreloque everything is sugarcoated. So you'll have to trust me."

Lux's heart soared, which surprised her.

"There's someone here who wants your heart, or something inside it," he continued. "And there will come a time when you must face her. It's my job to prepare you. I'll take you to the places and the people who can help. It's the best I can do. What do you say?"

"Show me Boreloque," Lux replied after a long pause. She felt overwhelmed.

"Lux, no one's accusing you of anything," Blaze said soothingly. "It's just who we are. But you *are* missing a piece of your heart, which I'm sure you can feel. And you *do* have one that's not yours. It's life. It happens. You'll get used to it."

"Is that why it keeps hurting?" Lux asked. "And how can someone survive without a heart? Wouldn't it kill them?"

"Amazingly, we can live with broken hearts and stolen souls. You and I are both doing a pretty good job." He squeezed her hand.

The mountains, lined with silver, loomed ahead. Clusters of pink clouds had gathered near the sun. They walked to a small hill further down the river where it split, one part into a larger lake and the other disappearing up into the mountains. They reached the divide and came upon a tiny, gurgling pool of emerald water.

"What's this?" Lux asked, mesmerized.

"It shows you something your heart needs."

"Does it work?" Lux asked eagerly.

"Of course. But I don't look often, and now isn't the time for you to do it, just like it wasn't the right time for the Cove. Don't go any closer."

Lux had knelt down near the pool. Blaze reached for her shoulder and pulled her back.

"I've been waiting for you for a long time," he said. "I need you to trust me."

As Lux stood up, she saw a shadow over her. But it didn't match up; it wasn't hers, and it didn't belong to Blaze. She looked around wildly, but saw nobody else with them.

FIVE

Album: A Thousand Suns

Track: Twelve

Darkness had fallen. Frigid rainwater rushed the street. Ember ran toward the flashing red lights, piercing the darkness. He reached the Tazos' driveway; his friends stopped close behind him and huddled together.

And then he saw her. Unresponsive, on a stretcher, with an oxygen mask over her face. A team of paramedics adjusted a brace around Lux's neck and then lifted her into the ambulance.

He was supposed to meet her at the Sour Enchantment. They were supposed to be together. If he'd just told her how he felt in that moment they had together, this never would have happened. But he'd been too afraid to risk being rejected by her again.

Arrabelle climbed into the back of the ambulance. "She must have fallen out of the tree house," she cried into her phone. The doors closed like a vault. The vehicle drove away, siren blaring.

"She'll be okay," Luther reassured them.

Ember knew he was only saying it so they could get through the show later. His soaked clothing clung to his shivering skin. He wanted to cancel the show.

"So, we should probably be on our way," Luther added. "Can you do this Ember?"

They watched Ember expectantly. He closed his eyes and pictured the broken leaves wedged into Lux's bloodstained hair. He used all of his strength to ignore the images of the girl he wanted to share a life with. This couldn't be happening.

"I just won't sing *her* song," Ember said. "That's all." He walked swiftly back to his house with his head raised high.

They piled into Jamison's black Jeep Commander and backed out of the driveway.

"Wait, stop," Duffy said. She opened the door and ran back into Ember's house. She returned a moment later with an arm full of clothes. "You can change when we get there."

"What about you?" Ember asked.

"I grabbed one of your shirts. I'm fine."

They drove across town in silence; fourteen eternal minutes. When they reached the parking lot of the Sour Enchantment, nobody moved. Ember finally cracked his door open, but went no further.

"We can go to the hospital after the show," Duffy said. She turned to the boys and nodded.

Ember's breath caught in his chest.

"Duffy, I need you to sing for me tonight." He got out of the Jeep and slammed the door.

"Okay," Duffy said, eyeing Jamison, Tanner, and Luther.

"Maybe we shouldn't do this," Tanner said. "I don't trust him right now."

"Go ahead and cancel, Tanner. I'll kick you out of the band myself!" Jamison shouted.

"She has stage fright!" Tanner yelled, pointing at Duffy.

"She'll be fine!" Jamison snapped. "Ember will be on stage."

"We're doing the show. Duffy, you can do it. You'll be okay," Luther said.

They all got out of the Jeep without another word, retrieved their instruments, and faced the rain again.

Ember had locked himself in the bathroom at the back of the venue. He ran his fingers through his hair and stared hard through the mirror into his own bloodshot eyes. He held back tears of fear and regret. He kept shaking his head as if none of what he'd seen was real.

It was only now that he realized the depth of what he felt for Lux. What he'd always felt for her. And now he was about to lose her. Maybe he already had. If he was honest, he'd never had her in the first place. He'd held on for so long, and for what?

A fist pounded against the bathroom door. "Get it together, man. People are arriving," Jamison shouted firmly. "We go on in half an hour!" He pounded the door again. Ember absorbed the wretched emotions threatening to spill over and put on his stage face.

The crowd in the Sour Enchantment was deafening. Astor Dane took the stage. He held a glass of whiskey and a freshly rolled cigarette in one hand and grabbed the microphone with the other. The boys and Duffy stood behind him in the shadows.

"Good evening. Thank you for braving the weather," Astor said, his Irish accent taming the crowd. "I promise it will be well worth your effort. Please welcome Falling Like Ember! I hear they're giving you something a bit different tonight, so enjoy. Cheers!"

The lights dimmed to blue, making the audience glow. Everyone upstairs leaned over the balcony and sipped their drinks. Ember walked forward, with Duffy close by him. He stared into the crowd. He was supposed to share his soul with them. They deserved a good show. Jamison cleared his throat very loudly and plucked a string on his bass guitar.

"Thanks for coming out tonight," Ember whispered. The crowd cheered.

"We're honored to fill in for Rodrigo. In case you came just to see him, he will return next Saturday. I know he's older and has a great beard that I'm super jealous of, but we'll try our best." Ember chuckled. Duffy looked back to Luther for consolation, and he nodded.

"Anyway. Do you ever have one of those days that you think is going to end so perfectly, but instead," Ember breathed heavily into the microphone, "it's tragic." He looked past the blinding lights. Whispers swept through the crowd.

"That's the kind of day I've had. So we're going to try something different. Miss Duffy Raven will be on lead vocals tonight. I think she's just smashing, so please give her a warm welcome." The crowd screamed in approval.

Duffy forced a smile and turned again for confirmation from the guys. Her gaze shifted back to Ember and their eyes locked. He left her then and sat down at the piano. She faced the audience. The music began.

Duffy performed Falling Like Ember's entire set list. She improvised a number of times, but nobody seemed to notice. Luther and Jamison took turns accompanying her with harmonies, though all eyes were still on Ember, who was hiding in the shadows.

Ember stared at his hands resting on the piano keys. His mind wandered back to that afternoon. It felt like so long ago. She hadn't run from him. Why hadn't he persuaded her to stay?

In the middle of the last song, Ember tapped the microphone at the piano to signal the sound tech. The spotlight landed on him. He imagined Lux in the audience, the only one there, watching him just as she'd planned to. And he sang, with a voice that was broken and raw, what had begun of their story.

We found love; there was just too much at stake
Our fears took over, so we tried to erase
The moments that brought the truth
A life together, me with you

So you didn't stay; you forced me to walk away
Didn't let me look back
You never gave me anything to hold on
And now you're gone

One night I caught you with your guard down
Shoes untied and heart tied up
Then later I found you lying on the ground
The broken in your heart wouldn't keep me around

Told myself I'd wait forever; that moment came too soon
And you didn't stay; you forced me to walk away
Didn't let me look back
You never let me hold on
And now you're gone

Ember left the stage, ignoring the cheering crowd. Luther, Tanner, and Jamison eyed one another. Duffy turned to them helplessly.

Jamison ran after Ember. He reached in his pocket and handed over his Jeep keys. Ember nodded and slipped out through the back door.

"That was the best show they've ever done!" a group of girls near the stage was discussing excitedly. "Who did he write that song for? What's going on? Is he single? Is he with Duffy? What *was* that? Best show ever."

"What happened?" Arrabelle Tazo ran straight for Ember when he walked into the hospital waiting room. Her eyes were worn with grief. "What do you know?" He became consumed with one paralyzing thought.

"Is she...?" Ember's voice caught in his throat. Mr. and Mrs. Tazo approached him with curious yet concerned expressions. Arrabelle held his arm tightly.

"I was with her earlier in the afternoon. The storm was moving in," Ember explained nervously. "I was leaving for our show when I heard the ambulance. Please —" He was pleading with the parents of the girl who meant more to him than anything in the world, but they had no idea. Ember couldn't look away from all of the sapphire eyes that mirrored Lux's so perfectly.

"We don't have a lot of answers yet," explained Mr. Tazo. "She's not stable." A heavy weight immediately lifted off Ember's chest, but was replaced by a new one. "We can only assume that she fell from her tree house. It was a bad fall. We don't know how long she was there before Arrabelle found her. There's intracranial pressure, a swelling in her brain. The doctors administered a drug that may have caused the seizures," he said. Ember was too afraid to ask any more questions.

"Her left elbow is broken, and so is her right ankle. A branch punctured the side of her waist, which thankfully missed her kidney by a few millimeters. Her face is pretty bruised. Her neck —" Mr. Tazo choked up. "They don't know anything for sure yet."

"She's in a coma," Arrabelle cried, and buried her head in her father's chest.

"So far there's...minimal brain activity," Mr. Tazo said, his chin quivering.

"We walked home from school together," Ember recalled. "I wanted her to come over. She was going to come to the show tonight."

"Ember?" Mr. Tazo hesitated a moment. "You've grown up."

"Yes, sir."

"Thank you for stopping by. We're glad she has you."

"Will you let me know when there's an update?" Ember watched the Tazo family. All he could see was Lux in each of them.

Mr. Tazo pulled a business card from his wallet and handed it to Ember. "We'll be here until further notice. Give me a call in the morning, okay? Thank you, Ember."

Ember woke frequently during the night, wondering where he was. He stared out his bedroom window at the tree house in the yard next door. He hadn't paid attention to it before now. His cell phone rested on his pillow, even though he knew Mr. Tazo didn't even have his phone number.

A pallid sunrise lured him out of bed. It hadn't been a dream. The only alert on his phone was a group message from the band.

Luther: songs?

Duffy: I'll Find a Way, Rachael Yamagata.

Jamison: Going To California, Led Zeppelin

Tanner: Beautiful Things, Gungor

Luther: In the Orchard, Tiger Army.

Ember typed a title into the message box, but then he deleted it. He wrote again. Deleted the letters. He finally closed the message screen without replying, and listened to Linkin Park's "Iridescent" on repeat.

"Hi Mr. Tazo," Ember said before the phone had even reached his ear. Three days had passed. They had exchanged numbers and spoken frequently. During that time, reality had sunk in. The Tazos had quickly accepted Ember into their family. Nobody asked specifics about his relationship with Lux, and he didn't tell.

"Glad you answered," Mr. Tazo said. "Can I swing by your house before you leave for school?"

"I'm, um, at the hospital," Ember replied uncomfortably. There was a pause on the phone. Suddenly he wondered if he'd over-stepped his boundaries.

"I'll come there, then. Meet me out front."

Mr. Tazo drove Ember to school. He explained that Principal Jacobs would be making an announcement to the student body, and that it was okay to talk about Lux. Then he continued to say how important it was to carry on with life as they knew it, which Ember didn't understand at all.

♪

Ember hopped in the passenger seat of Jamison's Jeep after a very long and tiring day. He'd visited each of Lux's teachers, even though they all already knew the story.

"You seem better," Jamison observed approvingly.

Ember leaned his head back against the seat. "Yeah."

"Good for you. Ready for practice then?"

"Actually, I'm meeting Lux's dad at the hospital. Could you drop me off?" Ember asked. "You guys can still practice at my place."

"Damn. Thanks, man." Jamison's eyes were like saucers. "Maybe we'll find a new headliner, too!"

Duffy opened the door then and climbed in. Luther was behind her. She observed the boys and then glared hard at Jamison. Not another word was spoken.

Ember met Mr. Tazo in the main waiting room of the hospital. He hadn't yet seen Lux, because she was still in the ICU.

"I didn't want to tell you this over the phone," Mr. Tazo began. Ember's heart raced. "Lux had an unexpected surgery this morning after you left for school. It was a simple procedure to reduce swelling. They also scheduled a follow-up surgery for this Thursday to repair some nerve damage they found."

"But did she wake up yet?" Ember interrupted.

"She hasn't woken up, Ember. All we can do is wait. They've

told us to look at this as a protective measure her body has taken against the injuries. The upside is she feels nothing. If she were conscious, she'd be experiencing tremendous pain. They told us to get back to our normal lives as soon as she's stable from the surgeries."

Ember didn't know how to react. He couldn't imagine life going back to normal. He didn't understand at all.

"Do I still get to see her today?" he finally asked. The thought of it had kept him anxious all day.

"Are you sure you want to see her like this?" Mr. Tazo asked. Ember nodded.

They walked into a dark room. Machines were beeping and displaying charts and numbers that Ember didn't understand. Then he saw her: a small, unmoving figure lost in a rigid bed. Unrecognizable. As he moved closer, Ember saw that nearly all of Lux's face was covered in thick bandages and wrappings. Even her eyes were covered. A large tube was protruding from her mouth, a smaller one was coming from her nose, and yet another from the top of her head. The little bit of her face that was visible was covered in deep scrapes. A brace held her neck in place. Her left arm was set in a thick cast, and her right arm was bound by a cluster of tubes and wires.

Mr. Tazo pulled a chair up next to Lux's bed. He carefully picked up her left hand, and swept aside the little bit of hair that was free. Ember observed the exchange, and a lump the size of a baseball formed in this throat. Mr. Tazo cleared this throat and motioned for Ember to join him.

Suddenly, he wondered how Lux would feel if she realized he was seeing her like this. Terrified, he approached the bed.

"It's okay," Mr. Tazo assured him. Ember stood at the side of the bed, too afraid to reach out. He remained silent while the seconds passed and his mind raced.

"Mr. Tazo?" A nurse walked in the room holding a flip chart. "Your wife has arrived. We'd like to go over the results of the last few tests while we've got you both here." She smiled sympathetically at Ember.

"Of course." Mr. Tazo took one last look at Lux and walked toward the door. "Ember, I'll be back soon. Do you want to leave?" he asked.

"No, go ahead." Ember tried to smile but couldn't. Mr. Tazo nodded and left the room.

Ember sat down in the chair. He thought of their last walk home. He thought about all the things he'd wanted to say to her for so long. He thought about the fact that she may never wake up again to hear him tell her what he thought of her, and how much he cared for her.

"Why?" He found himself reaching for Lux's hand as he denied every tear that fell. He rested his head on the side bar of the bed and released the last bit of strength he'd been holding onto. He pleaded. Nothing happened. She had to wake up. He sat up and wiped his face with his sleeve.

"Don't leave," he whispered desperately.

After a week and one more minor surgery, Lux's bandages had been reduced a number of times; finally her face was visible again. Scrapes were turning to scars. She was healing.

Ember visited the hospital every day after school, his guitar in tow. The Tazos fussed over him. They always kept him up to date on Lux. Each day he convinced himself that she'd come back, to her family, to him, to life. A life that was good. And he would be there when she did.

SIX

Album: Beautiful Things

Track: Two

Lux knew there had to be more: substance, a past, a future, a story. She couldn't shake the feeling of emptiness, or the shadow that seemed to be following her. But she was in Boreloque. With Blaze. She was distracted and intrigued and excited. Every time his hand touched hers, she sensed a deep, dark connection. There was something about him.

They moved away from the water and up a hill that overlooked more rolling hills. Lux continuously looked behind her; the weight on her shoulders was growing heavier.

Blaze looked to the sky. He pulled something from his pocket. He grinned and showed Lux a tiny, shivering star in the palm of his hand. It was so brilliant, she had to look away. But she could still see the image behind her eyelids.

"Don't let go," he said.

She grabbed his forearm just as she felt her feet leave the ground. They were whisked into the wake of the shooting star and flew so quickly that she seemed to leave her screams behind. They followed the trail of stardust, which absorbed into their skin. Blaze looked over at her and smiled. They went higher and higher, and finally they neared a billow of pink clouds and landed on what looked like cotton candy. Their feet sank slightly below the surface. She caught her breath and looked around in disbelief.

"Dreamer's Lane," Blaze announced. They moved and rose two to three feet with each step. Lux peered over the edge and saw Boreloque below. It was majestic. Also...she could fly.

Transparent walls began rising around them. Frameless, messy colors and images collided together and swayed distortedly in the breeze. Lines and contrasts melted in and around each other. Radiant galaxies smashing into coffee mugs and billowing flowers colliding with the moon; broken hearts melting into music notes and a soft sun burning into the crashing waves.

A gleaming, golden door rose up before them. The door had a great big knocker with the face of a lamb carved at its rounded wrought iron base. Blaze eyed Lux expectantly. She reached for the door knocker, but before swinging it back, she noticed the etching: "In like a lamb, out like a lion."

The door burst open forcing delicate particles of cloud out of the way. A man stood in the door looking at Lux excitedly. "She's here!"

"Hello, friend." Blaze cleared this throat, smirking slightly. The man stopped doting and turned to him. He was dressed similarly to Blaze and looked about the same age.

"She's younger than I expected," he observed. He had dark hair and eyes and bronzed skin.

"Lux, this is York," Blaze said. "He keeps Dreamer's Lane safe."

"Come along, Lux," York called as he strode ahead, and Blaze went ahead of her to catch up with him.

"She landed at the Crossroads," Blaze muttered to York.

"That's no surprise, is it then?" York said.

Blaze fell back and joined Lux again. He held her hand and pulled her along. She was having a bit of trouble staying above the clouds on her own.

A new, iridescent door appeared before them. York pulled a ring of keys from his pocket and sorted through them. Many of the keys, Lux noticed, were shades of crimson. He held up a large pearly one and unlocked the door. It swung open to reveal a white room with a small gate guarding something in the center.

"Should we bring her to the Twirlyfines, then?" York asked. Blaze nodded.

"Twirlyfines?" Lux asked.

"The Starlets," York said nonchalantly.

"Keep an eye on her. I'll meet you there," Blaze instructed. "I've been summoned again. I need to return before dark."

"I'll keep her safe," York said. "And I'll get in contact with the Seven Sisters. We may need them."

Blaze nodded reluctantly. "I'll find you at the park." Then he fell into the clouds and was gone.

"No!" Lux screamed.

"It's just fine." York chuckled and strode toward her, kicking up soft puffs of pink around his feet. "He's taking care of something. He'll find us again."

"He could have said goodbye," Lux said, and crossed her arms. She stared blankly at York. He grinned.

"Let's become friends, then," he suggested. He led Lux to a circle of couches in the white room. They sat. She stared at him. She was thinking about Blaze.

"I must say, your mind is quite vivid," York said. He gazed around the room and then nodded approvingly. "I'm impressed."

"Thanks. Where did Blaze go?" Lux asked, distracted.

"He's visiting an old friend." York smiled. "We'll meet him again soon. So we should be on our way to see the Twirlyfine Starlets."

"Who are they?" Lux asked. The images colliding on the walls around them were growing darker, as if nighttime was setting in.

"They're the ones without mothers and fathers. Anyone you meet here who can fly grew wings because they needed to. Maybe someday you'll have wings, too. Come. We'll take the funnel down."

York stood up, and Lux followed him to the gate at the center of the room. She gazed into a shimmering funnel, stopped in her tracks, and shuddered. She knelt down, gripping her hands to her head, and a cold sweat ran over her. The weight on her shoulders doubled. She felt York pull her away from the funnel.

"I don't want to fall," she whispered. Blinding pain returned. She was paralyzed. Everything was darkness. Then as soon as it had begun, it dulled.

"Lux. You're safe." York looked away as he spoke. "You'll be okay." He knelt down next to her and patted her back.

*

Blaze and Venia were face to face again. This time he waited for her to speak first. He knew she'd want confirmation and an update. Not about the girl, but about how well he was persuading her to trust him.

"Does she look well?" Venia's voice finally shattered the silence.

"Yes," Blaze said. "Just confused."

"Is she beautiful?" she asked. He nodded. "Sure of herself?"

He hesitated, then shook his head.

"But, lovely. Just like you always were," he said before he could stop himself.

Venia stood up and walked away from her throne. Blaze followed her into a room where lights shined along the far wall that was covered by a curtain. Venia stood in front of the curtain and faced Blaze.

"I'm not sure you can do what I have asked of you," she said.

"I'm here before darkness has fallen." Blaze shrugged. "I'm honoring our deal."

"So because I can't trust you, I've changed my mind." Venia turned around and ripped the curtain away from the wall. Blaze stared at the wall in dismay. He turned his face away.

"What have you done?" he whispered.

"Bring me what I need from her. I don't want to see her face." Venia walked slowly toward Blaze. "You know what to do. I told you before. Don't bring your memories into this place!"

Without warning she lunged for him. His head hit the ground, and he felt her hands tighten around his neck. He felt piercing, relentless pain as she gripped his jaw. Just before he lost consciousness, his body went numb, and he was thankful.

York and Lux sat at the edge of the spinning funnel, their feet dangling into it. Lux's pain had subsided, but it was settling in.

"I'm fine," she said. She smiled weakly. "I'm ready."

"All right, then. We're simply going to jump in. The force will hold you against the wall. You won't fall far," York explained. "I'll hold your hand."

They plummeted momentarily. Lux's stomach flip-flopped wildly, but she was quickly bound in place against the funnel. She wanted to cover hear ears from the terribly loud sound of wind, but she couldn't move her arms. A moment later, loud popping noises filled the space. Two winged girls, one blonde and one brunette, rose up on either side of York, fluttering weightlessly. They began a curious stare-down with Lux that lasted until the funnel eventually unwound on the ground. It lowered them onto the grass, leaving remnants of funnel dust behind. They'd landed near a pond.

The beauty of the two winged girls grew brighter as they moved toward Lux in order to get a better look. They were glamorous, confident. Their eyes were on her like fireflies against a summer night sky.

"Now that we've reached Cloverleaf Pond," York explained, "we'll wait here for transportation."

"How do you know it's her?" the brunette one asked York. "I can't tell."

"Where's Blaze?" the blonde one inquired. "He's the only one who knows."

"Yes, where *is* Blaze?" Lux crossed her arms indignantly. "Off with another girl?"

"He shouldn't have left her," the brunette said. She glared at Lux, which only increased her beauty.

"Don't get spicy," York said. "It's almost time to celebrate. I think it's time you introduced yourselves to lovely Lux. She and I have become great friends."

The brunette glared at York. The blonde remained indifferent.

"Fine then. Lux, these are the Twirlyfine Starlets, Hepburn and Harlow." York looked around curiously. "There's a third. Where's Hayworth?"

"Pleiades told us Lux is trouble," Hepburn, the brunette, said. "Nobody knows if she's the one. Are we supposed to do away with her?" Lux froze.

"Of course not," York replied. "Girls, Lux is *just* who we've been waiting for, and think of how long you've been waiting." The girls watched Lux warily.

"Either way. It's time for the party," Hepburn said. She blew a whistle hanging from her neck.

At the sound of the whistle, three smaller winged girls with flushed cheeks and darling smiles rose up from under the water in lily pad boats. They reached the shore and tumbled out of the boats, skipping over the surface of the water onto the sand.

"Pinwheel, Clover, and Bubble, meet Lux," York said.

"The party is waiting!" Bubble tugged at Lux's arm excitedly and motioned toward her lily pad boat. "You're riding with me! Let's go!" Everyone followed Bubble and Lux to the pond and got into the boats. Lux waded into the water.

"Who's the party for?" She asked as she took her seat in the boat next to Bubble.

"The party's for you!" Pinwheel squealed.

"But, why?"

"Because you're finally here," York said.

Lux looked at the incredible beauty surrounding her in every direction. She was beginning to feel that she couldn't possibly take it all in. It was almost enough to make her forget the darkness still hovering over her. Almost.

She watched everyone surrounding her and began to feel as fearless and weightless as the Twirlyfine Starlets looked. Everyone cheered. The boats gurgled as they cut through a maze of reeds and rocks in the pond. Lux felt the cool breeze on her face. She closed her eyes and stretched out her arms. Bubble laughed. Their voices echoed far and wide across the water. They moved toward an island that looked like a garden of lights.

But the feeling of elation didn't last. A deep, terrified scream rang over Lux's laughter. It erupted in the distance and radiated through them. The water began to murmur like an upset stomach. Lux grabbed the side of the boat; her heart was pounding. The lily pad boats sputtered to a stop. Everyone looked to her, terrified.

Only York remained composed. He turned to the setting sun behind them. "Not to worry. Blaze was just fixing some things. See?" The light faded rapidly behind the mountains and darkness fell completely.

"Why did he need to do that?" Hepburn asked.

"You see, Lux was discovered at the Crossroads —"

The Starlets gasped in unison, and plunged into the dark water with violent splashes. When they resurfaced, their wings pulled them back up, drenched and shaking, and they found their way back into the boats.

"Will Blaze know where to find us?" Lux asked, alarmed.

"In fact, Blaze should be joining us any minute," York said.

"Lux, there *is* someone who can explain the Crossroads!" Hepburn said through chattering teeth.

The final sliver of daylight quickly hid itself behind the purple mountain cap, and night was upon them.

"Don't you worry about the Crossroads, little one," York said.

Lux settled back into her boat next to Bubble. They soared over the glassy water toward the twinkling island.

As they got closer, Lux could see the glow from the island had turned out to be lanterns hanging from ancient, winding tree branches. They reached the weedy shore that rose far above the water. They secured the boats next to other boats that were already docked.

All around them, tiny spheres of light illuminated the steep path upward that led to the main part of the island. Some lights even followed them. The group stayed close together as they pushed their way through long plants and winding vines. They whispered and nudged each other as they went. Harlow and Hepburn each held one of Lux's hands until they reached a clearing. The base of the island appeared to be a thousand year old tree, whose seemingly infinite branches twisted, bent, and curled up and around into a sphere. It created a protective dome that enclosed the entire island, but still allowed a speckled view of the night sky.

"Where are we?" Lux was in awe, as if everything else she'd already seen and touched was nothing compared to this.

"We're home," Harlow said. She blew a kiss into the air, sending a soft dollop of shimmer into the breeze. The shimmer moved around the island, making their presence known. Heads turned. Harlow's wings fluttered softly, and her feet left the ground.

Lux heard the subtle strumming of a guitar, smelled the richness of fruit and flowers, and felt a warmth in the air from a crackling fire. Colossal branches hovered over them protectively. Plush, scarlet couches nestled against the base of the tree trunk, sank in to its roots, and wound up into the branches. Tables overflowed with a feast.

The lanterns were lit by fireflies and fairies that also flew among the tree. Swarms of them lingered among the vast branches, and they generously offered their light to the party guests. The fireflies made soft whistling sounds so beautiful that Lux wanted one to call her own and stow it away in a secret place. Perched above the couches were petite, lustrous birds, so white they were almost lilac. They congregated up the twisting vines, which wound around the expanse of the island. They, too, whistled, but an airier, sadder sound escaped their beaks.

A fire was burning at the far end of the island, beyond the tables of edible arrangements, and far from the brightest lights. It was enclosed within a pile of round stones. The embers became part of the sky as they wandered aimlessly away from their home, slow dancing toward the stars.

On the opposite end of the island were the brightest, most lush flowers Lux had ever laid eyes on. They bloomed vibrantly and swayed enticingly. Hundreds of pocket-sized fairies nestled in the flowers, which were also their beds. The fairies played and fought wildly amongst themselves, laughing and shouting, their voices never ceasing. Their energy seemed to feed the sources of light. With all their might, the fairies tugged at smaller flower petals, and greedily devoured bites of the luscious brightness. Their iridescent stomachs glowed in the same shades as the flowers they swallowed.

"They're stronger than they look," York said, approaching Lux. She hadn't realized that she'd wandered off by herself.

"They're beautiful," she said.

"They're remnants of a war that took place here long ago. They don't die off quickly or easily." York knelt down and picked one up. It struggled, but then stood in his open hand and stared indignantly at him. "That's good. We still need them, you see."

"What for?" She asked moving in for a closer look at the fairy. It winked at her.

"We'll certainly need them again someday," York explained. "You see, they fight the demons. That's what fairies are for. And only demons can kill them." York set the fairy back on the ground near its home and faced Lux.

"Blaze will tell you more about it." He nodded and backed away. "I'll leave you two for a moment. I'm going to let Fender know everyone's made it safely."

"Fender?"

"He keeps the park and the fairies safe," he said. Then he left her.

Lux felt the dark presence again. Everything in her sight dimmed. And what had he meant by "you two"? She looked swiftly over her shoulder then. Blaze. He said nothing. She didn't need him to. She turned to him, and found herself wrapped in his arms. Wherever they were now, this was where she wanted to remain.

"We've been waiting for you!" Pleiades called from the scarlet pillow she was nestled in. She stood, and everyone joined her over at the table.

Blaze took Lux's hand, and led her to the crowd. She noticed a lot of new faces, and wondered how many people lived here. There was a redhead sitting between Hepburn and Hayworth; it must be Harlow. She also noticed a number of men sitting around the table; they looked similar in age to Blaze, but everyone seemed noticeably more carefree than him. And they were all drinking a lot of Cove.

Blaze sat across the table from Lux. Everyone helped themselves to a feast of fruits and vegetables, steaming bread, and luscious desserts. Lux was about to reach for a piece of cake, when she caught Blaze's eye.

"Where were you?" she mouthed. He shook his head, but didn't answer. Lux noticed Pleiades then, at the far end of the table. She was laughing delightedly and downing one goblet after another.

"I'd like a goblet of the Cove, please," Lux said loudly. Everyone cheered and raised their glasses. Blaze's face fell.

"He still hasn't given you the good stuff?" A daunting voice belonging to a monstrously muscular man moved in next to her. He put his arm around Lux and introduced himself as Joplin.

"I know, I know. He thinks he actually has a chance with you." Joplin chuckled.

"What's that supposed to mean?" Lux asked heatedly, glancing at Blaze, who had looked away.

"Joplin! Don't start." Pleiades stood up, holding a goblet in each hand. She made her way to them, and shoved in next to Blaze. "Blaze says she can't know too much yet."

"Plei, it's inevitable!" Joplin argued. "He can't protect her. She landed at the Crossroads."

Pleiades seemed to have already forgotten what they were discussing. She emptied another goblet. Joplin directed his attention to a bracelet on his wrist and twisted the beads strung around it. Seconds later, a vat of the Cove hovered above them. Joplin winked at Lux. He grabbed her empty goblet and the liquid flowed into it.

"You should at least have fun while you're here, darling." He pushed her plate aside and set the full goblet in front of her. Everyone halted their conversations and watched expectantly.

"Do it. Drink," Harlow whispered. She blew a soft cloud of shimmer onto Lux's face.

"Don't fight it," Hepburn added.

"Blaze," Lux said, swirling her finger in the liquid. "Give me a reason not to drink this. Say something."

Blaze looked pleadingly at Lux. Finally, he closed his eyes.

"Drink up before he stops you!" Fender shouted.

He patted Lux on the back and pushed the goblet closer to her. Lux stared intently into the goblet. She wrapped her fingers around the stem. Why wasn't Blaze trying to stop her? She was entranced by the aroma under her nose.

"If you came here to forget, then this is the way," Pleiades said between sips. "It's a fresh start. This is your moment!"

"I don't think I *do* want to forget," mumbled Lux. "I don't know why I came here." She realized then that her desire to for real memories overpowered her desire for the Cove. She pushed the goblet away and stared at Blaze. Everyone grew silent, so all that could be heard were birds, fairies, and the crackling fire.

"She is the one," Hepburn said.

"What is it you want to remember?" Clover asked. "Because you'll only forget what no longer matters."

"I don't know what matters," Lux countered. "Shouldn't I find out before I risk not ever knowing?"

"Good evening." A man similar in stature and attitude to Joplin approached them. "Sorry I'm late, Fender. I had a slight delay in locking down the Fire Lodge. Who's this?"

"Hendrix, Lux has finally joined us." Joplin stood up and tossed the man a goblet.

"Move," Hendrix said immediately. Everyone on Lux's side of the table moved down. He sat down next to her. "What's wrong, kid?"

"Nothing," Lux replied quickly and glanced at Blaze.

"No, there's something." Hendrix lifted Lux's chin and examined her face carefully. "What you're about to do won't hurt any of us. You've been warned by someone who's different. Trust me; you'd rather be like us than like him."

"Why can't you people just say what you mean!" Lux shouted. She glared at Blaze. "What are your feelings for me? Just tell me! Say something."

After a moment, when he still said nothing, Lux got up and stormed away from the table. The real reason she was frustrated was that Blaze's silence only added to his appeal. She needed to know him.

She wandered back to the garden of fairies. She knelt down and watched them. Even they seemed to know their purpose, who they were. She wanted knowledge. She wanted her heart to be full, and for it to stay that way.

The fairy she'd met earlier flew toward her. It fluttered near her face and then backed away, beaming at her. It was charming. Lux slowly moved her hand forward, careful not to startle it. It twirled and laughed; shimmer flew from its mouth, and then it landed on her hand.

The tiny feet, no bigger than raindrops, burned instantly into Lux's flesh. Startled, she fell back and instinctively seized what had caused her pain. And then she let it go. She stared down in horror at the lifeless creature still in her hand; its wings shattered.

"No!" She pleaded in a hushed voice. She looked around frantically; no other fairies were paying any attention to her. And she was out of sight of her friends. "Wake up!" she cried.

The footprints were still burning deeper into her hand; the pain was tremendous. She held the dead fairy close to her face and whispered for it to look at her. She said sorry. But sorry didn't bring it back. She closed her eyes and prayed that when she opened them again, the fairy would be okay. But when she did, she felt a shadow move over her again. She opened her eyes and saw darkness around her. Weight. Pressure.

Lux could not let anyone know what she'd done. She felt despicable, afraid. Finally, she hid the fairy in her pocket. She had to hide the burn on her hand, or everyone would find out who she really was. She couldn't think straight, didn't know what to do. So she ran. She ran until she heard the music again. The music brought her to the fire.

Lux stopped and stared into the flames. She closed her eyes and took a deep breath. The fire warmed her face. What was she afraid of? Herself. Her capabilities, her strength. But most of all, she was afraid of not understanding who she was. And now she had something to hide. Her hand throbbed, but she clenched her fist to conceal the evidence.

Hendrix joined her by the fire and handed her a goblet. "He wants you, too. And that's not something you'll forget by drinking this, Lux."

She looked into his eyes, and decided there was no point in avoiding it any longer. She took the goblet and began to guzzle. There was a buzzing sensation somewhere between her head and her chest. The goblet her lips had kissed was soon empty. She was dizzy with satisfaction and smiling effortlessly. The darkness remained, only she no longer cared. The darkness wasn't so bad. She wiped the traces of remaining liquid from the edges of her lips and chin. The pain in her hand had numbed.

Lux understood Pleiades perfectly now. She viewed Blaze differently, too. She grinned at Hendrix, who was watching her intently. She felt no regret; she felt fine. Nobody would find out what she'd done. And then she noticed someone new. In the distance on the other side of the fire was a young man strumming a guitar. His face was hidden. She turned to watch him, shivered, and crossed her arms.

"Notice the zephyr yet?" Harlow asked as she approached the fire and refilled a goblet for Hendrix. She stood next to Lux. "You feel it, and that's when you know you're home. It stays with you."

"Zephyr?"

She watched the young man playing guitar again. Zephyr. Something about him was familiar. He would be the one to tell her just why she was in Boreloque. She knew it. They'd all been right; the Cove didn't make her forget. Instead, everything was illuminated.

Lux moved closer to Zephyr. He didn't move. He didn't acknowledge her. If only she could see his face. Behind the smoke and ashes rising from the flames, he looked ghostly. She wanted him to notice her. But he continued to play.

Like lovers that cross paths only in the stars
Once in a lifetime, twice gone too far
When you're finally ready to give me your heart
I'll have already left you behind

A thick ember rose from the fire and floated toward Zephyr.

"Look out!" Lux shrieked, but the ember died out just in time. Zephyr didn't seem to hear her. His song ended and he paused for a moment before embarking on a new melody. She heard new footsteps. Hendrix and Harlow had left her, but York was approaching.

"Maybe it's time for you to rest," he said. "We've prepared your bed in the Twilight Trees." She considered sleep but felt bound to Zephyr's music. She felt a strange connection to his words and his voice.

I had a dream of you and me,
still together fifty years away
I knew one thing, I loved you endlessly
You promised me what we could be someday
And I believed

"I know this!" Lux exclaimed, ignoring York. He watched her for a moment, nodded, and then retreated back to the lounge area. All York could see was a girl staring into the fire.

"The flames trigger her memory," Pleiades commented as they all watched Lux from the lounge. "I'm more concerned about someone at this table. Blaze. Why haven't you spoken?" Then, upon looking closer, Pleiades finally noticed his condition. He slumped down on the table and lost consciousness. She rushed to his side.

"*Venia,*" she said, and shuddered. "Call the Seven Sisters!"

She knelt down next to Blaze and examined his face. Thick, careless stitches became visible from his mouth. He gained consciousness again and cried out in pain. She grabbed the knife from his belt and carefully pressed it between his lips, breaking the stitches apart, one at a time. She gathered her skirt and wiped the blood from his face.

"She's jealous," Pleiades explained. She kept his mouth open far enough to pour in the Cove, then worked quickly to cut the remaining stitches. She held his hand and whispered soothingly in his ear.

"Joplin, call for the Pan Storm," Hendrix instructed. "York, make sure Dreamer's Lane is in lockdown. Fender, we're safe here, right? She can't get to —"

"Get to us now. Don't worry," Blaze raised his arm. He sighed heavily. "She can't get to us. And she won't try." He leaned forward toward the ground and spit out a mouthful of blood. Pleiades hushed him and forced him to drink.

"Venia made a new deal. She wants me to deliver Lux's heart to her," Blaze said. No one answered. "I feel for Lux. I didn't know if I would, but I do. Venia can't know."

Lux was still entranced by Zephyr; she'd seen and heard nothing back at the lounge. She was sitting in front of the fire listening, and letting the music seep deep into her heart. She unclenched her fist and looked discreetly at her hand. The wound was still there. She just couldn't feel it, which was strange, because it was moving deeper still. The flesh around the burn was turning dark. She closed her hand again and drank the Cove.

"What was that song?" She ventured around the edge of the flames again toward Zephyr. He still hadn't made eye contact with her. She offered up her goblet, but then he turned his back on her completely. She took a sip and contemplated. The sip turned into a gulp, and soon her goblet was empty. She returned to her spot near the fire and saw she finally had company again.

Everyone was arriving and finding places to recline around the fire. Lux glanced once more at Zephyr. She considered explaining the melody she recognized somehow, but when she looked in his direction again, he had vanished. She already couldn't quite remember the music, yet she couldn't forget it, either.

"More to drink?" Hepburn offered. Lux obliged. She sat next to Blaze, who looked ashen and weak. He was sipping from a goblet. She watched him for a moment before speaking.

"You don't have to tell me your feelings for me. But tell me about the Crossroads. If I'm a thief..." Lux paused. "How do I fix it?"

"You need to find out who you stole from," Blaze whispered. His words were muffled, because his hand was covering his mouth.

Lux leaned closer to the fire. She didn't yet realize the man whose heart she had indeed stolen was sitting next to her. She'd stolen from him long before she'd arrived in Boreloque, in another time and place. But his heart had traveled with her. Because love is unrestricted, it knows no restraint.

"And then you'll know your purpose," Blaze said. "And you won't need to be here any longer if you don't want to. You'll be free."

SEVEN

Album: The Road To Red Rocks

Track: Four

"You're pretty attached to the Tazo girl." Mr. Sweeney looked up from a magazine, and his reading glasses slipped down his nose. "Don't you have homework? Practice?"

Ember had walked in the front door to find his father sitting in the dimly lit parlor. He'd never pictured his father sitting at home alone, waiting.

"We have a connection. We always have," Ember said, realizing the attachment to Lux couldn't be explained. He didn't understand it himself. Mr. Sweeney closed the magazine and stared at Ember.

"Don't get too close."

"Too late!" The comment enraged Ember. He ripped the magazine from his father's hands and threw it to the ground. "She's going to wake up!"

"Ember. You haven't practiced in a week. And what about school? If you fall behind —" Mr. Sweeney rubbed his forehead wearily. "Where are your friends?"

"I'm not falling behind!" Ember shouted. "I do my homework at the hospital, and the guys understand. I've been writing a lot of new music."

"Was she your girlfriend?" Mr. Sweeney asked. "I don't understand."

"I'm making up for lost time. That's all I can tell you."

"Come home at a decent hour. I just don't want to see you hurt."

Ember and his father had lived like roommates for years. Specific rules had never quite been established. He agreed to his new curfew, but the next morning he left for school an hour early.

What he hadn't expected when he arrived at the hospital was to see Anya Jensen already sitting next to Lux's bed. How had he forgotten about her? She was the link between him and Lux.

"Hi," Anya said. She stood up suddenly and released her grip on Lux's hand. Her eyes were puffy. She turned away from Ember and faced the window.

"What are you doing here?" Ember asked, ignoring her brokenness.

"I needed someone to talk to." Anya faced Ember again and forced a smile. "She's a good listener these days." Fresh tears welled up again. Ember didn't know what else to do, so he dropped his things and hugged her.

"You can talk to me, too," he whispered.

They moved to the couch and sat together.

"How often do you come here?" Anya finally asked.

Ember was too uncomfortable to answer. After a long silence, it was clear both of them were thinking too deeply about too many things too early in the day.

"Let's skip," Ember suggested. Anya nodded in agreement.

They didn't move for hours.

Outside the sky was blinding white. Sweater weather had

turned to coats and scarves with the rising of the sun. Nurses came and went a few times every hour.

At one point Mrs. Tazo stopped in with fresh flowers and a new pair of pajamas for Lux. Delighted to see both Ember and Anya, she returned with refreshments and a game for them. She didn't stay; she had to get back to the spa. But she made them promise to come over for dinner that evening.

By early afternoon, Ember and Anya had grown restless. Neither of them necessarily expected any changes from Lux in that moment, but they were both silently plotting ways to wake her up.

"I have to tell you something about Lux!" Anya blurted out unexpectedly.

"Then we have to go," Ember said. "Now." He stood up abruptly and grabbed her hand.

"Where are we going?"

"Apples and Worms. I'll drive."

They made their way to the door, pulling on their jackets as they went.

Ember opened the passenger door of his truck for Anya and swept fresh snow off the windshield.

"I hope you don't mind Mumford," he said. He started the car and turned up the music. "This live album is paramount."

"I know. Track four was my alarm clock this morning," Anya said.

"No way!" Ember's face lit up. "Me too." They smiled at each other.

"I guess we're meant to be friends, then," Anya said. "Because I listen to Christmas music eighty percent of the year, so you caught me on an off-day."

"Well, now it's our song."

They drove through Briar Heights listening to "Ghosts That We Knew." Ember put the song on repeat. They parked outside of Apples and Worms Diner, but neither of them moved.

"But this one is your song; it's you and her," Anya said to break the silence. Ember turned to her with a desperate look on his face.

"I can't talk about her in front of her!" he exclaimed.

"I feel like she hears us, too." Anya smiled softly.

They walked into the diner and slid into a booth.

It was like an awkward first date, but the person they were both awkward about wasn't there. They stared at the menus.

"Great day to ditch school, huh?" A waiter in his thirties smiled over them. "What can I get you?"

"I'll have the caramel apple malt," Ember said, and cleared his throat. "And a burger with everything on it." He looked over his menu at Anya. "Sorry, I should have let you go first."

"I'll have the chocolate chip cheesecake pancakes. And *hot* syrup. And hot cocoa." She eyed Ember. "Lux's signature order."

"Forget mine. I'll have what she's having," Ember said. The waiter stared at both of them as if they were crazy, then stalked away.

"So, what happened at the beginning of ninth grade?" Ember asked anxiously.

"I remember that day, and I'm still as confused as you are." Anya gazed out the window.

"There was so much I never got to say to her." Ember followed Anya's gaze.

"We are opening Pandora's Box. You understand that, right?" Anya said anxiously. Ember nodded, then stopped.

"Wait. What exactly is Pandora's Box?"

"You haven't taken Mythology? Lux signed up to take it next spring, just saying," she said. "Anyway. Pandora's Box comes from Greek Mythology. Pandora was the first woman ever created. She was given a bunch of gifts by other gods; she had it all. When two of the super-important gods got in a super-big fight, she was used as bait, and given this beautiful box, but told never to open it. Of course, she was curious. Actually, that was one of the features the gods gave her when they created her. She couldn't help herself; she had to know, so she opened the box."

"Then what happened?"

"The box was filled with all the evil in the world. She tried to close it again, but couldn't; it was too late. The evil escaped."

"So she was left with an empty box?"

"No. There was one thing left at the bottom. Hope," Anya whispered. They were leaning closely toward each other now.

"So you're saying, if we talk about Lux, we're going to find out a bunch of bad stuff. But once we do that, there will still be hope," Ember said. "So we actually *need* to do this."

"You're too much, Ember Sweeney." Anya's eyes were wide. "I mean, talk about finding a silver lining."

"Isn't that what you meant?"

"Sure. So should we open the box?"

"I've been ready for years."

"And by the way, we can never tell her about this."

"Yeah, that's why we're here!"

"She would kill me right now if she knew this was happening. She couldn't even handle that we talked about her paintings."

"But, why?" Ember demanded.

"And if I ever told you what a smoke show she thinks you are..." Anya shrugged. "But every girl thinks so."

"Shut up."

"You *are* a pretty guy."

"Her paintings are all over school. It's public information," Ember said, ignoring her.

"Exactly," Anya said.

Maybe it was too much. Maybe he should walk away now and forget about her before they opened any box. But he couldn't; he needed to know.

Anya took a deep breath. "Where did you go to middle school?"

"Briar Day."

"Lux and I went to Morrison. She was a big deal there. Kind

of like you are here. She got a lot of recommendations to attend BHA."

"I didn't really know her then."

"Well, she won this big contest and the painting was purchased by an editor who used it as a book cover. It was re-painted on a wall at Morrison Prep. It was in the papers. It was paramount."

"I remember."

"She was *so* excited. And proud. She had confidence, you know? Her paintings were so full of life, just like her. And at that time her family was everything to her."

"Her family seems great. They've been so nice to us."

"To *us*, sure. Let me ask you something," Anya said, her voice rising. "Where would your dad be if you were in a coma?"

Ember stared at his hands. The thought had crossed his mind. Why weren't Lux's parents constantly by her side?

"Anyway," Anya continued quickly. "After she won the contest, she overheard all this stuff her family said behind her back. She wasn't meant to hear any of it, of course."

"What stuff?"

"Listen, they love me like their own kid. Which is great, since I don't have parents. I only have an older brother who bought me a loft in town where I basically live alone, because he travels for work. Anyway, I can see you like them. But the Tazos have no idea what Lux is passionate about. It would be like your dad not knowing you're into music. They don't see art as a way to earn a living; therefore, it doesn't exist. They're not proud of her. They compared her. They doubted her. They judged her. Behind her back. So, that's what she overheard. They won't acknowledge her talent."

"Oh." Ember was crestfallen. He thought about the pain this must have caused Lux.

"The Tazos didn't actually want her to go to BHA to study art. They had different ideas for her future. Something more professional. When it came to her talent, they looked the other way," Anya said.

The waiter set down their meals and left.

"Don't get me wrong," Anya continued casually. "I do love the Tazos. But, because of them, she's tried to suppress who she is in order to get them to accept her. I don't even think she realizes it, either. It changed her. And now, who knows? What will it be like if she wakes up?"

"*WHEN* she wakes up —"

"They probably hope she won't remember anything, so they can make her who they want her to be." Anya shook her head. "Sorry, but it's true. Anyway, that's what our twenties will be for, right? To grow up, move on, start over, and repair ourselves from childhood."

"Why can't they see how talented she is?" Ember asked.

"Well, you're definitely her biggest fan," Anya said, through a mouthful of food. "So do her a kindness. Talk her up to her parents while you've got the opportunity. Tell them how you want to use her work." Anya shrugged. "Talk to them about your album."

"I will."

"It won't be easy."

"It can't be more difficult than the last two years with Lux."

"Arrabelle doesn't get it, either. Lux has always lived in her shadow." Anya continued to talk between shovel-loads of food.

"What's the big deal about Arrabelle? Lux is cool."

"I know that. And you know what else?" Anya hesitated. "I wish Lux was here in my place."

"Me, too. Not that I don't like your company."

"Anyway, now you know the family dynamic. The first day of ninth grade was the day Lux and I officially became best friends. And she told me about you."

"Best week ever," Ember said. He sighed loudly.

"Well, something changed in her during that welcome assembly. You were on stage. She ran out before the end of your song." Anya sighed. "She never heard your dedication. She never could explain herself."

"She didn't see it on social media or anything?" Ember asked doubtfully.

"No," Anya said. "She never sees what's happening on social media. She just doesn't care about it."

"It was that night." Ember stared out the window. "I found her back home. She'd run away from me. She screamed in my face, *who do you think you are!*"

"She did...?"

"I'll never forget it. I've been asking myself that question ever since."

"Well, who *do* you think you are?" Anya asked. "Maybe that's what she's been waiting to hear. Maybe she wants to know the real you."

"I wrote her a note that weekend. I told her how I really felt. I said I'd wait as long as she needed, because I could tell whatever it was, it was something significant," he said. "But I never got to give her the note. The next time I saw her, she tried to make me promise to never speak to her again, to pretend she didn't exist. She told me she hated me."

Anya set her fork down and pushed her plate away.

"She never told me that. I'm sorry. For whatever it's worth, I don't think she meant it."

"Wait a second," Ember said suddenly. "*You* didn't ever like me, did you?"

"Seriously? Finish your food! Can't you *see*?" Anya shook her head and rolled her eyes. "This isn't about me. Or you." She took another large bite. "It's about her. Her family. Proving herself. And even if I did like you, would I ever say it, or act on it? NO!"

"You're assuming a lot right now, and it's just rude!" Ember retaliated, stuffing his own mouth with food. "I wasn't asking because of ME. I was asking because one of my friends likes you! And we have a rule!" Ember rolled his eyes.

"I'm not rude! Who likes me?" Anya asked eagerly.

"Oh, of course you want to know." Ember crossed his arms.

Anya became very quiet. She frowned. She finished her pancakes.

"When you put someone up on a pedestal, it makes you smaller," she said. She wiped her mouth with a napkin. "That was her thing. Family, Friends. She was always looking up. And you. She put you on a pedestal. She admired you. In her mind, she wasn't worthy. Eventually she buried herself." Anya shrugged. "And, you know, when someone's on a pedestal, you expect more of them, you just do. It's a flaw, but it is what it is."

"So, for two years now, it is what it is?" Ember said with his mouth full.

"Yes."

"That's terrible."

"Well, when you're buried, you have no strength in your spine. You need help getting back up," Anya said. "She's just not there yet. I told her all the time: 'you know, Ember Sweeney is nothing special.'"

"Oh, thank you."

"Calm down, it never worked. She's not stupid. Just scared," Anya said. "Aside from that, and when she's not panicking about the future or you, she really is so fun. And happy."

"Lovely. I'm the source of her unhappiness."

"Usually only when you start dating someone new."

"What about that first week? What about that? It was perfect. You said it's about her family. So it's not about me, then?"

"Girls are complicated, Ember."

"Or you're complicating a simple story."

"She's tried to ignore and forget you all this time. But you won't go away."

"You *really* know how to flatter me, Anya Jensen."

"*Don't* go away, Ember. You two deserve a first chance, at least."

"Have you told her that?"

The waiter appeared with the check.

"But I want dessert," Anya interrupted him before he could talk. "We'll take two root beer floats. Thanks."

"Be right back." The waiter crumpled the receipt as he walked away, muttering about the weirdos from BHA.

"I have told her that." Anya winked at Ember. "Many times." She reached across the table and touched his hand. "She just hasn't believed me yet."

At that moment, Jamison walked into the diner with Dylan Black and Alex Spencer. Ember waved them over.

"Hey Dylan," Anya said. "Did you take notes in Accounting today?"

"Mr. Medcraft let us watch *The Godfather*," Dylan said.

"We got to watch *Empire Records* in Ms. Rehberger's class," Jamison interrupted.

"Mr. Hemme's class watched with us, too. Why weren't you there? What's going on with you two?" Dylan looked slightly confused. He glanced from Jamison to Ember. "We were just talking about you."

"About me?" Anya replied, confused.

"What's this?" Tanner had joined them.

"Hi, Tanner." Anya smiled sweetly. "How was the Mythology exam?"

"We're talking about Lux," Ember blurted out.

"Really?" Tanner watched them uncertainly. "Have fun." The guys followed him to an empty booth.

"He's your best friend, right?" Anya looked in their direction.

"Tanner is the one who likes you. And this looks like we're... you know," Ember said. Anya's eyes widened.

"Oh. No. NO."

"Yeah, I know, NO." Ember shook his head.

"He likes me?" Anya was beaming. "Like, how much?"

"A lot. It's legit."

"Oh, I can't wait to tell —" Her face fell.

"And we're back where we started." Ember sighed. "Let's take the dessert to go."

"Wouldn't that look worse?" Anya asked.

"Yes." Ember looked over at the guys. It was obvious they were discussing the present scenario. "But it's not like we can fix it now."

"Says who? You're Ember Sweeney! I'm so let down," Anya said dramatically. "You are not living up to the rumors I've heard about you. Aren't you *cool* about everything? Friends with everyone? Nothing gets to you, yet you care so much? You're honest and can fix any misunderstanding?"

"Where do you get your information?"

"Piper Speedman. Duh. But, it's common knowledge! Written on bathroom stalls! You know what's strange? Right now you actually remind me of...her." Anya watched him inquisitively. "That's what it is. She's changed you! She's in your head. But, it's okay. I can fix this." She stood up suddenly, and walked across the room to the other table.

"Hi, guys." She smiled confidently. Alex, Jamison, and Dylan smiled back politely. It was clear that Tanner was upset.

"Cool necklace, Anya," Dylan said helplessly.

"Thank you. It's my own design. What were you saying about me?"

Nobody answered.

"You said you were just talking about me," she continued. They all looked at Tanner.

"Can I just sit down? Okay, thanks." She moved in next to Dylan and Alex, facing Tanner. She crossed her arms on the table.

"Tanner, Ember and I were here to talk about Lux Tazo. We're going to spend time together, and we are going to be very good friends," Anya said. "I'm sure you can try to understand what we're going through together. Lux is my best friend. He's in love with her." The guys looked across the room at Ember, who was watching awkwardly.

"So, please know this. I don't like him. He doesn't like me. But he is in love with my best friend. And you know what? I have a thing for *his* best friend. You *are* his best friend, right Tanner?" He nodded uncertainly.

"So, don't be upset with Ember," Anya warned. "All I'm going to say is, if you asked me out on a date, or brought me flowers, or wrote me a song, I wouldn't deny you. I'm awesome, and I know I deserve the best. I'm also looking for the best, and I like you."

The guys were speechless.

"Anyway, we need to get back to the hospital now. I just told Ember some things about Lux's personal life that he needs to process." She stood up. "Be nice to him. He's more sensitive than I realized. See you tomorrow, guys."

Anya left the table and returned to Ember, who was staring wide-eyed.

"Well, let's go! We have homework to do," she said. She walked to the door of the diner, forgetting about their dessert and their bill. She turned back to wave at Tanner, who quickly waved back. Ember dropped cash on the table and rushed after her.

"That was paramount," Ember said, after they'd gotten into his truck. Anya laughed.

"I just acted like *you*. The old you."

"I don't know if I was ever that good."

"Oh, you were. I saw it. Just never with Lux."

"Never with Lux. She terrified me."

"Now we're getting somewhere!" Anya said happily. "This is a good place to be."

"Terrified? I can't say I agree. What would Lux think of that?"

"I'm quickly finding out that you overthink everything, Ember Sweeney."

Anya and Ember spent the rest of the afternoon doing their homework in Lux's hospital room. They didn't talk. The conversation at Apples and Worms had been cut short. But Ember understood that they had, indeed, opened their Pandora's Box.

Anya set down her *History of Fashion Week* text, and stretched. She watched Ember, who looked lost in his thoughts. Her eyes fell upon his guitar. She stood up abruptly.

"I have to go call Mrs. Tazo. Double check what time we should get there for dinner. And can you give me a ride home tonight?" she asked.

"Absolutely," Ember said, not looking up. Anya left the room, but remained on the other side of the closed door. Moments later, she heard his guitar. He was singing to Lux.

Heartbroken tears streamed down her face. Terrified wasn't such a good place to be. She had a sinking feeling in her gut: reality. How long would he continue sing to her? Anya couldn't ignore the inevitable. She had to prepare to say goodbye.

It was the beginning of a beautiful friendship. She realized she was going to have to be the strong one of the two. She was willing to do it. For him. She could smile.

That evening, Ember and Anya joined Mr. and Mrs. Tazo for dinner. Behind the smiles and the kindness, it felt very lonely. Snow had gathered throughout the day. When they returned to Ember's house so he could drive Anya home, Mr. Sweeney stopped them.

"I don't want you driving tonight, Ember," he stated. "Anya, you can stay here. I'll call your parents."

"I don't have parents," Anya said matter-of-factly.

"Well, then I'll be your parent tonight. You're staying here. The guest room next to Ember's is ready. And you two make sure you finish your homework."

Mr. Sweeney made them tea and then went to bed. The two finished their homework in the kitchen. They didn't seem to have much more to say; they were tired.

Eventually, they climbed the stairs and said goodnight. Anya crawled into bed in the guest room. The weight of the day began to fall heavy on her heart. She tossed and turned. Finally, she got up, grabbed her pillow, and tiptoed into Ember's bedroom.

"You okay?" Ember whispered and turned over in bed. He was typing a message on his phone.

"Yeah," she whispered. She curled up in the chair at the end of his bed, and pulled a blanket over herself. "Goodnight."

"Night." Ember said. He continued to type.

Ember: Last song you listened to today?
Duffy: Jealousy by Cary Brothers.
Luther: Yellowcard. Sing For Me.
Tanner: ...Enchanted. Taylor Swift.
Jamison: HA!!! Nightswimming. R.E.M.
Tanner: Whatever, Jamo. Ember said we can do a cover.
Jamison: I'd cover any Taylor song. Tell. no. one.
Ember: Belief by Gavin DeGraw.

Ember could hear Anya crying, even though she was trying to hide it. He put his phone down. He gathered his blankets and pillow, and moved to the other end of his bed to be nearer to her. He reached for the box of tissues on his bedside table and handed one to her.

"Goodnight," he said. And eventually they both found sleep.

EIGHT

Album: Chariot - Stripped

Track: Six

"You called, Blaze?" A wispy voice resonated from above them in the trees. Seven petite, angelic girls were perched closely together on a branch, and the birds surrounding them chirped incessantly. Pleiades stood up and the girls flew down to meet her.

"Spindle, he'll need your remedy. The wound is deep, and it will leave scars," Pleiades said. She stood up, and the girls flew down to meet her.

Spindle, the tallest of the Seven Sisters, nodded at Pleiades and then glanced curiously at Lux, while her sisters surrounded Blaze.

"Oh, hello," she said to Lux. "We're the Seven Sisters. I'm Spindle. And they are Larrissima, Ursa, Pillion, Jupiter, Titania and Carina. What brings you to us?"

Lux suddenly felt uncomfortable. She sensed Spindle knew something about her. She smiled politely and made sure to keep her hand hidden.

"I landed at the Crossroads," she said importantly, just as everyone else had said it about her or to her. She drank from her goblet.

"Interesting," Spindle replied. "I'm sure you'll find your way back. But for now, we'll bring you to our home." She smiled, but watched Lux closely, eyeing her from head to toe.

Spindle put her fingers to her lips and whistled a long, drawn out melody. A muted, chugging sound erupted in the sky, and a multitude of stars above them and beyond the island parted. The breeze blew in what appeared to be a flying pirate ship, and the fire grew fierce.

"All aboard!" shouted a deep voice. "SS Pan Storm: onward to Folly Falls, home of the Seven Sisters." A man aboard the craft saluted them. The ship hovered just above the ground, and a rope ladder dropped down for boarding.

"I've got you." York went ahead of Lux and helped her inside. "Zwicky, this is our guest, Lux." The man tipped his hat, grinned, and hung a tiny flute necklace around her neck. York led her to a row of cushioned seats.

Hendrix and Joplin boarded next. They helped everyone else inside the ship, while Zwicky stood by and handed out necklaces. When they were ready for takeoff, Lux found herself nestled between Hepburn and Bubble. Blaze was facing her, resting on a cushion between Pleiades and Spindle.

Fender boarded the ship last. "I'll have to stay behind," he said. "One of the fairies is unaccounted for."

Lux's heart stopped. Her hand throbbed again. She watched everyone's reactions. They were murmuring, confused, concerned, looking at one another uncertainly.

"Call us back if you need us," Joplin said.

"Hopefully she's just off sleeping somewhere," Fender said. "It's happened before."

Fender climbed back down. The ship began to rise into the sky. Lux breathed a small sigh of relief, but guilt began to set in. She looked around to see if anyone had a goblet full of the Cove, but they'd all left their drinks by the fire.

"Sweet dreams Ember Park," Hepburn whispered. "Keep our fairies safe and sound." Something stirred inside Lux. She felt for just a moment that she'd been to the park before tonight.

"Welcome friends," Zwicky said. "This should be an easy ride. When you need your Float Coat, just blow your whistle."

Lux held tightly to her whistle, wondering what a Float Coat was. She momentarily forgot about the corpse in her pocket. The ship rose into the air and they sailed swiftly through the atmosphere.

A distant star went supernova and left a spiral trail as it shot across the sky. More stars moved in the wake of the ship. They sailed into a cloud, splitting it apart, and blanketing the passengers in dew. Ember Park had disappeared behind them, but a new cluster of twinkling lights appeared ahead.

The ship took a sudden nosedive. "Ready your whistles!" Zwicky shouted. The sounds flowed together harmoniously. Lux found when she brought the whistle to her lips, it played its own enchanting tune when she breathed into it. As they moved closer to Folly Falls, tiny white bears with thick pearly wings came splashing up from a sphere of waterfalls.

The Float Coats arrived at the Pan Storm. Each one flew toward the sound of their song. Blaze was taken first and six of the Seven Sisters flew along with them. Spindle waited with Lux. Lux's Float Coat found her, nuzzled its warm nose on her cheek, and purred. She gingerly climbed on its back and wrapped her arms around its neck, as everyone else was doing. The breeze swept them away from the Pan Storm, and they continued off into the darkness. She closed her eyes and listened to the creature purr as they flew down toward a circle of waterfalls.

The temperature changed suddenly and a wall of warmth

greeted them as they reached Folly Falls. Lux and her Float Coat soared above so she saw waterfalls, cliffs, and dimly lit caves. Spindle remained near. The other Float Coats began dropping their passengers into the water. Her own Float Coat dove toward the heart of the falls and moved very close to the water's surface. She let go, and with a splash, plummeted deep into the warm pool.

She opened her eyes under the water. Her Float Coat was swimming away, its fur waving slowly with the current. Families of sea horses passed by and mingled with water fairies who were having an underwater tea party. Lux was careful not to touch any of them.

She surfaced for a deep breath, noticed Spindle flying away into one of the caves, and breathed a sigh of relief. She looked around at all of the waterfalls, and then beyond them at the twinkling sky. She felt so small. But she also felt at home, somehow.

Harlow, Hayworth, and Hepburn approached her wearing matching mysterious smiles.

"You're coming with us, Lux!" Hepburn called.

Harlow and Hayworth each took one of Lux's arms. They pulled her up out of the water, their wings fluttering madly. Higher and higher they rose until they were perched atop the highest waterfall, overlooking Folly Falls.

The girls sat down on a ledge, and their feet caught the rushing water. The Starlets pointed out where the Seven Sisters lived, as well as Float Coat Cavern. The home of the Seven Sisters was nestled above the caverns in grooves among the cliffs. The rooms were lit up by fireflies. Hammocks were situated between thick vines, and hung below large lanterns. Next to their home was Float Coat Cavern. The creatures spent days sleeping under the shade of the falls, so they could watch over Folly Falls at night. Lux could see their large eyes blinking in the darkness. Each had their own space with names above beds. Plush vines sporting indigo flowers hung across the front of their rooms as curtains.

"Truffle is your Float Coat now." Hepburn had followed Lux's gaze.

"Mine?" Lux grasped her whistle. The girls nodded.

"Mine is named Saffron," Hepburn explained. "Harlow's is Olive, Hayworth's is Hazel. Oh, and yes, Blaze has one, too; Sage. There's one for everybody." Lux watched the Float Coats; some still circling over Folly Falls.

The girls were distracted by an enormous splash below. Their friends were cliff jumping. They were splashing around in the water, laughing, and cheering each other on. Then Lux saw Bubble, Pinwheel, and Clover swim away from the crowd. They went behind one of the waterfalls into a cavern.

"You can't see him from here," Hepburn said suddenly. Once again...where was Blaze? She began to feel as though everyone was keeping them apart, so she wanted him even more.

"He's in the grotto; it's farther back in the cavern," Harlow said.

Lux scanned the glowing caves behind the falls, wondering which one of them he was in. The more she thought about him, the more desirable he was.

"He'll be good as new by sunrise," Harlow assured her.

"What's wrong with him?" Lux asked.

"Nothing we can fix." Harlow looked away. "He needs the care of the Seven Sisters." Lux felt jealous of the Seven Sisters. She wanted to be the one caring for Blaze.

The Twirlyfine Starlets stood up in unison. Hepburn turned to Lux and winked. "There's no room here other than for you and your thoughts." They waved goodbye, and dove in.

Jealousy. Desire. Concern. Curiosity. Lux found herself alone. Her heavy mind clouded the view. She watched across the falls as a few of the Seven Sisters arrived home. They curled into their beds and extinguished the lights. She needed to find Blaze. She peered over the edge of the cliff and decided it was time to jump. She didn't want to be alone with her thoughts. She stood up, stared at the twinkling sky, and felt the balmy breeze on her neck.

Lux backed up a few steps and then ran forward at full speed, her toes digging into the grass. Before she knew it, nothing was underneath her feet and she was plummeting into the vast midnight, where she could only see shadows of bobbing heads. She soared into the water like a broken bird, arms stretched out as far as they could go.

When she surfaced and smoothed her hair back from her face, blinking water out of her eyes, everyone was cheering. Then they all turned to watch the next person jump. She turned to swim toward the shore. But suddenly, the weight on her shoulders grew heavy again. Lux began to lose strength. She felt far away from everyone. She couldn't take a deep enough breath to call for help.

Then something brushed against her foot in the water. She gasped and looked around wildly, seeing nothing. A moment later, it happened again. Her body jolted and she was pulled under, swallowing a mouthful of water on the way down. Panicking, Lux choked, inhaling more water, as she fought against the force pulling on her, but it was quite strong. With a spurt of adrenaline kicking in, and a sharp pain in her side, Lux swam back upward, fighting her way to the surface. And then whatever it was went away. She opened her eyes and realized she was now at the edge of the falls. She reached for a rock to rest against. She choked and vomited. Even holding onto the edge, she could barely stay afloat.

Lux finally caught her breath and looked back at her friends. They were all still cliff diving and cheering. Why hadn't anyone noticed her struggling? Where was Spindle? She crawled out of the water and sat on the rock. She felt something warm on her leg: blood. Deep claw marks ran from her shin down to her ankle. She stood up and steadied herself and then felt the gash in her side, too. She tried not to panic. Blood was everywhere now.

Pinwheel flew over to Lux from behind one of the caves. "Follow me," she whispered excitedly. She paid no attention to Lux's wounds. "They're in the Sugar Bath."

Lux's heart skipped a beat despite her pain, confusion, and growing fear. She followed Pinwheel into a domed candlelit cavern carved from stone, limping and leaving a trail of bloody footprints behind.

"Come in!" Bubble floated over next to Clover to make room for Pinwheel and Lux. None of them seemed to notice Lux's condition.

"Where's Blaze?" Lux demanded anxiously, her eyes darting around. "I need to see him right now. Can you help me find him?" The girls smiled and nodded.

Clover grabbed candles from the chandelier above the pool and distributed them. Lux held out her left hand for one, having forgotten about the burn the fairy had left on her. Clover noticed the evidence, which was now spreading toward her fingers and onto her wrist. She eyed Lux warily for just a moment but said nothing. Lux nervously clutched the candle and followed the girls into the dark. Wax dripped onto her hand, and it stung, but not as badly as her other wounds, so she ignored it. They departed the domed room and went deeper into the cave. She could hear a drip echo in the distance. Damp moss tickled her feet.

"Don't fall," Pinwheel whispered, as they reached another cavern entrance. They hid behind a rock formation that separated the new room from their dark path.

"He was in here," Clover said.

"He's gone," Bubble said. Her voice echoed. They stepped into the light where there was another pool. This one was swirling instead of bubbling and smelled of lilac. "They're all gone. That's okay, more room for us." She sighed happily and wasted no time getting in. Pinwheel and Clover joined her. Above them hung another chandelier holding at least fifty candles, swaying and dripping wax into the bath. Lux was afraid of immersing her wounds, but the bleeding had slowed, and since the girls still hadn't acknowledged her condition, she decided to join them. She lowered herself in slowly; at first it hurt, but then the pain eased.

Bubble handed Lux a goblet of the Cove. She drank. Her muscles relaxed and her body numbed.

"I could sleep right here." Lux yawned. She felt comfortable, settled.

"You haven't even fallen into bed yet. Just wait for the Twilight

Trees." Clover closed her eyes and leaned back.

"Let's call for our Float Coats," Pinwheel said. She sighed, and her head nodded slightly.

"They need to stay here." Bubble yawned.

"I'll call for the Pan Storm," Clover mumbled as she dozed off.

Lux's mind began to race. Part of her felt exhausted, and the Twilight Trees sounded incredible. But what if she went to sleep and it all disappeared? Where was Blaze? And what about Zephyr? What would it be like when she woke up? What if someone found out about the fairy? She felt her pocket. The corpse was gone.

"You're interfering with Blaze's heart." Pinwheel opened her eyes suddenly and studied Lux intently. "He's hurting, too. Your hearts are connected."

Lux blinked a few times. Her mind went starry. Pinwheel handed her a goblet of the Cove. She drank quickly until it worked again, until she felt calm about everything.

"We'll talk about that tomorrow. This day has felt like thirty," Bubble said.

Clover appeared to have fallen asleep, but Lux wondered if she was just keeping quiet about what she'd seen on Lux's hand.

Bubble climbed out of the tub and left the room. She returned a moment later with Hendrix. He scooped Clover out of the water and carried her out of the caverns. Pinwheel followed them. When Lux got out of the tub, she looked down at her foot; there was nothing there, not even a scratch. She felt her stomach. Nothing. She pulled up her shirt and searched for the gaping wound that had been there moments ago. Clean. She gazed down at her empty goblet. Then she saw everyone far ahead of her, nearing the entrance. She rushed to catch up. But she saw her bloody footprints were still stained on the ground.

"Midnight snack?" York was waiting outside the cave with Joplin. He handed Lux a vine of berries.

"It's midnight?" She asked.

"Long past," York said. "We can only hope to fall into our beds before the light appears again." They left the others behind then. They climbed many short flights of stairs within the caves, passed one wing of Float Coat Cavern, and continued up.

"How long has it been today?" Lux wondered.

"A few sleeps worth, at least," York said. "So everyone should rest well tonight, especially Blaze."

"I get him in the end, right?" Lux asked suddenly. She stopped walking.

York turned around and grinned at her. They exchanged a long look. Finally, he continued up the remainder of the stairs, and she followed him. They stepped onto a matted, grassy trail and were no longer in Folly Falls.

"Would you like to say goodnight?" York asked finally.

"Yes, I would." Lux felt timid. She sensed a taste of the Cove would help, but more than that, she needed to see Blaze, to know he was real.

"I'll send him over," York said. "Once he's well enough."

Lux frowned, but continued to follow him. They entered a forest lined with paths lit only by the sky. York carried a lantern which held safe a family of fireflies. The stars seemed to be rotating around Boreloque, dancing with one another. Surrounding planets bobbed up and down as the stars pushed them aside. Lux yawned deeply. Her eyelids began to feel heavy.

The trail began to slope and they reached a hill. Tree branches hovered and waved in the subtle night wind. Sparkling champagne lights appeared ahead of them. They came to a cliff, and followed it until they reached a bridge.

"Careful." York gripped Lux's hand and moved ahead of her. They crossed the rickety bridge, which dipped low and wobbled. Lux continued straight ahead, holding tight to the rope. It was a very long bridge, but she suddenly smiled at the thought of falling; what could possibly be down there?

Finally they reached the other side and followed another beaten path through the trees. The lights were growing clearer and larger. They stopped underneath a massive tree with lanterns hanging from every branch.

"Your sleeping quarters," York said. "The Twilight Trees."

"This is where everyone sleeps?" she asked, again thinking of Blaze.

"Most of the girls sleep here. And the guys live in the Pram. See over there?" York pointed into the distance. Lux saw a cluster of dim blue lights. "It's very rugged compared to this more delicate tree." He winked at her. Lux saw the skyline beyond the Pram changing from black to a subtle indigo.

She gazed up the gigantic, winding tree at the tent-covered living spaces. The lights in the Twilight Trees were subtly pink, and everything else was a soft white. She could hear the chatter of girls nestling around in their beds.

"So, this is where I leave you. Your bed has been prepared. The girls will help you." York turned and was gone.

A winding ladder was attached to the tree. Lux began to climb. Had she always climbed into bed? She began to shiver. Her clothes were wet and clinging to her.

"Lux?" Heads peered out from their nests and smiled at her.

"Is she here?"

"She made it!"

Harlow peeked out from far above and pointed. "That's yours, just there on the right."

Lux climbed a few more steps and leaned in to examine her bed. It was round like an egg and caved in, just big enough for her to cuddle in, and it was filled to the brim with feathers. Surrounding the bed and hanging from the branches above her were tiny lanterns just like the one York had carried. Each housed families of fireflies. The families in her lanterns peered out of the glass to get a good look at her.

"They're not prisoners," Hepburn insisted, leaning over her bed. Lux stared into the glass lamp. "We set them free when the morning comes, and they play all day. This is their home. They want to be here near us. They come back on their own whenever it gets dark."

Lux noticed a shelf next to her bed. On it was a neatly folded white gown. Next to the gown was a small vial of the Cove. She drew sheer curtains around her bed and changed. She drank the vial and fell into her soft bed of feathers, which enveloped her securely. She sighed peacefully and closed her eyes. She was content. She didn't even think to wait up for Blaze. Or wonder about Zephyr. Because she would stay forever.

The lights faded as the fireflies drifted off and light snoring replaced whispers. Lux had just dozed off herself when she heard a rustling beneath the tree. Soft music filled her ears. Her flesh warmed, and a lullaby put her soundly to sleep. Images floated aimlessly through her mind. Pleiades den, Dreamer's Lane, Ember Park, fairies, the burn on her hand, nearly drowning, her wounded body, and a very confused heart. She slept deeply for a very long time.

NINE

Album: The Hotel Cafe Presents...Winter Songs

Track: Two

Lux had fallen into a deeper coma than originally thought. The extent of her brain activity had been misleading. This was difficult for Mr. and Mrs. Tazo to accept, but instead of spending more time by her side, they became busier than ever with work. They didn't seem to know what else to do. Only Ember and Anya were with Lux constantly.

"We're not giving up. But we have reached the four week mark." Anya had arrived at the door of Lux's hospital room and hid behind it. The doctors were speaking with Lux's parents. "We haven't seen any significant changes or improvement."

She heard Mr. Tazo respond then. A knot grew in her throat. She took a deep breath. She couldn't be a kitten, not now. She needed to be strong.

"The full team wants to schedule a meeting to look at what

the future holds if nothing changes in the next month," the doctor said.

Anya had tried to be positive, especially in front of Ember. He had enough hope for both of them. But she was afraid; she didn't see how this could end well. Every day she lost a little bit of hope. She saw the situation for what it was: bleak.

"Some doctors would say now is the beginning stages of the cut-off time. If she hasn't woken up by now, chances grow smaller every day," the doctor said. "But she could find her way back. We can't predict the future of a coma patient. Her wounds are healing and her body is stronger than we'd expected."

"Don't tell the kids," Mr. Tazo said finally.

Anya left the doorway. She wandered slowly through the wing of the hospital that had become like a second home. She found herself in an empty stairwell. She leaned against the wall, stared out the small window where the last light of day poured in, and wept. She didn't want them to see her like this.

Then she realized this was how Lux would behave. She finally understood. Lux had hidden her feelings only to protect everyone else. Her family was fragile. Lux had just wanted to be strong. All this time....

Anya hadn't exactly lost Lux. But she was in the process of losing her. There was no way they could discuss it or hash out the details. It wasn't fair. There would be no closure or last conversation. It was all unfolding so slowly. They weren't at odds, but they were fighting against something together, something much stronger than either of them, even stronger than Ember's love for Lux.

How much strength did Lux have left? Was she even fighting? Was she just waiting for everyone to let go? Anya feared her own suspicions; maybe she and Ember were fighting alone. Maybe it was time to say goodbye. She left the hospital unnoticed.

Just after darkness fell, Anya arrived home. She unlocked the door to a modern flat with high ceilings and concrete floors in the heart of Old Towne Briar Heights. She stood in the entrance and looked at the shadows falling on the walls. She started to think about the holidays. Thanksgiving was just around the corner. What would Christmas be like? And New Year's? Summer vacations. Birthdays. Life....

> Anya: So tired. If You Can't Sleep. She & Him. On repeat.
> Goodnight Ember.

She didn't want to be awake any longer. She turned her phone off. She ignored homework and dinner and thoughts of everyone she knew, or had ever known. She was exhausted. She was alone. She needed a break. The circumstance had consumed her.

She wandered into in her bedroom, covered the windows, and crawled under a pile of blankets on her bed. She closed her eyes. Her face stung. Her head pounded. Her body ached and chilled. Her heart was bursting and imploding all at once. There was nothing but pain. So much pain. She slept restlessly against cold pillows soaked through with tears.

The families of fireflies had been set free. Time and time again, in fact. Float Coats grazed and aged. Fairies grieved. The sun glistened over Folly Falls, Ember Park, forest treetops, and other places Lux didn't know about yet. Flowers bloomed and Boreloque thrived, as enchanting as ever.

The lullaby that had lured Lux to sleep was still playing. She did not wake when everyone else did. She slept through the daylight and on through the night; many nights, in fact. She only stirred when the music paused, immersed in the depth of slumber. She needed nothing. This was home. She was comfortable right where she was. She had not one care in the world. She knew nothing else, not even a purpose or a passion.

Except that…

She felt a whisper in her ear. *I hate you*, it said.

Lux woke suddenly. Something was holding her down. She was trapped in her bed. The feathers had burned, and what was left of them dug into her flesh. She couldn't move her arms. She opened her eyes and saw she was covered in the skeletons and dust of fire-flies. The lamps hanging above her, their homes, were shattered and empty. Her hand had blackened up to her elbow. The burn in the shape of footprints had rotted through her hand. She tried to scream, but blood gurgled in her throat. She was alone in darkness. She couldn't breathe. The weight on her shoulders covered her whole body now. A force was pressing down on her chest and she felt her lungs give way. She stopped breathing. Something screamed in her face and pried her mouth open. It was trying to get in. She felt her heart pause.

TEN

Album: Volume Two

Track: Thirteen

Ember and Anya continued to spend time together with Lux every day after school. He never did ask about the day she hadn't met him at the hospital.

Of course, Anya was now also sharing her time with Tanner, too. A few days after their interaction at Apples and Worms, he'd shown up at her locker before lunch.

"I don't have a song for you. Yet," Tanner began.

Anya crossed her arms, but smiled.

"Mr. Besser lent me *Pulp Fiction*. And then Mr. Jorgensen overheard us talking, and he lent me *The Way Way Back* and *High Fidelity*. I haven't seen any of them, but I want to, and I was thinking —"

"Yes." Anya interrupted. "I'll watch a movie with you."

"Yeah?"

"Of course. Coach Spurz actually just lent me *The 'Burbs*. He quotes it all the time. Super weird, but I'm intrigued." She closed her locker, and stared at Tanner expectantly.

"Ask her to CRT, man!" Jamison shouted as he walked by them.

"Right," Tanner said. He shoved his hands in his pockets.

"Why are you so nervous?" Anya asked. She giggled. "I thought we established that we like each other."

"I don't know! It's because you're confident! You're super nice!" Tanner said. "You're just different from other girls."

"Good. So are you going to ask me to CRT?"

"Yes. I'm sorry."

Anya touched his arm. She nodded and smiled. "It's okay."

"Anya, would you like to have lunch with me?" Tanner asked. He took a deep breath. "And hang out during Common Room Time?"

"I can't. I have plans."

Tanner's face fell. Anya laughed.

"I'm kidding! Of course. Yes," she said sweetly. "Lead the way."

Every day after that, Anya and Tanner spent lunch and CRT together. They were a good distraction for each other. Anya didn't worry as much about Lux. Tanner didn't think as much about how Ember was acting. And Ember was forced to socialize with his other friends.

Tanner was supportive and understanding about how much time Anya spent at the hospital. But still, he questioned their new relationship every time he saw Anya and Ember leaving school together. Or arriving at school together. Or talking quietly in a corner.

Ember seemed to have forgotten about Falling Like Ember and his best friends. Tanner just happened to notice it more than anyone. Luther and Jamison noticed the change in Ember, but neither of them had a girlfriend spending all of her time with Ember Sweeney. In fact, Luther was experiencing the exact opposite situation for the first time in his life. He spent all of his time with Duffy now.

Tanner found himself waiting around a lot. Waiting for the guys to practice. Waiting for Anya to confirm plans. Sometimes she promised to meet him in the afternoon. But sometimes the afternoon turned into the evening. He waited. What could he say without becoming the bad guy? So he kept it to himself.

Tanner: Songs.

Luther: How Does It Feel? by Avril Lavigne.

Jamison: Really?! What, another cover?

Luther: Yes.

Jamison: Fine, I raise your Avril with an Amy.
You Know I'm No Good. Winehouse. Let's cover that.

Tanner: I raise you both and win this round.
Adele. When We Were Young. But we don't need a cover.
We have an original. Remember Duffy Raven?

Ember and Anya were sitting on the couch in Lux's room, as usual. He turned to her, and she removed her earbuds.

"What are you listening to?" he asked.

"Brandi Carlile. Heard of her?" she said. Ember shook his head. "Listen to this one. It's called "The Heartache Can Wait." It's from a compilation album." She handed him the earbuds and started the track from the beginning. When he finished listening to the song, he picked up his phone.

"I'm adding you to our group text. I like your style," Ember said.

"Wow, really? That's exclusive!" She perked up. She began browsing the music on her phone.

"We're exchanging songs right now. Share." He nudged her phone.

Anya: Falling Apart by Matt Nathanson.

Tanner: ...Oh hi, Anya. At least I get to "see" you this way.

Anya: You can see me or text me any time. What's your song?

Tanner: Lost+ by Coldplay with Jay-Z.

Duffy: As It Must Be by Joey Ryan.

Ember: When Will I by Monte Montgomery.

It was Ember who the adults worried about most. He sang to Lux when he believed nobody else was listening. He'd grown self-conscious about others hearing his music, which was quite unlike him. But the song he sang was leverage.

Anya had become protective. She didn't want Ember to know what she'd overheard between Lux's parents and the doctors. She began to lie in order to pick up the slack where her own dark thoughts hovered. She smiled at Ember when he seemed most sad. She warned him not to give up hope, because she knew a miracle would happen. She felt terrible; he believed her.

One evening during yet another late autumn record-breaking snowstorm, the two of them were with Lux doing their homework. Mrs. Tazo had insisted on bringing them dinner.

"This whole town is going to be snowed in," Anya said. She set down her books and gazed out the window. "It hasn't snowed this much in a hundred years."

"Let's tell Mrs. Tazo not to come," Ember suggested, writing notes as he spoke. "We can get snacks out of the vending machine."

"No. You know how she is."

"Yeah."

"Pretty, isn't it?"

"Wonderland."

Anya yawned. She'd woken up early that morning for a student council meeting. The weather only intensified her exhaustion. She curled up on the couch and decided to rest her eyes for just a few minutes before Mrs. Tazo arrived.

Ember grew distracted. Finally, unable to successfully complete his Music History paper for Mr. Jorgensen, he set his work aside. He debated. One minute. Two minutes. Five minutes passed. It was safe. He covered Anya with his coat, then pulled a chair next to Lux's bed. He removed his guitar from its case and faced the girl who'd bewitched him in her sleep.

Our souls crossed paths, entangled in the stars
There was a deep foretelling in our hearts
The universe knew
You would be my light, And I would be your fire

We could be anything, maybe just everything
If you took a chance on me
Please don't leave me waiting, a man can be so weak
But when I see your eyes, a warm breeze covers me

So wake up my sweet darling, get on with your life
The world here is waiting, and you are my light
When you open your eyes, sapphire and emerald collide
And together we're so alive

It's been cold here without you, the warmth is gone
Every night I lie wondering just what went wrong
But I wake up and see you, you've come around again
And I hope that at least we can be friends

In my dreams, we've been there and back again
The best life has happened
And you never ran, you always took my hand
And we took the flight to the rest of our lives

So wake up my darling, get on with your life
The world here is waiting, and you are my light
When you open your eyes, sapphire and emerald collide
And together we're so alive

Anya couldn't wipe the smile from her face or the tears from her eyes. She didn't want to be awake. Her insides were crumbling. She listened and prayed to dream of something comforting.

Six weeks had passed.

Still no changes, other than the fact that Lux's parents were around even less. They now dropped by only for updates or to deliver fresh flowers. Lux's room looked like a florist shop with arrangements, stuffed animals, and homemade get-well cards. Ember now viewed Lux's parents just as Anya did. He felt resentment, but he didn't know where there was room for it in his mind or heart. And then there was Arrabelle. He couldn't quite figure her out.

While Arrabelle appeared to have returned to her normal life a few hours away, which from what Anya and Ember could see, consisted of graduate school, well-attended parties, and a variety of casual boyfriends, she did stop in every Saturday for a long visit. She also sent Ember text messages quite regularly. She asked for updates, mainly. But she also sent him links to songs.

Listen to this she would write, usually very early in the morning or very late in the evening. Ember listened, analyzed. He never asked why she sent him the songs. Sometimes he replied, but not always. He fought it, but he wanted to let her in.

One afternoon Mr. Nickel visited, and he brought one of Lux's paintings.

"I entered this in a statewide competition last week," he said after he'd hung it on the wall. He took a step back and they examined it.

"What are her chances?" Ember asked.

"I won't lie, Ember. This is not her best. But I wanted to contribute something."

They sat on the couch and watched Lux.

"What's the deal with Arrabelle?" Ember asked suddenly. Mr. Nickel adjusted his position on the couch and his brow furrowed.

"She's always been a good friend of mine," Mr. Nickel began. "She has a good heart."

"Yeah, but — I mean, you know how they are, right? Their parents?" Ember struggled to make sense of what he wanted to say without saying it.

"Arrabelle Tazo," Mr. Nickel said, moving his hands over his beard.

"She sends me music sometimes," Ember said.

"Like what music?"

"Mostly older stuff."

Ember opened the messages from Arrabelle on his phone and handed it to Mr. Nickel.

Arrabelle: Still Fighting It by Ben Folds.
Arrabelle: Evan and Jaron. The Distance.
Arrabelle: It's Only Love That Gets You Through. Sade.
Ember: Thanks.
Arrabelle: Set the Fire to the Third Bar. Snow Patrol
& Martha Wainwright.

"She wants to get along with everyone," Mr. Nickel said. He finished scrolling through the messages. "Including her parents. If there is a common ground, she will find it and build on it. She knows she can speak to you through music."

Ember nodded. Mr. Nickel stood up then and pulled on his jacket. He walked over to Lux's bed and took her hand.

"I know Lux struggled with her parents and with her sister. I know Anya is her best friend. I know you and Anya talk." He let go of Lux's hand then, and walked to the door. "So I know what you're getting at. But now is the time to let people in. Please give Arrabelle a chance. She's much more a part of your life now than I think you realize."

Friends from school visited, too. They were often greeted by both Ember and Anya, which caused even more talk at school. Was Ember in love with Lux, or were Ember and Anya a couple? Hadn't Anya been hanging out with Tanner in the Junior Common Room every afternoon? Weren't Tanner and Ember best friends? Weren't Anya and Lux best friends? And what about that Duffy Raven? Where had she disappeared to? What was going on? Of course, Jamison enjoyed clearing up the rumors, and telling everyone to mind their own business.

Ember and Anya still only talked about Lux in places other than the hospital. Their first lunch together at Apples and Worms had uprooted Ember's ideas of Lux's family, so he hadn't demanded answers again. Something about all of the information terrified him. He thought of Lux differently now, too. She was more than just a dream. She was a real person, complex and deep, with both shadows and light. He wanted to be a part of it all. That was all he'd ever wanted.

Finally, one afternoon the doctors did sit down with Ember and Anya. They urged them not to have any expectations. The hospital staff felt sorry for kids with so much hope. It wasn't appropriate to let them believe so blindly. There was a very good chance Lux would never open her eyes again. Even if she did come to, the brain damage could be severe. She might never leave the hospital.

"I knew I'd find you here." Tanner was standing in the open doorway of Lux's hospital room. Ember had expected to see Anya or one of the Tazos. The room was dark, except for a lamp on in the corner. Tanner turned the overhead lights on and walked in.

"We need to talk."

"Hey." Ember let go of Lux's hand. "How's it going?" He stood up.

"Anya sent me. Jamison wanted to be the one to talk to you, but she wouldn't let him. You know, he's the mean one. Luther's the business-minded one, so he wouldn't be very nice right now, either. And I'm, apparently, the messenger," Tanner said. "The one who just waits on everyone now. So here I am." He shrugged.

"No, you're the nice one. And the super smart one," Ember argued.

"Remember the benefit the last Saturday in November?" Tanner said, ignoring him. "We agreed to it in August. We need you."

"Right, sure." Ember glanced at Lux uncertainly. "Which one is it?"

"Sweeney!" Tanner grabbed Ember by the arm and shook him. "She's not going anywhere. We can't wait around anymore, okay? You cancelled the Halloween show, and guess what? Nothing changed. And nothing is going to change today. Or tomorrow. You're awake and she's not!" Tanner shouted. "You've put our weekends at the Sour on the line. I mean, Astor is trying to be understanding, but you're letting it all go. Don't we have a say in this?"

"Yes, you have a say —" Ember began, but Tanner wasn't finished.

"We're on Thanksgiving break! If this situation was reversed and she felt the way about you that you feel about her, she wouldn't think this is okay. You just sitting here every day and letting everything else around you fade away. You're throwing your life away! Get out of here. This isn't healthy. I don't know why all these stupid adults in our lives are letting you get away with this! But I won't let you." Tanner's voice was shaking. "You have a big life ahead of you...with or without her. You were created for so much more than this. It's time to come home."

Ember hadn't realized Thanksgiving was approaching. He was afraid to be away, but his friendships and the band were depending on him. Tanner was right; Ember had ditched them. He needed to step away from the life he'd created with Lux, and not just for the weekend.

"It's your choice." Tanner shrugged and shook his head.

"Okay," Ember said nervously. "My house after school tomorrow."

Tanner's jaw dropped. Ember's heart was beating so hard in his chest, he was sure Tanner could see it. But he played it cool and shoved his hands in his pockets.

"I'll tell the guys," Tanner said uncertainly. "See you tomorrow." He looked back at Ember when he reached the door.

"Cool," Ember said. He'd always kept his cool, but now it felt unnatural. He wasn't cool. He was a mess.

"Oh, wait." Tanner turned around in the doorway. "We're out at noon tomorrow. Last day before break. So should we come after school, or will you be here?"

"We'll go to my place like we always do," Ember said confidently. "Want to grab lunch at the Sour?" He felt sick to his stomach, but smiled.

"I'll call Astor and tell him to expect us," Tanner said.

Ember sat down next to Lux again, feeling guilty and worried. Maybe he could visit her before school. He thought about Tanner's comment. Why hadn't any adults intervened? Resentment grew deeper into his heart. Fine. If they wouldn't stop him, he would stop himself. It was time to cut himself off.

"He must have drifted off. But he's not in the way at all. It's nice for her to have someone here," one of Lux's nurses said to Ember's father. They stood in the doorway of Lux's room.

"It won't happen again," Mr. Sweeney said.

Ember stirred. He could hear his father's voice. He collected his thoughts and realized where he was. He was in trouble. His head rested on the side of Lux's bed next to her leg; his hand held hers, and his guitar was on his lap. His neck was sore. He was afraid to open his eyes, but he sat up and saw his father standing over them with his arms crossed, looking very concerned. It was after midnight.

"So this is Lux," Mr. Sweeney said. There was nothing else to say. Ember stood up stiffly and put his guitar away.

"Sorry. I didn't mean to." He rubbed his eyes, out of sorts.

"You worried me," Mr. Sweeney said.

Ember followed his father out of the room. He didn't look back. *Maybe,* he thought wearily to himself, *she'll wake up when I'm gone. The next time I come back, she'll greet me when I walk in. Or even better, she'll be at home, and I can walk next door to see her.*

On the drive home, Ember checked his phone for messages.

Tanner: Home. Dierks Bentley.

Jamison: Home. Michael Bublé.

Luther: Home. Foo Fighters. (And Jamo is fired.)

Duffy: Home. Jack Johnson. (Seriously, Jamo. When did you start liking Michael Bublé?!)

Jamison: Fine, then! Ozzy. Mama I'm Coming Home.

Anya: Home by Phillip Phillips.

Ember: Edward Sharpe & the Magnetic Zeros. Home.

BHA held a tradition of serving brunch on early dismissal days. So when Ember got out of his Music, Cinema and Culture class with Ms. DuWaik, he headed toward the cafeteria to meet up with everyone.

"Duffy wants to know if she's invited today, too." Luther cut Ember off in the hallway before they reached the cafeteria. He sounded protective.

"What?" Ember thought he'd heard incorrectly.

"I want to know, too."

"What's going on?" Ember asked incredulously. "Where is she?" He realized he couldn't remember the last time he'd seen her. Luther hesitated.

"You haven't talked to her in weeks."

"Will you give me a minute with her?" Ember asked.

"You're not the only one having a hard time right now."

"I'll make it right."

"Make it right." Luther crossed his arms.

Ember and Duffy had been like siblings for ten years. And now here was Luther interceding for her. She hadn't bothered him and he knew the truth; Anya had replaced her. But he knew if there was anyone who could make sense of the situation, it was Duffy.

The cafeteria was packed, but Ember knew Duffy would be sitting with her girls. He spotted her in the center of the room. He threw his arms around her, and initially, she backed away. But he waited. Finally, she smiled. Sadly, but it was still a smile.

"I miss you, Raven!" Ember exclaimed, but then lowered his voice. "I love you. I'm sorry. I miss you." He buried his head in her shoulder. "Come over."

Her face lit up and crumbled at the same time. She hugged him back and didn't let go. Her friends Selma and Belle sighed wistfully.

"I'll come to your locker after brunch," Duffy said.

"Good. And we have to figure out what you're going to wear to the benefit," Ember added.

"Why does it matter what I'm going to wear?"

"Do you think I don't remember our last show? You were the star. You're stuck with us." Ember hugged her again and kissed her forehead. Then he dropped his messenger bag in the empty seat next to hers and left for the brunch line.

ELEVEN

Album: Three Flights From Alto Nido

Track: Four

Lunch at the Sour Enchantment officially reunited Falling Like Ember. Astor was the only one there when they arrived. He was listening to music while he washed dishes and cleaned the main bar area. The band and Anya joined him at the bar.

Duffy and Anya sat together and seemed to get along well, which Ember had been hoping for. Astor began to tease the two girls mercilessly about his best friend, so they were forced to team up.

"Is Mr. Nickel coming for lunch?" Duffy asked.

"Oh, yeah!" Anya added with great interest. "Don't you guys hang out here a lot?"

Astor handed each of the girls a bottled water. His eyes narrowed.

"You girls and your teacher crushes." He laughed at them. "Tell me, what is it about him that's so sexy?"

"WHAT are you talking about?" Anya laughed. "I don't know what you're talking about at all."

Duffy blushed and remained silent. She moved her chair closer to Anya.

"You're both in love with him! It's obvious," Astor continued. "Your poor boyfriends. You both date members of a band, yet you're in love with an art teacher."

"They'll be fine." Anya waved nonchalantly toward the members of Falling Like Ember, who were having their own discussion.

"This is the problem with girls. You're so confusing, and you never want what you can easily have. To be honest, *easy* and attainable is probably the best thing for you, because it probably also just translates to *nice* and honest," Astor said, and threw a bar towel to the ground. "But girls don't like *nice*, and once you finally get what you do want, and let me add that I'm sure you took the long, tearful road to get it, you change your minds."

"Stop it!" Anya said. The girls were laughing with Astor.

"Is this conversation even about us?" Duffy asked.

"You got me, Duff." Astor winked at her. "I'm talking about my girl. Well, she's not mine —"

"We're good listeners," Anya piped up. She leaned in closer. "Who is she?"

Just then, Jackson Nickel walked through the doors of the Sour. The girls froze in horror and grasped each other's arms. He went right for them.

"What a lovely surprise," Mr. Nickel said, smiling brightly. "Almost all of my BHA favorites!"

"I'll say!" Astor laughed. The girls cowered together. Ember, Jamison, Tanner, and Luther laughed at the girls, too.

"Mr. Nickel's here! Isn't this great, girls?" Tanner spoke up and wrapped his arm around Anya.

"Duffy thinks so," Luther agreed. He kissed Duffy, who was blushing fiercely.

"What have I missed?" Mr. Nickel asked.

"Nothing paramount," Anya said quickly.

"What do you call it, Anya?" Ember asked. "A smoke show, right?" He knew he could get away with teasing Anya, or anyone else there. They were all just surprised enough to have him in the room interacting with them.

"Yes. Smoke show." She rolled her eyes and shook her head. "I'm right! Am I not?" Anya looked to everyone for agreement. Duffy had buried her face at this point. "He is!"

"Food's ready!" Astor announced, and he began to pass out burgers and fries.

"Astor, can we put on this playlist I made?" Duffy asked, changing the subject.

Astor watched her inquisitively for a moment. "Let me see it."

"Sure," Duffy said. She opened the playlist on her phone and handed it to him.

"GIRLS LIKE ME LIKE ME"

Milkshake	Buddy
Juicy	Emily Wells
Whatever You Like	Anya Marina
Wicked World	Laura Jansen
Little Toy Gun	HoneyHoney
Sinners	Jim Bianco
The Quiz	Hello Saferide
Us	Regina Spektor
Charlie	Kenneth Pattengale
World Spins Madly On	The Weepies
Wonderwall	Ryan Adams
Just Another	Pete Yorn
The Luckiest	Ben Folds
It Was Always You	Moto Boy
Let's Never Stop Falling In Love	Pink Martini

"You're legit, Duff," Astor said. He adjusted some settings on her phone, and the first song began to play over the speakers throughout the club. "We could hang out." She blushed again.

Ember watched his friends while he ate his burger. They were smiling, laughing, and discussing music and movies with Astor and Jackson. It was a nice change to be with them in this environment again. But it wasn't long before his emotions caught up with him. He stood up and pulled Anya aside.

"I just need to know one thing," Ember whispered subtly, but he looked slightly obsessive.

"I already know what you're going to ask me. I know that look," Anya said. "You've been thinking about that this whole time, haven't you? Take a deep breath."

"Well, did she?" Ember moved his hands as if to rush the conversation.

"No, Ember. Lux didn't crush on him like all of the rest of us. She never, ever saw Mr. Nickel like the smoke show we all see him as. Trust me, I asked her more than once. But she grew up with him. It's different."

"How could I compete with that?" Ember asked in a panic.

"Get it together. Listen to yourself." Anya took a step away and pulled him with her to make sure nobody could hear them.

"Are you sure? I mean, he's pretty great. Look at him!" Ember looked over his shoulder. "Plus, they share a love of art —"

"Why are we having this conversation? She saw him as a big brother," Anya whispered. "That's it. They're like family. Like you and Duffy. Those lines would never be crossed between them. How many times do I have to tell you? It was *always*...you." Anya pushed Ember back toward his seat, then sat down by Duffy again.

Eventually, the band and the girls made it back to Ember's house. The guys seemed genuinely happy to be practicing again. They laughed and joked like they hadn't in a long time.

Around sundown, after a couple hours of practice, Luther suggested they take a break. The guys found Duffy and Anya in the kitchen making Thanksgiving centerpieces. Ember found a variety of snacks in the pantry, and distributed them on the table.

"Who wants cider?" Anya asked. Everyone obliged. Tanner joined her. He sat on the counter next to the stove. Luther, Ember, and Jamison sat down at the table with Duffy.

"You two are really cute," Duffy called over to them.

"So are you." Luther moved closer to Duffy and kissed her.

Ember couldn't have been happier for his friends, but he felt alone.

"Jamison, would you kiss me?" Ember asked.

"Sorry bro. I'm going after Piper Speedman right now," Jamison said, and shrugged. "She's a total smoke show."

"Please, no!" Anya whined.

"Don't ruin my game, Anya. I want her to be my New Year's date. We're hosting a sick party at the Sour Enchantment!" Jamison turned to Ember. "We *are* still playing that night, right? No matter what?" Everyone else turned to Ember.

"No matter what," Ember said.

"I'll be making my move in the next couple weeks," Jamison said.

"What about Francesca Guerrero?" Anya said.

"Or Gigi," Duffy suggested.

"What's with the Guerrero sisters, anyway?" Jamison asked.

"First of all, they're all super sweet —" Anya began.

"Dude, they're two sets of twins, and one year apart," Luther said. "They're —" He glanced at Duffy, then winked at her. "They're just cool."

Duffy rolled her eyes and smiled.

"Yeah, okay. That's paramount," Jamison said. "Side note, I thought Fran was still hanging out with Dylan Black."

"She's not," Duffy confirmed.

"Listen, I need to call Bella Guerrero to discuss the fall fashion show, anyway," Anya said. "So I'll get an updated status on all of the sisters. I'm going to set you up with one of them by New Year's.

But no Piper Speedman. And by the way, don't you dare hurt a Guerrero sister, or I will hurt you. Be nice."

Jamison said nothing but offered Anya a terrified look.

"What are the decorations for?" Ember asked, deliberately changing the subject. Of course he wanted Lux to be his date to the New Year's party, but he knew better than to say it.

"For the dining room table. Here. Tomorrow," Duffy said. She exchanged an uncertain glance with everyone at the table.

"Thanksgiving, man," Luther added.

"Your dad invited all of us and our families for Thanksgiving. Lux's family, too," Anya explained. "So we can be with you."

"Paramount," Ember finally said once everyone else had started talking again. He watched his friends interact, and realized just how much he had missed being with them. He was overwhelmed with both happiness and emptiness. He couldn't choose both worlds. He didn't know how to let go of Lux, and he wasn't sure he should. But something needed to change.

Mr. Sweeney came home from work that evening to find all of Ember's best friends, including Ember, watching *Almost Famous*. He was delighted to see them. Anya and Duffy proudly showed off the Thanksgiving centerpieces. Mr. Sweeney then showed the girls a recipe for a dessert he planned on making for Thanksgiving. He ordered Japanese take-out for everyone, and the kids stayed late into the night practicing. It was obvious he was happy to have them all back home again.

Ember woke up early on Thanksgiving morning in a panic. He felt a million miles away from Lux. He couldn't hear the machines confirming that her heart was still beating. He knew he couldn't go see her. But he knew he might see her family. Somehow that was something.

The main meal was to begin at two in the afternoon, but almost everyone arrived early for brunch. The kids were excited to continue where they'd left off the day before.

The kitchen, decorated by Duffy and Anya, was quite spacious with large windows allowing for natural light from the backyard. The adults spent the morning meal prepping. They discussed their various careers and commitments, while kids popped in and out of the kitchen frequently for caramel rolls, fruit, and croissants.

Ember and his friends hung out downstairs in the band's practice space, which also opened into an entertainment room and a billiards room. Tanner's younger brother Tristan, and Luther's younger sisters, Vaughn and Victoria, had joined them, too. Everyone loved that their parents were hanging out together for once. They decided it should be a yearly tradition, even into their college years.

"Dinner's ready." Arrabelle stood at the base of the stairs. Three guys were standing with her. One of them wrapped his arm around her.

"Happy Thanksgiving, Arrabelle." Ember found himself relieved to see her. She made her way through the crowd of their friends and hugged him. She turned to introduce everyone.

"Falling Like Ember, meet the hottest new band out of Europe: Medici. This is Talon, Abel, and Falcon."

"Yeah, we know of you guys!" Tanner stepped forward.

"We love your music," Luther chimed in. Everyone began to introduce themselves and ask questions. Arrabelle used the moment as an opportunity to pull Ember aside.

"I thought I'd see you at the hospital," she began.

"Oh. Yeah, I had to help my dad get ready for the party," Ember replied quickly. He felt ashamed. "So you were there? How is she?"

"Same," Arrabelle said. "Listen, I have something for you. It's in my car."

Ember followed her upstairs and they left the house unnoticed. He walked with her down to the end of the street and around the corner to the Tazos' driveway. She opened the trunk of her car, then handed him a large, heavy box. He peered inside. He was speechless.

"I thought you'd want this stuff. I thought it would mean something to you. My mom was going to throw everything away," she said. Ember reached into the box and touched Lux's clothes. He stared back at Arrabelle.

"The housekeeper found two messenger bags in the backyard when she raked the leaves that weekend. I think I pieced together which things go into *your* bag and which things were hers. You did lose your bag, didn't you?" Arrabelle asked sincerely.

"Y-yeah, I did," Ember stammered. He'd completely forgotten about all of it, except his journal. He'd gotten new textbooks and a new messenger bag soon after they went missing. It had never occurred to him that any of it could be linked to Lux.

He set the box on the ground and pulled out his bag. There was the journal. Just like that. He couldn't believe he was seeing it. His most coveted possession, recovered. He hadn't even gone looking for it. Immediately, he opened it to the spot where he kept a note. It was missing. He glanced at Arrabelle, his heart pounding.

"I meant to get it to you right away, but I forgot. I just thought maybe this will help inspire you to find what you're looking for," Arrabelle stated. "You know, help you finish your songs."

"What do you mean?" Ember asked. He began to feel frustrated, self-conscious.

"I know you're not her boyfriend. Your number isn't even in her phone. You had one class together at school. You sat on separate sides of the room. She never talked about you or to you. I spoke with her days before the accident, and there were NO boys in her life at all. *Who* are you, Ember Sweeney?" Arrabelle crossed her arms. "What's your deal with my sister?"

"Maybe she didn't want to tell you about me. Maybe she didn't want to tell you anything," Ember said. Arrabelle was right and he knew it. But there had to be evidence somewhere of a connection between him and Lux.

"I've never known a guy like you. You're the most popular high school student in this state, and you're pretending some random girl in a coma is your girlfriend. Every girl wants you. You spend day and night just sitting there with her. What's that about?" Arrabelle stared him down. "I just need to know."

"*Random* girl? Wow. I don't know who you think I am, and I don't care. I can't explain it, and I don't have to. She's going to come back to me, to you, to all of us. I don't care what those stupid doctors say. She will wake up, and I'll be there when she does. And you won't be because you're you, Arrabelle. Get over yourself." Ember grabbed the box and turned down the driveway.

"Wait!" she called after him.

He stopped. He was disgusted. He hated her.

"You guys didn't even care about her!" he yelled. "If she wasn't like you, she was nothing! What's going to happen when she wakes up, huh? She's the most talented girl in our school. But she hides it; she's ashamed because her family doesn't believe in her. You don't even believe she'll wake up!" Ember shouted angrily. He'd been bottling his anger, and had just needed a reason for his outburst. "Don't you see?"

Ember's words had clearly stung Arrabelle. He couldn't believe he'd even spoken them. This wasn't him. Her expression changed, weakened, as if Lux's reality was sinking in at that very moment. She leaned against her car.

"You're the one who found her. It was you who saw her lying there. Go to the hospital and hold her hand," Ember said quietly. "See how it feels when she doesn't hold yours back. Maybe you need to say goodbye. Or tell her you're sorry. But you can't pretend it's not happening. Your parents — they don't even come around anymore."

Arrabelle covered her face with her hands.

"Arrabelle, look at me," Ember pleaded. "Lux might never wake up. And then *my* life will be over. I'm too far lost in this to get out. There's no reason both of us should take the fall if she doesn't make it. I'm not asking you to be strong. I'm asking you to accept it. You have to face this."

"It's almost time for dinner," she said finally. Her chin was quivering.

"Fine. Great." Ember picked up the box again. He was furious. He couldn't even look at her. He walked down the driveway, and she followed.

"You'll want to check the back left pocket of the jeans in that box when you get a chance," Arrabelle called after him softly. Ember nodded, not ready to speak and not ready to look.

They reached the front door and faced each other. Ember closed his eyes and took a deep breath.

"Okay," he said. He turned the doorknob.

"Ember. Did you get the last song I asked you to listen to?"

"Yeah."

"Have you listened to it?"

"No, I haven't. I was hanging out with my friends for once."

He opened the door, and without another word, they returned to the celebration.

He went upstairs to hide the box in his bedroom. He set it down on his bed and stared expectantly. He couldn't look in the pocket or he would not return downstairs. But he did take out his phone and re-read the text messages Arrabelle had sent him. As he was scrolling down, a new message appeared.

Arrabelle: Down. Jason Walker.

Arrabelle: Come Home, OneRepublic & Sara Bareilles.

Everyone gathered around three tables in the dining room that afternoon. They gave thanks and kept the conversation light. Food was passed between tables and plates were filled.

Ember noticed Arrabelle eyeing him across the table a few times, but he ignored her as best he could. His friends could all tell he was upset about something, but they assumed it was about Lux, so they said absolutely nothing.

Between a football game and the first Christmas movie of the season, nighttime crept upon them. Ember and his friends cleaned up the kitchen. They sang songs and danced around while finding places for dishes and food. He invited them all to stay over that night. He was feeling less angry and increasingly strange about Arrabelle and the box. He felt the only way to fix these things was to go to the hospital and talk to Lux. So he needed the company of his friends, even if they didn't know why.

They camped out in the entertainment room. Sleeping bags, pillows, and blankets covered the couches and every inch of the floor. They sorted through movies to watch and listened to old records. Eventually, all of the parents said goodnight and left.

After raiding the fridge around two in the morning and stuffing themselves once again with a final Thanksgiving feast, everyone started to nod off. One or two people at a time fell asleep while they lay in the dark talking. They discussed a summer tour, traveling through Europe, going to college, and staying together forever. Soon, just Anya and Ember were awake. The two of them vowed that the next time they did this, Lux would be with them. It was an uncomfortable agreement.

Around four in the morning, Anya had finally drifted off to sleep. Ember, who was still wide awake, snuck out of the basement and crept up the two separate flights of stairs to his bedroom. The sky had cleared, so the moon shone into his bedroom window, illuminating the box on his bed. A new message appeared on his phone.

Duffy: Comes and Goes (In Waves) by Greg Laswell.
Are you okay? Come back to bed.

He played the song and set his phone down. He looked out his window and noticed Lux's tree house next door. He held up her jeans, that were cut up and stained with blood and dried mud. His heart felt so heavy. He was so lonely. He didn't have the strength to find out what was in the pocket, even though he had a feeling he knew what it was. He dropped the jeans back into the box, and returned downstairs.

TWELVE

Album: The Symphonies: Dreams Memories & Parties

Track: Six

Lux finally awoke to the sound of rain falling and distant thunder clapping. She didn't open her eyes immediately, but listened while still nestled in her bed. She stretched and smiled, thinking of the splendor she was enveloped in, the beautiful world she was now a part of. She thought of her new friends; she felt as though she'd known them her whole life. And she'd just experienced the best sleep of her life. She had no memory of past evils or nightmares, but the weight on her shoulders lingered. It would go away with a goblet of the Cove.

It then occurred to Lux that she could hear nothing but the rain. No voices. She sat up and gazed around; the beds were empty. She stretched her arms wide, and knocked something off the shelf into her bed. She couldn't see where it had fallen, so she stood up and moved her hands through the feathers until she felt a folded piece of paper. It opened up to reveal a map of Boreloque.

She examined the map and began to feel quite adventurous, but she wasn't properly dressed. She looked to where her nightgown had been the night before, and sure enough, there was her new outfit, along with a raincoat and an umbrella. She changed into a pair of loose-fitting, pale pink cashmere pants, which rolled up to just below her knees. Then she pulled on a flowing, white, sleeveless top. She tightened the waist of her pants with the rope provided, then pulled her hair into a messy bun.

She pulled on the raincoat and dropped the umbrella over the edge of her bed. Then she folded the map, stuck it between the rope and her pants, and began her descent.

Halfway down the tree, Lux stopped. She felt strangely about what she was doing. Something had triggered a foggy thought that refused to surface completely. It rang like a dull, distant bell that wasn't loud or clear.

Pleiades appeared below then, dressed in a ruffled green raincoat, and holding a matching umbrella.

"Hi!" Lux waved and continued down.

"I snuck away to check on you," Pleiades said, looking over her shoulder.

"Why did you have to sneak?" Lux asked, opening her umbrella.

"We're supposed to let you sleep."

The girls ventured into the forest.

"Where are we going?" Lux asked as they reached a dirt path.

A sly smile covered Pleiades' face. She grabbed Lux's hand, and they ran through the forest.

"I want to show you something," Pleiades said, winded. "Something secret."

They reached a downward slope and stopped. Lux had to grab a tree branch to keep from slipping. Pleiades carefully inspected the area, then motioned for Lux to follow. They reached a very small clearing and approached a moat; beyond the moat was a large tree.

"The Pram." Pleiades pointed toward it. The Pram was at least twice the size of the Twilight Trees; the tree structure itself was much older and larger. Each living space consisted of small tree houses. There were more than Lux could count, and they went higher than she could see, some hidden by branches or clouds. The roof of each rickety little house had a slate blue A-frame tent, and each had a porch area with chairs. There were stairs between each of the individual houses, and small torches throughout that emitted blue flames.

"What's this?" Lux asked, suddenly giddy. Pleiades said nothing, but grabbed Lux's hand again. They moved quickly over the moat, then hid behind another tree. Pleiades grabbed a stone from the ground and tossed it high up into the branches.

"Good. Nobody's here," she said. They moved to the base of the tree, where there was a rope hanging instead of steps. They began to climb.

"He lives at the very top," Pleiades explained as they climbed.

When they finally reached the top, Lux's arms and legs were shaking. They took turns jumping from the rope onto a wide, blue cushiony chair on the porch. Lux swung the rope and leapt. The entire porch rocked back and forth like a swing when she landed.

The first thing she noticed when they went inside was a spout just like she'd seen in Pleiades' Den. The wall was lined with goblets. The beds were made of wool. Weapons cases were next to every house entrance, covered in dust. There were no fireflies, only blue flames emerging from tiny lanterns on bedside tables. Hidden compartments with hand-carved knobs covered the tree trunk. Maps and markings covered the walls. Each compartment opened into a small door. There was a large, round compartment next to each bed. Lux knew this was Blaze's home. She was afraid to look behind any doors. But the compartment by his bed was the first place Pleiades went for.

"There are clues and memories everywhere. He's got yours," Pleiades said, dropping her voice to a whisper, "and this is against the rules. But since you're lost, I'd like to help."

Lux sat back in the chair and let Pleiades' words sink in. She wasn't lost. She was home. She wouldn't worry about pain ever again. Or sadness. Or loss. All of that was nothing.

"Aha!" Pleiades exclaimed, pulling the door open. "I can't believe he left it unlocked! I thought I'd have to break in," she said casually. She pulled the box out. "Lux, this will bring back every memory."

Lux quickly covered her eyes before she saw. "I don't want to know! Whatever Blaze has hidden, he's done it for a reason. I'm not supposed to see it!"

"I think you should," Pleiades prodded. "I've told him from the beginning, it will only help you more if you have your memories."

"No!"

"Oh, fine. I'll put it back."

Lux waited until she heard the compartment door snap shut again. She breathed a sigh of relief and opened her eyes. The breath escaped her lungs. Pleiades had tricked her. She was holding a folded piece of paper with Lux's name stained through. Something within Lux struck like lightning all the way to her soul. She screamed. Pleiades placed her hand over Lux's mouth and shushed her.

"Why did you do that?" Lux's voice was muffled.

"It's for your own good! So, what does it mean to you?" Pleiades asked eagerly. She returned the note to its rightful place. Then she observed the room, and walked to the door. She pulled the spout, but nothing was in it.

"Honestly, Blaze! Where's your Cove stash?" She began thrashing around the room.

"I don't know what it meant!" Lux said, distraught. She turned away from Pleiades.

"Then maybe we should leave," Pleiades said. "Because every single space in this tree contains your memories. Not one drawer or compartment is empty."

"What…?" Lux said. "So what about this one?" She pointed to a smaller drawer near Blaze's bed.

"It's one you brought here with you."

What if she did look? Nothing could make her want to leave; she was certain. But why were her memories stored *here*, of all places?

"Maybe I just want to see a few."

"Are you sure?" Pleiades opened the compartment containing the note again, and Lux took it. She looked at it, but didn't open it. She turned it over.

"Can I keep it?"

"No. And by the way, do not tell Blaze we were here. Or any of the guys."

"But it's mine."

"Well, no," Pleiades said with a waver in her voice. "It's not. I'm not supposed to talk about it. Only Blaze should."

"Why?" demanded Lux.

"It has to do with the Crossroads. Remember, you arrived with something that wasn't yours. And something had been taken from you."

"*You* guys stole my memories!" Lux shouted, appalled.

"We haven't stolen anything from you," Pleiades assured her. "We're just keeping things safe and preserved. Now please, keep your voice down. Your memories are only here so nothing bad happens to them. If you take one from this tree, it will disappear forever. But, I don't think there's harm in looking."

The longer Lux kept the note in her hand, the more she wanted to take it and run, even if she was afraid to look inside.

"Fine," Lux agreed. "Let's just get out of here."

"And I'll put this back." Pleiades yanked the note out of Lux's hand. They exchanged a tense look. "There we go," she said. She closed the note back into the compartment. "Blaze will never know."

"How is your best friend, by the way?" Lux asked curtly. "I'd love to actually see him."

"You'll see him," Pleiades assured her. "And he's wonderful. A breath of fresh air, as always."

"Speaking of, I have a question for you. A serious one," Lux said. "And I want it kept between us. What's the deal with…Zephyr?"

"The zephyr…?" Pleiades eyed Lux curiously. "Hmm. I'm not sure. I guess it should make you feel at home. Safe. Warm. Ask me again after I get another drink of the Cove. And that's our next order of business. We must find some."

They climbed out of Blaze's house and bounced from the cushiony chair on the porch to the knotted rope. They climbed down until Pleiades moved onto a staircase between two small houses. Pleiades led her down and around the winding staircase, then into a hollow. Lux could see through and past the tree to the other side of the forest.

Then Lux spotted a very small door, the tiniest she'd seen yet. She instinctively pulled on the knob, and the door swung open. Inside the compartment was a pile of paintbrushes. She picked one up and touched the bristles with her fingertip. She couldn't explain her desire to keep it, but she needed to. She needed it more than she needed the note.

"No! You may not take it, Lux! Especially not this. I'm sorry. Hand it over. I'm protecting you," Pleiades said. "This was a bad idea. I thought we were going to have fun, but now you want to keep everything." Lux did want to keep everything. She wanted to open every door on the tree.

"Fine." She reluctantly set the paintbrush back in its place. Suddenly, Pleiades knocked her to the floor, and she scraped her hands on the way down.

"Stay down," Pleiades warned, touching her finger to her lips. "Someone's here. We have to escape."

"Splinter," Lux said, and looked at her fingertip.

"Let me see," Pleiades said, and grabbed Lux's hand. She saw the burn, and the darkness around it. She glared at Lux.

A deep voice called out for them. The voice grew louder, but Lux couldn't distinguish who it was. What if they got caught? She tried to push Pleiades away from her so she could peer over the edge of the stairs for a better look.

"I knew it. Someone's come looking for us," Pleiades whispered. "And we'll talk about *this* later," she said. She shoved Lux's hand away.

The tree began to shake slightly; someone was climbing the rope. She hoped more than anything it was Blaze.

"How are we supposed to escape?" Lux whispered. "Who is it?" But Pleiades shushed her.

They'd been spotted. Someone shouted; it wasn't Blaze. Lux panicked and jumped from the stairs onto the porch of the nearest tree house, but she missed her step. She reached for something to stop her fall but there was nothing. Her scream was heard throughout Boreloque. Everyone would know she'd woken up.

THIRTEEN

Album: Over You

Track: Three

The morning following Thanksgiving was largely uneventful. Ember had only slept two or three hours. After a breakfast of more leftovers, everyone went home to sleep again for the day. They agreed to meet up again that evening for practice.

Ember retreated to his bedroom. He tried to sleep, but Arrabelle was sending him text messages again.

Arrabelle: Travis. Love Will Come Through.

He listened to it. Over and over again. Damn her. It gave him hope. It was all too much. There was more to Arrabelle. She was trying to reach him, and he didn't like it. He lay in bed all day tossing and turning. What else was there to do if he couldn't be with Lux? But sleep never came. Too soon, the doorbell rang.

The guys and Duffy were back. He couldn't breathe. He'd have to pretend again.

They practiced all evening. The guys could see Ember was distracted, but they tried to ignore it. They discussed the upcoming show as if everything was normal, as normal as it could be. Anya had said she was too tired to hang out, which meant she was at her flat, alone. Ember wondered if she'd gone to see Lux. He wondered if he should talk with her about Arrabelle. Something told him not to.

The next day, Saturday, was the day of the show. Ember's thoughts were out of control at this point. He was losing an internal battle. He tried to convince himself that if he stayed away long enough, Lux would just come home. He'd never need to go back to that hospital. The place had taken a toll on him.

He sat up in bed and looked out the window. The sun shone through the sparse tree branches, which it hadn't done in what felt like weeks. He decided to go outside.

The backyard was a foot deep in brittle scarlet, russet, and olive green leaves. Sporadic piles of snow had settled in for the winter, refusing to melt. Ember began to rake the leaves into piles around the yard. The sun warmed his face. It felt good. He'd been raking for nearly an hour when he looked up and his eyes fell on the tree house. He'd never been in the Tazos' yard.

He peeked through a hole in the fence. It didn't look like anyone was home. As he was about to climb over, Ember noticed something shining. It was a thick, iron doorknob at the back corner of the fence. It was a passageway connecting their property lines, covered over by old, winding branches. He'd never seen it before now. He swept a pile of leaves out of the way and pulled at the gate. Old branches cracked. The ground was uprooted as the gate slowly creaked open. It clearly hadn't been opened for many years.

Ember felt like a stranger again. He crossed over into the yard. He approached the immense oak tree towering over the Tazo home, its branches swaying over the Sweeneys' property line. He walked around the trunk to where steps were nailed in. His heart sank.

A weathered pink shoe was hanging by a jagged lace just below the entrance to the tree house. *Careful, your shoe's untied.* Ember suddenly remembered his own words, some of the first words he'd had the courage to say to Lux in a very long time. The shoe blew softly in the breeze. It was still hanging on after all this time. She'd fallen far. A chill covered his body. He climbed the crooked steps, and stopped when he reached the shoe. He pulled it free, then continued to climb.

"What — that's mine!" Ember exclaimed when he climbed into the tree house. His favorite album *Raising Sand* rested against a record player. His name was written on the cover in Duffy's handwriting.

Then he noticed the tree house itself. *Magical.* He moved into a room of paint supplies. The walls were covered in stunning abstract images. Half-finished projects were strewn about. Near a mess of paintbrushes was a handcrafted brown leather journal. He returned to the central round room again, noticing a kitchen and piles of books lined up under a window. The window had a perfect view of the backside of his house. He quickly scanned the books, noticing *Catcher in the Rye.* They would need to discuss Phoebe.

The walls in the last room he found were covered with homemade frames. There were no photographs in the frames, but quotes, by van Gogh, Picasso, da Vinci, Monet, Bob Ross, Frida Kahlo, Andy Warhol, and Banksy. Ember sat down on one of the oversized pillows on the floor and read each of them. The quotes shared themes of dreams, doubt, pain, and light. He concentrated on the last quote he read.

Music fills the infinite between two souls.
~Rabindranath Tagore

A new song idea flooded his mind. He needed something to write on. He rushed to the room with the paint supplies and picked up Lux's journal. He paged through until he reached a blank page, and began to write furiously. What flowed from the ink to the page wasn't just lyrics; it was a letter.

He turned the filled page, and heard Lux's voice loud and clear when he read:

"I want to paint like I used to...carefree and with love, with nothing else on my mind, especially him. Especially. Him."

"Ember! Sweeneeeeeeeey!" Jamison's voice rang through the atmosphere and into the tree house. Alarmed, Ember thrust open the tree house window.

"I'm over —! I'm —! Uh, I — BE RIGHT THERE!" he shouted.

He didn't know whether he should rip the pages out of the journal, or bring it with him. He reasoned that Lux would never know he'd had it, that he'd put it right back. He stuffed the journal in the back of his pants, and left Lux's shoe behind. He was almost to the ground when he heard Mrs. Tazo's voice. Startled, he lost his balance and fell. Her scream hurt his ears.

"I'm okay; I'm fine!" Ember got up and rushed to hug her. "See? Look."

"Come inside," she said, composing herself after a quick glare. Ember followed her into the kitchen.

"Sit." Mrs. Tazo motioned to the bar stools and walked to the refrigerator. She handed him a bottle of water, then opened one herself.

"Is everything okay?" Ember began to wonder why he was sitting in Mrs. Tazo's kitchen. They hadn't discussed Lux on Thanksgiving.

"That's what I want to know. Are you okay?" She watched Ember suspiciously.

"Yes."

"The nurses asked me where you've been." She cleared her throat. "You were there every day, and then —"

"My friends kind of lost it on me," Ember interrupted. He gazed out the window at the tree house. "We have a show tonight, and I've already missed a lot of practice. There's a tour and an album release set for next summer. I'm sorry," he said. He took a long drink of water.

"They're right." She smiled sadly. "That's your future."

"I'll be back. I just need to get through tonight," Ember said. He watched Mrs. Tazo's expression, wondering if Lux's condition could ever truly change the Tazo family. Maybe he was hoping for too many things that might never be.

"Have you seen this?" Mrs. Tazo pulled *Future Edge Magazine*, which must have been addressed to Lux, from a pile of mail, and flipped to the back. There was picture of the band with a half page article below it. He took the magazine from Mrs. Tazo and stared at the picture. Falling Like Ember looked cool, united, and not at all unhinged and falling apart. He thought of the words he'd seen in the tree house: *Music fills the infinite between two souls.* It had to work.

"How is she?" Ember finally asked.

"Nothing's changed, Ember," Mrs. Tazo said, then quickly turned away. "And I'm needed at the spa." She grabbed her purse and smiled at Ember. Her composure scared him.

"I should get home. The guys just came over to practice."

"Of course, honey. Have a great show!"

He was almost to the gate when she called after him. "Ember, wait!" She rushed into the backyard. "Do you need anything tonight?"

Standing in the open door between both properties, he hesitated. "You could come to the show. Maybe just stop by, or something."

"We'll be there," she said immediately. "Oh, and next Thursday —"

"Yeah?"

"It's the Holiday Kick Off in Old Towne; the spa is on the committee. Would you be interested in performing at the outdoor arena by the ice rink? We'll pay —"

"Yes." Ember didn't even let her finish.

"Great. I'll get you the rest of the details by tomorrow."

They said goodbye then, and Ember closed the gate.

"Look what I found." Ember stood before Luther, Jamison, and

Tanner in the parlor, holding the box from Arrabelle in his arms. Still more shocked than excited, he pulled the items from the box for them to see. Tanner grabbed the journal and paged through it.

"Where did this come from?" Luther demanded as he grabbed the journal from Tanner. Tanner then went for the messenger bag. Jamison sat back and watched.

"It was all in Lux's tree house," Ember explained. When they stared blankly back at him, he continued. "Arrabelle gave it to me. I wasn't going to show anyone, but then today I found Lux's shoe hanging from the tree. And inside the tree —"

"Wait, wait, wait a second." Duffy entered the parlor through the kitchen. She sat down on the floor by the fireplace. "*Lux Tazo* had your stuff? This changes everything!"

"Maybe she stole it," Jamison suggested.

"The only thing she ever stole was my heart," Ember said. The guys snickered. He ignored them, but felt immediately stupid for saying it out loud.

"It's a sign!" Duffy said excitedly. "I'm calling Anya."

"Why isn't Anya here?" Ember asked. "Where is she?"

"Don't put ideas in his head. He's obsessed enough as it is," Jamison said, a hint of bitterness in his tone.

"There's no way to be sure until she wakes up," Duffy said. She reached into the box and pulled out Lux's clothes. She looked to Ember for an explanation.

"It's what she was wearing that night," he said.

"Strange," Duffy said. "Why would Arrabelle give you these?"

"She said — Wait! Check the pocket."

Duffy reached into the back pocket of Lux's jeans. She pulled out a note. Lux's name had bled through like a water stain. Ember walked over to Duffy and took the note. Everyone was speechless. He opened the note and read it through.

"It's my letter." His heart was pounding. "Do you think she read it?"

"This is big time. She'll just have to tell you herself when she wakes up," Duffy said.

"Seriously, stop saying she's going to wake up," Jamison muttered, rolling his eyes.

"Dude, shut up," Tanner said, glaring at Jamison.

"Jamison!" Duffy shook her head.

"All right, enough. We need to go over the December calendar." Luther stood up and grabbed his planner.

Ember ignored them all. He thought back on what had happened between him and Lux two years earlier, and for the first time he accepted the possibility that she may have said she hated him completely due to her own fears or doubts.

"Did we agree to the Winter Wonderland show the weekend of Christmas?" Tanner asked. "Or is it too much with New Year's at the Sour?"

"Wait," Ember interrupted. "Mrs. Tazo just booked us for next Thursday. The Holiday in Old Towne kick-off event thing."

"Are you sure?" Tanner asked. Ember nodded. Everyone exchanged glances.

"Great," Luther said. He wrote it in the calendar. "As long as we get paid. And on that note, we should cover a holiday song."

"Anyone opposed to "Christmas Lights" by Coldplay?" Ember asked. Everyone looked at one another, shrugged, and nodded. "We also need to learn "Auld Lang Syne" for New Year's Eve."

♪

Falling Like Ember put on a great show that night at the benefit; it was like they'd never spent a day apart. There was a different mood between them, which included a safe distance, but it also renewed Ember in a sense that he knew his purpose. However many strings were currently attached to his purpose didn't matter.

During the next week, life began to feel normal again in the strangest way. The band practiced every day after school, they spent lunch and CRT together, and their group texting was constant. Ember's mind was still flooded with questions and doubt, but he was getting better at covering up his emotions. He directed his energy into deliberately not thinking about Lux Tazo. He was learning to smile again, to pretend he was cool with everything.

On Thursday night, the band arrived at the arena in the town square for their sound check. The side streets had transformed into a marketplace with homemade goods and festive foods. The whole town was lit up. Vendors would be around every weekend until Christmas. While the band waited, they mingled with locals and checked out the booths.

Ember left the group and walked toward Tazo Spa, hoping to say hi to Mrs. Tazo. Instead, he ran into Arrabelle. Even though he'd seen her just a week before, it felt strange. She didn't ask any questions about the box or the note in the pocket of Lux's jeans, even though he knew she must have read it. She explained that she was helping her parents with the booth for the spa. He thought that was strange, too. The two walked a bit further from the spa and found a hot chocolate stand. He turned around and saw the arena stage from a distance. Tanner, Jamison, and Luther were setting up. A large crowd had already gathered.

"You seem quiet," Ember said. He couldn't hold back with her anymore.

"Don't worry about me, Ember. Get up on that stage and be first-class." Arrabelle nudged his arm. "This is a good moment in your life. Be in it."

"I have a sound check right now," Ember said. "But I'm going to find you after the show, okay?"

Arrabelle nodded. She nudged his arm again, then pushed him away.

Falling Like Ember was the last of three bands to perform and they got the best response. Once they were on stage, Ember looked out into the crowd and saw a lot of his friends and teachers. But all he could focus on was Arrabelle. He moved to the keyboard for the next song and heard his phone. He had to look.

Arrabelle: The Fray. How to Save a Life.

He searched for her in the crowd again, but she had gone. He quickly texted her back.

Ember: The Fray. Never Say Never.

The show wrapped up just in time for the weather to arrive. The black sky had turned a warm golden hue as the night carried on. Snow began to fall as the festive crowd left for warm homes. The band loaded their equipment into Luther's SUV; it was already late, and they still had school the next morning.

"I'm going with Anya. See you tomorrow," Tanner said. He ran back toward the stage.

"I'm going to find the Tazos." Ember looked over his shoulder and scanned the streets, realizing he still hadn't seen Mr. and Mrs. Tazo.

Duffy climbed into the front seat and slammed the door. A thin wall of snow fell from the window. Luther got out of the car with an ice scraper as Ember began to walk away.

"Wait a minute." Luther stopped him. "You'll be at school tomorrow, right?"

"Where else would I be?" Ember asked. Luther offered a withering look.

"You have that look in your eyes. Anyway, we're getting noticed," Luther said. "Our audience is growing."

"I know that." Ember shoved his cold hands in his pockets.

"Our platform isn't about you going after some girl in a coma who you don't even know. Remember how we started out and what we're about," Luther continued steadily, careful not to speak loudly enough for Duffy to overhear. "I heard a lot of people talking tonight, about you and Lux. But you need to realize that even *if* she wakes up, it may not turn out like you're hoping. And you'll still have to play." Luther finished removing the snow from the car. "You're a headliner, Ember. But the guys and I have been talking, and —"

Ember looked at the new message on his phone.

Duffy: Walk Away. Over You. Jay Nash.

"Thanks for a good show tonight, Luther," Ember said. Duffy was watching them closely from inside the vehicle. He left without looking back. He didn't look for Arrabelle or her parents. He didn't see the point in avoiding Lux any longer.

He'd left her for his friends in order to prove he was still there for them, still cared, and could still play; he was, he did, and he could. But it still wasn't enough. The more time he spent with them, the more opportunities they took to remind him that he was fighting a losing battle and loving the wrong person. There was no pleasing them. Each of them had made it a point to tell him he was wasting his time. Duffy was too connected to the guys, and even Anya felt far away for some reason. He was on his own.

Ember walked down empty streets, leaving his footprints behind in fresh snow. He listened to the songs that had been sent to him that day. When he reached the hospital an hour later, covered in snow and shaking from head to toe, he stopped in the cafeteria for hot tea.

He returned to the place he should have been all along. He felt terrible about himself because he hadn't listened to his instincts. He'd listened to everyone around him when deep down, he knew better. He knew what was right. He'd allowed everyone else to tell him their version of what should happen in his life, what he should expect, what to believe, and what he should or shouldn't do. It had gotten him nowhere. It had left him alone. And it hurt.

FOURTEEN

Album: Blink

Track: Three

"I've got you!" York caught Lux in his arms. Her terror was replaced with relief upon seeing an endearing smile on his face and hearing Pleiades' delighted laugh.

"She needs to see Blaze," Pleiades said immediately.

"She needs the Cove. I can see it in her eyes," York said.

"Why didn't Blaze visit me last night?" Lux demanded. "You said you'd send him over! Does it have something to do with Zephyr? I did hear music."

"She keeps mentioning the zephyr," Pleiades muttered to York.

"Lux, you slept much longer than just last night," York said. "Last night was days ago. He's checked on you many times since that night."

"He has?" Her heart soared.

"He's always been with you; you never had to worry."

"Well, where is he now?"

"That's why I'm here; I'll take you to him."

"Yeah, let's get out of here." She was still shaken up from the fall and suddenly didn't want to be so close to her memories. Her hand was throbbing again.

"He's been quiet today," York said. "Waiting for you."

"We'll have a reunion!" Pleiades said excitedly. "Another party! And we'll drink the Cove!"

"*You,* my darling!" he said to Pleiades, "are in trouble. But I'll deal with you later." Pleiades simply laughed at him.

They climbed the rest of the way down the tree, then followed a trail that Lux recognized led back to the Twilight Trees. They veered off at a bridge, turned toward the mountains, and headed uphill. Dandelions flourished in wet grass that reached past their knees. The grass was plump with the weight of raindrops. It was now only drizzling, although the sky was still gray. They arrived at the edge of a cliff. Lux saw two dangerous ways down: a rock scramble or a steep bamboo water slide.

"I'll go first," Pleiades said, removing her raincoat. The slide was splashing warm water in all directions. When she sat down, vines rose from around the edge of the slide and wound around her wrists. She was then propelled by the force of the water and disappeared below them.

"It's your turn, then, isn't it!" York called. Lux nervously pulled off her raincoat and tossed it aside as Pleiades had. She looked at him uncertainly. "You'll be just fine." He patted her on the shoulder. "Like you were in Dreamer's Lane."

Warm water sprayed Lux as she sat down on the slide. The vines wound around her wrists; she told herself the sooner she got to the bottom of the slide, the closer she'd be to the Cove. And Blaze.

"Wait, I'm not ready!" She turned to him again, but a surge of water pushed her and she was off. She dropped straight down. The vines held her in place, but she felt her body drift off the slide to meet with chilled air. She plummeted into a ravine of jungle and pools; it looked like a much smaller Folly Falls.

She'd fallen hundreds of feet in just a matter of seconds when the slide made a sharp twist, turned into a dark tunnel, and slowed down. The vines loosened around her wrists. The slide was moving slightly downhill at this point, and Lux sat up. She could see a tiny light in the distance, and the ropes holding her in place had taken on an orange glow. She was in an old mineshaft. Just above her head flickering light bulbs hung so that she could see shadows of what she was passing through. The slide continued to twist and turn like a maze.

She could hear whispers of insects, which were quickly washed away by another rushing wave. She glided down the next steep hill, the vines tightening again. Water forced her on her back and rushed over her face but quickly cleared away as the slide started winding again.

Spritely laughter echoed ahead when Lux came to a halt in a small pool. The slide twisted upside-down and around so now she was facing in the opposite direction. The water swept her up in a wave that pushed her in one last, swift movement. She was outside again. The current pushed her straight up the slide, then flowed back down as she continued to rise slowly. Soon she was sitting at the top of the slide, but on the other side of the ravine. The vines unwound from her wrists, and she stood up, dripping.

"What did you think?" Pleiades was already lounging in the grass nearby.

"Paramount...just like everything else," Lux said, once again overwhelmed. York arrived a moment later.

"Doing okay, then?" he asked. She nodded, and he patted her back. "Everyone's at the Ventino. Let's get going." He walked ahead of the girls.

The three of them walked together through another small, forested area and came to a clearing. A massive rust-colored boulder was before them. York led them around to the other side. There was a door knocker with the face of a lamb, just like the one in Dreamer's Lane. Again, an inscription below it read, "In like a lamb, out like a lion." York reached over Lux and rapped at the door while she stared at the words. The door opened.

The girls went in ahead of York. The place was one large room that was quite open and went low into the ground. Hammocks hung and woven rugs were spread over the floor. Along the walls were copper pipes and a swirling vat that was producing the Cove. Everyone was drinking. Harlow, Hepburn, and Hayworth appeared together, each with a goblet for Lux.

She took the first one and drank as fast as she could. Her senses illuminated, and her veins swelled with assurance. She scanned the room in search of Blaze. She still didn't see him, so she started on the next goblet and found an empty chair in the corner. York sat with her.

"Where is he?" Lux asked urgently. She needed to see him, to know what she'd experienced with him had been real. She was starting to feel confusion between what was actually happening and what might be just in her imagination. York looked very satisfied with her question.

"He'll be here." He set down his goblet.

"It's just that the longer I'm away from him, the more I care; the more I want to know him and be with him." Lux took a long sip and thought, *I'm starting to think he's unattainable.*

"I have a question for you. But, give yourself a minute to think about it," York said softly. "What's worth fighting for?"

Lux considered the question, but it seemed quite off the topic of Blaze. Nothing came to mind. She closed her eyes. The paintbrush she'd found in the Pram appeared in her mind. She focused on it. Then, like a bolt of lightning, she saw herself hiding someplace dark, holding the paintbrush, and crying. She threw it. She wanted to make it go away. It caused pain. She heard screaming. She felt scorn. Another lightning bolt struck, and the image went away. She opened her eyes and stared at York.

"I'm afraid to fight," she whispered. York nodded.

"What if you weren't alone?"

"I don't know what's worth fighting for," she said uncertainly.

"Would you fight for Blaze?"

"Yes." She looked wildly around the room. "Why? Where is he?"

"It was just a question." He touched her arm. He pushed the goblet she was holding toward her mouth.

Of course she'd fight for him. But why would she ever need to?

Hendrix and Joplin walked into the Ventino then.

"Let's pack up and get out of here. Something's not right," Hendrix announced. "Could be a storm."

Everyone hurried to gather their things.

"A storm?" Lux asked York, but he'd left her to join Hendrix outside. "What about Blaze?" She dropped her goblet, but nobody seemed to notice.

"Ready, Lux?" The Twirlyfine Starlets flew to her.

"Help! Where are we going?" Lux asked frantically.

"To the Fire Lodge! You'll love it," Harlow said. "Drink up!"

"Please. Where's Blaze?" Lux whispered desperately. The Cove wasn't working as well as it had before.

"We're going to see him now!" Hepburn said.

Everyone had scattered. The girls were the last to leave the Ventino. The Twirlyfine Starlets and the Lily Girls flew ahead of everyone else, leaving Lux with Hendrix and Joplin.

There was a small opening in the clouds, and Lux spotted Dreamer's Lane. The rain continued, and it got colder with every step. Raindrops turned to ice and then softened. Snow began to fall. It quickly covered the ground, but their footsteps stamped it out along the trail. Pleiades fell back from the group and pulled Lux aside.

"I never did ask you," she began, "how did you sleep?"

"Good, I think," Lux said. She couldn't stop shivering. "The singing put me to sleep."

Pleiades glanced curiously at Lux. "Do you miss Blaze?"

"Yes —"

"He misses you, too."

"I want to see him," Lux said carefully, remembering when he'd first held her hand at the Crossroads, as if he'd been expecting her, as if he knew her.

They arrived in an open field and the clouds around Dreamer's Lane had cleared. Snow continued to fall on them. A white funnel moved slowly down from the champagne floor of Dreamer's Lane. Once the funnel had reached the ground, they walked into it, a few at a time, and were whisked up to the sky.

Like the first time she'd arrived in Dreamer's Lane, a door rose up in front of them. Everyone was watching her, waiting. Lux approached the door. The now familiar inscription, "In like a lamb, out like a lion," was written under the face of the door knocker. And now she was staring at a lion, but she could have sworn it was a lamb last time. The words had faded, and the letters F.L.E. were etched over the top. She didn't remember that being there the first time, either... *How long have I been here?* Her hand twitched; she pulled the heavy door knocker, and it swung back. It echoed loudly throughout the skies, and the door swung open. There stood Blaze.

"Well, are you coming in?" he asked. He appeared to be perfectly healthy, and quite happy. He had eyes only for Lux. She felt helpless. She couldn't move her feet or find her voice. The feeling in her stomach had paralyzed her. His alluring smile took her breath away. Everyone bounced past Blaze through the door until finally only the two of them remained.

There was something about him. He was in her head, in her heart. The loud chatter behind them faded into the sky. Blaze took the last step toward her. She threw her arms around him and didn't let go.

"I need you," Blaze whispered. He sighed heavily.

"I know," Lux replied. She knew something was coming, just not what. Somehow she'd known it would come to this all along, and somehow they would be together forever.

"We'll talk soon. Just us," he said. She nodded.

He broke away from her and they returned to their friends, who were walking ahead. She grudgingly realized this wasn't the time or place to steal Blaze away, in a world where she was a guest and he was the star. So she smiled. She knew he wouldn't leave her again.

The snow continued to fall in Dreamer's Lane. They made their way down a hill into a village and approached the main street. The last bit of daylight faded and street lamps flickered on as fireflies and fairies returned home, seeking shelter from the snow.

"It's truly beautiful, Lux. You've outdone yourself," York said. "I think you're getting closer to what you need to figure out." He pointed behind her. The sky had cleared in the distance, revealing the last splash of sunlight. She was captivated by the colors.

"What do you mean?" She didn't understand. The colors were clouded over again, and the snow fell harder.

"It's...yours," Pleiades explained simply. "This is all your creation. We're in your world."

Lux offered a blank stare. She began to feel anxious, and pushed her way out of the crowd and away from the view.

"Blaze?" she called. He took her by the arm, and she threw herself into his embrace.

"We'll meet you at the Fire Lodge," York said. "You two should talk." Everyone else moved on ahead of them again.

"You're going to be okay," Blaze whispered.

She thought of the paintbrush. She tried to push it to the back of her mind, but it only became more dominant.

She needed to know who she was, her purpose. She wished that everything that ever needed to be said between the two of them could be said right then and there. She wished she could see her life, or their life together, twenty years in the future, and know just the right thing to say. Or maybe it was just one word. But she still needed something from him. And that something was everything.

"So, where do we go from here?" she asked, in hopes that he would answer something along the lines of, *we go to forever*. She couldn't imagine existing without him now, and she refused to be separated from him again. But then she was distracted by the sound of music, just like she'd heard in the Twilight Trees. She backed away from Blaze and looked around for Zephyr. He was nowhere to be found.

"Come. Sit," Blaze said. Snow had gathered on the clouded floor, and he swept it away. "I have a story to tell you."

She sat down next to him, shivering.

"It's time you learned about Venia," he said. His voice was lower, more serious. Lux became anxious; whether it was because she was alone with Blaze, or of the growing darkness, she wasn't sure, but the mood had changed.

"What's Venia?" Lux whispered.

"*Who* is Venia," Blaze corrected her. "She's —"

"Is she who you've been away with?"

He hesitated, then nodded. Hurt and jealousy threatened to erupt in Lux's heart.

"It's not what you think," he said. "But it's hard to explain."

Somehow, somewhere, she'd felt this way before. Words were nothing when she could picture actions of betrayal. It depleted her of joy.

"Lux, you have to trust me," Blaze said. "We're her prisoners. She's stolen from us, stolen something that doesn't permit us ever to leave. I'm not even supposed to be telling you this."

"Oh, that again!" She replied, incredulous. Her spirits lifted. "This whole idea of thievery; I'm not sure we're on the same page —"

"Lux."

"You can't tell me you're prisoners *here*!" she laughed. "Prisoners of what? A perfect life? Happiness? What could she steal, your imperfections?"

"Quite the opposite, actually," He said, and hung his head.

"The point is, we have to overcome her. I need to know if you're willing to fight with us, with me."

"Of course," she said. "Anything..." Their breath moved into the thick, damp air. Snow continued to fall on them.

"Once upon a time, Venia was different. She wasn't Venia at all," Blaze began. "But she was always powerful. She had strength. She brought me here. I was the first one. Eventually she let all of us in. But then there was a misunderstanding that hurt her very deeply. She turned on all of us. By doing that, she became blind to any good left in her, so everyone else's goodness was magnified. It drove her mad. She was overcome by jealousy, and the hurt she felt turned into anger, and then into hate. It destroyed her from the inside out. She tried to kick everyone out. We fought back, thinking we could help her. It started a war. We wanted to prove to her that love wins, and it heals. But she won, at least temporarily. She's still hiding, still plotting. Never satisfied. You see, Lux. It's not over between us."

"It's not over," Lux repeated. She was trying to understand the importance of what he was saying, but his words weren't quite sinking in. She was just so glad to be reunited with him, finally.

"If all goes well, you'll be safe, and we'll be freed," he concluded.

"And then what?"

"Once we're free, the possibilities are endless. We start new."

"Good. What are we waiting for? Where is she?"

"Below. In her lair. She won't come out, so we'll go to her," Blaze explained.

"Why won't she come out?" Lux asked.

"She's protecting...something."

"What's she protecting?" Lux began to feel annoyed. *Out with it already!*

"You have to see it to believe it."

"Okay, so let's distract her! Whatever she's stolen, we'll take it back. How can we lose against one person?"

"We're weak. The Cove is just a trick. It makes us feel better off than we actually are. It kills our pain. This place, this world; it's a cushion. We are literally sitting on clouds, because you somehow knew that's what we'd need to survive. So, that's what you created."

Lux shook her head. Now Blaze was being ridiculous. The whole conversation was dragging on and beginning to feel a bit absurd.

"Blaze, we can do this. Or I'll do it myself. We can't be afraid."

"There's a lot more to it. More than you can understand right now, until you see it for yourself. I'm the only one here who can get to her. We'll go together."

"What exactly has she stolen? How bad is it?"

"It's bad."

Blaze stood up and reached for Lux's hand. When she reached for him, he saw the burn on her palm. It had spread up past her wrist and along her fingers. He yanked her hand closer and examined it.

"Who else has seen this?" he asked urgently.

"A few people," she said uncomfortably. She pulled her hand away.

"It's too late..." he muttered. "Why didn't you tell me?"

"Because you were never around when I needed you!"

Blaze ripped a bandana from his arm and wound it tightly around Lux's hand. Then he grabbed her by the arm, and they walked on.

A light switched on ahead of them, and Lux could see the Fire Lodge, torches surrounding it. When they reached the door, she stopped him.

"I'll fight," she said. "If it's a matter of the heart, that is worth fighting for. Especially if it's yours."

Blaze closed his eyes. "Well, we're out of time," he said. "So I hope you're ready now."

The door swung open. The rustic cabin was crowded with bunk beds, a fireplace in the corner, and a very large table in the center of the room. They were all connected and carved from the trunk of one massive tree. Maps, notes, keys, trinkets, and goblets covered the table. Lux joined her friends, who were gathered there.

Fender stood up and pulled Blaze aside. Lux moved to the other end of the table so she could listen in.

"I've got news. I hope it's not too late," Fender muttered.

"There's not much more time," Blaze replied.

"How can we get more time?"

"We can't. The end is here."

"Are you just going to stand by?"

"I'll have to. I have my limits," Blaze said. "Just remember you're all safe in Dreamer's Lane. What's the news?"

"It's about Lux. Her condition."

Blaze didn't answer.

"She's as good as yours," Fender said. "But —"

Lux turned to approach them, but Joplin stood in her way.

"Have a sip." He handed her a goblet, filled to the brim. The froth was too enticing, although she knew he'd deliberately distracted her. She drank, but kept her eye on Blaze.

He walked to a bookshelf in the corner of the room, removed a large book, and brought it to the table. He lifted the cover. Within the pages was a secret storage box. In the box was a folded piece of paper. Blaze unfolded it and placed it on the table. A map: Boreloque Underground. Venia's lair.

The storm picked up outside. Wind howled down through the chimney. Heavy snow fell over the Fire Lodge, and the burning lights in the room were losing their romantic flare. Lux noticed Blaze was avoiding looking at her. She watched him for a very long time, as everyone else bustled around and talked over him.

"I can't do this," he said suddenly. He crumpled the map and threw it across the room. Everyone became quiet. Lux stood up. She picked up the map and placed it back in front of Blaze. She gazed intently into his eyes.

"I'll be with you," she said. "You will face this, and you will succeed. We'll be together, and we'll build on that. No one and nothing will crush us."

"You don't know what you're saying," Blaze whispered.

"Exactly. And she doesn't need to know!" Pleiades shouted. "She *can't* know! She needs to be protected now."

Lux stared at Pleiades. She wanted to ask questions, but instead she ignored her instincts. Nobody was quick to give information anyway, and she didn't have time to play their games anymore. Her job was to help Blaze. She sat down to study the map and tried to remember every place she'd been.

"There's a cave; it's below Folly Falls," Spindle said, pointing to a place on the map. Lux hadn't even realized the Seven Sisters were with them, until now. She hid her bandaged hand and looked up at everyone joined around the table. "It's a secret passage. It goes under the Pram and around the backside of the waterfalls of Haven Hollow. It will lead to a cave where you can hide as long as you need to."

"And in the forest by Pleiades' Den, there's a well. Follow the stream," Fender offered.

"It's the other direction," York cut in. "You haven't been there. But you'll find it. It'll help." He smiled softly at Lux, as if he was saying goodbye.

"Clover Cove. It's near Ember Park Island and the Clover Leaf Pond," Bubble chimed in. "If you swim low enough, you'll reach another entrance that leads up to a cave. That's also in Haven Hollow. It's along the edge of Venia's Lair, but we're pretty sure she can't touch the water."

Lux thought of her experience in the waters of Boreloque so far. She knew she would avoid that route if at all possible.

"And just blow your whistle if you need to get away. Your Float Coat will come for you," Zwicky said reassuringly.

Lux clutched the whistle around her neck. She began to feel as if they were all saying goodbye like they thought it was over. It wasn't over. It was just the beginning. With Blaze, she could do anything. She was hopeful.

"Lux," Pleiades said, and reached for Lux's bandaged hand. "Do not go to the Pram. Not until it's over. Promise me."

"And if you ever find yourself back at the Crossroads," Blaze quickly added. "If I'm not with you, do what you can to save yourself. Follow your instinct. Your soul will never lie to you. You'll know what to do." He looked away and stared at the map. "There's a reason you landed there. It's your biggest clue, and it's all I can give you. Remember who you are. You do know, deep down. Remember who you are right now, in this moment."

"Remember, Lux," Pleiades said pointedly.

"Let's go, Blaze," Lux said. She stood up and walked to the door. She would always remember how she felt then: hopeful, strong. They were going to defeat Venia. She would fix it all, restore what had been undone. If this was, in fact, her creation, it was going to be one she was proud of.

FIFTEEN

Album: Eyes Open

Track: Eight

Ember heard voices when he left the elevator, which struck him as odd. It was late. He pushed open the door to Lux's room, looking over his shoulder for any sign of nurses or doctors. He was still shaking from head to toe, still covered in snow.

"What's going on?" Ember stood in the doorway, unable to move. Mrs. Tazo approached him and buried her face in his shoulder. He stopped breathing. He'd only seen her like this on the night of the accident. He tried not to panic, but then noticed Mr. Tazo looked even worse than his wife.

"Tell me she's okay —" Ember choked out the words.

Mr. Tazo joined them at the door and pulled his wife into his own embrace.

This was it. It was out of their hands. Maybe it always had been. He wandered to the foot of Lux's bed.

"I knew I'd find you here." Anya's voice filled the silence. "You came back to her —" She stopped dead in her tracks in the doorway, and immediately began to cry.

Ember didn't have the strength to reach her. He stayed where he was, unaware that he was holding Lux's foot.

Time stood still in the worst possible way. Even when the doctors came into the room to speak with everyone together, it was as if Ember was hearing it through a humming, crackling speaker. He didn't know who was saying what; his stomach was turning, and he was seeing stars.

"We're so sorry —"

"As we discussed, she went downhill sometime around Thanksgiving."

"We haven't seen any improvement."

"It's time."

"Diminished brain activity..."

"Say goodbye —"

"If you need to talk..."

"You have forty-eight hours."

"You can say goodbye, each one of you..."

"We've all agreed."

"NO!" Ember shouted through bitter tears, as bile rose in his throat. "I haven't agreed!" He backed away. "You don't even want to save her; you never did! How could you let this happen?"

He threw a vase of wilting flowers to the ground between his feet and Lux's parents. He was disgusted by their tears. He would never accept it. Never.

"You're killing her! This is your fault! You gave up!" Ember shouted through reluctant gasps. He couldn't stand to look at them any longer.

Anya reached for him, but he backed away.

He ran through the hallway, then down the stairs, and out the front entrance of the hospital. He was already out of breath, but the winter wind embraced him. He continued to run, salty tears freezing to his burning cheeks. The only thing clear in his mind was that she'd gone downhill around Thanksgiving, when he'd stopped coming to visit her. It was actually his fault. He stumbled into a snow bank and vomited.

Ember ran again until he reached Lux's backyard. He climbed up into the tree house. He turned on *Raising Sand*, then crawled across the cold floor to the bean bag. He reached for the shoe that the damn girl should have tied when he told her to, because then none of this would have ever happened. He cried away the evidence, the truth, and the inevitable. Nothing had ever hurt so much in his life. Nothing would ever hurt this much again.

He stayed in the tree house all night, coiled in the same spot, listening to *Raising Sand* over and over again. His exhausted body fought each moment, as if it knew it shouldn't go on any longer. He prayed for the music to carry him away. In the dark, cold hours that his friends and family searched for him, nobody ever thought to look in Tazo Castle.

Mr. Sweeney, along with Ember's friends and their parents, stayed up all night waiting, pacing, searching. He was just a hidden passage and a property line away. If Ember had looked out the tree house window, he'd have seen Anya and Duffy sitting together on his bed. He'd have seen the guys and their parents milling around his kitchen. If he could see through to the other side of the Tazo home, he'd have seen Arrabelle in her childhood bedroom, alone and weeping on the floor near her bed.

A frosty, bitter light broke through the branches and in through the tree house windows. Ember was still in the corner of the main room of Tazo Castle, wrapped around a pillow and nearly frozen. He hadn't slept, but behind his closed eyes he'd seen images of nightmares. The one he loved, whom he'd poured his soul into saving, and whom he'd never had a real chance at a life together with, would soon be dead. He couldn't save her any more than he could save himself. The sunlight was his enemy, and time was his foe. The doctors had said forty-eight hours, and he'd just wasted eight of them. He hated everything.

"I tried" were the only words he could muster into the walls of the tree. He sat up and looked around the room for what felt like would be the last time. His body hurt terribly and was drained of the will to carry on. His eye caught a picture frame hanging on the wall, the one whose words he'd believed in so much. *Music fills the infinite between two souls.* It felt impossible to stop believing; it had become a part of him. He pulled the frame off the wall. Then he recognized the flaw in his plan. There was no time in infinity, and he'd been given an expiration date. The music would live on, long past Lux's life, and long past his.

He picked up his phone and scrolled through the missed phone calls and messages. He read the ones from his friends and Arrabelle, but ignored all the others.

Tanner: In My Arms. Plumb.
Duffy: Maybe It's Time. The Milk Carton Kids.
Luther: D'Artagnan's Theme. Citizen Cope.
Jamison: Acoustic #3. GooGoo Dolls.
Anya: Back to December/Apologize/You're Not Sorry.
Taylor Swift.
Tanner: All Around Me. Flyleaf.
Jamison: Toad the Wet Sprocket. Windmills.
Luther: Radiohead. Karma Police.
Tanner: Plankeye. Goodbye.
Duffy: Ember, come home.
Anya: Where are you?

The messages were hours old, but he couldn't reply. He didn't know what to say. He moved on to Arrabelle's messages.

Arrabelle: Ember. I don't want you to be alone right now. Where are you?

Arrabelle: Fade Into You. Mazzy Star.

Arrabelle: Have A Little Faith In Me. John Hiatt.

Arrabelle: If You Were Here. Cary Brothers.

Arrabelle: Over the Rainbow. Ingrid Michaelson.

Thankfully, his phone shut off before he could read on. Ember slowly and calmly climbed down the tree, the picture frame in one hand and Lux's shoe in the other hand. He left the backyard unnoticed and began the walk back to the hospital. The world seemed empty. No cars passed. The snow that had fallen overnight was untouched. He had less than two days left with her. And he wasn't going to leave this time, not until she was put to rest.

Ember stood outside the hospital, knowing that the next time he walked out the doors would be to get ready for Lux Tazo's funeral. He was numb. He felt as if pieces of his heart had seeped out with each tear that left his body. He looked at his watch and saw the date. Two months ago, he'd invited her to a show because he'd written a song for her, but she never made it to the show. He hadn't gotten to sing for her, not the way he needed to.

Suddenly, he had an idea. Adrenaline surged through his body. Instead of going inside and returning to Lux's side for the last time, Ember ran again. After another bone-chilling and breathless trek, he burst through the doors of Briar Heights Academy. Friends called after him, and teachers tried to stop him. He didn't even stop for his best friends, who were huddled in a corner together. Jamison, Tanner, Luther, Duffy, and Anya watched, stunned, as Ember ran past them, oblivious to the fact that they, too, had been awake and distraught all night. The first bell rang. Ember barricaded himself in the principal's office. He leaned his head against the door to catch his breath.

"Sweeney! Where have you been?" Dr. Jacobs rushed from his desk. "Are you okay?"

"I need your help," Ember said desperately, out of breath,

shaking. "I have thirty-nine hours…they're letting her die," he admitted for the first time out loud.

The principal hung his head. "I know." He pulled out a chair for Ember. They sat together.

"I need everyone to sign a petition," Ember pleaded. "To stop them from letting her die like this."

"Ember, I can't do that. We both know it's not our decision," Dr. Jacobs stated sadly. "We don't want to make this any harder for them —"

"For *them*? They don't care!"

"Ember —"

"Fine, I figured you'd say that. How about this? I wrote some songs for Lux. I want everyone here to hear them, before she's gone. I'll play one last time: the last show she never got to see." Ember set the photo frame from Lux's tree house on the desk. Dr. Jacobs read it and remained quiet.

"I just need this. I need to play for her. Please. Astor Dane from the Sour Enchantment will set it up. I want everyone to see. Everyone should get to say goodbye."

"So you'd like to put on a show in our auditorium?"

"It'll be a farewell show."

Dr. Jacobs leaned back in his chair and didn't answer for a long time. The silence was deafening in Ember's mind as he realized that each minute at school was a minute away from her.

"Do Lux's parents even know about this idea?" Dr. Jacobs finally asked. "I mean, everyone was out looking for you all night. Police are involved. I need to call your father —"

"It won't be a problem," Ember said hastily. He had decided it would happen one way or another. "They'll let me. But the show won't be here. I'm going to be with Lux."

"Oh. No, I'm sorry. That could never work, Ember! Maybe you could do a show here, but even that — I don't have experience with something like this. I'll get e-mails, phone calls — it would be a legal issue for the hospital. I don't have a good feeling about it."

"You don't have a good feeling because one of your students is about to die." Ember paced the room. "Did she not sit here in this chair with you three years ago when she was accepted into this school? And in that moment you promised her a glorious future. At least, at the very least, let her have that kind of departure."

"Listen. If Lux's family and doctors approve this, which I highly doubt they will, then I'll let your show stream in the student lounges. I want a personal phone call from one of them immediately. I don't know what else to say. I don't know how else to help you. But, if this will help you deal with it —"

"Yes! It will. Thank you. I'll have Astor call you soon. And can you announce it? Let them know it's a farewell show. They'll know what it means." Ember's hoarse voice caught in his throat.

"Okay, fine." Dr. Jacobs sighed loudly. "I'll stream it in the auditorium and cancel classes. And if they don't let you do this at the hospital, the stage here is all yours. You're right. Everyone should say goodbye." Tears had welled up in the man's eyes as he witnessed Ember's desperation. "And I need phone calls, or it's not happening."

"Please call my dad. Tell him I'm sorry." Ember stood up. "And can you tell my friends what's going on? My phone died."

Dr. Jacobs stood up and walked Ember to the door. "I will," he said.

Ember left the office. The hallway was empty now. He broke into Duffy's locker and took her phone. He left school and called Astor to explain his plan.

The first phone call Dr. Jacobs made was to Mr. Sweeney. He assured him that Ember was okay, and on his way to the hospital. Then he called Anya, Duffy, Luther, Tanner, and Jamison into his office. He explained what was going on, and suggested they join Ember at the hospital if the farewell show was approved. He sent them back to class, but promised he'd update them as soon as he knew anything.

"I'm not leaving until she's gone." Ember had arrived back at Lux's hospital room. He couldn't bring himself to apologize. Mr. and Mrs. Tazo and Arrabelle were squished together on the couch where he'd spent the past two months. Mrs. Tazo started sobbing all over again. Arrabelle rushed over to Ember and embraced him.

"I came to say goodbye," he whispered.

"I'm so glad you're okay," she said, and hugged him tighter.

"I need to do something. And I need you to hear me out." Ember broke away from Arrabelle and faced Mr. and Mrs. Tazo. They approached him.

"All this time I was trying, hoping...to bring her back. With music. Every day I would come here and sing the same songs, hoping she'd recognize home, something familiar, or me. I believed it would work. Obviously, it didn't. Now I just need a proper goodbye. So, I'm going to play a farewell show for her. If you'll let me."

"Let him do it," Arrabelle said. He nodded his thanks to her.

Ember explained his idea to the Tazos just as he'd explained to Dr. Jacobs. He promised that Lux would remain out of sight of the cameras. Nobody would even know he was in her room. After a lot of questions and uncertainty, they agreed to Ember's idea. But they still needed to get approval from the doctors.

A lawyer representing the hospital met with the Tazos and Ember. They sat together in a small room with a round table and swivel chairs.

"You can call me Kyrie," she began, and smiled warmly at Ember.

"I'll be representing Ember, should the need arise," Mr. Tazo said, shaking Kyrie's hand. "And, of course, my daughter."

Kyrie presented the legalities of the situation, which Mr. Tazo was able to discuss and agree to quickly. No names, no faces, no details of the hospital or of Lux's situation would be revealed. Astor would need to leave when visiting hours were over, which meant the show would go no later than 8:00 that night. Ember hastily agreed to everything, too. He was running out of time.

Astor Dane arrived at the hospital shortly after the meeting with Kyrie ended, and papers had been signed. He'd brought sound and film equipment, as well as a keyboard for Ember. Ember's guitar was already there, where he'd abandoned it the night before. They got to work setting up a makeshift stage in the corner of the room by the window. Then Astor set up his laptop and the camera near the door. The Tazos waited in the hallway.

"Astor, could you ask Dr. Jacobs to play "The Fighter" by Gym Class Heroes while everyone's walking into the auditorium?" Ember asked, determined and distracted and disoriented.

"I'll call Jackson," Astor said. "He can have Mr. Besser or Mr. Jorgensen do it."

"Then for my intro, will you play "The Greatest" by Cat Power?"

"I'll get it ready now. Then I'll call Dr. Jacobs to give him the go-ahead."

"Thanks. I'm ready."

Ember sat down in the old familiar chair he'd spent the past two months in. He waited while Astor made the phone calls. His hands began to shake. He realized this music was so much more personal than anything else he'd composed. He'd never intended to share it with anyone other than Lux. But here he was.

Astor adjusted the camera one last time. He checked the soundboard and opened a website on his laptop. He opened the door and invited the Tazos back in. They were accompanied by Anya, Duffy, Jamison, Luther, and Tanner. Ember's heart stopped. There was no going back now. The room was crowded. The friends and family huddled in the far corner by Lux's bed. A nurse had followed them in to check on Lux, and when she left, Astor gave a thumbs up.

Once Dr. Jacobs had gotten the go-ahead from Astor, he made an announcement to the school. He instructed the entire student body and all teachers to meet in the auditorium immediately. "The Fighter" played over the loudspeakers as soon as the announcement was finished.

The auditorium lights dimmed when every seat was full. A massive screen lowered down over the stage and a projector turned on. Teachers gathered in a line against the back wall of the room. The song ended.

Ember's face lit up the screen. Students whispered loudly and quickly, trying to figure out what was happening, wondering why he looked so disheveled.

"Hi, I'm Ember Sweeney." His voice boomed and echoed through the auditorium, silencing everyone. He'd always had the power to silence a room.

"Many of you don't know the real story or have heard only rumors. But there is a story, and now it has an end. So it's ready to be told. I'm here today because of Lux Tazo. I've been with her almost every day since her accident two months ago. And I'm with her now."

"I fell for Lux a long time ago and waited for the right moment for too long. She was never my girlfriend. Because before we ever had a chance, something happened between us; something went wrong. She wouldn't even look at me. She acted like I didn't exist. She told me she hated me. And she made me promise to pretend she didn't exist either."

"Until the day of her accident. We started over that day. Even so, we didn't get the chance we deserved. But we'll always have the sunrise."

"The rest of our lives was supposed to start two months ago today. Then I would have been okay with those two crappy years. I invited her to the Sour Enchantment. Some of you were there that night. But she never showed up, and I knew she wouldn't be walking through those doors. I'd just watched an ambulance take her away. What I'd momentarily grasped was instantly gone. In one moment. Just like that." Ember took a loud, deep breath. He held up the photo frame: *Music fills the infinite between two souls.* The words covered the screen.

"But I thought if I just sang to her, over and over and over again, she'd recognize the music. She'd find a way. I know; we're kids. I'm just a kid. But that doesn't make this any less. And even when pain changed us, we still tried. So, here we are. Out of time. I just thought everyone deserved to say goodbye. I don't know how else to end this. But this is my last show." Ember closed his eyes, struck a chord on the keyboard, and began the first song.

Something happened then at Briar Heights Academy. Even before the end of his first song, the lights in the auditorium rose and flowers were brought in. Once the flowers were arranged, Mr. Nickel and a few other art teachers brought Lux's paintings to the stage. The paintings were arranged on easels surrounding the flowers and facing the audience. Astor had added an image of Lux to the bottom corner of the screen, so her face appeared next to Ember's.

Many of the kids at BHA hadn't yet faced death, and certainly none of them had ever watched it unfold like this. A life was coming to a bitter end, but that didn't stop them from hoping. By the end of the second song, a few students began to mingle. Dylan Black brought his paintbrushes to the stage and tossed them near the flowers, which started a wave of dedications and mementos. The Guerrero sisters led the lacrosse team to the stage and left a stick and gloves. Lux's name was written on both, and "fighter" was next to her name. Keepsakes were added to the stage one by one. Notes and letters were folded up and added to the collection. Piper Speedman brought a few film students together and they documented what was happening. Ember continued to play in the background.

Ember's introduction had shocked Mr. and Mrs. Tazo. As he spoke, everyone shifted uncomfortably and avoided eye contact. Everyone except for Arrabelle. Ember felt helpless, but he needed to be honest about everything. He caught Duffy's eye a number of times while he spoke. He watched his friends whispering to each other. He finally decided to get on with the show when he noticed Mr. Tazo staring at the ground, his hand covering his mouth.

After the first hour of the farewell show, Lux's parents left the room. Nurses came and went, caring for Lux just as they always had. Arrabelle stood close to Astor, and Ember's friends watched from the corner.

Ember picked up his guitar and began a new song. He looked at his friends, his voice caught in his throat, and he looked away. His eyes burned. But something caused him to look again. One by one, each of them held up a piece of paper with a song written on it.

Duffy: Empty by Ray LaMontagne.
Luther: Waiting For the End. Linkin Park.
Tanner: Walk On. U2.
Jamison: Full of Grace. Sarah McLachlan.
Anya: Top of the World by Patty Griffin.

Across the room, both Arrabelle and Astor held up pieces of paper, too.

Arrabelle: Hear You Me. Jimmy Eat World.
Astor: I Won't Give Up. Jason Mraz.

Ember read each one and fought every tear. He nodded at them and forced a broken smile. They motioned their goodbyes and quietly filed out of the room.

"Look at this." Luther held up his phone as they stepped into the elevator. "Everyone must be streaming the footage from their phones." Everyone else took out their phones to see for themselves.

"And this." Duffy held up a picture someone had sent her of the stage.

"Astor's streaming it from our website, too. He didn't tell Ember, or us," Jamison announced. Tanner held up his hand to stop Jamison from saying anything more.

"Just let him sing," Duffy concluded. "Let him be. We won't tell him."

They got off the elevator and made their way to the hospital entrance.

"We should add something to the stage," Luther said. His phone rang. He answered and his jaw dropped. He was silent for a long time.

"I'd love to accept, but — I'll do what I can once we think the time's right. I'll call you back." Luther put his phone away. "That was Armada Records. The story has blown up on social media. Apparently the world is watching footage of this farewell show. It's all over the news. This woman just asked me if we've Googled ourselves this morning, and if we're represented."

"We're not discussing anything business-related," Tanner interjected. "Not here or now."

Anya remained at the hospital.

Now it was just her, Ember, and Lux, like it had been for the past two months. The room felt oddly quiet. Nobody had asked how she was doing, not even Tanner. It was nobody's fault.

She'd stuck around. She was the true best friend. She'd taken on Ember's pain and had tried to be the strong one, willing to face reality. She had nothing left to give. She crawled gingerly into the bed with Lux, closed her eyes, and pretended that it was Lux who was comforting her.

"I spent all night looking for him," Anya whispered. Reluctant tears slid down her flushed cheeks. She was as exhausted as Ember. "I'm so mad. But I can't lose you both."

"He loved you. I wish you could have seen how this all turned out. It would have brought back the old you. The real you." Anya sighed, exhausted. "I miss you," she said, and her face crumbled.

"This one's called "Very Best Friend," and I wrote it about Anya Jensen. She's the best person I know. She's been here every day, too. She sat on the other side of this door and waited when she knew I needed to be alone. And she may just be the one with the most to lose when this is all said and done. So, when you see her again —" Ember picked up his guitar. "Be good to her. Be the kind of friend she is. Bold. Purposeful. Kind."

Anya cried hard into Lux's shoulder, hiding her face from Ember. She still didn't want him to see how much pain she really was in. But of course he knew. And only he knew. He turned to her as he sang.

A friend like you is the best, the very best
Never wavers, always put to the test
Your open arm is always reached out
It's time for you to take a bow

Take a bow
Cause there's nothing I can do for you, for you
To make this all better, to take it all away
I'll always think of you when the music fades

And when it came down to you and me and her
You reached out, in your silence your voice was heard
And it was like water down a stream
Steady and constant, solid and free

The girl with the light always knew, always knew
What the rest of us saw in you

And when it came down to me and her
She walked away, but her eyes promised forever

Take a bow
You're beautiful, the best, the very best

If we could have souls like yours and if we could open the doors
If we could share ourselves and not hold back
But give it all and think about the space that we make
And the space that we take and the place where we blame
We could all be changed

Ember watched Anya, using Lux Tazo as a shield. He understood. When the song ended, he announced he was taking a short break. He couldn't watch her any longer.

SIXTEEN

Album: Speak Now - World Tour Live

Track: Fifteen

Lux's hand began to throb again. She could feel Blaze's anxiety. Hot sweat dripped between their entwined fingers. They were close now. She could see almost nothing as they crept through the eerily quiet forest.

"I want you to never forget, Lux..." Blaze stopped walking. "You're my light." He held her close and kissed her forehead. "You came here for a reason, and you'll always be a part of me."

She nodded. He still wasn't making himself clear, but at least they were together. They reached the dead tree marked by strands of long black hair; the entrance to Venia's Lair. Lux's heart pounded hard with anticipation. She knew the plan. She would distract Venia by simply showing up alive, while Blaze searched for the stolen items. There was no assumption that Venia would harm Lux; she needed her. So the plan was that they would be introduced and have a little chat.

"You'll go first. I'll be right behind you." Blaze pushed Lux in front of him then, a bit harshly. Something about his touch didn't sit quite right. "You ready?" he asked. She hesitated for a moment, nodded, sucked in a deep breath and jumped into the tree hollow, which turned into a rough and winding slide.

All she could see was darkness; her breath caught in her throat. Her body crashed against the walls of the slimy, rotting tunnel. A crimson glow grew in the distance and she knew she was close. There was nothing to grab onto and she couldn't slow down. The stench made her gag. She landed hard on the broken ground. She fought to stand up and stumbled.

Trying not to breathe in the smell, she observed everything in the crimson night. It was barren and ugly, illuminating only fragments of death, the remnants of demons and ghosts. She moved forward and heard a low growl. She took a few steps over a mound of ashes, coughed, and breathed in a thick cloud of dust. The growling grew louder.

Then Lux stopped dead in her tracks. Sense flooded her mind as trust abandoned her; it was a trap. Blaze had sent her here. There was no way out. He'd sent her to die. But, why? It didn't add up. Her heart raced as courage dwindled. Bile rose slowly into her throat.

Somewhere ahead Lux heard glass shatter; a door slam; and a horrid, shrill screech. She trudged through the forest of dead trees, whose branches scratched her arms as she went. Her heart sank. She had no defense, no plan but survival and dependence on the one she loved. She became livid with herself for believing in him. How could he?

"Lux!" She heard a desperate, hushed voice behind her. Her heart plummeted, soared, filled, emptied, and stopped.

She heard him moving toward her. "Where did you go?" he asked.

"I thought —" She threw her arms around him.

He pried her arms away from his body and led them forward in silence. It felt very strange. She hadn't been given enough information. She'd trusted too blindly. But then Blaze took her hand again. She caught her breath. It would all be over soon.

They shuffled along tree stumps and holes in the cracked ground. The path cleared and they stood before a ravaged and shackled structure. Something was familiar. Lux knew this place; she'd been here before. Maybe in a dream. The windows were blown out and shards of glass covered the ground. She hung back when she saw the salivating, mangy lion guarding the door.

"Don't make eye contact with...anything," Blaze said. He gripped her hand tighter and pushed through the entrance, past the glaring lion. The inside of the structure was thick with fog, and it was difficult to make out anything clearly. Ghostly noises came from unseen sources. In the foyer was a grand, winding staircase. Pieces of the stairs were caved in and stained. Her hope sank lower with each step and each staggered breath.

"VENIA!" Blaze thundered, startling Lux.

The rumbling growl turned into a scream. Lux suddenly wanted to abort the mission. This wasn't what she'd expected.

"Come in," Venia snarled in a low, dripping voice from somewhere above them. Blaze led Lux into a room off to their left. A silver light shone in a back corner, illuminating an empty throne.

"She's hiding," Blaze whispered, taking long and deep breaths. He gazed around in every direction. Finally, he led Lux back into the sanctuary, to the base of the winding staircase. He pointed up the stairs, and motioned for Lux to keep quiet. She nodded, unexpectedly terrified.

"What is she?" Lux whispered. Blaze shook his head. He pulled her closer. They climbed the creaking stairs, slowly, cautiously. The staircase wound around and they faced another flight up. She stared up at the top of the staircase and gasped.

Venia.

She was perched at the top of the staircase, looking down on them, hovering like a ghost. She was so thin, her bones protruded from her ashen, decaying flesh. Her clumps of stringy hair hung limp and framed her emaciated face. She had large, pale eyes that were sunken to the back of her skull. Teeth were missing and visibly cracked, and her crazed smile terrified Lux beyond death. Most terrifying of all was that Lux recognized her.

"I want to go!" Lux cried. "NOW!" Blaze ignored her and pulled her along. He seemed entranced by Venia.

"Yes, that's right. Twirl her," Venia instructed Blaze, her voice crackling.

Blaze did as he was told. Feet stumbling and face crumbling, Lux tried to gather her thoughts. Where could she run? This wasn't the plan. Blaze was supposed to be off by now, finding what Venia had stolen.

"I knew you wouldn't be able to do it," Venia sneered. "But I've waited so long. I'll do it myself." Blaze nodded.

"I'm so sorry Lux," he whispered. He grasped her arm tightly, hurting her. "Maybe someday you'll understand. It's our only hope for the future." And then he pushed her with a strength so fierce, she flew up the stairs and landed facedown at Venia's feet.

Lux was so shocked she didn't move. She'd hit her head. Warm blood flowed down the right side of her face. A throbbing pain grew instantly to pounding. She closed her eyes. Her mind was blank. She'd lied to herself. She couldn't save herself or anyone else. She was no one's heroine. She wasn't brave or strong. She wasn't even a victim. She had stupidly, willingly, blindly walked right into this predicament. That's what hurt the most. The one she'd grown to love had betrayed her, offered her up to die. Why?

"She's yours!" Blaze screamed. "Go ahead! Do to her what you did to me, but give her back. DO IT!" He sounded out of his mind. Lux didn't understand. He wanted her back?

"You STUPID fool, Blaze," Venia spat. "You agreed to something, remember?"

He shook his head. "We make deals all the time."

"It was a long time ago." She revealed a thick rope and pushed it over Lux's neck. Lux was frozen in fear and the pain was too much to give into.

"But we had a different deal!" Blaze screamed. "When she arrived, you —"

"I'm not talking about our most recent deal; I knew you couldn't do that. Just try. Remember back to our first encounter. Or perhaps you've ingested too much of that pathetic substance that brings false happiness, and you've forgotten like the others! You deserve to be alone." Venia laughed hysterically. "I told you I hate you. I told you to forget I exist. But you refused. You never gave up. And you should have. If you had just stayed in your own world…"

Lux peered down at Blaze though swollen eyelids. He looked lost: speechless and frightened. And her heart unexpectedly broke for the man who'd betrayed her. She tried to raise her hand out to him, but her fingertips only trembled. Tears fell, burning into her wounds, mixing with blood that flowed onto her cracked lips. She tasted iron and salt.

"No…" Blaze pleaded weakly. The strong and quiet leader Lux thought she'd seen in him did not exist in this place. In fact, she'd never seen it in him, she'd only hoped to. She no longer knew him. He was at the mercy of hate.

"I have no use for you, Blaze. I never needed you. I just needed the girl. Be gone now with the zephyr. Forever." Venia waved her hand at Blaze. Her robes flowed around her wispy frame. Blaze cried out, but Lux could no longer see him. *Zephyr*, she thought. Everything turned black.

Lux opened her eyes. She was huddled on the ice cold ground in the corner of a dark room, her limbs bound by heavy, rusted chains. Everything was blurry. The last thing she remembered was Blaze throwing her to Venia, but for some reason she still loved him.

She propped herself up on her elbow to observe the room. It looked like some sort of scientific lab. She recognized the backside of the throne in the corner. Tubes and wires extended out from it and led to glass jars, labeled, and filled with an unrecognizable substance. She decided there must be over a hundred jars, only a few of which were empty. Some of them glowed and bubbled over and released something through the tubes every so often. If only she could read the labels.

She tried hard to focus for a very long time. Finally, her eyesight cleared just enough. She was able to make out a label on one of the jars. It said "YORK." There was something else below it, too small for Lux to read, but it was a single word. Whatever it was, it must be what Venia had stolen.

Then comprehension hit her like a brick. She felt the weight, saw red, and finally succumbed to her shattered heart. She could hear Blaze's voice burning in her ears, a resentful echo. And she knew. Venia had stolen their hearts. Everyone's.

Why hadn't Blaze come for them? What could be more important?

Lux used the strength she had left and nudged her way closer to the other side of the room. She needed to see the jars more clearly. She knew she was next in line and it would be painful.

Lux remembered her first moments in Boreloque, when she'd arrived at the Crossroads and been accused of thievery, of stealing this very thing. A heart.

But she, Lux, was also missing something. She could still hear Blaze screaming while Venia laughed hysterically at his pleading. Where was he now? As she slowly made her way across the room, she began to think of the Pram. She wished herself there. With the comfort of her memories. The letter. The paintbrush. Clues.

But there was nothing to set her free from this. Nobody was coming to help her. She was on her own. She had to escape. She closed her eyes and traced the trail to the Pram in her mind. She needed to get through the forest, to the islands and past the mountains to whatever was on the other side.... The mountains.

She edged closer to the rows of glass jars. Hearts pumped within each jar, some soft, and some spewing their contents steadily. The descriptions below each name became clear. Qualities. Attributes. The best of each. The hearts spat their essence through the tubes, which traveled to one large vat at the base of her throne. Venia had not simply stolen everyone's hearts, she was feeding off of them.

What if she simply disconnected the tubes? Would the hearts stop beating? How could she restore them? How would she get past Venia? Where was Venia? She couldn't be far. Lux had a lot of decisions to make, and quickly.

Suddenly she realized this wasn't about her at all. She needed to fix this, fix them. And then she'd leave Boreloque. Venia hadn't gotten to her. Lux had never been so thankful to know she wasn't home.

She read each label. *Optimistic. Peaceful. Brave. Loyal. Genuine. Generous. Honest. Kind. Bold. Fearless. Gentle. Humble. Protective.* And then she saw *Blaze: Patient.* Yes, that was the thing about him. She wished she could start over with him. She continued to read all of the names, but kept glancing back at his. Maybe she could save only him. Maybe that would undo everything. She'd been convinced, even as she'd tumbled into Venia's Lair, that this was home. But now she was certain from the pit of her clenched stomach that she'd been wrong, and that gave her the freedom to leave it all behind.

Finally she came to the end of the rows of jars. The last one was empty. It said *Lux.* But there was no description. What would Venia want of her?

"Ah, she's awake." Venia's raspy voice slithered through her broken teeth. Startled, Lux rolled over and faced her. The silver light behind her throne switched on and cast shadows on the room. Venia stared at Lux as though she didn't know what to do with her.

"What do you want from me!" Lux screamed. She struggled to free herself, while Venia watched. "What are you doing with their hearts? Tell me!" She had just as much anger as fear inside of her now.

"Yours still isn't ready," Venia said, "but this is helping." She seemed to be losing strength. She clutched her throne to remain upright. Lux wondered how much time they had.

Venia grasped a lever on the side of her throne. She pulled it. There was a grinding sound and the boxes grew brighter. The tubes filled with a thick, dark substance and began to slowly extend toward the throne. Venia laughed until she coughed and a disgusting gurgle escaped her throat. Lux was repulsed.

"Stop! Wait! Venia. Let's make a deal," Lux said hastily. She would gladly pay for it later, if she could just make a difference now.

"A deal?" Venia was intrigued.

"Yes. Let me go now, and I'll just give you...my heart. You can have it! But you need to give me time first, like you just said!" Lux said. Sweat poured from her scalp.

"I get your heart, anyway." Venia seemed disappointed. "What kind of a deal is that?" She tapped her fingers together.

"Fine! You get it anyway, I know that," Lux said. "My friends have told me what you're doing," Lux lied. "I know everything. But, you won't have to let me go once you have me again. I'll be yours. You can keep all of me!" Lux knew she was selling her soul to the devil, but she didn't care anymore.

"You certainly did arrive at the Crossroads, didn't you?" Venia's voice lowered. She seemed intrigued. "And your *friends*, you say?" A faraway look blanketed her expression. Lux glanced at the jars and the tubes. She had only moments.

"Your *friends*, as you call them, are not what they seem," Venia said heavily. "Your *friend* Blaze promised your soul to me long before you arrived. I knew you'd be coming here. You were always meant for me, and me alone. I sent him to lure you in, so then he could live. All he wants is to live. Without you weighing him down. That's all any of them want. He wants nothing to do with you."

She may as well have offered herself right then and there. But she fought. She had to believe that Venia was lying.

"Even if they're not my friends," Lux's voice rose indignantly, "that's not Blaze's deal to make. Only I can give you my heart. Only I can give myself willingly, in order for you to truly have what you want, in the quality that you want it. Let me go now, and I'll return without a fight. But, if you don't — I'll never give you what you want, I promise you. You'll never be satisfied; neither of us will." She was losing her breath.

Venia slowly reached for the lever. She hesitated, then shut it off. The contents in the tubes slowly retreated to the jars they belonged to. Lux couldn't believe it. Maybe there was a chance.

"I'll let you go. But you promise you'll come back...?" Venia smiled as if she knew something Lux didn't. Lux didn't care.

Venia slithered off her throne and inched toward Lux. She pulled a key from her robes and unlocked the chains, which fell loudly to the ground around Lux. A chill ran down Lux's spine. The way Venia was looking at her —

But she was free! Lux stood up quickly. She felt tremendous pain, and the weight on her shoulders had never been heavier, but she ignored it.

"What are you waiting for?" Venia's wicked smile was replaced by a repulsing glare, and her ghostly blue stare followed Lux.

"I don't know what I'm waiting for," Lux answered as she slowly backed up, making her way closer to the jars. "Oh, yes, I do. This!"

Lux grabbed Blaze's glass jar and ripped the tubes from it. She ran as fast as she could out of the room, not looking back. She escaped the structure and ran through the dead forest, then back to the tunnel she'd tumbled from upon her arrival. Stairs were there now; she climbed. Venia's terrifying screams echoed throughout Boreloque as Lux hurried away.

She desperately wondered what to do next. She was, after all, returning to someone, or maybe everyone, who'd betrayed her. She reached the top of the tunnel and was now on solid ground. It occurred to her then that she was near the Crossroads.

SEVENTEEN

Album: Come Home - Single

Track: One

Word of the farewell show traveled fast. Local news teams had shown up to both the hospital and the school, attempting interviews. But faculty and teachers at Briar Heights Academy were protective. When Luther, Tanner, Jamison, and Duffy arrived back at school, they were rushed inside. They found all of their classmates still there, even though classes had been cancelled, and students from other schools were also dropping by with memorials and condolences. Parents arrived in nervous hordes, unsure of what to do.

Ember still had no idea the effect his decision was having on the world. And it wouldn't have mattered if he did; he was doing this for Lux. He was glad he'd decided to take a break, though; he was losing his voice, his fingers were calloused and cracked, his eyes burned, and he hadn't eaten since lunch the day before.

He sauntered into the hallway and grabbed a sandwich from the nearby food table someone had set up. He couldn't even taste it. It was dry against his tongue, but he knew he needed it if he wanted to finish. All he really wanted to do was go back to the tree house and hide until he wasted away. He was grateful no one had found him there, and that he hadn't revealed to anyone where he'd been all night. Tazo Castle would be his new refuge.

As he swallowed the last bite of bread, Ember realized he'd need to say goodbye on his own, alone. He had enough sense to realize that even though he was presenting a farewell show, it was still a performance. She deserved more and so did he. He was just terrified to face the moment.

♪

When the band reached the auditorium, they were greeted with endless questions. They had no answers to give, but somehow their presence helped calm the crowd. They approached the stage together and examined the collection dedicated to Lux. There were things for Ember, too.

Jamison, Luther, and Tanner sat on the edge of the stage together, watching everyone in the auditorium. Duffy joined the Guerrero sisters, her friends Selma and Belle, and a few others of Lux's friends.

"Look at all these people. Her friends," Luther muttered. "I feel...guilty."

"Why?" Tanner asked.

"I know why. Because we didn't even try to know her. Each of us had at least one class with her. Ember talked about her, or at least he wanted to, but we got tired of hearing it. She walked by his house every day and none of us ever talked to her," Jamison said.

"We don't deserve to be here," Tanner said. "This belongs to Ember."

"I keep wondering…was she really this great girl and we wasted an opportunity to know her?" Luther asked. "Or was she just… any one of us here in this room?"

"That's the problem. Everyone in this room thinks they're somebody great," Jamison said.

"Everyone does have something to offer, though," Tanner cut in.

"She didn't promote herself. That's why we didn't notice her. Was she great? Who knows? Doesn't matter now," Jamison concluded.

"Ember sure seemed to think so," Tanner said.

"I guess I don't understand what *great* is," Luther said, shaking his head. "But Ember has always seen the best in people. He saw something that we didn't. We were too busy. And he was patient. He waited all this time. And look how it turned out."

"Well, to be fair, he was in love with her," Jamison said. "We weren't. Anyway, she was someone to Ember, so she should have been someone to us. We were wrong."

They sat together quietly, alone on the stage; always on stage, but now just part of a tribute.

"Guys…look behind you." Duffy was anxiously watching the screen behind them. Everyone else had stopped to watch, too. Anya sat at the piano now, and awkwardly stared into the camera. Jamison nudged Tanner and they turned to watch.

"I'm Anya Jensen," Anya's voice boomed over the speakers. Her face was flushed and swollen, but she smiled. The hundreds of people milling around the auditorium stopped their conversations. "Ember will be back soon. Anyway. I was thinking that most people don't get to say goodbye like this, you know? So we're really lucky, if you think about it. I've spent the past two months saying she'd wake up, planning the rest of our lives. But instead, I've gotten all this time to say goodbye. So, that's good. I just wish she could have seen how much people care. Not even just about her, but about everything."

Anya held up her journal then, opened it to a page near the

middle, and laughed to herself. "If she wakes up, she'll kill me."

"Poor thing still has hope," Jamison murmured.

"Lux and I shared a journal. We wrote letters to each other. I want to share the last thing she wrote. Ember doesn't know about this…but it will be his soon, because it's about him."

Anya… I can't get him out of my heart. I'm scared, even though all I want to do is run to him. WHAT IF IT'S TOO LATE?! I love someone I don't even know. Why did I run away from him so long ago? I'll never find a good enough answer. Because I was so wrong about everything… I saw the rest of our lives together. (This is so embarrassing, please destroy these pages after reading.) Anyway, I haven't been living, not really. I have things to prove to myself. Other people's opinions are overrated. I can't wait to undo the past and start over. Today. Tonight. I swear, the next time I see Ember Sweeney, I'm going to tell him I love him and tell him I'm sorry – and hope he feels the same. (Or, I'll just try not to run away.) And if he doesn't feel the same, at least I'll know that I didn't leave that mess before trying to move on, and we'll both finally have closure. I have my whole life ahead of me, with or without him.

Anya closed the journal.

"I've replied to that letter so many times now, the journal is full. My last response was, "HE LOVES YOU, TOO! DON'T GIVE UP! COME BACK!" I wanted to share this as a lesson. You never know the last chance you're going to have with someone," Anya said. She began to cry again but composed herself. "You can make all the plans you want, but we just don't know what our futures hold. So. Always take the opportunity. Live when you have the chance. Be nice. Be good to the people in your life. Accept them. Our lives are short enough, and way too short for being afraid. You have this moment to work with."

Ember opened the door to Lux's room in time to hear Anya's last words. But before he could join her, he heard another voice he recognized, so he closed the door again. Mr. Sweeney rushed down the hallway, looking worse off than Ember.

"Hey," Ember said uncertainly. His father embraced him.

"I'm so sorry," Mr. Sweeney whispered. "You're not alone." Ember's heart swelled, but he'd still never felt so broken.

"Dad, will you stay —" Ember couldn't finish his question.

"I won't leave you," his father said firmly.

Mr. Sweeney followed Ember into Lux's room. Anya was sitting in the corner again, out of sight, which meant the camera was still rolling and everyone in the auditorium at BHA must be expecting more. Ember quickly grasped Anya's hand before returning to his stage. Mr. Sweeney joined Anya and hugged her. Arrabelle and Astor returned then, too.

Ember closed his eyes to remind himself why he was doing this farewell show. He wondered if anyone was even watching. What had he'd gotten himself into? Why had he done this? Lux didn't even know, and would never know, that he loved her. At least everyone else knew. He needed to focus, to finish what he'd started.

"This one is called Someday a Mother," he murmured.

When you wake up, you'll be so strong
You'll have braved the storm
And wherever you were, you changed it for the better
Maybe you saved someone
Maybe you found my mom

And someday you'll tell the kids where you've been
And they'll ask to hear more
You'll share of fairies and tales
And you'll talk about your friends
And remind them great things are in store

News crews were waiting outside the hospital. Security stood at the doors. Protesters had gathered. All of this had only created more pain and trouble for the Tazo family, which was the farthest thing from Ember's intent. They were trapped inside the hospital. They were trapped in the decision they'd made to let her go. They seemed to have forgotten that they'd been given forty-eight hours to change their minds.

"Did we make the right decision?" Mrs. Tazo whispered to her husband in a dark corner at the end of the hall.

"I don't know. Maybe we should talk to the doctors again," he said.

"Should we stop Ember's show?"

"Yes. I know we agreed we'd do anything for him, especially now that — we're losing her." He choked up. "This needs to end. It's too much."

"It's not too late," Arrabelle approached them, determined. "You two made this decision without me. I should have a say, and I say no. Please, no."

"But where does that leave us?" Mrs. Tazo pleaded. "Back at square one. The only reason all of this is happening is because of Ember. Because he's saying goodbye."

"And then it's still over," Mr. Tazo added. "If his music stops and it goes back to how it was yesterday —"

"Everyone's hopes are up for nothing," Mrs. Tazo cried. "We know how it ends. Let it be over."

"We'll talk to the doctors again," Mr. Tazo said, taking Arrabelle's hand. "For you."

"She is *still* alive," Arrabelle said. Then she stepped aside and sent a message to Ember.

>Arrabelle: Lost Boy. Ruth B.
>...Take some time. Get away from this.

EIGHTEEN

Album: One Cell In The Sea

Track: Six

A voice Lux recognized sang from up in the trees.

She ran from the truth
Until the tears stained her cheeks
Then everyone knew what she'd done

She slowed at the edge of a clearing in the forest. She looked up into the branches and stared into the pale eyes of a ghostly boy, a boy she knew. He was strumming his guitar but something was different; now he was looking directly at her. He stood up on the branch, jumped from the tree, and landed next to her.

"Zephyr!" Lux reached out and touched his arm. He was real.

"If that's what you'll call me…" He smiled and touched her cheek. He wiped her tears away. "That's who I'll be. I'm with you. Always have been. There's no need to worry." He led her out of the forest.

"Where are we going?" Lux asked, still crying. They walked quickly. A weight began to lift from her chest.

"The mountain. Right now I need to take you as far from the Crossroads as possible." Zephyr squeezed her hand in assurance. "I won't waste time asking how you escaped, although I am quite curious. I was prepared to go down there and rescue you," he said.

"Rescue me? How?" Lux asked. Something clicked like a lock in her heart.

"I'll explain it all once we're safe inside. And I see you plan to save someone before you leave?" Zephyr pointed to the glass jar Lux was clutching. "I believe there's no greater act of love. So forget what you know of this place. Forget it all as fast as you can."

"Why?" she asked eagerly.

But as they returned to the place she'd come to know, she saw why. Boreloque was no longer. It had been terrorized, burned. There was no sound other than their feet over foliage.

"How long was I down there?" she asked.

"So long that everyone gave up believing you'd get out." He stopped them. He touched her face again. "They'll never believe you got out on your own, either. You've become a fighter." Even in his ghostly figure, he was bigger and stronger up close.

"I have?" Lux was surprised. "Is that what Venia needs from me?" They picked up their pace again.

"Venia doesn't need any more fight in her than she's already got. That's just what brought her down," Zephyr explained. "Love is your quality. That's what she needs. Just love. But you're too afraid to use it, so it's quite unused. You'll never be short on love, so don't ever be afraid of it running out, okay?"

"Okay," Lux whispered.

"Venia is terrified of you. You've triggered her memory. You're the most important thing she needs. But your love is only yours to give, and when you pointed that out to her, you exposed the flaw in her plan. It's the one quality she can't steal, fake, or recreate. She's very angry, as you can see by her retaliation method." Zephyr waved his hand around.

"She destroyed all of this because of me?" Lux was astonished and outraged. She would not let Venia get away with this.

"Yes. She thinks you're alone. And she thinks hurting all of this will weaken you," he said. "Because this is your creation. It was your safe place." He led her to the shore, and helped her through the murky water into a lily pad boat. He rowed them toward the mountain.

"That's impossible," Lux said. "I'd never seen this before. I don't even know how I arrived."

"But it felt like home, didn't it?"

"Not...immediately." But she knew he was right somehow. "Venia must know I'm not alone. You're here with me."

"Venia can't see me. No one knows I'm here but you." He winked at her. "I snuck in a long time ago."

"Oh."

"I promise I'll explain. But we need to settle your unfinished business." Zephyr pointed again to the glass jar Lux was holding. "Do you know what you have to do?"

"I don't know the exact details, but I don't care if I die doing it." She clenched her fist, then looked at her hand. The wound had blackened up to her elbow.

"Okay, then." Zephyr raised his eyebrows. "We'll try. Venia's been after Blaze for so long, but he's been out of love. Until now."

"So she can't get someone's qualities unless they're in love?"

"Exactly," Zephyr said.

"Does Blaze know this?"

"Just me. But Venia knew you'd trigger his memory, too. His heart. Only you didn't fall for each other as quickly as everyone had hoped and expected. You're both guarded. That's why you're here."

"And what if I leave? What will happen to him?"

"Without you, he'll wander. Forever. But if you succeed, everything will be restored. Some things will be undone. You'll see."

"I don't understand." Lux frowned.

"We're almost there."

Death was everywhere, yet he was calm. But when she looked at him, she felt calm, too.

"So because I didn't fall for Blaze, now what?"

"He left you to die and you're returning to save his life. What do you call that? Indifference? You've fallen far...deeply. And I hope you're the one to shatter every jar in that room of hers. It will change time, history, the future."

Lux nodded absentmindedly. She'd have to piece together so much more before fixing anything. She was going to have to get into Venia's mind.

"Is there hope for Venia?" she asked, feeling uncertain.

"She's afraid to die because she's alone. She's in denial. She does still understand a basic truth: love wins and good wins. At least in the end. She wants to be good. But her method is evil."

"Could she ever change?"

"She'd have to give everything back of her own free will. But, here's the catch: Venia is her own captive. It seems an impossible task. You're the last and only one who can help, but you didn't take *her* jar."

"How do you know I'm the last?" Lux asked.

"Because you were also the first," Zephyr said.

"So I need to go back there and get her jar."

"I haven't found any alternatives."

They were moving closer to the mountain. There was an opening at the base that led to a cave. They moved toward it, and as they reached the entrance, the dawn broke behind them.

"Where is everyone?" Lux asked. She looked in the sky for Dreamer's Lane, but saw nothing.

"You mean, where is *he*," Zephyr said.

Lux stared into his eyes. "I just thought maybe he felt the same way about me. I don't understand."

"He does love you. He just thought this was the only way. Because in another time and place you told him it was. He's known you for so long, and so much has happened between the two of you," Zephyr said.

"He's only known me for...moments," Lux stammered.

"Maybe that was enough time for him. But Blaze and Venia, they're complicated. You showed up. Memories surfaced. But that's what was going to happen all along. We all knew it."

Lux didn't ask what he meant, because she was distracted by something floating in the water ahead of them. Zephyr pushed one out of the way with an oar. Horrified, she stared into the deep. Dead Float Coats surrounded their boat. She picked up the whistle around her neck and blew it. Her Float Coat didn't show up. Reluctantly, she removed the necklace and dropped it into the water, then buried her face in her hands.

"We're almost there," Zephyr whispered.

He began to sing to her. She felt like she was in a dream within a dream. But she was very awake and in a very real place. The boat moved into the cave, naturally lit by a violet crystal ceiling and glowing aqua water. It remained untouched by Venia. They reached a dock. Zephyr got out of the boat and secured it to a rock. He helped Lux up, while she held the jar close. She followed him into a small cavern with soft chairs and candlelight.

He led her to a chair and covered her with a blanket. "Rest," he said.

She watched him leave, then took in the room. She was reminded of Pleiades' Den, a lifetime ago. She tried to relax and realized how sore her body was. Every joint and bone felt out of place. Her muscles and her eyes burned. She could hear distant screaming, even though the cavern was silent, save for a rhythmic dripping of water echoing somewhere. She covered her face with the blanket.

Zephyr returned with a bowl of berries. "Ask me anything now," he said.

"You didn't tell me where everyone is," Lux said, her voice muffled through the blanket. She just needed to find Blaze. She knew Zephyr could help.

"They're safe. And I don't think you'll see them here again." He sat down in a chair close to her, picked up his guitar, and began to strum. "I need to get you home soon."

Lux pulled the blanket from her face and sat up. "I am going to save him. Believe me." He nodded. He handed her the bowl, and she took a few berries.

"I have nothing but faith in you," he said.

"So how were you going to rescue me from Venia's Lair?" Lux asked.

"I'd have sent you home right then and there. From the depths." Zephyr smiled. "And I'd have gone away, ceased to exist."

"No, you can't go away. Stay with me."

"I'll be with you. I'll make sure you're home...before it's too late."

"Too late for what?"

"Someone's waiting for you back home. If you show up too late, you won't be there or here. You'll be sent some place new. Your fate will be decided for you."

"But you'll be with me? Wherever I end up?" Lux asked. Zephyr simply smiled. He stopped strumming and took a bite of an apple. She considered his words. He alone would be enough. "And why didn't you talk to me before? I saw you at the party. You wouldn't look at me. You left."

"You didn't recognize me. Not the way you do now. We both needed time," Zephyr explained. He turned his guitar over. He opened a hidden compartment and pulled out a small wooden box. Lux recognized it immediately.

"You took that from the Pram." She took another handful of berries. "It's mine."

"Someone who lives in the Pram took it from me. Regardless, yes it's yours. What's inside will send you home whenever you're ready."

"You said Blaze was out of love," Lux continued. She couldn't forget him.

"He was forced to quiet his heart. The one he loved did not want his love any longer, but he fought her." Zephyr began to strum again. "This went on for quite a long time. Finally he carried on in a state of brokenness, knowing he'd never heal if she didn't."

"Who is she?" Lux asked. She had an idea, but she wouldn't say it aloud. She shivered.

"You were with her recently." He set down his guitar and sighed. "So can I send you home now Lux?" He had grown serious.

"You're coming with me?" She confirmed. She gazed at the glass jar. Maybe everything would just fix itself if she stayed with Zephyr.

"If that's what you want." He handed Lux the box. She touched the jagged wood, thinking about what she knew was inside. It was the answer, and yet she was still waiting.

"Zephyr?" she asked. "Where's home?"

He shrugged. "Somewhere only you know."

Something subtle tugged at her heart. If he would be with her, it would be okay.

Lux unhinged the box. She touched the crumpled note and looked at Zephyr. His eyes slowly turned the color jade. She knew his smile, his voice. She knew home. And she was ready to go back.

"Will you sing to me?" Lux whispered.

She wrapped up in her blanket again. Boreloque began to fade. Home filled her heart. Memories. Childhood. Beauty. Firsts. Zephyr's voice reminded her of all she longed for.

She couldn't fight with anything
Evil with evil was hate for hate
But love overcame
And she saw the light
Love against love proved the battle that won
And she saw the light

That would call her home
What would be waiting for her was a life
A life that showed her she wasn't alone
And she saw the light
She was the light
All it took to ignite was a fight

Zephyr's ghostly figure transformed. He was no longer a secret. Everyone would know who he was, and who he was to her. Flesh. Spirit. Life. A spark. A flame in her heart. She couldn't stop staring into his eyes, which told stories of all she'd forgotten, and a future yet untold.

"How will you get me home?" Lux sighed peacefully as she listened to the music.

"With a kiss," Zephyr answered. He reached out and touched the hand with the burn and the evidence.

And the music stopped.

The glass jar next to her shattered. The beating heart inside spattered blood everywhere. Shards of glass lodged into Lux's face, neck, and arms. She screamed. She'd forgotten Blaze in the presence of Zephyr, who was actually Ember. He wasn't going to let her go so easily.

Zephyr returned to ghostly gray. He backed away from Lux. She picked up the heart in a panic. She heard screaming again and looked around wildly for the source.

"Please! Help me fix this!" She screamed. "I have to find Blaze!" Lux couldn't believe herself. She'd forgotten them. So easily. She could have saved them all. She still could—

"I'll help you." Zephyr grabbed the wooden box. They ran back to the boat and set off.

"You know where he is," she cried. She was damaged, bleeding, and dirty.

"It's not safe, Lux." He spoke over the distant screams.

"Of course not," she cried. She understood completely. Love

was worth the risk, worth fighting for.

They departed the cave and entered a blood red sky. But she knew now exactly where they'd find Blaze. Zephyr rowed the boat through the muddled water. His expression was somber now. He'd tried to protect her, tried to make it easy.

"Tell me about the Crossroads," Lux said desperately. Matter from the pumping vessel soaked between her fingers.

"We're almost there," Zephyr finally spoke.

"What will I need to do?" Lux pleaded. Again she tasted iron and salt. Her throat was dry. When they neared the shore, he jumped out of the boat to pull them in. They began the walk inland. Zephyr held his arm around Lux protectively.

"She's going to ask you to sacrifice yourself," Zephyr said. "That's what happens at the Crossroads. Exchanges."

"Exchanges of what?"

"She'll ask for your soul, plain and simple. Now that she knows she can't steal it, you're going to have to offer yourself willingly."

"And if I don't?" Lux argued indignantly, knowing full well she'd already promised herself to Venia.

"Well, it'll be you, or us. Everyone's known all along it would come to this. Arriving at the Crossroads was a sign that it would end this way if you didn't act on your feelings for Blaze. They tried to convince you, but it was obvious you were harboring feelings for someone else."

"Someone else? What do you call this!" Lux yelled, thrusting the heart in Zephyr's face. "It will always be Blaze!"

"What about me?"

She couldn't answer; she was too confused to make the pieces fit together. Somehow Zephyr was connected to Blaze, but how? Her head was pounding, her heart was breaking, and she wanted to give up.

They stood in a valley. Once they climbed to the other side, they'd be at the Crossroads. She felt sick to her stomach. How could she face them now? She'd left them for dead. Zephyr pulled her close. She couldn't separate the truth from the lies, or one person from another, or Boreloque from the other place. She was torn in every direction. She needed out.

They arrived at the Crossroads. Lux forced herself to remember what she'd learned of it. The state of her heart... Choices she'd already made... She was lost... Who had her heart? She hadn't found out. She was still a thief. It was too late for a remedy.

The red sky turned to ash. Rain began to fall. Lux couldn't wait any longer.

"BLAZE!" She screamed loud enough so that all of Boreloque would hear her. She couldn't be a kitten in the face of a mess that was her own making.

She heard Venia laughing, but she didn't let that stop her. Lux screamed Blaze's name over and over and over until she began to lose her voice.

And then she saw him.

Blaze appeared at the edge of the forest, near where they'd first met. Where he'd saved her. She wanted to run to him then, but her legs wouldn't move. She cried out, reached for him.

"I forgot the box," Zephyr murmured. "You need it. I'll be back." And he was gone.

"It's okay," she cried, fumbling with the heart. She stumbled to the ground. She closed her eyes. Time passed. Strength diminished. Then she felt something. Blaze was standing before her. She looked up at him. The darkness was closing in on them.

"Take off your shirt," she instructed. She couldn't waste another second. She glanced up again, and through thick tears, saw a bare chest with a fresh wound in the shape of an X, sewn sloppily with thick, dark string. She'd have to open it again. She pulled at his arm. He fell. She dropped his heart.

"I'll save you. You'll come with me!" Lux wept uncontrollably, leaning over him. She didn't care that he'd abandoned her. She loved him enough for the both of them. She would give her own heart before she'd let him die.

Lux ripped the stitching from Blaze's chest and separated the wound with her fingers. His labored breathing stung her ears. She picked up the heart. She saw something out of the corner of her eye.

Everyone else. Standing at the edge of the forest. Watching. Their expressions were empty. Chains bound their wrists. They walked slowly, methodically, in unison toward her and Blaze.

"It'll be over soon." Lux breathed fast and unsteady; she couldn't catch her breath. "I'm going to fix you. We'll be fine, all of us."

With all of her strength, she punched Blaze in the chest while holding his heart, causing him to convulse and scream out in pain. Flesh tore. She saw the horrified look in his eyes, and pressed her hands over the wound.

Everyone was moving closer, each of them carrying something. Her eyes were too swollen to see what it was. The earth shook. Venia's piercing scream echoed. She had surfaced. A storm erupted overhead, sending sharp rain driving into earth and flesh. Lux lifted her face to the sky. Rain washed away the blood, freed her hands, and cleansed her face.

"Why didn't you want to save us, Lux?" Someone out of the crowd murmured.

"You didn't love us?"

"Why did you forget us?"

"No!" Lux pleaded. "I'm back! Blaze! You understand!"

She tried to pull Blaze into a standing position. She needed Zephyr. Venia's scream grew closer. Everyone gathered in a circle around Lux and Blaze.

Venia swooped down from the clouds. She stood in the midst of the crowd and faced Lux. She glared menacingly. The edges of her garments blew in the wind and whipped Lux's face. Lux fell to her knees and looked away.

"The thing is," Venia hissed, "you did this to yourself. You did this to him." She rolled her head back and laughed hard.

"I love him!" Lux cried.

"You fool." Venia stopped laughing. "Stop believing in love. Look where it's gotten you. This is simple obsession. Do you think I didn't know your heart? You latch on to whoever is there, because you're afraid to be alone."

"I just wanted to make things right," Lux whispered, sinking to the ground again, bringing Blaze with her.

"Blaze's instructions from me were to create obsession in your heart. He succeeded. You see, Lux, obsession is stronger than love. It'll make you do things out of your own control. I took the best of him for myself, but you didn't even care," Venia rasped. "There is nothing good left, and you still want him."

"That's exactly what love is," Zephyr whispered in Lux's ear. He'd returned. He knelt down next to Lux and placed the box in her hand. "Don't let her get in your head. She knows nothing of love anymore. You're not like her." He took her hand. "And you never will be if you don't want to be."

"There's good in everyone, Venia," Lux cried. "Even after you've robbed us. Even in me. I saw what I'd done, and I came back." She looked past Venia to everyone. "That's love."

"I knew love more than you *ever* will!" Venia spat. "But I learned from it."

Blaze sighed heavily. His gaze remained empty. Returning his heart hadn't restored him. Lux couldn't understand what had gone wrong.

"I know what you're trying to do. You can't steal someone else's love and make it your own! You were loved even when there was no good in you!" Lux pleaded.

This angered Venia. She screamed. Suddenly Lux realized what everyone was holding, because their glass jars shattered in their hands. Every heart fell to the ground and absorbed shrapnel, while the bodies belonging to them bled and writhed. Lux felt the glass on her own body moving deeper into her skin. So delicate, yet so sharp.

"This is what you wanted," Venia sneered. "Everyone's gotten back what I stole. All except for one."

Before Lux knew what was happening, Venia had reached down and was choking her. Blaze was still between them. He lay in a heap, among the others.

"Pleiades, tell Lux the mistake she's made," Venia demanded, pressing her skeletal hands deeper into Lux's neck.

"Lux stole *your* heart. She gave it to Blaze," Pleiades cried to Venia.

Blaze's eyes opened wide. His gaze burned into Lux's. She'd unknowingly given him the heart of their enemy. She'd destroyed them.

Venia roared with laughter and stood up. She raised her gaunt arms victoriously. The wind from the storm strengthened. Sand from the shore crept over the hills and began to blow wildly around them. Lux covered her eyes and crawled away slowly. Suddenly she was numb. Her mind went blank. Her soul was empty. She was coming to the end of herself. Blaze reached for her arm. She saw a hint of recognition return to his eyes.

"You belonged to someone else all along," Blaze managed to say. "In another time and place. You pretended with me."

"I never wanted to hurt you," Lux said. But when she spoke the words, she wondered if she was speaking to Venia. She continued anyway. "I love you, but nothing makes sense. Maybe there is someone else; I don't know. There must be another time, another place."

"Lovers united, but only for a moment," Venia mused, standing over them.

"Don't be afraid," Zephyr moved between Lux and Blaze. He took Lux's hand. She pushed him out of the way and crawled back to Blaze, covering herself further in deep shards. She held him close. Time had run out. Rain washed over them.

"I'll do anything," Lux sobbed, hiding her face in his shoulder. "Take *my* heart."

"You both lose. Mine forever, never together. All mine." Venia licked her lips hungrily. She pulled Lux and Blaze to a standing position. Lux's knees buckled, but she held him up. "But I will be forgiving in one area. Grace *is* my name, after all. What would I be if I didn't offer it, at least? I will forgive you for the future. You are what makes me who I am. You made me strong. Don't you see? I'm you."

"Just take my heart and keep me! Let them go." Lux was losing the fight.

Venia suddenly thrust Lux aside and shoved her fist through Blaze's back. Every rib shattered as she grasped the heart inside him. She ripped it away with a vengeance, then proceeded to push it back through the front of his chest and held it up, lifting him off the ground. Lux's face was covered with his blood once again. Blaze hung lifeless, his face frozen in agony. Lux felt her own heart stop.

"Thank you for reminding me," Venia scoffed. "I still haven't gotten your heart. You keep saying I can have it, but you're still hiding from me. If you truly wanted to save your friends *and* your lover, the sacrifice is a *willing* soul. Come out, come out..."

There was a bottom line at the Crossroads. Evil. And in the end she just couldn't do it. She couldn't bring herself to sacrifice her own soul. Not for Venia. Not for anyone. The exchange wouldn't fix them. It would only buy her time. Full or empty, she knew it was time to go.

Lux tried to get up, to run from the scene. She slipped on the glass and wet grass, shredding her feet as she went. She fell on her back and the last bits of air escaped her lungs. Glass punctured her shoulder blades.

She'd landed by the Legend Pool. A lock of her hair slipped into the waters, which jealously pulled her in. Her face was immersed. Zephyr was by her side again.

"It's almost over," she heard distantly. She began to feel the earth below her thumping, beating methodically. The beat of a heart. Venia was approaching. This was it.

"Not yet, Lux," Zephyr whispered. He drew her head from the water, but the pool continued to fight and pull her back in. "Don't give in yet. Not yet." The water gave way. She surfaced to find his face touching hers. He kissed her forehead.

"Who are you?" Lux struggled to speak.

"I'm the one who wants you home," Zephyr responded.

"How will I know it's home?" She whimpered.

"You'll see me there. Remember the box," he implored.

"Tell Blaze I love him," Lux said, and struggled to breathe. "Tell him I'm sorry." Her body was limp. "And I love you..." She wanted to touch Zephyr's face, feel him there.

"We know now," Zephyr said. He leaned in close to her face.

"Who are you?" she whispered again. But she didn't hear his answer over the chaotic buzz. She needed to hear it. She needed to make sure before she left. "Don't leave me," she cried. She turned her head to see Blaze again. Pleiades had crawled over to him and was now holding him.

The pool tugged Lux back in again; it had changed, and the water forced her eyes open.

She saw a room. A small, cold room.

Zephyr was in the room.

But it wasn't Zephyr. It was, in fact, a boy she knew named Ember Sweeney.

But...he was with a girl she knew. Maybe it was Pleiades. But it couldn't be. It was all wrong. She couldn't be seeing that... them...together. The memories were broken, pieced together incorrectly. What Lux saw and what she knew, quickly caused a new pain, so agonizing that her own scream was unrecognizable to her. She didn't want to be anywhere now. She wanted to cease to exist.

She struggled, helpless against the swirling pool drowning her. She could no longer feel Zephyr. She breathed no more.

Venia appeared standing over Lux. She paused and craned her neck. She reached down and grabbed Lux's black, burned hand. She laughed hysterically.

"And anyone who saw this, *knew* how it would end. They knew and they didn't tell you. I had you from the beginning." And then she wasted no time ripping the soul from its home.

"THIS BELONGS TO ME, BECAUSE YOU ARE MINE! You. Are. Me. This is mine, and I am your future. The demon in you is just a piece of me." And with that, Venia swept away and everything was made clear. But Lux could do nothing about anything. It was too late. It was over. She was dead. The weight she'd carried around Boreloque, the pressure weighing her down, had finally crushed her.

Lux wished Zephyr would let go of her hand, now that she knew who he really was. If only she could see Blaze's face one more time, just to make sure. She didn't want to believe either of them were who they said they were. That would mean Lux was who Venia said she was. She was afraid again. Angry and bitter, hurt and alone, and filled with fear was such a wretched state to die, but here she was.

Then she heard a voice again, a song. She gave in, comforted by no control of her own. The afterlife was singing to her.

Come back to me, whispered the voice.

"I'm trying!" She wanted to scream. But she had no words. Who was calling? Who would want her now? Death wanted her.

She felt something. The sting of losing her heart. It was vast. She opened her eyes for one last look into the bubbling pool that had taken her life. A last look into the eyes of her betrayers. Now they were even. But they were all broken, and not one single thing had been fixed.

The pain of seeing home was not what she'd expected. It grew so much stronger than the feeling of the deepest wound Venia could inflict. Lux had to move. Somewhere. Somehow.

She ripped through the veil shielding her from the other world she was staring into. And then she found herself there. Boreloque was no more.

When you feel that warm breeze, you'll know it's me. It won't be dark forever, she heard as she broke through.

She breathed hard. Deeply. Cut. Burned. Pain. Healing.

Everything. Nothing. Dead. Alive.

Home.

Lux was back. She wondered instantly, desperately, if she could choose Boreloque again over what she saw. Boreloque was less painful than this.

She was on her back. Restrained. Not an ounce of strength to fight. It angered her. She closed her eyes again, trying to focus. How had she ended up here? She couldn't make a sound. She was restless. She struggled. To breathe. To find her voice. To be acknowledged.

Her head hurt from falling. Her heart hurt from losing. She had to make sense of what the hell she was seeing. What she was seeing was not what she'd left behind, she was sure of it. Ember and Anya together? This was wrong. This wasn't what she'd returned for. This wasn't the promise. But this was what she was seeing. She looked at him. The pain was too much. She closed her eyes again. She didn't want to see. She would rather be lost and empty, and somewhere in between.

NINETEEN

Album: Bleed American

Track: Six

Snow fell steadily from the darkening sky. On this late afternoon it created a blanket over Briar Heights. This would be her last night. Her last snowfall. Last show. If only she knew. Farewell.

School was officially dismissed for the weekend, but nobody left Briar Heights Academy.

Ember wanted to go home and sleep. Alone. Forever. He decided he'd rather accept the news from a distance. Now he found himself alone in the room with Lux again. It was eerily quiet. He looked out the window. Darkness. He turned toward Lux.

He just wanted them to see her. Sure, he'd be in trouble. But what more could go wrong? He didn't give a damn. She looked peaceful enough, even beyond the tubes and monitors. He wanted them to see her this way, not in a casket with a false sleep on her young face. Astor had slipped out again with Arrabelle, so he had a few minutes, at least.

"My plan was to wake her up," he said to the camera. "I believed she'd come back if she heard the same songs every day. Music unites us. It's why I do what I do...it fixes what gets lost and broken between us. But that's failing us now. Anyway, this is the first one I sang to her, and maybe it'll be the last."

Ember approached the camera and zoomed out so all of the room was visible. He took a deep breath, knowing he could be caught any moment. He picked up his guitar and moved a chair up next to Lux's bed like he'd done every day.

Come back to me
I wish you could see
How sad this place is without you
We need you

Back at BHA, the students, teachers, and parents were talking and mingling, while Ember stayed in the background. Duffy made her way back to the stage. She took photos of the tributes to Lux. She would show them to Ember someday. She could see by the look on his face that it would be over soon. It was time to get back. Tanner, Jamison, and Luther joined her and leaned against the stage facing the screen.

The auditorium went silent. Lux Tazo. Visible.

"What the hell is he doing?" Luther muttered.

"Of course. Ember's going rogue," Jamison said, and threw his hands in the air.

"Let's get back," Duffy said as she pulled her coat on.

"We need to be with him for the rest of this," Tanner said. He put his phone away.

"The rest of this?" Luther repeated. "No, he's done. This is over *now*. He knew better."

"Yeah, it's bad," Tanner agreed and shook his head.

"Tanner, you need to worry about finding Anya. She needs you. You think Ember Sweeney can be a shoulder for her to cry on right now?" Jamison said.

The rest of them hurriedly pulled on coats and hats. Tanner turned around slowly then, and stared at the screen. He shook his head. Again. And again. He watched very closely as Ember moved to the end of Lux's bed. A murmur grew throughout the auditorium.

"TANNER! Let's go!" Jamison shouted. But Tanner didn't hear him. Instead he reached for the nearest body, which was Duffy.

"How...?" Tanner breathed. Duffy looked at the screen, and blinked in disbelief.

"Help!" Duffy shouted frantically. "EMBER!" She covered her mouth with her hands. Tears fell as she rushed into Luther's arms.

"Call — Ember," Luther stammered.

Duffy, Jamison, and Luther pulled out their phones and tried to call Ember, who, of course was nowhere near his phone. Tanner made a different call.

"Anya, get to Lux. NOW!" Tanner demanded nervously. He began pacing.

Commotion spread through the auditorium. Everyone saw. Shouts and screams and cheers and gasps erupted among hundreds of people gathered. Everyone watched expectantly. The screen went black.

From inside the hospital, all was calm. But Anya, who'd been sitting on the floor in the hallway near the nurses station, answered her phone. She stood up slowly and walked into Lux's room. She dropped her phone. Ember looked at her, standing in the doorway, and his expression changed. He stopped playing.

"What is it...?" he asked. He couldn't look where she was looking. He was too afraid. He wasn't ready for it to be over. Tears streamed from her wide eyes, but her expression was blank.

Anya slowly moved toward Lux's bed. Ember finally turned and saw what she saw. He saw what the rest of the world was seeing.

Lux was moving.

She shuddered, tossing slowly, turning as if trying to break free of breathing tubes and intravenous drips and much too long a sleep. Lux's eyes fluttered. Anya and Ember stood at the foot of her bed, embracing each other and watching in disbelief. She seemed to make momentary eye contact with Ember.

It seemed everything was happening too slowly. Anya moved to the wall and pressed the emergency button. In seconds, doctors and nurses filled the room, as well as the Tazo family. Ember and Anya were shoved aside.

Lux continued to struggle, becoming hysterical, trying to break free. She was grabbing at everything attached to her and appearing to be in extreme pain. A few short, scratchy cries escaped her throat, but she revealed a sharp, strong voice. She was awake, alive. She was back.

"Get these kids out of here now!" a doctor shouted.

Anya and Ember couldn't move. They hadn't moved for two months. They continued to embrace, trying to catch a glimpse of what was happening. Ember closed his eyes. He couldn't stop shaking. A doctor moved out of the way just as Ember looked up again, and he got a clear view of her. Lux's eyes were open wide and she made distinct eye contact with him this time. She stared him down. Then her eyes rolled back in her head. Tears streamed down her face.

A nurse forced Ember and Anya out of the room. Ember's father and Astor joined them in the hallway, and a moment later, the rest of the Tazo family did too. Everyone huddled together. Nobody spoke.

Ember left the hospital that night feeling like a ghost, or at least as though he'd seen one. He felt much older. He felt lost, very lost. Over the past two months, something in the hope he'd held onto had carried him from youth into adulthood. It was like a warm wind, a zephyr. Then it quickly passed; the warm wind departed and he was left covered in chills. Knowledge. While he knew he should be ecstatic, he was shaken.

The Sweeney family, which now included Anya, was bombarded by news crews, who wanted to know anything and everything Ember would share.

"What would you say happened here?" A woman shoved a microphone in his face.

"Please, give him space," Mr. Sweeney said. He held his hand firmly and protectively in front of Ember and Anya.

"Have you spoken with Lux?"

"Does she feel the same way you do?"

"What does this mean for Falling Like Ember?"

"Are you in love?"

Ember was speechless. To begin with, it bewildered him that these people knew so much, or anything, for that matter. He couldn't imagine how anyone besides the students and faculty at Briar Heights Academy could know about his farewell show.

Someone pushed him into the backseat of his father's car. Anya got in on the other side, and Mr. Sweeney quickly followed. Ember rolled down the window slightly. Snow crept inside and fell on his cheeks. The news crews hovered around the vehicle.

"How do you feel?" One reporter shouted.

Ember faced the strangers pointing microphones in his face. He rolled the window down further and shivered as the cold hit him. Finally he just shrugged and shook his head. He was numb. He was out of words. He had nothing left to give. His father kept looking in the rear view mirror but said nothing. No one said anything.

Ember Sweeney had just poured his heart out to the world,

saying goodbye to a girl who was now not going anywhere. Lux had survived. This was the best news. But the best news still brought mixed emotions. It was awkward. The world felt small. He would be known for this.

When the three of them arrived home, it was only early evening, but it felt like the middle of the night. They stood in the parlor near the stairs. Anya handed Ember his phone, which had been charged. Hundreds of text messages were waiting for him.

"What can I do?" Mr. Sweeney asked. He grasped Ember's shoulder and hugged Anya. She finally broke down. Ember sat down on the stairs while Mr. Sweeney led her to the couch and covered her with a blanket.

"You live here now," he said. He smoothed her hair. "I don't want you living alone anymore. We're your family."

Mr. Sweeney turned to Ember, who nodded.

"I'm going to get her room ready," Mr. Sweeney said. "Ember, what can I do? Anything?"

"No," was all Ember could muster. He yawned and suddenly felt the weight of the world on his shoulders. He was exhausted. He hadn't hung his head until now.

"Get some rest. We'll sort everything out," Mr. Sweeney said with a tired but encouraging smile. Ember found no comfort.

"Okay." He nodded. He climbed the stairs behind his father.

"Ember?" Mr. Sweeney turned around. "Everything's going to be different now. It'll be okay."

Ember crawled under the covers of his bed and scrolled through the messages on his phone. He was looking for something from Arrabelle. But before he found anything from her, he read a group message from the band, which had just come through.

Duffy: Your Song. Ellie Goulding.
Jamison: Ho Hey. The Lumineers.
Luther: First Day of My Life. Bright Eyes.
Tanner: Blessed. Brett Dennen.

While he was debating what to share, Anya wrote in the group message.

Anya: Life Is Wonderful. Jason Mraz.
Ember: Let There Be Morning. The Perishers.
Ember: In Other Words. Ben Kweller.

He continued scrolling through until he found Arrabelle. She'd written a few times. But the most recent message was all he needed to see.

Arrabelle: You'll Be Okay. A Great Big World.
Arrabelle: Romeo & Juliet. Monte Montgomery.
Ember: Only a Man. Jonny Lang.
Ember: The Crossroads. Eric Clapton/Cream.
Voodoo Chile (Slight Return), Stevie Ray Vaughan
& Double Trouble.
Arrabelle: Somewhere Only We Know. Keane.

Ember turned his phone off again and rolled over in bed. He was too tired, too overwhelmed, for sleep. While he usually drifted off to a song, there was just nothing he could put into words or music that would make sense of his life in the moment. He needed silence. He tossed and turned for hours.

All of Lux and Ember's friends, and even those who didn't know them, went out and celebrated all night. They retreated to the Sour Enchantment, immediately reliving the story that was still unfinished. The auditorium at Briar Heights Academy went dark. Lux's memorial remained.

TWENTY

Album: Happenstance

Track: Five

Lux was awake for only a few moments that Friday night, but that was enough. She fell in and out of sleep for the next few days. She was in pain. She hadn't spoken, but was stable.

After the weekend of close monitoring, examinations, tests and assessments, the doctors were able to give a clear update to the Tazo family. They explained that there was some brain damage, but most likely she would eventually fully recover. She suffered from memory loss. But only time would tell, as she gained strength, what the extent of it was. Her recovery could take a long time. And her family would need to be patient and supportive. Furthermore, the doctors wanted to wait until Lux was more alert before anyone other than her family visited again. Her complete recovery was the new priority.

Mr. Tazo had called Mr. Sweeney from the hospital that

morning while Ember was still asleep. He explained everything he knew and ended with the comment that Lux was not ready for visitors. Mr. Sweeney, while an agreeable man, did argue that it was Anya and Ember who'd been by Lux's side daily, and it seemed unfair that they'd now been reduced to visitors. Mr. Tazo didn't disagree with him, but didn't stick up for them either. He did at least promise to call them whenever there was a change: an improvement, or something newsworthy. That was better than nothing.

Ember and Anya didn't attempt to visit the hospital. They were exhausted. They were snowed in anyway, which was a blessing in disguise for everyone. They stayed home, in their respective bedrooms, while Mr. Sweeney cared for them, bringing food and occasional updates.

School resumed as usual the following Monday. Everything at Briar Heights Academy seemed to fall back into place, but there was an underlying excitement in everyone's hearts. Together they'd witnessed a miracle. They celebrated while the ones they were celebrating had gone home alone. The students and staff felt united, unaware that the ones who'd united them seemed to be falling apart again. Nobody could explain it, so they couldn't stop talking about it. December fifth was now referred to as Farewell Friday. Had Ember really brought Lux back? Would she have woken up all along?

Ember and Anya stuck together at school, especially during Common Room Time. They felt strangely forgotten, even though everyone kept watching them. The week dragged on for them and flew by for everyone else. While the rest of Briar Heights Academy was finishing final projects and preparing for holiday break, the two best friends were standing by, just as they had been for the past two months. They just wanted to see her, and they were waiting for the call from Mr. Tazo that the time had come.

But that didn't happen. Instead, when they got home from

school one afternoon, Mr. Tazo was in the Sweeney's kitchen with Ember's father. He didn't appear sad or upset, so Ember sat down with them. Anya avoided them, but watched from the corner of the kitchen. She filled a tea kettle with water.

"I wanted to give you an update in person," Mr. Tazo said. Ember waited. Anya listened in, pretending to be occupied. She lit a burner on the stove and opened a box of tea.

"Lux is improving. Little by little, she's remembering. If she continues on this path, she could be home by the New Year. In the best case scenario, maybe even Christmas." Anya took a few steps closer to where they were sitting. "She'll still have physical therapy and rehabilitation, and things —"

"That's paramount," Ember said, trying to sound upbeat.

"There is one concern, though. It involves the two of you," Mr. Tazo said cautiously.

"What is it?" Ember asked immediately. Anya crossed her arms but said nothing.

"Lux seems to think, well, she's upset." He turned to Mr. Sweeney then, and he didn't look at the kids. "Apparently she does remember what she felt for Ember, and she does remember Anya... But she seems to think the two of them have had some sort of affair, and she feels very angry about it. She's convinced they both betrayed her. Now, we've tried to explain a few things to her...not the farewell show, or anything like that yet, of course. At the moment, however, she doesn't believe us, and she doesn't want to see Ember or Anya." Mr. Tazo turned back to them, a pained look on his face. "I'm so sorry, kids."

"What?" Ember shouted. "No!"

Anya ran from the room and up the stairs without a word. Ember decided to go after her. When he reached the top of the stairs, he saw that her door was closed. He went into his room and found the journal belonging to Anya and Lux on his pillow. He sat down on his bed and began to read.

The band arrived a few minutes later. Ember overheard Mr.

Sweeney explain to them what had happened. He stayed in his bedroom. The boys and Duffy agreed that they'd go down and practice, and leave Ember and Anya alone. This was difficult for them, because Falling Like Ember had become larger than life overnight, and they had a lot of things to discuss.

Ember hadn't exactly gotten the girl. And he hadn't even expected to get her in the end, but now the details were floating in the air somewhere, untouched. He was cautious. And he had to admit, the warnings the guys had given him during the two months Lux was in a coma had been accurate. With or without her, he had to go on. Falling Like Ember was not actually about Lux Tazo. It couldn't be. Especially now.

Anya: Maybe. Ingrid Michaelson.
Tanner: Bring My Love Home. Brendan James.
Luther: Send Me An Angel. Thrice.
Duffy: OK. Holly Conlan.
Jamison: Last Kiss. Pearl Jam.
Ember: Gone Gone Gone (Done Moved On).
Robert Plant & Alison Krauss.

"How about Christmas Eve at our place?" Mr. Sweeney and Ember were at the grocery store weaving through heavy traffic of holiday shoppers.

"With whom?" Ember asked carefully.

"The Thanksgiving crew. Everyone. What do you think?"

"What about the Tazos?" Ember asked nervously. Mr. Sweeney placed his arm on Ember's shoulder as they came around to the coffee aisle.

"We've survived so far, haven't we?" Mr. Sweeney said brightly. "It'll be okay."

"Okay," Ember said. "I'll tell everyone at school tomorrow."

"I'll call their parents. I'd like to host a neighborhood cocktail hour on Christmas Eve, too. Then maybe a big dinner Christmas day. It could be another new tradition," Mr. Sweeney suggested. Ember could see how much it meant to his father. They needed a full house for the holidays.

Two and a half weeks had passed since Farewell Friday. Tuesday arrived, the last day of school before winter break. The students of Briar Heights Academy had the next three weeks free. As usual, Tanner, Luther, Jamison, and Duffy joined Ember and Anya after school to practice and hang out.

"So, when's she coming home?" Luther asked. He stared out the kitchen window into the backyard.

"I don't know," Ember said. He left the room.

Everyone then turned to Anya, but she simply shrugged and stared at the ground. Then they heard Ember pounding on his drum kit in the basement.

"Well, who'd have ever thought it'd turn out like this?" Jamison exclaimed and laughed sarcastically.

"Can you be nice for once?" Anya glared at him.

"It's not over," Tanner said. He sat down at the table and put his arm around her.

"It's true," Duffy piped up. "This still isn't over. It can only get better..." she said.

"Maybe she'll be home by Christmas!" Luther offered.

"Yeah, right," Jamison said, and rolled his eyes. "Christmas Eve is tomorrow. *Don't* get Ember's hopes up. Hey, should we make "Girlfriend in a Coma" our opening song for the summer tour?"

Duffy shot out of her chair and walked over to Jamison. She punched him very hard in the face so that blood sprayed from his nose.

"That's enough!" she screamed. Jamison swore at her and ran into the bathroom around the corner from the kitchen. Everyone looked at each other and shared shrugs and smiles.

"How are we supposed to act if she does come home, or comes

here?" Duffy asked, as if nothing had just happened. "We should probably have a plan so we don't overwhelm her."

"Yeah, she hangs out with us now," Tanner added. "But she doesn't even know it."

Jamison returned then with a handful of tissue over his face. He glared at Duffy and sat down.

"Hey Jamo, how are things working out for you and Piper Speedman?" Luther asked pointedly.

"She's got some stuff going on right now," Jamison said defensively.

"Yeah, like spreading rumors about all of us," Duffy said.

"Can't wait 'til she's on the inside of this circle." Tanner whistled under his breath.

"It's just taking some time!" Jamison shouted.

"Exactly," Luther warned. "So how about you be a little more supportive about the Lux situation, at least for the sake of the rest of us, because we do care. Not another word. Got it?"

"Let's practice," Tanner said. He stood up and left the kitchen. The guys followed him.

Duffy stayed with Anya. Anya opened a box of craft supplies. The girls sorted through odds and ends for the centerpieces.

"Thanks for punching Jamison," Anya said casually.

"You're welcome. I'm not sure it will change him, though," Duffy said.

"Oh, it won't."

"How are you doing?" Duffy asked carefully. "Are you okay?" She gathered red and green construction paper, and debated between scissors and cutouts. Anya sat at the table and watched Duffy work. She shook her head.

"I guess not; I'm not okay. But I live here now. It's starting to feel like I have a family again, and that's amazing," Anya said. "I anticipated every scenario except for this. It was Ember and me. We were the ones who believed. Well, he did, and I pretended to. Now we can't even see her?" She shrugged sadly. "How could she ever think that we'd do that to her? And why does she think it?"

"Then it's time for a fresh start," Duffy said slowly. "That wouldn't be the worst thing, would it? She needs to know who both of you really are, and who we are, too. We have to try."

"We're talking about Ember Sweeney," Anya said. "All this time — she thought he was with you, Duff. This doesn't make sense."

"What if I talk to her?" Duffy suggested. "I could be the one to explain everything."

"You could try," Anya admitted. "I don't see how it could hurt now. But I don't know how you'll be able to reach her."

"Don't you dare give up! Not you or Ember. We've come too far," Duffy said. "If I've learned anything from this and from you two, it's to speak up. In the moment, right?"

When Anya didn't reply, Duffy set down her crafts and grabbed Anya by the shoulders. "Eventually she'll remember. She will know the truth! I won't let you give up. It's going to work out," she said desperately. She walked over to the kitchen window. "I'm going over there right now."

It was over before it started. Duffy shuffled back to Ember's house after a brisk exchange with Mrs. Tazo, who'd treated Duffy like a stranger.

Ember opened the door, saw the look on Duffy's face, and sat down on the snowy front step. He cleared a spot next to him and she sat down. She said nothing.

"I don't know if we can fix this one," Ember said. He stared at the ground, leaning forward, hands folded. Duffy leaned her head on his shoulder.

"This isn't how it's supposed to end!" she pleaded into the crisp air.

"I didn't make the right wish," Ember said. "I only wished for her to wake up, but I didn't follow through." His breath floated away.

"Make a new wish," Duffy suggested. "Don't wish for a happy

ending, because that still involves an ending. We all keep talking about the end. Why? Shouldn't this be a beginning? Make a new wish. That's all."

"Should I just be happy that I got the one wish?" Ember asked. "What more could we have asked for? If it's meant to happen —"

"Since when do you sit around and wait for things to happen? You're Ember Sweeney...take the stage!" Duffy punched his arm. "Ask for more. Ask for everything! Why not? This is not about *that* wish; we all made that wish. The whole world made that wish on Farewell Friday. And because of what everyone saw, they believed in the two of you; they believed in love. She woke up because of your love for her. I'll show her the evidence myself." She eyed Ember cautiously.

"Don't," Ember said. "Maybe I do just need an ending. I just need to know. Then I can move on from this." He sighed.

"No." Duffy's eyes welled up. "Don't sell yourself short. You are not alone."

Ember just needed to get to Lux, apart from her family. He needed closure, a final conversation. He would sit her down. In person. Yes, that's what he'd do.

TWENTY ONE

Album: Speak For Yourself

Track: Nine

Lux sat on the couch in a room that had apparently been hers for nearly three months. She stared out the window. She was alone, waiting for her father to pick her up and finally take her home. It was the morning of Christmas Eve. She'd been awake for three weeks. She was still quite physically weak, but well enough to go home. The doctors had decided that the best thing for Lux was to be re-introduced to her life there.

She was still confused. She had been very surprised to wake up in a hospital. With memory loss. It was a strange sensation; she wasn't sure what it was she couldn't remember, but she knew nothing added up, and it made her angry. The hardest thing of all was the image of Anya Jensen and Ember Sweeney in her mind. It was killing her. She didn't want to talk about any of it.

The weeks awake had filled quickly with rehabilitation,

tests, and therapy. But no one had come to visit her. As angry as she was, she wanted someone she knew to burst through the door and force themselves back into her life, and by someone, she meant Ember. She didn't know why, but she wanted him to fight for her. It took days after waking to find her voice, to form meaningful words, and to piece together her version of her life and her story. But everyone tried to convince her of a different story. She'd been in a coma for two months. Her life had been put on hold. That's where she knew everyone was wrong. So much more had happened than what everyone was telling her. It had changed who she was and how she would live from now on.

Lux remembered odd things. She told the doctors memories of being born, and about things that happened when she was just a toddler. She remembered when Arrabelle was a child. She remembered the family cat Fellini that died when Lux was three years old. And she was angry about all of it because what she was really frustrated about was how she'd left Boreloque. It did help to talk with the therapist about it, although she was reluctant at first.

"I needed to save them, especially Blaze. I love him," Lux told her therapist Patricia. "When I was there, I couldn't *not* love. But in the end, the more I gave, the more I lost. I believe Boreloque is real, but I don't know how to get back. And I need to go back."

"Who is Blaze?"

"Well, he's...he — he's connected to Zephyr, somehow. I thought Zephyr would never leave me, but he did. I feel stupid. He took a piece of me."

"Talk about Zephyr."

"He was with me the whole time. Until I...came back here. I don't know where he went. He was supposed to be here."

Lux tried to share as much as she could with Patricia, because she never wanted to forget Boreloque. She needed to get back to save everyone, and figure out what to do about Venia. But Boreloque faded a little bit with each passing day, even if the pain of it didn't. Patricia asked her to write about it. So she did, whenever she could, with as much detail as she could grasp. But writing didn't quite help. She had to find a way back.

After a week of talking only about Boreloque, the doctors attempted to introduce a new subject: Lux's life at home. Her family, Briar Heights Academy, hobbies, and friends. She didn't speak at all the first day. But by the next day, she was ready.

"I hate Ember Sweeney. And Anya Jensen." Lux crossed her arms. There was an unmistakable look of dismay on Patricia's face for just a moment. "And side note, they're *not* a good couple. They won't get along, and it'll never last. I don't even want to know how or why they ended up together. I really hate them both. And no, I can't remember why. But...he was supposed to —"

Choose me, was how she wanted to finish the sentence, but that didn't make sense. And every time she thought about Ember, she thought about how Blaze had betrayed her, and how Zephyr had abandoned her.

"I don't trust my family," Lux continued, taking advantage of the silence. "They don't believe in me. I don't need them."

"Why don't we take one step back? How do you know Ember Sweeney?"

"He's my neighbor."

"What about Anya Jensen?"

"She goes to my school. They both do."

"How do you know they're a couple?"

"I saw them together. Here. Right in front of me."

"Were you friends with either of them?"

"Maybe..."

"Did you ever feel differently about Ember before you hated him?" Patricia asked with a hint of desperation in her voice.

Lux stared at her. She couldn't answer because she had an overwhelming desire to admit her love for him. And that was absurd. She didn't think she should have any feeling for him...and anyway, she needed time to get over both Zephyr and Blaze.

"What's the last thing you remember before you went to Boreloque?"

"Leaves…"

"What color were the leaves?"

"Orange. And music; I do remember music. So much music."

"What kind of music?"

Lux shook her head. She wasn't sure. The thought of music frustrated her.

The doctors and the Tazos did eventually tell Lux that early in October, she had walked home from school with Ember Sweeney. She and Ember liked each other very much. She was supposed to go to his concert that night with her best friend Anya. Ember was going to ask her out, and she was going to say yes. But she'd fallen from her tree house during a thunder storm right before his show. And then she slept for two months. She found all of this hard to believe. Especially the last part, because she knew she hadn't fallen; she'd flown to Boreloque.

By now, Lux liked her therapist. Patricia listened intently to everything she said and didn't judge her at all. Lux was comfortable enough to say whatever she wanted. She could tell Patricia genuinely wanted to help. But Lux felt as though they were getting nowhere.

"There's someone I need to see," Lux said one afternoon during a session. "Can you get me out of here for a while?" She was sick of talking about everyone. She wanted to see someone, someone who'd always made sense, had always been real and honest with her. Patricia said she had an idea, and promised an answer by the next day. Lux lay awake half the night. She was excited.

"I found someone who wants to help you." Patricia offered a lengthy pause. "This person is willing to take you wherever you need to go."

"Who is it?" Lux asked, intrigued.

"Arrabelle."

"Oh."

"Hear me out. She wants to help you. She says she won't tell your parents. And she's called me every day to ask about how you're doing. Are you comfortable with this?"

Lux thought about it. She knew Arrabelle could help. It wouldn't have to be for long. It wasn't like they'd have to go shopping, or to the spa. And she liked the idea that their parents wouldn't know. She agreed.

♪

"Wait, I thought we were going to my school." Lux watched out the window from the passenger seat of Arrabelle's Audi S7.

"It's Saturday. He won't be there. But I know where he is."

They drove across town. Arrabelle kept busy with the music. She didn't say much.

"Are you two hanging out again?" Lux asked, suddenly guarded.

"I've been seeing a lot of his best friend lately, so you know how it goes. We end up in the same places." Arrabelle found another song and turned up the volume. "Listen to this. It reminds me of you."

Lux looked at the screen on the dashboard.

```
The Guy That Says Goodbye To You Is Out Of His Mind
by Griffin House.
```

One thing about Arrabelle hadn't changed. She'd always had the ability to find obscure older music that Lux ended up loving and applying somewhat obsessively to her own life.

They pulled into the empty parking lot of the Sour Enchantment and listened to the rest of the song.

"I can wait here..." Arrabelle offered. Lux thought that was kind of her. It wasn't the sister she remembered.

"Come with me," Lux said.

Arrabelle came around and helped Lux out of the car. They

walked very slowly to the main entrance and knocked. Astor opened the door. He and Arrabelle embraced, but said nothing. He whispered something that Lux couldn't hear. Then he hugged Lux. They walked inside and Astor closed the door behind them.

He was sitting at the bar.

"Jackson," Lux said timidly. He turned on his barstool and stared at her. He got up and walked toward her, looking worried. Then he glanced uncertainly at Arrabelle, who smiled and nodded. She followed Astor back into his office.

"Lux," he said softly. "Hey kid. You're okay?" He embraced her, and she thought she felt him crying. He backed away to look at her again and then helped her to a chair. She felt an urgency to tell him absolutely everything. She knew he would have the right words. He was her oldest friend.

"Well, I'm an escapee," Lux began. "So my time is limited. It's nice; my sister helping me out. I just needed to see you."

"How can I help?"

"Can you tell me about myself? I just…need to know who I am. Nothing makes sense. I'm so mad…" She began to cry. Jackson handed her a bar napkin.

"Well, you're sweet, kind, and a loyal friend. You are loved. You're a very talented painter," he stated. "And *you* have a lot to offer this world. But you struggle to believe in what you're capable of. You're learning to trust yourself and your instincts."

"Can I tell you something?" she asked. She would never tell her family, she felt like she had no friends share with, and something told her not to tell Patricia. "I just need to say it. Out loud."

"Anything."

"I loved him. I just did." Lux shook her head. Her heart broke all over again as soon as she said it. "I loved him."

Jackson sat back in his chair. "Lux, I've seen you shake your head a lot over the years. You know that doesn't change anything, right?" He was smiling. She laughed through her tears. "The things I just told you about yourself are true. Accept it. And if you loved someone before, is there a reason you can't now?"

"I know you hear the rumors, Jackson. Don't make me say it!"

"Say what? What rumor?" He pushed a plate of fries between them and she took a few.

"If you must know, I had a thing for Ember Sweeney."

"Such a casual confession. But, yes, everyone knows that," Jackson joked. Lux gaped at him. "I'm kidding! But I knew."

"Okay. So I liked him. Too much. And then this whole coma thing happened. And he went and moved on...with my best friend!"

"Where do you get that idea?" he asked. "Because I have been in school, and you haven't, and I haven't heard that at all. In fact —"

"I just know," Lux interrupted. "And I'm having trouble letting it go. Nothing helps. I can't make sense of it in my head. It's haunting me."

"I think you may be wrong."

"Well, what should I do?"

"Go to the source," Jackson said simply. "You'll be going home soon, right? He's next door. Find him. Tell him how you felt, or still feel. See where he stands now."

"I don't know...that's scary." Lux began to feel nervous. She smiled at Jackson although she was still so frustrated. She kind of liked the idea of seeing Ember face to face. Maybe she'd feel better if she yelled at him. Told him things.

"If you confronted Ember Sweeney, would it be the scariest thing you've ever done?" He asked.

"No," Lux answered quickly. She could think of much scarier things she'd encountered recently.

"So, how bad could it be? You have nothing to lose. I'm right, aren't I?" He nudged her, and she smiled sheepishly. Then she nodded toward the kitchen.

"What's with those two?"

"Something." He grinned. "Your sister was really worried about you. She's not so bad. I think she's quite fond of you."

Lux nodded.

"Oh, while I have you here, Lux. There's something else I want to talk to you about."

"What is it?" she asked. He seemed very serious all of a sudden.

"I entered one of your pieces in a competition. The one hanging on the wall in your hospital room." Lux's heart sank, but she didn't even know why. "It didn't win."

"Oh." She sat back and let it sink in. "Okay."

"And I think I may know one reason why," he began. "Can we talk about your work?"

"Sure," she said, feeling nervous.

"Before your accident, we discussed some things you were dealing with personally. I gave you homework. Do you remember?" he asked.

She shook her head. Not only did she not remember that conversation, but she didn't remember much at all about her own artistic ventures.

"Your style changed a lot over the last two years. It became very dark. I felt that you were holding back, and I think that was revealed in your work."

She nodded.

"Lux, I just want you to think about that. Decide how you want it to be going forward," Jackson said. "The homework I gave you was a challenge. To incorporate color again, and to remember how you felt about your talent when you first discovered it. We were going to find your light."

"Okay," Lux said finally. "Then I guess I'm still up for the challenge."

"Lovely," Jackson said.

"So...I'm a painter?" Lux asked curiously. Everything he'd said was new to her. She had no idea what he was talking about. But she was eager to return to the hospital and see her painting on the wall, which she'd never recognized as her own.

He sighed loudly and hung his head. Finally he nodded.

"You're amazing. Don't worry. I'll help you remember," he said. "You'll remember. It's part of you."

Lux felt a new sense of peace after her meeting with Jackson, even with the news of the competition. She was able to relax a bit, and not feel like she was losing her breath. Maybe this could be the opportunity to start over. She wasn't alone in whatever it was she was going through. She wanted to pick up a paintbrush.

"Hey, Kiddo," Mr. Tazo walked in the room where Lux was still sitting on the couch. He handed her a bouquet of flowers. He picked up her travel bag and a large box filled with cards and gifts. She walked past her bed and removed her painting from the wall.

"Ready to get out of here?" Mr. Tazo looked around the room.

She nodded. She was ready. Her nurses and doctors had already said goodbye and wished her well, even though she'd return the day after Christmas for physical therapy.

The drive home triggered memories Lux didn't expect to have. She didn't speak. She could feel her father watching her. Finally he turned on the radio: "I'll be Home For Christmas." She wondered about the last line of the song. ...*If only in my dreams.* She thought it was sad. Whoever was singing didn't ever get to go back home.

They turned onto the old cobblestone street, protected by massive, ancient trees, which were bare now, other than the fresh blanket of snow over the branches. Lux gazed out the window past her father as they passed Ember Sweeney's house. She pictured a pink bicycle in the front yard.

They pulled up the driveway and into the garage. They went inside through the laundry room. Lux was met with the smells of lavender, basil, and ginger in the sprawling kitchen, alive with greenery. She was home. The scents awakened something; suddenly she remembered much more. She remembered loneliness. She ran her fingers over the countertops. She walked through every room. The parlor was perfectly decorated with a Christmas tree that reached the ceiling and white lights and garland that hung everywhere throughout the house. The grand staircase smelled of peppermint.

"Are you hungry?" Mr. Tazo asked Lux when she returned to the kitchen. She shook her head and sat at the kitchen island.

"Mom and Arrabelle should be home soon with food. We can stay here tonight. But we've been invited to a cocktail party next door," Mr. Tazo said uncertainly.

"Next door, as in the Sweeneys' house, next door?" Lux asked, suddenly annoyed. He nodded. She didn't like it. "I'm tired," she said, and stood up.

"Is there anything I can get you?" he said, concerned. "I can bring you some tea."

"I'm fine, thanks." Lux left the kitchen and her father followed. As he helped her up each step, she looked at the pictures on the wall. She looked sad in all of them. She hated it. She wasn't sad; she was strong.

Once they reached the top of the stairs, they walked down the long hallway that led to Lux's bedroom. The door was open and the room was bright. A vase of fresh flowers was on the bedside table. She walked to her closet and saw all of the dark clothing. She needed color. Mr. Tazo wished her sweet dreams and closed the door as he left.

Lux covered herself with a blanket and stared out the window. Ember's house. She closed her eyes. Her mind was spinning. She began to remember just how much she'd felt for him. There was something about him, something she couldn't put her finger on. She shook her head and went to sleep.

When she woke from her dreamless nap, her bedroom was dark. There was a cold mug of tea on her bedside table. She lay in bed for a few minutes before moving, and thought about where she was. Home. She looked out the window again. Still snowing. All the lights were on now at Ember's house. Then she noticed Tazo Castle. Someone had strung lights and decorated it. It twinkled in the dark and illuminated the snow. It looked like the Twilight Trees.

A chill ran down her spine. It was time to get up and face her family before she succumbed to her thoughts and stayed in bed all night. She slowly made her way down the stairs. Her parents and sister were sitting quietly around a crackling fire, sipping mulled wine. She'd never seen them like this before.

"Lux!" Mrs. Tazo smiled delightedly.

"Welcome home." Arrabelle stood up and hugged her. "You look great."

"Hungry yet, Kiddo?" Mr. Tazo patted a seat next to him on the couch.

Lux felt okay enough about Arrabelle now, and she knew her parents deserved a chance. Things had changed. Even if they hadn't changed, she had. Plus, it was Christmas. She was happy to be where she was, genuinely happy. She forced herself to ignore Boreloque, if only for the night. She was back in Briar Heights now, and there was no way she knew of to change that.

"I'm starving," Lux said, and smiled. Mrs. Tazo perked up, and they moved to the kitchen. A feast of appetizers and desserts was waiting for them. They snacked and engaged in light conversation about the day. Lux drank hot cocoa and tried to ignore the loneliness she felt when she thought about Blaze, or Zephyr, or Ember.

"What do you want for Christmas, Lux?" Arrabelle asked slyly. Lux hadn't thought about it even once. Of course, she hadn't gotten anyone anything. She shrugged and smiled.

"We got what we wished for," Mr. Tazo murmured and kissed his wife. Lux wondered again just how serious her condition had been. She wasn't ready to ask for details.

"Can we just show it to her tonight?" Arrabelle asked suddenly. "We have a gift for you. I *know* you'll like it. And we had some help with it…"

Lux was curious. She turned to her parents.

"Why not?" Mr. Tazo gave in with a winning smile.

"Wait, just a second," Arrabelle said. She grabbed her phone and left the room. Lux finished the last sip of her cocoa. She couldn't help smiling. She was excited. It felt like the first time she'd been excited about something.

"Follow us," Mrs. Tazo instructed. Lux and Arrabelle followed their parents down the dim hallway leading to the garage. They walked past the library and into the round sun room at the end of the hall, which was quite separate and private from the rest of the house. The room was lit only by strands of Edison bulbs, so Lux couldn't see much. Where was her gift?

Arrabelle flipped the light switch. Lanterns hung from the ceiling and illuminated the room that had been transformed into an art studio. Blank canvases were stacked in the corner and five easels were set up. More paint colors than Lux had ever seen lined shelves along the walls. Paintbrushes, pencils, charcoal, sketch books, and a framed photo covered a large white desk. Lux couldn't believe what she was seeing.

"This is for me?" She asked in disbelief.

"Do you like it?" Mrs. Tazo asked nervously. They all seemed nervous.

"This is paramount!" Lux made her way further into the room and touched everything to make sure it was all real. Then she noticed hanging on the walls were photos taken of the paintings that covered the walls of Tazo Castle. She was overwhelmed and surprised and confused and truly hadn't ever expected something like this from her family. When had they started to care? Or support this part of who she was?

Lux ran her fingers over the paintbrushes and then noticed three tubes of paint on the desk: pink, yellow, and gold. She stopped and stared at the paint colors. She picked up the tube of gold. She smiled.

Next to the tubes of paint was another photo frame. She picked it up and read it over and over.

"Who went into my tree house?" she asked abruptly. Her parents and sister eyed one another. It had been Ember Sweeney who'd gone into her tree house weeks earlier, and they couldn't tell her that quite yet. The doorbell rang.

"I'll get that," Mrs. Tazo said, and hurried away.

"Music fills the infinite between two souls. Funny you picked this one." Lux stopped to wonder for a moment. "This is the only one of my quotes that isn't about painting. What made you choose it?"

Mrs. Tazo returned then with Astor and Jackson.

"Are we too late?" Astor said. "Arrabelle told us about the big reveal."

"Ah, she's seen it!" Jackson said. He grinned at Lux.

Lux looked around the room again, then from Arrabelle to Jackson. She threw her arms around him.

"I remember," she whispered.

She turned to her parents. "Thank you. This is what I love. It's what I want to do with my life. And I want you to be proud of me," she said. She wasn't afraid to tell them what had needed to be said for so long, because it was the truth. She knew there was nothing to fear if it was the truth.

Her father revealed the tiniest smile. Her mother looked worried.

"There's nothing wrong with me. This is part of who I am. It's not my identity, but it's a big part of me, and you'll support it if you want to know me. You don't have to agree with my choice, but you may not talk negatively about me anymore." She looked away from her parents then, who both remained silent. She looked at Jackson.

"I don't want to waste what I've been given," she said. "Don't let me forget that." He nodded.

"I'm proud of you," Arrabelle said. Lux smiled at her. Mr. and Mrs. Tazo nodded in agreement.

"Use this well, Lux," Jackson said. He and Astor backed out of the room.

"Did you come all the way here just for this?" Lux asked them. "Stay!"

"We were at the party just next door," Astor said. "We could all head back over."

"What do you say, Lux?" Mr. Tazo asked.

"No, let's hang out here tonight." Jackson patted Lux's shoulder.

The rest of the evening they played board games and ate popcorn and salted caramels. When Lux grew tired again, she said goodnight to Jackson and Astor. Arrabelle helped her climb the stairs for bed.

Lux lay in bed for over an hour. Her body was exhausted, but her mind was wide awake. She stared out the window and watched the party next door.

There was a knock at her door, and Arrabelle peeked inside.

"Can I come in?"

"Sure."

Arrabelle sat on the floor against Lux's bed. "Listen. Everyone's celebrating Christmas tomorrow at the Sweeneys'. Your friends want to see you. I understand if you're not ready, but — Well, you won't be alone. Jackson and Astor and I talked about it, and we'll look out for you."

"Can I ask you something, Ar?" Lux turned over in bed. "Who *are* my friends? I haven't heard from anyone. I thought I'd hear from Anya, at least."

"Trust me. You have many wonderful friends. And Anya is still the best of them. I just think everyone wanted to give you space. To remember. The doctors and dad and mom were worried."

Lux thought about how angry she was with Anya. Hatred and sweetness momentarily bubbled into her heart. It didn't make sense: Ember and Anya. She hated the thought of them together. She just didn't understand. But she couldn't let that control her.

That was their business. She had a life to get on with.

"You're different from what I remember," Lux said, yawning. "I like having you around."

"I'll always be around."

She wished secretly that Arrabelle would say something about Ember. But there was no more exchange of words. Lux felt a strange peace with Arrabelle nearby. She still felt something was missing, unfinished, and she knew it must have to do with Ember. Jackson was right. She would talk with him. In person. Yes, that's what she'd do.

"Good night, Ar. Merry Christmas," Lux whispered, then dozed off. One of many weights lifted off her shoulders that night, and she slept soundly.

TWENTY TWO

Album: Raising Sand

Track: Seven

"She's going to kill us both. I read her journal to the whole world. And you...gave a eulogy. It's so weird," Anya whispered. She and Ember watched out the window of the guest bedroom, which was now Anya's, as the whole Tazo family followed the sidewalk to the Sweeneys' house.

"I didn't give a...*eulogy!*" Ember shuddered.

"Whatever you say," Anya replied nervously.

It was Christmas Day. Lux had accepted the invitation to the party. Mr. Tazo had called ahead that morning to warn them. Now Anya and Ember were avoiding addressing the fact that Lux believed something romantic had happened between the two of them.

"Well, at least there's no way she's seen the Farewell Show. We would know. We'll just act normal, stay busy, and nobody will talk about it," Ember said tensely. "I've hidden the technology, newspapers, and magazines. And our website should be down for construction soon, too."

"I've told you ten times, Lux isn't on social media, so don't worry. She doesn't care about it. And let's not talk about how close you and I are now, okay?" Anya tapped her fingers against the window pane. "In fact, let's just stay away from each other today. Don't mention that I live here."

"Okay." Ember's sinking feeling returned.

♪

Arrabelle rang the doorbell. Mr. Sweeney answered with a warm welcome, and Lux watched her family take turns hugging him as they walked in. She stood back and watched curiously. When had they all become friends? Friends that hugged? Then Mr. Sweeney turned to Lux and smiled as if he knew her, which he'd always done. Arrabelle hung back with her.

"I hear you have some great eggnog brewing, Mr. Sweeney!" Arrabelle winked at him.

"It's ready and potent!" He laughed.

"Come on Lux, I'll sneak you some." Arrabelle nudged her. Mr. Sweeney chuckled. Lux enjoyed his laugh; it was welcoming. She smiled at him and stepped inside. He took her coat. She gazed around the house. It smelled of fresh bread and burning firewood.

Lux felt as if she'd waited to see it for a long time, but she didn't know why. She noticed a piano out of the corner of her eye and something triggered. She walked into the parlor and touched the piano keys, but stopped when she heard Anya's voice behind her. Anger. Pain. Betrayal. ...Forgiveness. Kindness. Newness. She took a deep breath and turned around.

Anya stood at the foot of the grand staircase and waved. Lux's heart swelled. She couldn't help but smile. She forced the lingering images of what she'd seen out of her mind. She missed her best friend.

"Hi, friend," Anya said cautiously when Lux approached her. They stood face to face, saying nothing as more people arrived, oblivious to the girls' first reunion in months.

"Hi," Lux said. "How are you? How's school? Lacrosse?" She shuffled her feet and crossed her arms.

"I'm good," Anya said softly and nodded. "It's good."

"How did the fall fashion show go?" Lux ventured.

"I actually passed it on to Bella Guerrero," Anya said, looking away. "I just had a lot going on."

Tanner walked in from the kitchen then and interrupted the girls by kissing Anya. Then he saw Lux and his face lit up. "Lux! Merry Christmas." He hugged her. "Oh, wow —"

"You know me?" Lux asked uncertainly.

"I do. It's good to have you back. You two catch up; we'll hang out later." Tanner kissed Anya again and walked away.

"Do I hang out with him? Are you two together?" Lux asked. She felt blindsided. Did Ember know about the two of them? Wasn't Tanner one of Ember's best friends? They were in Ember's house. Anya was suddenly giddy; she nodded.

"What about Ember?" Lux couldn't restrain herself. Anya returned Lux's question with a blank stare.

"Ember's fine. He thinks we're a good match." Anya said. "I've been waiting to tell you about Tanner. I've missed you." She was choked up and embraced Lux. Lux hugged her back but was still confused.

"Maybe you did talk about Tanner once…" Lux recalled a conversation.

"Yeah, I did." Anya giggled. "And now, these guys are our friends."

"They don't even know me, do they?" Lux asked. She couldn't remember being friends with Ember Sweeney's crew.

Just then Duffy burst through the front door with a pie and cider, her father beside her with champagne.

"You'll see. Oh, here's Duffy. You're going to love her." Anya smiled.

Lux had forgotten all about Duffy Raven. An entirely new bundle of memories and emotions came flooding back. So much must have changed between everyone. But, wait — If Anya wasn't with Ember, that meant he still could be with Duffy. Maybe it was actually Duffy she'd seen with him when she woke up.

And when had everyone become her friend? As Lux wondered these things, she was approached by Luther and Jamison, who greeted her just as enthusiastically as Tanner had.

Lux went along with all of it, although she was as confused as ever. She'd wanted to be friends with these people once before, but something told her she'd been afraid. Now she wasn't afraid of anything. She'd seen much worse than any guys or girls in Briar Heights could throw at her. There was nothing left to be afraid of. Duffy got in line for hugs, and the greetings started all over again.

"Happy Christmas!" Jackson and Astor walked inside. They approached the band, and then Arrabelle joined them, too.

Lux noticed Arrabelle talking with Jamison as if she knew him. And then she saw Duffy and Anya together, organizing centerpieces on the tables. But before she could ask any more questions about how everyone had become friends, Jackson pulled her aside.

"We're looking out for you." He ruffled her hair. "You're safe here."

"Thanks," Lux said. She felt relieved with him close by. "And I have something for you," she said. She ruffled through coats and bags near the front door, and then finally found what she was looking for. She revealed a small canvas and handed it to Jackson.

He touched the canvas, which was splattered with gold and yellow over pink polka dots. He looked at her, but didn't say anything.

"I'm on a different sleep schedule these days. I tried out my new studio sometime in the middle of the night," Lux said.

"It's five year old you," he said finally.

"I'm going to find my light," she said.

Jackson nodded. He hugged her. "This is lovely. Thank you. Best Christmas gift I could have gotten. Other than you, of course."

There were over thirty people gathered now, and the house was getting crowded. Four tables were set for dinner. Every counter was covered with food and drinks.

"Everyone grab a beverage and find your name at a table!" Mr. Sweeney shouted from the kitchen. He wove through the crowd quickly. He seemed to be looking for something. "I'll be just a moment," he said, walking away.

"You have to come down sometime." Mr. Sweeney stood in the doorway of Ember's bedroom. "It's okay. They're all having a great time. If she actually hated you, or really believed what she thought she saw, she wouldn't have come. She's here. That means she wants to see you."

Ember stared out the window. "Please Read The Letter" had played on repeat for the last hour, drowning out the voices downstairs. The moment had come and he couldn't face it. He couldn't face her. Not in front of everyone. He couldn't move. He'd lost part of himself during those two months in the hospital. She scared the hell out of him.

"I'll be right down," he said.

"Duffy made sure you're sitting at different ends of your table, if that helps," his father assured him. "And you're not near Anya, either."

It did help. Ember took a deep breath, glanced at the tree house again, and placed the note he was holding under his pillow.

Lux sat down with Duffy and Luther, who took turns chatting her ear off. Duffy had very deliberately introduced Luther as her boyfriend. Lux's doubt was forced to fade a little bit more. Everyone she'd attached to Ember was stripped away. Everyone was making sure Lux knew who the couples were, though nobody mentioned Ember's name directly. And where was Ember?

Suddenly, out of the corner of her eye, Lux saw him. He stood at the bottom of the stairs, more than just a memory, someone she couldn't possibly hate. But she was still angry and so hurt. She immediately reminded herself again that she'd faced worse. She would be okay. She was strong.

Ember Sweeney. She was in his home, at his table. His eyes burned into hers. He'd grown up, changed. He was more attractive than she remembered, more reserved. She felt her heart melt. He approached the table. His friends stood up and greeted him. He sat down next to Jamison, who patted him on the back encouragingly.

"Merry Christmas," Ember said.

"Merry Christmas," their friends replied in unison.

Lux simply smiled. She couldn't stop staring. Ember Sweeney. She couldn't look away. Those eyes. That voice....

Mr. Sweeney stood up then and raised his glass. "Welcome to our second holiday dinner of the season. We're so glad to share the company of friends, neighbors, and family."

Lux tuned him out. She thought about the recent holidays she hadn't been a part of.

"...It's really wonderful to have the *whole* Tazo family with us today."

Cheers rang out. Lux sat back in her seat. Everyone was smiling at her. Everyone except Ember. Her father was blinking back tears. Arrabelle, Astor, and Jackson cheered proudly. She shrugged awkwardly, but continued to smile.

Everyone at Lux's table stood up with their plates, and she followed them into the kitchen. She watched Ember, who was avoiding eye contact with her. She filled her plate and sat down again. Duffy was in the middle of telling her a story, and Lux kept smiling and laughing, but hadn't retained a word. Ember was staring at his fork. Lux wanted to say something. This wasn't like him at all. She knew it. This was more like…her.

The room was buzzing with chatter. Lux turned around and noticed all of the parents sitting together. They seemed happy and content. It was bizarre; not how she remembered them, either. She returned to conversations at her own table but kept an eye and ear on Ember. She began to wonder if he didn't want her there; maybe she was intruding. Maybe he didn't want to be friends with her. But everyone else apparently did. She shrugged, because she simply didn't care as much as she once had. She mixed mashed potatoes and cranberries together on her plate and smiled stupidly to herself when she pictured his face. Then she suddenly thought of Blaze. Her smile faded.

She glanced at Ember again, and this time their eyes met. He stood up. "I need to show you something." He nodded toward the stairs. Everyone watched as Lux stood up, without a word, and went with Ember.

She followed him up the stairs and into his bedroom. He closed the door. She saw her tree house through his window. Her heart pounded and her ears began to ring.

"I just wanted to say hello. Without everyone staring at us. This is…awkward," he said.

"I know."

He sat on his bed and patted the spot next to him. They sat side by side.

"Well, hello," Lux said.

"Hi."

"So you and I are friends, then?" she asked.

He nodded.

"I guess that's one of the things my memory must have lost."

He didn't reply. They sat in silence. They listened to the buzz of the conversations downstairs.

"I mean, we're friends *now*," Ember said, flustered. "All of us. You're just automatically part of it. It's hard to explain at the moment, and you and I didn't hang out or anything…until the day you fell. Do you remember?"

Lux shook her head. The last thing she remembered before her "fall" was an image of the Lara Rehabilitation Clinic. And the last thing she remembered before that was summer vacation.

Ember reached under his pillow and grabbed the note. She sideways glanced at it and her eyes grew wide.

"How did you get that?" Lux demanded. Her name had bled through the paper. She'd seen it before. It had been in Boreloque. She was sure of it.

"I have a better question. How did you get it?" Ember asked.

"I — I don't know." She shook her head.

"Well, let's just say I got it back." He smiled. "I was saving it."

"What is it?" Lux was so curious now, she moved closer to Ember.

"You haven't read it?"

"No. I don't think so."

The cautious, nervous walls they shared began to crack slowly. They were face to face. She could smell a sweet, woodsy fragrance on his skin. She'd remember it forever.

"It's a letter." Ember gulped.

"May I read it?" Lux asked. Ember stared at the note. Finally, he handed it to her. He ran his fingers through his hair. She unfolded its worn edges.

"It's from a long time ago," he explained. "From the beginning."

Lux,

The way I see it, a song is going to define us at some point, whether it's today, next week, or years down the road. Right now, I'd prefer it to be any number of Ed Sheeran songs. But I'm afraid we could turn out to be a Taylor Swift song, and that scares me. I don't understand what just happened. But we had a perfect week, and we like each other, and we should be together. Tell me why you're sad. I need to know because I love you. Yes, I said that. I'll wait forever, but I don't want to waste another minute of my life not being a part of yours. You can trust me. So, let's fix this and be best friends and get on with it. Stick With Me Baby

– Robert Plant & Alison Krauss.

Love, Ember Sweeney

Tears welled up in Lux's eyes. She read the note again to be sure. Her trembling hands were making the paper shake. What would have happened if she'd read this in Boreloque...? The note had crossed over into another time and place, and she needed to make sense of it, even more than she needed to address Ember's use of the L word. Love.

"I was afraid then. I didn't think you —" Lux paused, distracted. She felt another weight off her shoulders but still wasn't settled. "I don't think I ever stopped..." She couldn't finish her sentence.

Ember touched her cheek and moved in closer. She read the note again. She was torn. Because her heart was still torn apart. This was the last thing she'd expected. She knew it had to mean more.

"It's just that so much has happened," Lux whispered. "I'm still trying to figure it out."

Ember's face fell. "You're right, a lot has happened," he hastily agreed. He tried to smile but couldn't.

"I'm just still so mad at you. When I came back...what I saw — it hurts so much." She couldn't keep it to herself; she pictured him with Anya. "I can't make sense of it." Her blood boiled. She knew what she'd seen.

"Lux, you have to know that nothing ever happened between Anya and me," he said desperately. The color drained from his face. "I can prove it."

"I don't understand what I know...but I know what I saw." She couldn't explain it to him without explaining Boreloque, and she just wasn't ready to reveal that place. She didn't know how to. She knew her confusion and doubt wasn't solely about him, just like it hadn't been two years earlier.

"Then can we pretend you didn't read the letter?" He looked away.

"I don't want to do that," Lux said, raising her voice. For as much as she cared for him, she just couldn't sell him short, not like this. He deserved better.

"What do you want then?" Ember's voice rose. "I was there every day! I was the one! How am I supposed to just —?" He ran his fingers through his hair again.

"You were *where* every day?" she asked quietly.

"Oh — at school," he lied. "Waiting for two years. I should have gotten the hint. But, here we are," he mumbled.

"It doesn't count as waiting when you have dated almost every girl in our grade," she reasoned. It felt good to defend herself but also scary. And daring.

He said nothing.

"And it doesn't matter if *they* asked *you* out," she continued. "You still went out with them. You've never been alone. But I have. You don't even know what it's like to be alone."

"Yes. I do."

"Well. I guess there are things that both of us aren't able to tell each other right now, so let's just...can we be friends?" She couldn't believe that's what she was asking of him, when she somehow knew she also wanted everything and all of him forever.

"Friends." Ember turned to face her again, smiling sadly as if he'd just lost her all over again. "Of course."

"Good." Lux smiled. Her heart pounded. This was a disaster.

"Yeah, we'll hang out sometime," Ember concluded, and sighed. "Ready to go back down to dinner?"

"That's it?" Lux asked. This was Ember Sweeney; she didn't know what she expected from him, but she expected more than a halfhearted agreement to just be friends. She wanted him to stand up to her. But then it occurred to her that she had a history of turning him down.

"Yeah. You're mad at me anyway, aren't you?" He walked to the door. "Let me know when you're finished being mad. Then we'll talk about being actual friends. Let's go."

"Fine," she said, sulking. She met him at the door. They glared at each other. She wished he'd kiss her. But she didn't want that, either. She just wanted to see things clearly.

"You said you came back," Ember said suddenly. "Where were you?"

"I came back...you know, from my sleep." Lux tried to look confused. It worked.

"Well, I'm glad you're back."

Ember opened his bedroom door. They walked downstairs together. When they reached the bottom of the stairs, everyone in the room was watching them expectantly. She returned to her seat and looked to Ember for clarity or comfort, but he was once again avoiding her stare. Arrabelle, Astor, and Jackson promptly pulled chairs up near Lux. New conversations started and someone brought dessert to the table. Lux forced herself to ignore how she felt, but she couldn't wait to get back home with the letter and analyze every aspect of the past two years. She needed to set her memory straight.

She planned to face her lingering feelings at home that night. But she didn't go home that night. She stayed overnight at Ember's house.

Luther, Duffy, and Jamison had made a big fuss over Lux and told her she had to stay. Their entire group of friends stayed. They played games, listened to music, and talked late into the night, with Christmas movies on in the background. The guys picked up their instruments at one point, but Ember stopped them. He did, however, allow them all to sing Christmas karaoke. Then, at midnight, they exchanged gifts. They'd even gotten gifts for Lux.

"We thought this might be a good way for you to get to know us," Jamison explained.

"Someday, if you want, you can send us some, too," Duffy added. They'd made a playlist for Lux. She read the handwritten compilation, which included five songs from each of them, even Anya.

"While You Were Away..."

Duffy: Aha! -Imogen Heap, Paperweight -Joshua Radin & Schuyler Fisk, Under My Bed -Meiko, Fairytale Lullaby -Bombay Bicycle Club, Open Your Eyes (Deep Blue Songspell) -Bea Miller.

Luther: Float On -Modest Mouse, Hoppipolla -Sigur Ros, Uprising -Muse, Mine Is Yours -Cold War Kids, Here We Are -Dandylion Warpaint.

Tanner: Breathe In Breathe Out -Mat Kearney, Stars -Grace Potter & the Nocturnals, Wish for You -Faith Hill, Colder Weather -Zac Brown Band, Barton Hollow -The Civil Wars.

Anya: Anchor -Mindy Gledhill, Christmas Day -Dido, This Moment -Katy Perry, Baby It's Cold Outside -Colbie Caillat & Gavin DeGraw, Silent Night (Lord of My Life) -Lady Antebellum.

Jamison: In the Cold, Cold Night -The White Stripes, Hail Hail -Shovels & Rope, Little Talks -Of Monsters and Men, American Girls -Counting Crows, Seat Next To You -Bon Jovi.

Ember: I Still Ain't Over You -Augustana, Nothin' -Robert Plant & Alison Krauss, Ain't With You -Eric Tessmer Band, Don't Owe You a Thang -Gary Clark Jr., Stormy Weather -Etta James.

Lux was overwhelmed. She promised to make it up to all of them, but everyone made it very clear that having her with them was all they wanted. Eventually, she drifted off to sleep on the couch during a conversation with Jamison, her heart feeling unusually full.

It was the middle of the night when Lux awoke. She didn't know where she was. The room was black and the house was silent. She could hear light, steady breathing all around her. Then she saw a sliver of the moon out the window. She'd had a nightmare. She had to get back to Boreloque if she wanted a life in Briar Heights. It would be the only way.

Unless... She had an idea; she made a plan. She sat up on the couch, pushed down the mound of blankets she was nestled under, and stared out the window.

She was a painter. She was *the* painter. She would recreate her experience. That's how she'd fix it. That's how she'd share it. Paint it all as it was meant to be.

"Are you okay?"

Even in a whisper, she recognized Ember's voice. "Yeah." She lay back down. "Thanks."

She spent the rest of the night planning. She was going to paint Boreloque. Perfectly and wonderfully. There would be no Underground. No Venia. No shadows. No wounds. Boreloque would be free and beautiful and bright.

"How did you sleep?" Jamison asked Lux at breakfast the next morning. "How are you feeling?"

"That's it," Duffy interrupted. "Jamison is only allowed to hang out when Lux is around."

"Yeah!" Everyone else chimed in.

"I don't know what it is. She makes me want to be nice," Jamison said, and shrugged.

"I actually didn't sleep much at all," Lux said. Jamison looked concerned, and she giggled at him. "But it's okay."

"Me neither," Ember said, watching her.

"My doctors say I was in a coma. But...I wasn't." Lux fidgeted. "I went somewhere. And I want to show you. So I'm going to paint where I was. I haven't always been proud of my work, but this is important. And since you're all my friends, I need you to see it when I'm finished."

"Paramount!" Jamison said brightly and clinked his orange juice glass with Lux's.

"Can't wait!" Duffy agreed.

Anya kicked Ember under the kitchen table and mouthed something to him.

"We also wanted to ask you about designing the cover for our new album, if you're interested," Ember said nonchalantly.

The members of Falling Like Ember exchanged quick glances.

"Yes," Lux said excitedly. Something clicked when she thought of Boreloque and Falling Like Ember together in the same time, place, and sentence. She knew immediately she could create something great for them.

"I mean, after I finish this other project," she continued, sorting out the details in her mind. She felt inspired. "My project needs to come first. But, I'll have you guys look at a few pieces I've completed. We'll make sure it's a good fit and what you're looking for."

The band exchanged quick glances again but smiled and nodded.

"The album doesn't drop until May, anyway," Luther said. "Take the time you need."

"Speaking of May —" Ember paused. He looked at each of his friends. "I have one last Christmas gift, and it's for everyone. Well, it's a potential gift."

"What is it?" Luther asked eagerly.

"I got a call from the manager of that new band Wendy and the Boys. They want us to tour with them this summer."

Ember's next words couldn't be heard because everyone was cheering and talking so loudly. Luther immediately brought up the calendar on his phone. Tanner began pacing the kitchen.

Jamison hugged Lux. Duffy looked nervous but excited. Anya and Lux exchanged smiles.

"Wait!" Ember shouted. "Guys!"

Tanner sat down again, and everyone stopped talking.

"So, Wendy and the Boys are pretty huge in the U.K. these days. They'll be opening for Coldplay in the spring. Anyway, they want to host us in Europe for the summer. Since they're from London, that's where we'd start out," Ember said. All eyes were on him. "It would be eight weeks, about five shows a week. It would be a lot."

"What about the offers to tour in the U.S.?" Tanner asked suddenly. Everyone turned to Luther then.

"Well," Luther hesitated. "Suddenly, we have a lot of options here, too. A lot."

"Why is it suddenly?" Lux asked.

"Oh, uh —" Duffy stammered.

Everyone exchanged quick glances again, and this time Lux noticed.

"If we toured at home, then the girls could all come, too!" Tanner said quickly.

"All of the girls at this table are welcome no matter where we go," Ember said immediately. "It's already been approved." He glanced at Lux. She smiled nervously.

"Lux, the band has just been noticed a lot more recently," Luther explained. "This is our moment. So we just want to be sure we make all the right moves."

Everyone smiled at one another. They found themselves in a moment of silence, excitedly looking from one face to the next thinking about the possibilities.

"It'll all work out," Duffy said finally. "Let's revisit the options after winter break. I say we just have fun here together for the next two weeks."

Everyone raised their glasses.

Before Lux went home that morning, she asked Ember if she

could borrow the album *Raising Sand*. When she'd woken up the night before, she could hear it playing in her mind. She needed it for her project. It reminded her of Boreloque...and Ember. She needed to sit down and draw the lines.

"That album is actually in your tree house." He shuffled his feet and grinned.

"Oh, okay." Lux was too embarrassed to ask why. "Then can I get a copy of your album? It'll help me with the design process."

She sat on his bed while he copied all of the recorded Falling Like Ember tracks for her, and they casually discussed design ideas. She looked around his room and burned as many things into her mind as possible. Then she saw something in a pile on his desk.

"Why the hell do you have my journal?" she asked, alarmed. She rushed over to his desk and grabbed it, trying to recall just what she'd written on the pages.

"No! Wait!" He stood up, flustered. "I just needed it!"

She stared, wide-eyed, hands on her hips.

"Okay," he began quickly. "Yes, one day I went into your tree house. When I looked around and saw everything, I had a moment of inspiration. I needed something to write on. Then I heard the guys calling me, so I just grabbed it and took it with me. I swear, I didn't read...all of it."

"How much did you read?" She asked heatedly.

"Just one page. Promise." He slowly reached for the journal in her hand, but she pulled away. "Let me show you," he pleaded. "What I wrote is still there. I haven't even opened it again." She continued to watch him carefully.

"Nobody ever goes into my tree house." She handed him the journal. "So was it you who put up the lights everywhere in Tazo Castle? That's what it's called." She watched him page through the journal. Finally he stopped and opened it to the page where his handwriting was.

"Yes. It was me," he admitted.

"Well, I think it's beautiful," she said. She was still staring him down.

"Okay," he said, and paused. Then he handed over the journal with the page he'd written in. She read it. She touched the page. It was another letter.

"I'd like to keep it," she concluded. "I don't like to rip out pages."

"Fine, no problem," he said hastily. "Just know I didn't read it."

"Okay," she finally agreed. She could see the honesty in his eyes. And she was secretly flattered. She sat down on the bed again, and he returned to preparing his music for her.

When they'd finished, he insisted on walking her home.

"So, are you still mad at me?" Ember asked. "I mean, for everything before you found your journal in my room."

Lux nodded slowly.

"It's a little insulting," he admitted.

"I'm sorry. Don't give up on me," was all she could come up with.

"I never did." He hugged her.

"I'm just trying to be honest. I don't understand it," she admitted, but somehow felt peace. "There's just more about me and all of this that I need time to sort out."

"I'll wait," he said.

They said goodbye, and she made sure not to close the door until he was out of sight.

Lux went straight to her new art studio. She was thankful nobody was home to ask her how the night went, or how she was feeling; she was ready to get down to business.

Raising Sand was leaning against a new record player on her desk when she walked into her studio. She looked around curiously. Arrabelle...? She couldn't help but notice similarities in the way Ember and Arrabelle communicated sometimes. Something about it made her trust both of them a little bit more.

She listened to the album while sorting through colors and brushes. Boreloque was about to come alive again.

Ember Sweeney initiated the first group text message in a very long time.

Ember: The Brightest Lights. King Charles.
Duffy: Halo. Lotte Kestner.
Luther: I Will Possess Your Heart. Death Cab for Cutie.
Tanner: All We Ever Find. Tim McGraw.
Jamison: Howlin' For You. The Black Keys.
Anya: Heroes (we could be). Alesso.

TWENTY THREE

Album: MTV Unplugged v2.0

Track: Fifteen

Color stained canvas: carefully, carelessly, completely. Lux had rediscovered her passion. She was proud of it. Nothing to hide. Nothing to protect. She left the door of her studio open, and she hadn't set down a brush in three days. She was putting the finishing touches on Folly Falls when her father knocked on the door.

"Kiddo, it's time for your physical therapy appointment," he said, observing her work. Lux was glad for this, because she wanted to visit Patricia, too.

"I'll be right there."

She waited until her father left the room and walked over to her desk. She opened a spiral bound notebook to a page near the back. She had written the name Ember. Then a few lines below that, she'd written the name Blaze. A few spaces after Blaze, she'd drawn an arrow to the name Zephyr. She'd referred back those names often over the past few days. Something was growing in her mind. She wasn't quite ready to say anything out loud. Then she quickly wrote her own name, and drew another arrow: Venia. She took a deep breath.

"Lux! Come in!" Patricia said happily. "Look at you, walking on your own!"

"I feel stronger every day," Lux said, and sat down.

She described her Christmas to Patricia, beginning with all of the new friends she had, who, as it turned out, were dating each other. One of them was even dating Anya. And nobody seemed to be dating Ember. In fact, Ember had actually given Lux some sort of very old love letter. All of the supposed misunderstandings were now lingering in the air. Lux told Patricia that somehow things were better, even though she was still confused. Nobody seemed completely willing to confess or explain anything. There was a missing link. But Lux had decided that finishing the paintings would free her from Boreloque, and then she'd finally be herself. Then everything with Ember would fall into place, too.

"It sounds like you've really thought this through," Patricia said. "That's wonderful. I'm proud of you. And don't forget, I'm always here."

"I think I've reached a crossroads," Lux said. "I can choose to have faith. Or I can keep doubting. I feel like everyone's waiting on me."

"Don't rush anything, Lux," Patricia said. "You take as much time as you need. I think your friends will wait patiently. Whatever it is you need to do, that's not something you should put a timetable on right now."

Lux agreed with Patricia, but she was impatient with herself. She was trying to make her mind work faster than it was able or willing to; she didn't want to acknowledge that her mind, her brain, her body had experienced trauma. They weren't working together as they once had, which was difficult to accept.

Lux got home from the hospital that day feeling even more determined. She returned to her studio. She opened the notebook to the page with the names. After studying it carefully, she turned the page. She began to write her theory.

"I thought I'd find you in here," Arrabelle said as she walked into Lux's studio. The room was dim and the sun had disappeared. Lux was still sitting on the floor writing in her notebook. Arrabelle turned on a set of the Edison bulbs that hung across the ceiling.

"Hi," Lux said as she instinctively began to hide the notebook away. Giving it a second thought, she left it out. "What are you up to?"

"I was hanging out at the Sour." Arrabelle sat down on the floor with Lux. "And by the way, the record player is your Christmas gift from Astor."

"No way," Lux said, smiling. "I kind of love him. I always have."

"I know." Arrabelle sighed loudly. "He's a good one. So, listen. There's the New Year's show at the Sour. Falling Like Ember is headlining. Everyone will be there. I'll be there. All of the parents will be there."

"Parents?" Lux repeated.

"Yeah. Apparently it's a thing now. The parents and kids hang out and do holidays and events. Together. In the same place. At the same time."

"It's weird," Lux said. "But it's cool." Arrabelle nodded in agreement.

"So, what do you think?" Arrabelle asked. "I know you're not one hundred percent on Ember Sweeney, or even Anya, but — you can't miss it. It wouldn't be the same without you. You can be my date."

"Wait, you're going solo?" Lux asked, surprised. "You *have* changed!" Arrabelle laughed.

"Well, yeah," Arrabelle said. "I want to show Astor that I don't need to bring someone. That maybe I want *him* to be my someone. I know that I need to be on my own first in order for him to realize I'm serious. I don't think he trusts me."

"You and Astor?" Lux laughed again. "Yes, I'll be your date, with two conditions. One: I need the help of your musical knowledge. I'm making a gift, and I think you can help me. I need access to all of your music."

"Done," Arrabelle said immediately.

"Two: I want to let Ember know the same kind of thing you're letting Astor know." Lux took a deep breath. Opening up to Arrabelle and being honest was a new thing, and it still felt unsafe. But she knew she had to give it a chance.

"So you are one hundred percent about Ember, then?" Arrabelle asked.

Lux shook her head again.

"I honestly don't know, and it's hard to put it into words," she said. "But I know I need to show him that I do care. I know there's something more between us. It's my turn to reach out."

"Ember cares about you a lot, Lux," Arrabelle said.

"Apparently he loves me," Lux said bluntly.

Arrabelle smiled and nodded, a faraway look in her eyes. "I can promise you nothing happened between him and Anya."

Lux took a deep breath. She stared at her notebook.

"I know. I need to spend time alone with Anya, too. I think what gets to me is that I've just never seen him alone. I guess I know how Astor feels if he can't trust you," Lux said, and shrugged. "I mean, come on. Was it a coincidence that when I woke up I saw Ember standing in front of me with another girl? And Anya, of all girls? Maybe if someone would be honest with me and tell me why they were there in that moment that I opened my eyes..." Lux watched Arrabelle out of the corner of her eye.

"So..." Arrabelle stood up. "I will have your questions answered for you by New Year's Day, if you give me your New Year's Eve. It will all make sense. Until then, work on this; focus only on your project. Promise me you'll take the rest of the year for you, and this, and what you're creating. Can you wait a few more days?"

Once again Lux was forced to choose whether or not to trust Arrabelle. She was intrigued. If Arrabelle was promising something, Lux had no reason not to believe her.

"I can wait," Lux said. She followed Arrabelle to the door and turned on a few more lights in the studio. She put her notebook back on the desk, and picked up a paintbrush.

♪

Arrabelle got out of her car and waved at Ember, who was standing outside the door of Beans Coffee Shop. They went inside, placed an order, and found a table.

"Thanks for meeting me," Arrabelle said. "Ember, it's time to tell Lux about Farewell Friday. About everything. You're the one to do it."

"What about your parents and the doctors? It's like they don't want her to know," Ember said.

"Forget them. What you did for her is the first thing she should have been told. That's what brought her back! You're the reason she woke up."

"I don't know," Ember said. "You don't think she'll think I'm crazy?"

"She'll think it's amazing and sweet and just...love," Arrabelle said. "And it'll sound like Alabama Shakes. Or Twenty One Pilots."

"I didn't see this coming, but I miss hearing from you every day," Ember said. "Let's keep talking music."

"On that note," Arrabelle said, "can you help me decipher these songs from Astor?" Arrabelle handed Ember her phone, and he looked over the text messages.

Astor: Can't Get It Right Today by Joe Purdy

Astor: Come To Me by GooGoo Dolls

Astor: Love You 'Til the End by the Pogues

Finally, he handed the phone back. "He likes you. He's ready to settle down. But he's insecure. It's obvious you love him, but you always have a boyfriend. Plus, you're a little scary sometimes."

"You got all of that from these songs?"

"We talked about you." Ember smiled.

"Anyway," Arrabelle said, trying to hide a smile, "thank you. I'll think about that. And my advice to you: tell Lux. But give her a few more days with her art project. She's focused. I'm bringing her to the Sour as my date on New Year's Eve. So...we'll see you there."

"I'll be waiting," Ember said.

It was the last day of the year. Lux brushed the last stroke on her final piece "The Mountain" and stepped back to observe her work. She stood before twelve vivid paintings that had brought Boreloque to life. She held her breath and closed her eyes. She opened them again. She felt the same. Nothing. She still felt no closer to explaining where she'd been and what she'd been through.

Something told her she had to see Ember Sweeney immediately. She threw on a coat and boots and walked around the corner to his house. It took her much longer than it should have, because she still felt quite a bit of pain in her ankle. She was impatient.

She stopped short before knocking on the door. The door knocker was a lion. Although a lion was common for a door knocker, what she saw was "In like a lamb, out like a lion." She was no longer a lamb. She wasn't a kitten. She wasn't afraid.

Lux knocked on the door. A moment later, Ember answered.

"Hi!" He took a step back, surprised. "How are you?"

"I just need to know you're not going to be with anyone else at the Sour tonight," Lux began, flustered. "I mean, if you are, fine. But just tell me. Are you going with anyone else? Like a date?"

"No," Ember answered quickly. "I'm going alone."

"Well, I'm going with my sister," Lux said. "But Anya told me about dinner at Apples and Worms, too. So maybe I'll see you there."

"I'll save you a seat," Ember said. "How are the paintings coming along?"

"Listen, I had to do this project for myself. I had to prove to myself that I could live up to what I know I'm capable of. It's not just about painting. I want to believe in myself. I guess it's not an overnight thing..."

"No, it's probably a lifetime of working through things in your mind...every day. Over and over," Ember suggested. "That's how it is for me with music."

"Yeah, exactly." She paused and thought about what he'd said. "Also, I'm making you a mix," Lux said. "I'll bring it by soon."

"Paramount," he said.

"See you tonight." Lux took a few steps back down.

The same distant tug on her heart that had been present since she'd woken up from a deep sleep remained. Blaze would not let her go. Zephyr would not show his face.

"Ember, I just want you to know —" Lux paused, and took a deep breath. "It was never actually you I was confused about. All this time, I was fighting against myself. I'm my own worst enemy. I pushed you away, and I'm sorry. I needed to believe in myself before I could let someone else believe in me. And I felt like you really did. And that scared me."

She took another step back. Sharing her heart and being honest with Ember still hadn't fixed it, although it helped a little. All she wanted to know was peace, that she was in the right time and place with the right people, doing the right thing. Where she belonged. Ember smiled.

"You're going to run again now, aren't you?" he said.

She nodded. She had to admit that somehow he knew her well, but she didn't understand how. Suddenly frustrated beyond her control, she instinctively knew just where she needed to go. She ran. To the safest place she knew.

Tazo Castle was just as Lux remembered. She turned on the heat and plugged in the kettle. She nestled into the beanbag chair and glanced at the space on the wall where her favorite quote had once hung. "Music fills the infinite between two souls" had been replaced with something handwritten that said, "Come back to me."

She ripped the paper off the wall. Ember. She recognized the phrase, but couldn't place it. It wasn't from his letter. It wasn't what he'd written in her journal. Maybe it was his lyrics? She powered up her laptop for the first time since the ground had been warm, and decided to peruse the Falling Like Ember website. She could find their lyrics there.

She found the website, and read the page intro — again and again. She became numb. Then terrified. On the main page was a video link titled, "The Farewell Show." She clicked it.

♪

"Ember! Come in." Mrs. Tazo hugged him. Since they'd celebrated Christmas together, she treated him as if the days between December fifth and twenty-fourth hadn't happened. He removed his navy pea coat to reveal a black fitted long sleeved top over dark blue skinny jeans and scuffed leather boots. He wore a brown leather wrist cuff, and his ears were slightly gauged. His hair was pulled into a messy bun. He looked ready for the stage.

"Look at you!" Mrs. Tazo said brightly, always appreciative of a perfect appearance.

"You're coming tonight, right? My dad said you're all meeting at McCauley's Pub before the show," Ember said.

"That's right! What time do you perform? We want to get some footage."

"We go on at ten, but — wait, where's Lux?" Ember lowered his voice and looked around.

"Not sure," Mrs. Tazo said. "I just got home. I can't remember what she said her plans were." They walked into the kitchen. "Lux!" she shouted. No answer.

"She still doesn't know anything about the farewell show, right?" Ember whispered.

"Nope. She's been so wrapped up in her painting thing again." Mrs. Tazo waved her hand. "I bet that's where she is. She hasn't left her new studio in days."

Ember followed Mrs. Tazo down the hallway. The door was open. The room was empty, but Ember's jaw dropped when he saw Lux's paintings. Awestruck, he walked into the studio. Mrs. Tazo walked among the paintings to the desk and picked up Lux's phone.

"Typical." She laughed and shook her head. "She left her phone here. And she only turned it on for the first time today. Anyway, she has no idea about her celebrity status, if you will."

"I asked our site manager to remove the show from the website," he said.

"You should be the one to tell her anyway, don't you think?" Mrs. Tazo reasoned nonchalantly. He nodded but felt like she'd once again slipped into the role of surface and perfect.

"Well, I just wanted to check in and say hi," he said. "If you see Lux, tell her I'll see her tonight."

"She must have gone to Anya's."

"No, Anya is living with me now. And she's with Tanner and Duffy and Luther right now."

"Oh. Well, Lux doesn't know Anya's living situation then, does she?"

Ember shook his head. They conveniently hadn't needed to tell Lux that Anya was now her neighbor, too. They wanted to wait until things were more settled for Lux.

"Well, I need to get up to the spa so I don't miss my nail appointment. See you at the show, honey!" Mrs. Tazo walked Ember back to the front door.

Ember returned home. He felt uncomfortable with the way Lux had left him earlier that day. He waited. Darkness fell. Everyone would be at Apples and Worms by now.

"Hey, we're all here waiting!" Anya said when he answered his phone. "Where are you?"

"Yeah, I'm on my way." Ember tried to sound nonchalant, but he felt anxious and stupid. He ran to the garage and jumped in his truck.

When he showed up at Apples and Worms, he saw Arrabelle seated at the table with the band.

"Where's Lux?" Ember and Arrabelle asked each other in unison.

"I thought she was with you!" Ember exclaimed anxiously. "Wasn't she going to the show with you tonight?"

"I thought she was doing dinner with you guys first!" Arrabelle said. "I told her I'd meet up with her after. That's why I came here."

"I thought she was still painting or with Ember," Anya said. "Don't worry. I'll find her." She stood up and buttoned her coat. "Arrabelle, go back to the Sour and help Astor and Jackson set up. Ember, you guys finish dinner and relax for a minute. It'll be fine."

Ember's optimism dwindled. He handed Anya the keys to his truck.

♪

"Did you find her?" Ember asked. He'd already called Anya twice, but this time she was calling him. They were in the middle of a sound check, and he walked off the stage.

"No, I just called to tell you...you'll be okay. I'll find her. She will be there."

He sat down at the bar. He ran his fingers through his hair.

"I just, I think I'm done," he admitted. "I can't keep doing this. I'm...mad."

"Okay, then! Be mad! Don't let her scare you. She's no big deal," Anya said, and chuckled. "We've reached the bottom of Pandora's box."

"We have?" he asked uncertainly.

"The best is yet to come," she replied.

Lux was still holed up in Tazo Castle, unaware of time, of the world outside. It was almost like being in Boreloque.

She knew everything now.

Almost everything.

She saw what Ember had done for her, and had watched their story unfold. She listened to his music and knew every word. She saw herself dying. She saw herself wake up. She saw doctors push Ember and Anya away. They were the ones who had been with her the entire two months. They embraced because she was back in their lives. Because they were afraid. Because they both loved her.

Lux became inconsolable. She needed to get to Ember. And to Anya.

The sky was black and the air frigid, but she trampled through the crunchy snow, still dressed in sloppy old clothes that were stained with paint. The air stung her lungs. She was still too weak to run; sharp pain moved through her legs, and her ankle was throbbing. She thought of Venia. She thought about her theory.

She was an open book with a broken spine. But so was he. It would be okay.

Lux had reached the edge of the Juniper Creek neighborhood when Ember's truck turned the corner, slid on a patch of ice, and then screeched to a halt. She leapt out of the way and fell into a snowbank.

Anya jumped out of the truck and ran to Lux. "What are you doing!"

Lux wept, and Anya held her. There was nothing to say. It had all been said. Finally, they walked back to the truck, and sat in silence for a long time.

"I'm sorry I read our journal," Anya said finally. Lux laughed through her tears.

"I'm glad you did. And I'm going to write back tomorrow in a new one. But right now I need to get to the Sour Enchantment." Lux straightened up in her seat, focused.

"Yes, you do," Anya said. "Ember's worried all over again."

"I have to see him!"

"Don't worry."

"I'm sorry I doubted you," Lux said.

Anya nodded and smiled but said nothing. Her pain had run deep. It wasn't something she could shrug off.

The Sour Enchantment was more crowded than Lux had ever seen it. It was the first appearance of Falling Like Ember since Farewell Friday. The first act had started. Ember was in the green room doing interviews, so he had no idea that Lux had arrived.

Anya and Lux were noticed immediately. Someone from the press approached them and asked for an interview. This drew more attention; photos were snapped and questions were shouted.

"How do you feel?"

"Are you and Ember a couple now?"

"Do you remember the fall?"

"What do you think of Ember Sweeney's music?"

"Will you be touring with him?"

"Have you seen the farewell show?"

"When can we see your artwork?"

"What are your plans, now that you've been given a second chance?"

"Is that Lux Tazo?"

While they were blindsided by the attention, the girls were both distracted by a bigger story. Anya stepped forward and took Lux's hand, and they made their way through the crowd. Astor pushed people out of the way then and escorted the girls into his office.

"Sorry about that, ladies," Astor said. He handed each of them a bottle of water. "Ignore the press, just decline to interview. They're everywhere."

Lux quickly observed Astor's office. The walls were covered with signed photos of famous musicians and bands. Countertops were covered with paperwork and half-empty bottles of expensive looking whiskeys. There was also a faded photograph of him and Arrabelle from high school. She smiled.

"I've set up a new VIP section for you and any other friends you want who aren't in the band. It's upstairs overlooking the stage. Nobody will be able to bother you there."

"Sorry, Astor. I didn't mean to —" Lux began.

Astor raised up his hand and stopped her.

"Didn't mean to become famous while you were sleeping?" He laughed. "Darling, people just want to see you and know you're alive. They fell for you like Ember fell for you." He picked up a small glass and finished the amber-colored substance inside. "You gave the world hope. Even me."

Lux began to think about the farewell show again, about how broken Ember had been. Anya took her hand.

"And now, it's our time to celebrate," Anya said excitedly. "I have my best friend back. You're back."

"Yes!" Astor said. "And I'll take good care of you both. Follow me."

The girls followed Astor closely. He shielded them from the crowd, and soon they were walking along a back hallway that Lux had never known about.

"Lux, Ember told me you missed dinner, so there are appetizers and drinks set up, but let me know if you need anything else. All the parents are at the upstairs bar if you need them. Arrabelle and Jackson are somewhere around here, too. Falling Like Ember is about to go on." Astor stopped and faced the girls intently. "Ready for this?"

"Wait. Does Ember know I'm here?" Lux asked.

"He's been in interviews. I can try to pull him aside," Astor offered.

"No, no. I'll get to him," Lux said. "Don't tell him."

Astor smiled. "Brilliant. Now are we ready?"

"Ready!" Lux and Anya answered in unison. Astor hugged them both.

"You are making me *so* much money tonight. I love you!" He shouted. "And I love your sister, so put in a good word for me, little Tazo."

"I already have," Lux said. "And thank you for the Christmas gift."

Astor winked at her. He led the girls up a stairway at the end of the hall, and down another narrow hall. The walls were covered in graffiti and signed by all of the bands who'd played shows at the Sour. As they neared the VIP room, Lux spotted Ember Sweeney scrawled on the wall. She moved her hand over his name.

Astor opened the door to a room with big couches and sparkling lights. A hot chocolate bar was set up against the wall. Desserts were piled high. The far wall was open and overlooking the stage. Lux closed her eyes for a moment and shook her head. It felt like Ember Park.

"There she goes again, shaking that head." Lux looked up. Jackson and Arrabelle were sitting at the bar in the corner. "What are you wishing away this time, little Tazo?" Jackson teased her.

"It's too good to be true," Lux said.

"But it is true. And there it is," he said.

"What?"

Jackson stood up and walked toward her. "Your light." He enveloped her in a hug.

"Jack, can you help me track down their friends?" Astor asked. "They'll need different wristbands. You'll recognize them before I will, and I want them up here before the show starts." Jackson left with Astor, so it was just Lux, Anya, and Arrabelle.

Lux looked down at what she was wearing. Very old black and white striped leggings. Black snow boots with fur popping out the top edge. A once white sweater dress, now splashed with every color of the rainbow. Plaid leg warmers were makeshift mittens that reached her elbows. Hanging from her neck was a bulky multicolored paisley scarf. Under a blue beanie, her hair was in a messy side braid with flecks of paint dried into it, and a small brush was sticking out of her hair. She looked at Arrabelle. Perfect. Put together. Tailored. Gorgeous. And Anya. Daring. Bold. Flawless.

"Arrabelle?" Lux asked timidly. "Do you think we could trade outfits? I mean, this is kind of a big night for me, now that I'm here, and —"

"If you want to." Arrabelle touched Lux's braid, and looked as if she might cry. "But I think you look perfect. This is who Ember Sweeney fell for." Lux stared into her sister's eyes, full with sincerity, and for the first time she saw a resemblance. She nodded and decided to trust her.

"This is you, Lux," Anya agreed. She looked at her phone then.

> Ember: Let Your Loss be Your Lesson. Robert Plant &
> Alison Krauss.
> Luther: Centuries. Fall out Boy.
> Tanner: All This Time. OneRepublic.
> Jamison: Golden Years. David Bowie.
> Duffy: Two Is Better Than One. Boys Like Girls.
> Luther: That's so pop cult of you, girlfriend!

"I need a song," Anya said. "And I need one from each of you, too." She showed Arrabelle and Lux her phone.

Anya: Auld Lang Syne ~The Hotel Cafe Artists.
Anya: (Lux's choice... Fight Song, Rachel Platten.)
Anya: (Arrabelle's choice... Crawl by This Way.)

Arrabelle showed the girls a new message on her phone.

Astor: Good Things by The BoDeans.
Astor: Sometime Around Midnight. The Airborne
Toxic Event.
Arrabelle: Hands Down. Dashboard Confessional.

The girls approached the railing that overlooked the stage. They could see the whole club around and below them. Downstairs was packed; the bar area to their right was even busier.

A crowd of their friends pushed through the door then, accompanied by Astor and Jackson. All of them ran for Lux. Nicolette, Isabella, Francesca, and Gabriella Guerrero, Dylan Black, Sally Gallik, Brynna Lowe, Claire Berry, Daniella Dawson, Piper Speedman, Selma Baldwin and Belle Madison, Perry Jordan, Phoenix Bruhn, Cannon Casey, Austin Amos, and even more new friends associated with Falling Like Ember that Lux was just meeting.

Excited reunions ensued as Lux embraced each of her friends. They'd been waiting. She'd gotten a second chance. Her heart was on the brim of bursting, and she hadn't even seen Ember yet.

The music started and they all moved to the railing to watch Falling Like Ember perform the last and best show of the year.

"Happy New Year's Eve!" Ember's honey drip voice boomed into the microphone. Lux's knees wobbled. He was scanning the main level and hadn't noticed his friends upstairs. "How are we doing?" He shouted. The crowd roared. "Great. Let's get on with it."

Ember looked around at the guys and nodded. The band played a new song, something different than Lux or their friends had ever heard. It was bluesy with a little bit of rock. Ember looked angry.

Yeah she broke me
The girl just tore my heart

Yeah she got to me
She throws it in my face
Tells me she hates me
But keeps me close anyway

Makes me want to head to the crossroads
But she already stole my soul
Yeah she stole from me
Woman turned out to be a gypsy

Then she begs me
Please don't give up on me
Well I can't girl, but I want to
Oh, damn girl confuses me

But she's fresh in my mind and strong
Like a shot of Irish whiskey on my tongue
Why don't ya take from someone else
I've cried myself to sleep enough

I thought she was my baby
She stole my pride and joy
And her sister tells me
Oh, don't give up

But she broke me

The song ended, and while everyone cheered, the crowd hushed quickly. Murmurs were heard throughout the venue, and Lux heard her name over and over. Then the band went into a rendition of "Little Wing."

"He seems...upset," Lux said, turning at Anya. Suddenly she felt nervous. Who else could that song have been about, other than her? And now "Little Wing?" That was one memory she had retained. She hadn't worn that hoodie since the day Ember noticed it.

"He's fine," Anya said casually. "He thought you ditched him at dinner. He's fine."

"He did...?" Lux asked, anxiety sweeping over her.

Ember sat down at the piano and adjusted the microphone. He gazed into the crowd again. "I have relentless hope. And it can be painful. But, it's how I'm inspired to write music. This next one is a song I sang to someone every day for two months. Because I had hope."

The crowed engaged in hushed discussion.

Paint me a sunrise, I'll sing you a song
Don't let me lose you before we're both gone
I know the place where you belong
And I've waited so long
for you

So come back to me
We could be anything, just everything
Please don't leave me waiting

Something jolted inside of Lux. This was her song. *Come back to me*, Ember sang. And then strangely, the crowd sang along. They knew it. But so did she. Because it was Zephyr's song. She took a few steps back, then ran. She left the room and rushed down the narrow hall, Ember's words echoing all around her.

She was frantic. She couldn't breathe. She could hear her friends behind her yelling her name. She reached a door at the end of the hallway. She opened it. She was now above and behind the stage. She could see Ember below. She saw a ladder. Her heart leapt into her chest. She crawled across a thin floor that led to the ladder, slowly turned around, and climbed down. She then stood in the shadows behind the stage where nobody could see her yet.

Come back to me, left Ember's lips again.

She watched Ember from the shadows and knew; he was Zephyr. He was Blaze. He'd been with her in Boreloque. He'd gotten her out alive. She had no doubt. Of course, this also meant that she was Venia. But she wasn't afraid. She knew she would sort that out someday. What mattered now, in this moment, was that he had never left her. He'd kept her safe and alive and brought her home with this song. She moved forward slowly, out of the shadows and onto the stage.

Chaotic, shocked cheering came from the audience. Tanner, on the drums, noticed Lux first. His face lit up. She smiled and waved at him, and a calmness settled over her. She walked toward Ember, and Luther and Jamison saw her. They smiled and moved aside so she could walk past them. Duffy and Ember were at the very front of the stage. Ember's eyes were closed, but Duffy noticed her. She quickly hugged Lux and backed out of the way.

The noise and the audience faded away. Nothing was left but a spotlight on Lux and Ember across an empty stage.

Ember stopped singing, but kept strumming, his eyes closed. Duffy and Luther picked up where he'd left off. Lux finally reached out and touched Ember's arm. He slowly dropped the guitar so it hung on his shoulder. He took a deep breath and ran his fingers through his hair. He turned and opened his eyes. The crowd was deafening. He stared at Lux as if she was a ghost.

"We'll always have the sunrise," she whispered.

Ember took Lux's face in his hands and kissed her so strongly, she couldn't tell herself apart from him. The band played on.

She remained in his embrace until the song ended. Ember raised their hands together in the air, and then the two of them left the stage while the cheering continued.

"You were with me the whole time," Lux said quickly, once

they were behind the curtain. There was so much she wanted to say and explain. "You kept me safe. Alive."

"You have no idea how long I've waited for you," Ember whispered. He held her and rested his forehead on hers.

"There are still a lot of things I need to explain, things you'll need to know," Lux began. "Things I need to do someday...and I don't understand it yet —"

"But for now we have this moment to work with. There'll be time for that tomorrow. And the next day, and the next day." Ember pulled Lux closer and kissed her again.

"MIDNIGHT!" screamed voices from the VIP lounge upstairs. Lux and Ember's friends were cheering.

Ember's phone buzzed and a message from Arrabelle came through. He looked at it and winked at Lux. He led her back to the stage. Hats and horns were passed around the venue along with sparkling glow sticks. Cheering continued. He showed the band the message on his phone, and they nodded. He waved at Arrabelle. Then he brought Lux with him to the piano, and they sat together.

"Astor, go find your girl!" Ember shouted into the microphone. "It's almost midnight. She's waiting."

The audience continued to cheer. Falling Like Ember set their instruments down and performed "Auld Lang Syne" a cappella. Every voice in the Sour Enchantment joined in.

The show ended. A new year was upon them.

Jamison, Luther, Duffy, and Tanner left the stage and mingled with the crowd. Ember and Lux remained together at the piano, oblivious to all the photos being taken of them. He touched the paint on her face and in her hair.

"How is the project coming along?" he asked.

"I thought I was finished," Lux said. "But there'll be more to add. Someday."

Ember nodded. "There's something I need to show you," he said.

"I saw it. All of it." Lux said. "I was wrong about you."

"I know you were," Ember said. He winked and kissed her.

"I love you," Lux said. In that moment there was nothing truer.

Their night ended with the New Year's Day sunrise. Astor Dane had allowed the band and their friends to stay and celebrate. Arrabelle and Jackson and a group of their old high school friends all stayed, too.

Lux and Ember returned home as the dawn was breaking. They went to her tree house, nestled in mounds of blankets together, and fell asleep to *Raising Sand*. Lux drifted off while she thought back on days of staring out her window into Ember's house.

Ember Sweeney had stolen her heart, and she'd stolen his. But stealing had become sharing, and there would be no giving back of anything.

Someday Lux would tell the whole story of Boreloque. It appeared she'd lost. But she would return someday. She would find a way. Until then, she knew any unfinished business would follow her. But love would always be on her side. That was all she knew now, in this moment, and it was all she needed.

Ember drifted off to sleep and he was content. Unseen things had proven to be real, tangible. Music had filled the infinite between two souls.

TWENTY FOUR

Album: X

Track: Six

I think everyone has unfinished business, in this life...and that. Maybe the goal is not always to finish it, but to find the path that leads us to understanding why the business was ever at hand in the first place. Maybe that way we can learn about ourselves enough to help others learn about themselves...and right now, I feel like helping others is what I need to do. That's why this happened. I had to get to know myself, and accept myself, and love myself, in order to see that. Everyone struggles with one thing or another...but nobody needs to get stuck.

Lux finished writing the words in her journal, then shoved it under her pillow. She started the first track of *Raising Sand* on her phone, turned off the bedside lamp, and went to sleep.

"Lux, there's no translation for your name since it's already of Latin origin." Ms. Albright, the Latin teacher from Briar Heights Academy, smiled over her glasses at Lux. "What's your middle name?"

"It's Grace," Lux answered. She smiled at Ember, who was sitting next to her. He winked at her.

"Perfect!" Ms. Albright's eyes lit up. "We'll call you Venia!"

Hearing that name knocked the breath from Lux.

The world became dark and quiet. She was falling.

Lux felt her body spinning; her head was aching; she was cold. And alone. She stood up in a dark room and pressed her hand against her throbbing forehead, trying to stop the pain.

She moved forward with careful steps, her arm stretched out in front of her, but couldn't find a door.

"…Ember?"

The echo of her voice startled her. Light appeared. Flickering lights rose and fell above her head and she felt her legs carrying her uphill. She wasn't at Briar Heights Academy. She wasn't in Briar Heights. She wasn't home. She was back.

"Blaze!" she screamed. There was no answer.

"Help me!" she whispered urgently to the tiny birds, swooping down in front of her to offer light. She didn't understand how she'd returned. But now that she was back, she knew she had to find Venia.

Lux continued to call for Blaze, but he never did answer, and neither did anyone else. "York! Pleiades! Harlow! Bubble! Joplin! …Zephyr!" She called every name until she'd nearly lost her voice.

She stopped. She waited. She was ready to face the worst of herself.

"VENIA!"

The ground shook. She stumbled and fell. The birds swarmed around her, chirping madly. Lux heard a shrill scream in the distance.

She ran as fast as she could through the dark forest. Her bare feet throbbed as they slipped over sharp rocks and dirt. Sweat poured from her brow, streaking her dirt-stained face. This was her only chance.

She reached the hollowed tree that marked the tunnel down to Venia's Lair, but stopped and looked around. The Lair had taken over Boreloque. Lux turned around and ran until she reached the clearing that had become the setting for her most vivid nightmare.

Venia was at the Crossroads sitting on her throne.

"I've been waiting," she said. She sounded weak.

"I know what your name means." Lux gulped and tried to catch her breath. She knew it was now or never, or Venia would survive and follow her back home to Briar Heights.

Venia's face fell into a pained stupor. She growled under her breath, her bloodshot eyes rolled back in her head, and she writhed uncomfortably.

Lux saw the hearts of all her friends, thumping violently in glass jars behind the throne. The jars were scattered carelessly across the ground and connected to the throne by tubes. As long as Venia lived, there was still time.

"It's over!" Lux cried. "You don't win. Not like this. Give up now, and I can restore what you've stolen. You had love, and you didn't accept it. You tried to fill that void with everything else, and it didn't work. It won't ever work. Give up!"

Venia screamed. She leaned forward in the throne and covered her ears. She began ripping her hair out, and her teeth were cracking loudly. Her scream grew louder. Even if she did have a change of heart, she was too weak to separate herself from what she'd stolen, so Lux knew she needed to set the souls free.

Lux ran behind the throne. Each jar had three clear tubes running from it, and they were all leading to the back of the throne. It was much more intense than Lux had remembered the first time she saw it. She followed one set of tubes to find they were all directly connected to Venia's body. To the back of her neck, her shoulder blade, and below her ribcage.

"Stop trying to be strong, it won't get you anywhere," Lux pleaded. She debated what to do with the tubes. "Stealing beautiful things won't make you beautiful! It will only make you a thief."

Venia snarled, unable to break free, as her entire body slowly crumbled.

Each heart was expanding rapidly now and threatening to shatter the glass. Lux thought of Blaze, then Zephyr. And Ember. Were their hearts among those in the jars surrounding her? Tears blurred her vision, and she fell to the ground, still holding the tubes.

"I have to kill you," Lux said, weeping. "You aren't grace. You never were, and I won't let you destroy me, or the people I love. I don't have to become you. I was created for more than this. I am worth more. I will not let you win." She ripped the tubes from Venia's body with all the strength she had.

Venia's throne shook violently. Her scream was reaching levels Lux had to block out in order not to black out. She ran full force toward the back of the throne and pushed it off its pedestal. It fell over on its side, and everything stopped. With no breath left inside her, Lux fell facedown. Thousands of rabid bats departed from the trees. A multitude of fairies came down from the sky and chased the bats. Then, silence.

The sky remained dark. It wasn't clear how much time had passed. Things like time had never been clear in Boreloque. Lux sat up. She looked down at the jars strewn about. Empty. There was no evidence of hearts anywhere. She crawled slowly to where Venia lay withered in the chair. Her skin had fallen off in patches, and parts of her skull were visible. She had torn her eyes out. Lux took the cold hand that had once stolen her very soul, once been a part of her. She wrapped her arms around the corpse.

Lux woke up in a cold sweat. She was on the ground next to her bed; she must have fallen out of it. She reached for her phone and saw it was only 2:37am. *Raising Sand* was still playing on repeat. She didn't want to go back to sleep. She pulled on a robe and crept downstairs to her art studio. She turned on a lamp, then after gathering the darkest paint colors she owned, placed a blank canvas on an easel.

After a few hours, Lux picked up another blank canvas and started with black and then crimson. She didn't know how she ever thought she could reveal Boreloque without Venia. Venia had shown Lux exactly what she didn't want to be. She was the darkness that Lux no longer needed to fear and would never become. She was a shadow that would never be seen moving again. She deserved a space on the wall as a reminder.

The sun had risen and Lux was staring at the work she'd produced during the night. In contrast to the rest of the Boreloque series, which now hung on a wall near the art department at school, these were dark and heavy on her heart. But they were essential to tell the whole story. They were part of the process. She felt relieved.

Mr. Tazo appeared at the door of Lux's studio. "You're up early. To paint the Lara Clinic?" He stepped inside for a closer look at the paintings. "Is that the inside?" He shivered and shook his head. "Great job." He kissed Lux on the forehead and left the room.

Lux backed up and examined the paintings again. Her heart skipped a beat. She'd painted the Lara Rehabilitation Clinic. He was right. She told herself to remain calm. She took a photo of the paintings on her phone and ran upstairs to get dressed.

She changed quickly, then grabbed a CD off of her night stand. She'd made Ember a mix two months earlier, but until this moment, couldn't fully explain the music she'd chosen. She looked over the list of songs once more before she left.

Haunted –Taylor Swift; Stand Still, Look Pretty –The Wreckers; All For Believing –Missy Higgins; One Moment More –Mindy Smith; Not Over You –Gavin DeGraw; A Place For Us –Tyler James; We'll Be A Dream –We The Kings & Demi Lovato; What's This? –Flyleaf; Alice (Underground) –Avril Lavigne; I Don't Believe You –Pink; Jar Of Hearts –Christina Perri; Secrets –OneRepublic; This Is Home –Switchfoot; Kashmir –Led Zeppelin; Crossroads –Avenged Sevenfold; Heart Shaped Box –Nirvana; Coming Undone –Korn; Thnks fr th Mmrs –Fall Out Boy; You're So Vain –Marilyn Manson; Paralyzer –Finger Eleven; Strength Of Heart –Venia; Fighter –Christina Aguilera; Almost Lover –A Fine Frenzy; Grace –U2; Ghosts That We Knew –Mumford & Sons; Killing The Blues –Robert Plant and Alison Krauss.

Lux followed the road with the view, to the last memory she had of her life before the fall; a road she hadn't followed in five months. The cobblestone ended. The road ahead was still broken up, flooded with muddy water and dirty piles of leftover snow. Then she saw it.

The building still appeared slightly enchanting. She was once again drawn to the gates. Towering trees were covered in snow and protecting the grounds. She stood at the gate, her breath floating through the wrought iron posts. She took out her phone and compared the painting to what she was seeing.

Her version was darker. Being held prisoner in Venia's lair, in her own darkness, was her deepest fear. However, there was nothing to fear now. She stared at the building. She'd once been afraid of belonging inside, but she didn't belong here. She was no longer haunted. She was free.

Lux knocked on the front door of the Sweeney home. Ember opened the door, wearing pajamas. His hair was sticking out wildly in all directions. Yawning, he took notice of Lux's distress, and ran his fingers through his hair. He smiled. Before either of them spoke, he stepped out the door and enveloped her in a hug and kissed her.

"Promise me you're not going to run away when I explain this, because I know it's going to sound crazy. You'll just have to trust me," Lux said, then took a deep breath. "Trust me today, and in the future." Ember simply smiled and sat down, patting the brick step next to him. She swayed back and forth a moment and then sat next to him.

"Good morning," Ember said, and kissed her again. He took her hand. "If I'm not mistaken, you're the one who runs away from me."

"Morning. So. I've told you all about where I was while I was — you know, in a coma. I told you about the people I met there. I told you how…you were there. And how you brought me back. You were with me the whole time."

"Yes, I literally was."

"Actually, I didn't tell you everything. Some things happened that affected the future. Our future. Before I tell you more, I need you to promise me you'll never, ever give up on me, no matter what happens. Promise me we'll always be together, Ember." Lux squeezed his hand.

He smiled calmly and rested his head against hers. "Lux, I can't promise you that."

"What?" Maybe she'd heard him wrong.

"I won't promise you that. We had completely different experiences recently that brought us back together, and it's changed our lives in a good way." He hugged her. "But I'll never forget that I already had to let you go once. I had to accept that you wouldn't be a part of my life anymore. So, I can't promise that we'll always be together, because I know that it's entirely possible for — well, we're just not in control as much as we'd like to be. We don't know what the future holds. But I do promise to never give up on you."

Lux sensed a change of heart within Ember. His response caught her off guard and felt a bit too rational. It was grown up. The silence grew between them when she had no response to his reasoning, but she knew he was right. There were no guarantees.

"All right then," she said quietly.

"Well, tell me about our future," he said, winking. She couldn't deny him, even when she didn't like the words he said to her. She thought about her dream the night before and what she'd painted because of it. She focused.

"Okay. I left out someone important. Remember how I met someone I think was you in the future? Well, the future me was there, too. Her name was Venia. That's my middle name in Latin," Lux explained.

"Grace?" Ember frowned slightly.

"Yes. She didn't let anyone love her. She hurt a lot of people," Lux said. "She became evil."

"That's not you, Lux," Ember answered firmly.

"It was once, and you were the one to point it out. I know it's not me now, because I think, I hope, I learned from her. You have to know that it could have been me. Maybe it still could be someday," Lux explained. "I hope she never surfaces again, but if she does, please find a way to show me how to love again. Don't give up on me."

Ember sat back, raised his eyebrows, and ran his fingers through his hair again. Lux thought for a moment he might call her crazy, but both of them knew better than to use that word against each other.

"If I hadn't fallen, I really could have turned into what I saw in her. It makes me glad. I'm glad all of this happened," Lux said.

"What about this makes you think it's in the future?" Ember asked.

"I know because…I saw you there. You were older, maybe

twenty years older, I don't know. It was definitely you. You and I were torn apart. I was always trying to find you, trying to get closer to you."

"You mean Blaze?" he said.

"Yes. I fell for you there, too. That's why I didn't think I needed to come back here...back home. When you betrayed me, it was because you were so attached to the other me, the me you'd known forever, to the me that had become Venia. I forgave you, and Venia hated that. She killed me. That's when I woke up."

"Last night I went back. I killed her," Lux said. "When I woke up, I painted the rest of Boreloque, the part I left out." She pulled her phone out of her pocket and showed Ember the paintings. He said nothing.

"You recognize it, don't you?" Lux asked. Ember nodded.

"This is, was, my fear. I tried to fix everything, but I don't know if I did. The only way I can know for sure is if I find a way back again," she said.

"How did you go back last night?" Ember asked after a moment of hesitation.

"Ember, there's something about that album. *Raising Sand.* Listen, I know this won't make sense, but it takes me away to another place and time. I don't know anything about time portals, but maybe if there's something along the lines of a music portal — I wish I could show you."

Ember crossed his arms and stared at the ground.

"Something happens when that music plays," she said firmly. "And you don't have to believe me, but please don't think I'm crazy. And please don't look at me the way I know anyone else would if I ever told them, which I don't plan to, ever. Not even Anya."

"Music portal?" he said finally.

"The thing is, I fell for you, and then I discovered that album," Lux continued. "Maybe I was listening to the album when I fell from Tazo Castle. Last night I fell asleep to it, and when I woke up, I was on the ground."

Ember remained silent.

"When it comes to Boreloque, I know one thing; you were with me from the beginning," Lux said. "I want you to be with me until the end. I just need to know that whatever we face, we'll fight together, not against each other, and not in two different worlds."

"Wherever we are, I hope there's not a lot of fighting," Ember said finally, smiling. She could see he was trying to lighten the mood.

"That's why I say...just promise me you won't give up on me," Lux said. "Let's make a deal. If twenty years goes by, and I forget you, me, us, this right now, everything that's happened, please remind me. Don't let me forget."

"I don't make deals, Lux," Ember said.

"Oh." She wanted too much for him to understand exactly where she'd been.

"It's just that everything you've told me about this place, Boreloque, it does remind me of the song "Crossroads." That song is about someone selling his soul in exchange for talent." He sighed loudly. "I don't ever want to hear about you selling your soul, not in exchange for anything. Not even in a dream. So, a deal, no. But a promise, yes. I won't give up. You won't ever have to question that."

"Okay," she said after a long pause. She hadn't even realized what she was saying. He was right; she didn't want to make a deal. That's something Venia would do.

"So, we're going to be together in twenty years?" Ember nudged Lux. She glared at him, but had to laugh. She was just glad he wasn't running away at this point.

"Yeah. You're stuck with me. That's what you get for saving my life."

"I'm never writing you a song again." He kissed her.

"Speaking of, here's this," she said, and handed him the CD.

"It's about time! So this is the soundtrack to your life?" he asked.

"It's more like the soundtrack to where I've been," Lux said. "I can finally explain the last couple years."

"Paramount. Let's go listen to it." He stood up and took her hand.

"Wait." She hesitated. "I just told you...everything. Now what? Where do we go from here?"

She felt as though she'd asked him this before. She needed a real answer. She needed him to be a man. She needed to see Blaze in him.

"We listen to the music," Ember said calmly. "Then we follow the moonbeams and fairy tales through the darkness, and we go to forever."

The End

About the Author

Christina L. Schmidt resides in Denver, CO. She spends time with friends and family, and weekends in the mountains.

Visit her on the web at
www.christinalschmidt.com
Facebook: AuthorChristinaLSchmidt
Twitter: ChristinaLS5
Instagram: ChristinaLS5
Pinterest: ChristinaLS5